THE LOST CENTURY

THE
LOST
CENTURY

A NOVEL

Larissa Lai

Author of *The Tiger Flu*

ARSENAL PULP PRESS
VANCOUVER

THE LOST CENTURY
Copyright © 2022 by Larissa Lai

ARSENAL PULP PRESS
Suite 202 – 211 East Georgia St.
Vancouver, BC V6A 1Z6
Canada
arsenalpulp.com

The publisher gratefully acknowledges the support of the Canada Council for the Arts and the British Columbia Arts Council for its publishing program, and the Government of Canada and the Government of British Columbia (through the Book Publishing Tax Credit Program) for its publishing activities.

Arsenal Pulp Press acknowledges the xʷməθkʷəy̓əm (Musqueam), Sḵwx̱wú7mesh (Squamish), and səl̓ilwətaʔɬ (Tsleil-Waututh) Nations, custodians of the traditional, ancestral, and unceded territories where our office is located. We pay respect to their histories, traditions, and continuous living cultures and commit to accountability, respectful relations, and friendship.

This is a work of fiction. Though historical personages are represented, they are represented as characters in a novel, and their thoughts and actions are the products of the author's imagination. Generally known historical facts are adhered to as closely as possible, although in many cases they are imaginatively .elaborated and sometimes presented on a different timeline from the actual historical timeline. The truth served by this novel is narrative truth. It is not scientific or historical truth.

Cover and text design by Jazmin Welch
Edited by Catharine Chen
Copy edited by Rebecca Rosenblum
Proofread by Alison Strobel

Printed and bound in Canada

Library and Archives Canada Cataloguing in Publication:
Title: The lost century : a novel / Larissa Lai.
Names: Lai, Larissa, author.
Identifiers: Canadiana (print) 20220211485 | Canadiana (ebook) 20220211493 | ISBN 9781551528977 (softcover) | ISBN 9781551528984 (HTML)
Subjects: LCSH: World War, 1939–1945—China—Hong Kong—Fiction. | LCSH: Hong Kong (China)—History—Siege, 1941—Fiction. | LCSH: Hong Kong (China)—Social conditions—20th century—Fiction.
Classification: LCC PS8573.A3775 L67 2022 | DDC C813/.54—dc23

For those to come

Typhoon Shelter
YOU ASKED
June 30, 1997

The Typhoon Shelter Restaurant is a stone's throw from the Tin Hau MTR station, but you really have to look to find it, hidden as it is on a narrow side street and eclipsed by buildings so tall they scrape the clouds. But Ophelia Tang's great-aunt Violet Mah knows the way. They trudge up the hill through the rain under their commemorative umbrellas in blue and yellow, pausing just long enough to take a quick photograph at Tin Hau Temple Road Garden No. 3, with its little shoji-screened shrine and carved stone lamps. They left Auntie Macy Cheung Koon-Ying's flat in the Mid-Levels later than intended, and Ophelia wants to get back before 4:30 to watch Governor Chris Patten depart from Government House and board Her Majesty's Yacht Britannia. It's June 30, 1997, the last day that Hong Kong will be a British Crown colony.

The wind blows in at an angle, and the two women are getting drenched, eightysomething and twentysomething alike. The steady rain intensifies and threatens to become a deluge. Eager to get inside, they scramble in their squelching shoes. Water begins to descend in sheets and splash hard on the pavement. They huff for breath as the hill grows steeper.

At last, they arrive. The sliding doors roll open, and their faces are hit by a cool, air-conditioned breeze. Their nostrils, mouths, eyes, and ears flood with the scent of seafood, chilies, and fried garlic. A grumpy, tired server greets them and guides them to a table near the tanks, where all manner of sea creatures crawl, swim, or float.

There's a clock on the wall with a graphic of a girl's face on it. She's got turquoise skin, little white freckles, and pink hair. She sports big yellow sunglasses and pop art lips. The hands of the clock circle her nose. She gazes at them impassively, a glamorous space alien from a stellar future no one can yet dream. When the clock strikes midnight, Hong Kong will become part of the People's Republic of China under the slogan "One country, two systems," recalling another midnight almost thirty years prior, when Britain let go of a different jewel in its burnished crown, with different but related consequences. The restaurant is only half full, unusually quiet because everyone is either at home watching the pre-handover festivities on TV or down at the waterfront under their own blue-and-yellow umbrellas trying to stake out good spots from which to observe the official ceremony later. Though no one but Ophelia is listening, a New Romantic band called Cri de Cur, popular a decade ago, comes on over the tinny sound system. Safety pin through her lip, the lead singer Donna Wannabe croons, "You say you've never been so happy / but you look so goddamn sad." They find a table and sit.

The grumpy server brings a pot of bo nay cha, the kind that is well known to cut grease. "Yiu mut yeh?" she asks. "What do you want?"

Great-Aunt Violet says, "This place specializes in typhoon-shelter-style crab, Feelie. So we'll have that first, okay?"

Ophelia nods. "Smells good."

"Spicy, extra spicy, or super spicy?" the server asks in impeccable English.

"Extra spicy," says Great-Aunt Violet. "Super spicy would be too much, I think. A little heat is good, to draw out the deliciousness. But too much, and you can't eat the dish."

The server nods, scribbles, and vanishes.

In the back, dishes bang and clatter. The crab-pink lights in the dining room flicker. Outside, the rain pours down in torrents, making a temporary river of the narrow street.

Ophelia looks expectantly at her great-aunt.

Great-Aunt Violet crosses her eyes at Ophelia, as if to say, "Why me?"

"You promised you'd tell me," Ophelia says.

Great-Aunt Violet sighs.

Why is it that the grandchild most distant from the history is the one most interested in it? Do you think you can bring it back? You can never have it back, and thank goodness, because it was a miserable time. Why do you want to look? I don't want to look. My generation endured so yours wouldn't have to. You have other options. You should use the advantages you were given to do something useful.

You want to know about my sister, your grandma? You want to know if it's true that she murdered your grandpa? Where did you even hear that story? Well, it might be true, and it might not be true. Who is to say? So many years have passed, Feelie. It's long over, and Hong Kong is a different place. Why do you want to know? What good will it do for her or for you now?

And why does everyone want to know about her and nobody cares about us? Always, it's Emily, Emily, beautiful Emily. Emily the beloved. Emily who suffered. Emily who had children. Emily who died for our sins. Well, she's not around anymore. She died. I'm alive. So you're stuck with me, and what I remember, and what I'm willing to tell. Sorry about that, but that's life. Sorry I'm not her.

Yes, she was beautiful. Yes, she was kind. Yes, she cared a lot. No, she never got justice. Who gives an onion pancake? That's how it goes in this life for most of us. You think you're special? You aren't special. The past is not going to come whirling back to you the way you want. Doesn't it already reek of mildewy brown wainscotting and mothballs? Old incense and rotten oranges? How spoiled are you, anyway? You're just going to have to take it how it was, with everything that's missing—everything I don't remember, everything I was never told, everything I never saw. Also, everything I don't care about and everything I don't want to tell. That's it. Like it or lump it. I'm just one old lady, one cranky old lady with a faulty memory, a big ego, and all my confabulations. Too too bad, too too sad, so sad for you.

Raymond? He lived with us until he was twelve, and then he took off. I don't know where he is. Why does everyone ask me? I don't know. He was troubled, and then he was gone. Why don't you ask me about Macy? Didn't Macy pay for your plane ticket? Aren't you staying in her beautiful flat in the Mid-Levels? Didn't she pay for your education, and your condo in Vancouver? Wasn't it Macy who invited you here to watch the handover of Hong Kong from the British Crown to the People's Republic of China? Didn't she also help arrange the adoption of your new daughter from that orphanage in Qinghai?

I can tell you Macy's story because Ting-Yan and I raised Macy, and Macy stayed. Macy was a good girl who became a good woman. A smart girl who became a rich woman, a kind woman who takes care of her family. We treated Raymond and Macy the same, but Raymond took off. Too much of his messed-up parents in him, in my humble opinion.

It wasn't our fault Raymond left. If it was anyone's fault, it was Emily's. Emily's fault and Tak-Wing's fault. Tak-Wing was an asshole and Emily was a romantic fool. Why does everyone ask about them, and not Tak-Wing's younger brother Tak-Tam, who was good and kind, and who died so young? Why does no one ask about his father, Old Mah, who poisoned his own people with opium packaged as a cure for opium addiction? Why does no one ask about Old Cheung, who tried so hard to do what was right for his family and almost destroyed it by trying so hard? Why does no one ask about Old Lee, one of the early South China communists? Or his wife, Siu-Wai, and her friend Yim-Fong, who gave their lives to the movement only to be purged before the new country was ten years old? Why does no one ask about Morgan Horace, the Jamaican revolutionary and rum importer, whose beautiful visions were dashed to the dirt? Or Isadore Davis Wong, who facilitated the passage of so many refugees to Free China and the rescue of so many Allied soldiers as a member of the British Army Aid Group, and who was left stranded in Hong Kong with a large family and no home for his pains? Why does no one ask about the Irish professor of Chinese history, Kathy Duffy, who helped so many young Chinese women find their way in the modern world? Why does no one ask about Tanaka Shigeru, the civilian translator torn apart by what the Japanese Imperial Army did to his classmates and friends? Why does no one ask about William Courchene, the Métis soldier from Saint-Boniface who brought Raymond into this world? Why does no one want to know about Lee Ting-Yan, whom the handsome prince didn't want to marry? Why does no one ask about me?

What has Macy been saying to you? Macy is a good person, but she doesn't know diddly-squat. She doesn't have a clue. She is good with money, but stupid about human beings. Lots of Hong Kong people are like that. They find the past unbearable, so they drive as hard as they can into the future without understanding how their ignorance of yesterday creates a miserable tomorrow. Macy can be like that. I can't believe that she thinks Emily was a murderer.

Emily was not a murderer. You don't understand the whole story. I'll tell you what she did, but you can't tell a soul.

The crab arrives, his otherworldly face deep-fried and facing them with all the wisdom of sea and wok. He waves his antennae at them in the air-conditioned breeze. Beside his wise and knowing face sits a massive claw, bigger than any Ophelia has seen in her life. The head itself is propped up on a heap of fragrant crab pieces still in their bright orange shells, but smashed with the flat side of a cleaver so it's easy to get the meat out. Deep-fried garlic, chilies, and shallots are piled to overflowing atop the crab. The whole concoction smells irresistibly delicious.

Out on the street a car alarm goes off. A customer rushes out of the restaurant to see if it's hers, and the shock of rain hitting her face makes her shriek as the sliding doors close. Ophelia glances over, glad to be inside.

"Here," says Great-Aunt Violet, plunking one of the juicy claws onto Ophelia's plate. "Try this. Best in Hong Kong."

1936-1937

CHAPTER 2

TUITION

December 12, 1936

When I was seven and Emily was eight, our father announced his modernity. "You can marry, or you can go to university. I've put aside a decent sum for each of you—wedding gift or tuition, your choice."

There was no real choice.

It was obvious who would receive the money as wedding gift: beautiful Emily, lovely as the moon in spring, gorgeous as a pink peony at the height of bloom, even at seven. What Emily had received in beauty, however, was taken from her account in wisdom. Worse, it was eclipsed by her vanity. The only knowledge she had, and the only knowledge she cared about, was the knowledge of her own beauty. Her beauty was immense, and her knowledge of it deeper than the South China Sea. She understood that beauty was a kind of currency better than money, at least for women of our generation. She knew she had to use it to get what she wanted, everyone else be damned. If only she'd had the wisdom to make better choices. But no one talked about choices in those days—that's a Generation X thing. My generation talked about desire and death, and got plenty of both.

It was obvious, too, who would receive the money as tuition: yours truly, Violet Mah, bright as the sun and sharp as the edge of a pork cleaver, but ugly as the butcher's chopping block. I mean ugly: square face, pointy nose, small eyes, gigantic mouth full of teeth so big they barely fit. You think I'm ugly now because you think all old ladies are ugly. It was more obvious when I was young.

In looks, I took after my father, but looks matter less to a man. My father was wealthy. He made his money in gambling; this whole cursed colony did, one way or another. But I mean he was a casino man, first in Macau, then in Hong Kong. Not as successful as Stanley Ho, but good enough to make a few investments. With a Singaporean school friend, Yeo Chooi Koon, he started an anti-opium pill company called Dream Horse to help our people recover from the scourge of dragon chasing imposed on us by the British a hundred years ago. Father and Yeo believed that a special recipe for a Tang dynasty elixir of immortality, which included magical ingredients like cinnabar, realgar, arsenolite, malachite, and magnetite, could cure the people of their dependence on opium. Not that I am in any place to denigrate the value of opium. My father's grandfather made his fortune selling it as a comprador for Witt-Weatherall and Co., and his father (my great-great-grandfather) was the famous taipan Mr Henry Witt-Weatherall himself, though this is seldom discussed in polite company, because my great-great-grandmother was Chinese. Because Witt-Weatherall never claimed my great-grandfather, he became Chinese, like his mother. After that, Witt-Weatherall was no longer around to claim any descendants, and all marriages were Chinese. So we are Chinese too, and do everything the Chinese way.

"What a headache trying to remember them all, ViVi!" Emily said once upon a time, when I was fifteen and she was sixteen. She dabbed her wrists with a bit of Chanel Bois des Iles. She liked that one better than the Chanel No. 5 that all the other girls wanted. She had sophisticated tastes. "A new world is coming in which we will be free from all those dreary, oppressive old ancestors—just you wait and see."

The smell of a distant forest and languid flowers rushed to my nose. "Don't be so disrespectful, Emily," I said. "There will come a time when you'll wish you could remember."

"I really doubt I'll ever care."

"Someone you care about will care."

"Don't be such a bore, Violet."

Some people say we don't look very Chinese because there were compradors in the families of some of the Chinese wives, too, including my mother, Eunice Liu Hei-Yu. But what is Chinese in this moving, changing, twisting world? If I took my father's money for tuition, was that still Chinese?

I was so shocked when he made the offer again, when the reality of one option or the other seemed sooner and more likely. I loved my father, but in those days, relationships between fathers and daughters were more distant than they are now. When I was little, he lived with us at the Stable, the first house he bought with his casino money. But when Dream Horse began to do well, he bought a house for himself just around the corner, the Kimblewick. So he wouldn't be distracted, he said, by the sounds of things that were women's business. I saw him perhaps once a week for Sunday dinner, during which he would dispense wisdom to all members of the family.

"A woman should put others first, herself last," he'd say. "When she does something good, she shouldn't cluck about it. When she does something bad, she shouldn't deny it."

But other times, he was more progressive. "Women should have the right to education. And when China comes into her own, women should have the right to vote."

Whether the wisdom was conservative or progressive, it was always stated firmly and with authority. We never knew how to respond, so we just ate quietly.

Sometimes he'd give us his opinions on the politics of the day. He admired Sun Yat-Sen, but worried that Chiang Kai-Shek was a despot. He thought the Communists had some good ideas, but mistrusted their zeal. When we were young, we thought China was very far away and only half listened to his ideas about it.

My mother was the one who translated his offer into details that made sense. She invited me to drink tea and eat melon seeds in her room, at the little rosewood table she had for entertaining exactly such conversations as these. "If you want to marry, your father and I will arrange for you to marry his business partner Yeo's oldest son in Singapore. By all reports, he's a very nice young man."

"But is he good looking?" I asked. I split a melon seed with my giant front teeth.

"No." She didn't say any more than that, but I had already been to literature class. I could read subtext. *How could someone as ugly as you possibly expect to marry handsome?*

"Didn't think so," I said. "Maybe Emily will marry him."

"I've suggested it to her. Yeo has two sons. You could both marry into the family, if you wanted. When it's time, the four of you could inherit Dream Horse and carry it forward into this bright new century." She poured a little cup of tea for each of us.

"If I were to marry, I'd want to marry for love." I tried to sip, but the tea was much too hot and burned my tongue.

She looked at me the way a sage looks at a common person. Paused for way too long. "That's what Emily says too."

"Mama, no one will marry me for love, no matter how much I love them."

She sat there, uncomfortable, trying to think of something kind to say.

I said, "Only the beautiful get to marry for love. Only the beautiful can be modern. In love, at least. The ugly must take arranged marriages because that is the only way they can marry at all."

"You always were the cleverest of my children, dearest Violet," she said.

"The clever, ugly, and modern go to school." I sipped again. She had put little rosebuds in the tea, and their sweet odour filled my head.

"I would have liked to have gone to school. I'm smart, like you, but my father was not modern. He arranged my marriage. I suppose he was modern enough to ask me beforehand how I felt about it." The sorrow in her beautiful face was very romantic. What did she ever really have to worry about?

"And so you married Father for his money?"

"Don't talk like that about your father. He is a good man. A kind man."

"A wealthy man who looks like a horse."

"Violet!"

"I'm sorry, Mama."

"I know you don't think so, but it's possible to be two things at once. Your father is both wealthy and kind. In a husband, these qualities are more important than good looks. If you decide to marry young Master Yeo, you will come to understand this when you are older."

"I don't want a husband. I'll take the tuition. I want to help people. I'll study medicine, continue our family's commitment to the health and longevity of the people." The University of Hong Kong offered a bachelor of medicine, and a slightly older friend of mine, Lai Po-Chuen, was one of the first women students in that program at HKU. She was halfway through the degree and enjoying it.

My mother smiled.

"If I understand you at all, child, this is the path of your greatest happiness."

"I know, Ma. It's also my only real choice. I just wish there was more than one real choice."

She died of tuberculosis shortly after that. Before she died, she tried to arrange for my father to take a concubine so he wouldn't be alone after she was gone. In the old days, men were free to take more than one wife as long as they had the means to support more than one family. It was almost expected, particularly among businessmen, who did it as one way among many to show off their success. My mother went so far as to choose an eighteen-year-old orphan girl called Ada Ng Yeuk-Hai from the Po Leung Kuk home for wayward women and girls.

But Father said no, that he would remain true to her memory.

This made her weep, out of love for him and out of grief for herself.

Because she was crying, Old Mah wept too.

What we didn't know was that he was already courting somebody else, a sing-song girl at Tim Nam Teahouse at Wing Lok Street and Bonham Strand, where he stopped on his way home from work many days of the week. In those days, rich men did what they wanted, and Old Mah was no exception. That's Confucian patriarchy for you! Aren't you glad you don't have to live in such backward times?

The songstress was blind, as many in that profession were. It was a profession that poor people put their daughters into as a matter of tradition and livelihood, since it was harder for them to be married off. Don't be so judgmental with your sociology degree, Ophelia! I know it wasn't right. But it was the shape of the world then. The sing-song girls had much better lives than a lot of women in old Hong Kong.

The blind singer Polly Tsai Mei-Gwan was smashingly beautiful. I mean really gorgeous, like a cool breeze blowing over a misty mountain. The fact that she couldn't see and so didn't know this just made her all the more beautiful. The good Christian orphan Ada Ng was simply no competition.

When my mother found out, she was stinking mad. I mean howling mad, and bitter as that smelly herbal medicine we had to drink when we were sick, the kind that boiled for hours in a crusty clay pot.

"How could you betray me like that?" she wailed. "You don't love me! You never loved me! What kind of modern husband are you? None at all! A modern husband does not take part in these barbaric feudal practices!" She tore her hair, cut up her beautiful cheung sams with ragged scissors, threw her perfumes and powders at her vanity so hard that its perfect moon-shaped mirror broke. She was very ill at the time, so it was amazing that she could rage so hard. Don't underestimate how tough those women of the 1920s were, Feelie! She was tough! Ten times tougher than you or me, even though she was so sick.

After that hissy fit she threw, though, she declined fast. She got sicker and sicker. Her face grew hectic and hot. She grew thinner and complained that her bones ached. She coughed up green phlegm tinged with blood, and then she just coughed up blood. By then, Father had already married Polly Tsai Mei-Gwan and set her up in her own house in the Mid-Levels, which Second Mother Polly dubbed the Nest. Mother couldn't do anything about it. She died shortly after that. I know Father felt regret, because he asked us to keep her room intact, and he still came and slept there sometimes. So extravagant when there was such a shortage of space in Hong Kong! But now rich Chinese people leave empty flats and houses all over the world. No wonder communist ideology took hold in China! His grief was both extravagant and neglectful—it was Emily and me who were asked to nurture and honour it, to keep it alive. I do think he really loved our mother, but death and dying were such a regular part of life in those days, for rich people as much as for poor people. As were second and third wives, even while earlier wives were still living. Women were just expected to accept it. He kept her in his memory, but he also continued to move forward.

Second Mother Polly was a kind woman. But she was also tough, pragmatic, and astute. She always treated me and Emily well, but kept us at arm's length. As the daughters of the first wife, we posed a minor threat. Until her position in the family was consolidated, she didn't want us too close. She set to work having children and making sure that Father was on her side. She was young when she married him, not much older than us. Is "gross" a sociology word, Ophelia? I don't think it is. I'm not saying it was good, I'm just saying it's how things were.

She had a son right off the bat, then two daughters, then three boys in a row. She gave them classical Chinese names I can't remember anymore, as well as whimsical English ones: Power, Pretty, Pineapple, Pirate, Purple, and Peanut. Those are my half-brothers and half-sisters—you met Uncle Peanut last week at dim sum, remember? Father was overjoyed because it meant his family line was assured. He didn't exactly neglect me and Emily, but let's just say we were on our own a lot with only poor Amah, our childhood nanny hired from a nearby village when Emily was born, to watch out for us. Driver Lim and his wife, Auntie Lim the geomancer, were there, too, but they weren't much involved in our actual upbringing. To say Emily ran amok was a major understatement. She took Mother's death as personally as she took Father's neglect and did everything fun and bad that she could dream up. As time went on, Mother's intact bedroom

21

became spookier and spookier, and Emily ran wilder and wilder. As for me, because I felt sorry that Emily had no mother, I mothered her. I knew that I wanted to be a doctor, but I put my own dreams aside because I didn't know well enough to look out for myself. Though I hadn't caused it, I felt guilty about my mother's death and wished I'd been gentler and more diplomatic with her.

The other unspoken truth in my family, besides the equine hideousness of my father and me, was that the pills Dream Horse made did not promote the health and longevity of the people. To the contrary, they made people ill. We branded the pills to appeal to people's commitment to themselves as Chinese and to the idea of China as the Middle Kingdom.

Lots of Hong Kong people wanted retribution for the Opium Wars—the great humiliation that allowed the British to continue taking tea and silk out of China, while imposing opium on its people and gaining Hong Kong as a British Crown colony to boot. But Hong Kong was a tiny fishing village before it was a British possession. During the Qing dynasty, with the rest of Xin'an County, it was subject to mass evacuations on pain of death. When the evacuation edict was lifted, it was repopulated by some of the same Punti people who had been forced out, and some new people. The Punti called them "guest people" and let them live only on the least fertile mountainside land. These were the Hakka, like Old Cheung, like your Auntie Siu-Wai. On top of those hatreds, Ming and Qing dynasty loyalists still struggled against one another. And the Triads played a big part in the enforcing of loyalties. Loyalties overlapped and diverged like rain and wind. And it's not like the divisions went away after the British came. We're such a fractured lot, and the fractures keep getting worse and more tangled up.

The coming of the British suddenly made Hong Kong a centre of trade—legal, illegal, and everything in between. The British called it the gateway to Asia. You might call it the door to another dimension, the door that, once opened, changed the continent from one thing to quite something else. Some people dreamt of getting rid of opium and, in so doing, closing the gateway and bringing back the past. But which past? I don't want the past in which the emperor neglected the well-being of the people, women were property, everyone feared their neighbours, and no one had enough to eat. Do you? Other pasts are possible. There were times when women could be scholars, and fair-minded magistrates took the interests of the people to heart. But all pasts are only dreams, unless you have a real way of making them present. That's what I think. In the meantime, the British brought us another way. But now they are heading out, and things are going to be different yet again. Well, nothing can stop the world from turning. But what's that old saying? The more things change, the more they stay the same.

Though Old Mah didn't want the Qing dynasty past, he was a canny enough businessman to recognize that people were nostalgic for it. He branded our Dream Horse products to remind them of it. His advertising slogans called out, "Close the Gateway!" "Strong, Peaceful, and Self-Reliant!" What he didn't advertise was that the secret ingredient of the Dream Horse pills was opium itself, albeit modern opium and not traditional poppy tears.

The new kind of opium—the kind we put in Dream Horse products— was opium that had been distilled and refined to make two modern drugs: heroin and morphine. Heroin was cheaper and was the primary ingredient in our most popular product, Dream Horse Red. We also sold a more refined version for a more refined clientele, Dream Horse White, which contained morphine in addition. In the early days, there was another line, too, called Immortal Carp, which came in two colours: black and gold. There was a very special version called Carp's Eye, which was glossy white. Each pill had a little black dot on it so that it looked like a 3-D cartoon fish eye. These incorporated special ingredients from a traditional recipe for an extra-potent elixir of immortality: mercury, arsenic, and strychnine. To smoke them was an immense pleasure. It made the smoker soar with phoenixes through the clouds. But after an old man from the village of Wong Nai Chung in Happy Valley died of a heroin overdose combined with heavy-metal poisoning, Father had to go to court. He was fined enough money to buy that man's family a very nice house in the village of Tai Hang, while Father spent three months in Victoria Gaol. After that, we stopped making the whole Immortal Carp line. The cheapest one, Dream Horse Red, was what sold best anyway.

According to all the old stories, I ought to have been jealous of my older sister, Emily Wai-Yee, for having all the things I did not: fine features, pale skin, dark eyes as gorgeous as those of the Cantonese-speaking movie star Lee Yi-Nin in *The Modern Bride*. In truth, I was not. I admired her and looked up to her. I willingly involved myself in all her exploits. Sometimes, because I could see she was not too bright, I saw it as my duty to take care of her. If she wanted to slip the eagle eye of Amah and the safety of our home in the Mid-Levels to go the flower market and charm a free peony from the flower sellers, I'd go with her to make sure she didn't get hurt or abducted. When she wanted to stow away in the trunk of Driver Lim's brand new motor car and go for a joyride, I stowed away with her so she wouldn't get in trouble alone. If she wanted a roll of haw flakes or a handful of White Rabbit candy, I'd sneak it from Mama's purse for her. When she became vain in her teens, I'd buy her hair clips, face powder, and Florida water. I once even got her a lipstick, but Mama said Emily was not that kind of girl and took it away. After Mama died, Emily found the lipstick in Mama's vanity and started wearing it again. And again, I took it away. Though I was a year younger than her, she had no one but me to look after her anymore. But then she went and cut her hair and had it permanently waved. There was nothing I could do about that. My sister was beautiful and innocent. She had a mischievous streak, but because of her beauty, the mischief was often more charming than annoying, though sometimes it was annoying too.

When she declared her intention to marry Cheung Tak-Wing, the handsome cricket-playing son of the Hong Kong Cricket Club's head cook, I became very worried. Our father had one enemy in this world, and that was Head Cook Cheung, because Head Cook Cheung was the son of the man from Wong Nai Chung Village who died of opium poisoning after smoking our Immortal Carp. My usually kind, solemn father was mad as hell. "The damn English!" he said. "They take care of their own and don't give two hoots about any Chinese, even if what we do is no different from what they do." We were at the Kimblewick at Second Mother Polly's urging, and both of us were terrified. We almost never visited Father in his private abode, that glossy European house with its arched gateway and wide verandas. The interior was decorated in an elegant but austere Chinese style. And of all its rooms, his office, in which we visited him, was the most elegant and austere. He sat behind an ornately carved desk on a throne of hard rosewood.

"Cheung is also Chinese," Emily squeaked.

"Yes, but he's one of their Chinese. A servant, a lackey, without nerve or enterprising spirit." Behind him, traditional Chinese paintings of his esteemed mother and father gazed at us with disapproval.

"You don't know that," Emily said, finding her nerve. "Cheung is a man from the villages. His prospects were always limited. He's worked hard and done well for himself."

"That's my other objection," said Father. "Of course, I want you to marry for love, but must you love beneath your station?"

"That's not the way love works, Father," said Emily, in a soft but steady voice. "Love doesn't know class. Besides, you have no idea what Tak-Wing is capable of. He played football in the Berlin Olympics! He's going to be someone."

"I forbid it," Father said. "I didn't teach you to be free so you could shame and humiliate me."

I interjected on Emily's behalf. "It's not freedom, Father, if you take it back when we decide to exercise it."

His face was red and hot. We weren't supposed to talk back—the fact that we did, however meekly, posed a real dilemma for him. Father struggled so hard to be a modern Chinese man, but he didn't fully know how.

He had learned how to be Chinese from his mother, because his father had wanted to do everything the English way. "Tell her," he said to me, "tell your sister to choose anyone except that dreadful Cheung boy."

"He isn't dreadful," I said, remembering the baked Alaska Tak-Wing had treated me and Emily to last week at Jimmy's Kitchen in its brand new Pottinger Street location. I couldn't believe that fancy restaurant had let us in, but Tak-Wing had learned the graces of aristocracy, and they didn't dare refuse him. The baked Alaska had impressed me mightily—a towering heap of snowy meringue on fire, which gave way to a mountain of cake, ice cream, and chocolate sauce once a fork was stuck in. Every element was a novelty: the burning rum (imported, and not something a Chinese woman would normally drink); the meringue (imagine the luxury of time to beat egg whites to such a froth); the ice cream (dairy products were exotic and slightly off-putting until one developed a taste for them, but they were also English and therefore fancy); chocolate sauce (which is not really a Chinese taste); cake (which we traditionally steamed rather than baking); and most of all, the miraculous combination of heat and cold, which could only be achieved using strange foreign appliances that we did not have in our own home and wouldn't have known how to use even if we did. "He's a lot of fun. And like Emily, he's nice to look at. They make a good match. You have to decide, Father, whether you're a modern Chinese or an old Confucian patriarch. If you're the modern Chinese you want to be, you have to let Emily do what she wants." My behaviour was outrageous for a Chinese girl of good family. But Mother was not around anymore to make me do better. We had Amah, of course, but because she was not our mother, we ran roughshod over her with little respect for her thoughts or feelings. I regret that too now, but she is long gone. I tell her so sometimes, when we go to sweep her grave. I hope she hears me.

Amah said, "Poor Old Mah. You raised your daughters to be too clever. And then you left them to their own devices."

Father knew it was true. He spent what little time he had away from his business with his second family, not so much because he cared for them more than he cared for us, but because Second Mother Polly was there to make sure that he did. He often felt guilty about neglecting us and annoyed at Amah for holding him accountable.

"You will not disobey me," our father said. "I've never denied you anything in your lives, my two precious daughters. And to repay me, you've grown spoiled and insolent. I won't have it. I just won't." He didn't shout, but the restrained softness of his voice was more frightening than if he'd railed to the heavens. He was right about us being spoiled, though. We were so shocked at the newness of his behaviour that we stood frozen in place, utterly unsure what to do. We knew that proper daughters feared and revered their fathers. But because we had lost Mother so young, and because we seldom saw Father, we had never properly learned how to talk to him.

He took hold of the little glass cat that Emily had given him as a birthday gift several years before and hurled it at the wall. There was a fearful thunk, then it shattered into a thousand pieces.

We fled the room.

CHAPTER 3

STEAMED FISH

February 16, 1937

No one ever asks a steamed fish what it wants. Everyone wants to eat it—it's prized above many other more complex and interesting dishes—but no one ever asks it what it wants. They all ooh and sigh when it comes to the table. Fresh, steamed, swimming fish! Ho yeh, ho yeh, very good! Very good and very expensive, often twice the cost of any other dish on the table, and sometimes even three times, if it's a particularly plump and juicy fish. Steamed until it's just done and its pale flesh comes barely free of the bone. How did the old cooks know how to do that without sticking in a chopstick and testing? Don't ask me, I'm useless in the kitchen. If you want to *know* something, ask my clever sister Violet, who reads books and goes to university.

Steamed fish knows nothing. It has to be served unmolested and scantily cooked, that's how you know that it's fresh. That's how you know the cook has skill. They leave the head on. The eyes are boiled white so children can chew them like candy. The cook pours good quality soy sauce over it, properly fermented in the old way, with no sugar or anything else added, not like the soy sauce they make these days with chemicals, salt, and caramel colouring. Proper sauce is made with soy beans, wheat, salt, and water, fermented with a special yeast, then strained and pressed. It's poured over the fish with a little good quality peanut oil, shredded ginger, and green onions. That's it—simple, so you can tell the fish was alive just moments before cooking. In fact, a good restaurant still takes the live fish to the table in a pan, and as it flaps and gasps for air, everyone oohs and aahs and says, "Yes, yes, very fresh, ho sun seen!" Sometimes the kids don't like it, especially the ones who were raised in Canada. What fools. They want their food brought to them already cooked and cut up, don't show me where it came from, just bring it to me hot and smooth and ready to eat! But if you don't see where it came from, how can you know you're not being tricked? That's what all those packaged, ready-to-eat foods you can buy these days at Wellcome are—neat little tricks for the spoiled and stupid who don't know any better. In my day, if you couldn't see it alive and flipping before it was cooked and served, you couldn't be sure what those sneaky cooks might bring you. Those sneaky, crooky cooks like Tak-Wing's father, Cheung Chiu-Wai! You never know what a cook like Cheung Chiu-Wai might do in the kitchen with that fresh fish; someone like him might still swap it out for another one, smaller and less fresh. There would be no stopping him from doing that, but the point of showing you beforehand was that it would give you at least half a chance of being able to tell when it came to the table. A gasping fish is a sign of the restaurant's honesty. That's why it has to be just barely cooked too. A discerning customer like my father Mah Chin-Pang could tell. He would look sternly at the live fish when it was brought flopping in its pan, and even more sternly at the cooked one to make sure it was the same fish.

But no one asks the fish if it wants to be fresh any more than they ask it if it wants to be eaten. Just as nobody asked me if I wanted to be beautiful. Nobody asked me if I wanted to be a girl, and nobody asked me if I wanted to be pretty. I know my father thought that he could marry me off to the son of his business partner, Yeo, to consolidate his business and make sure it would last into the next generation and the generation after that. Or maybe he thought he could marry me off to one of the sons of the Ho Tung family or one of the sons of Shouson Chow, should they have deigned to be interested in my tender meat. I was that pretty—it's not bragging, it's the truth carefully assessed by my father, my mother, my horse-faced sister, Amah, Driver Lim, Auntie Lim, Second Mother Polly, and all the little half-brothers and half-sisters who came after my mother died. I was the kind of woman through whom alliances and fortunes could be made. They knew it, and I knew it. Everyone knew it—that I was like a fresh, steamed fish that could impress guests and satisfy family members as long as it was cooked until the flesh came just barely free of the bone.

But just because no one asked me what I wanted doesn't mean I didn't know. I knew, and I knew very well. I wanted what I wanted, and what I wanted was love. And lucky for me, unlike other pretty Chinese women before me, it was a time when Chinese women could want, and Chinese women could love. A little secretly, a little shamefully, but they could. It was the Dirty Thirties, the Nanking decade, when republicanism was alive and well in China, everyone was full of hope for real freedom, Shanghai was still roaring, and here in the British Crown colony of Hong Kong, though Chinese and British people lived quite separate lives, everybody was fashionable and everybody had a club and a hobby—tennis, cricket, Cantonese opera, mah-jong, dancing. Me, I loved all of those things, sports and the men who played them—tennis especially, though cricket was all right too. Unlike my father, who clung to everything Chinese in spite of how Western he already was, I embraced Western things. But I loved Chinese things too—the Cantonese opera with its moon-gazing maidens, its slender scholars, its just magistrates, and its angry warlords. I loved the stylized high-pitched voices, the red, white, and black makeup, the all-male casts, and the brightly coloured Imperial-style clothes. I fell in love with the men who played the female roles—many young women did in those days, though you weren't supposed to talk about it. I loved to eat melon seeds, sip oolong tea, and play mah-jong late into the night too. I loved the clacking tiles, the gossip, the old ladies who knew about the most shocking scandals, the pretty young things who would sit for a round or two before losing patience and slipping away to dance the lindy hop, the quiet husbands of the gossiping ladies who played reluctantly to make up the necessary group of four after the young things had slipped away. I *was* one of those pretty young things. I loved to dance more than anything else in this sad and fleeting world. I loved to dance, and I loved to sing. I especially loved to dance at the Repulse Bay Hotel to the music of Nick Korin and His Swing Band. I loved the gala nights, the tea dances, and the dinner concerts at the Gripps in the Hong Kong and Shanghai Hotel, and the Rose Room at the grand Peninsula. I loved the tiffin concerts, too, put on by George Pio-Ulski and His Classical Quintette, where they'd play highbrow stuff like Weber's *Oberon*, Mendelssohn's Piano Trio in D minor, and European popular music like Ralph Benatzky's "Mein Mädel ist nur eine Verkäuferin." Later, when the war got going in China, I loved the charity balls and fundraisers for the Far East Flying Training School, the British Prisoners of War Fund, and the Free Schools for Boy and Girl Refugees. Yes, I knew there were big arguments, small skirmishes, and then eventually a real war that unfolded in China. I knew, and I tried not to think about it. I was young, okay? I wanted to love and have fun while I could. Because it would have been unseemly to go alone, I dragged my poor sister Violet around everywhere I went, though she wasn't much fun. She was so ugly that no one would ask her to dance. She'd find the darkest corner she could to sit by herself until it was all over. I longed for better company, and better guidance.

But my mother was dead, and my father was caught up in his business life and the life of his concubine, who had borne an unusually large number of children. As long as he didn't find out about it, which he mostly didn't, I was free to do what I wanted, and what I wanted to do was dance. Of course, I didn't have a lot of pocket money, and it was expensive to go the Repulse Bay Hotel. Violet and I weren't like the beautiful expatriate people who lived their beautiful expatriate lives in such places. Though my family wasn't poor, we were still Chinese. And Chinese people were only grudgingly allowed in these places. If I wanted to go out every weekend, I'd have to be more resourceful. I dreamt and planned as I played my records on the gramophone I had begged Father for by way of Second Mother Polly. I had all the latest records from Parlophone and Rex, which I bought at the Tsang Fook Piano Company. I had Victor Silvester's Harmony

Music playing "Dicky Bird Hop." I had Gino Bordin playing "Charm of Hawaii." I had the Phil Green Orchestra playing "Sweet Muchucha" and "The Peanut Vendor." But what I loved most was the music coming out of the Canidrome in Shanghai played by the trumpeter Buck Clayton and His Harlem Gentlemen. Actually, Clayton didn't have roots in Harlem at all. He was born in Kansas and made his name in a taxi dance hall in Los Angeles, but we all take on a little mislabelling sometimes so people can place us better. He played *Rhapsody in Blue* and "The Very Thought of You." I sang along and discovered I had a voice. And also that Clayton had a Chinese counterpart called Li Jinhui, whose daughter was a famous singer. That could be me, I thought. I practised a few of my favourite Shanghai jazz standards: "Rose, Rose, I Love You," "Waiting for You," "By the Suzhou River." But my favourite was a Yiddish song popular in Germany: "Bei Mir Bist Du Schön," made famous by the Andrews Sisters. I sang it as I showered. I sang it as I walked with Amah down to Central to get vegetables and meat for dinner, while I helped her hang laundry and put out the garbage.

One day just before lunar new year, when all the little shops along the steps down to Central were festooned with plum blossoms, lucky sayings in gold characters on red paper, and bright lanterns over the doorways, we walked and I sang. Two men strolling in front of us turned around. One was tall and dark skinned, the other pale and slender. "Pardon me," said the pale and slender one, in perfect Cantonese.

"Oh!" I stepped back. People didn't usually talk to one another in the street, not then or now, but the men were in a festive mood. Were they drunk? Down the steps in front of us, a shopkeeper and his two sons set off a long string of firecrackers.

"We don't mean to startle," said the tall, dark man, also in perfect Cantonese. Not drunk. And very well spoken. "I'm Isadore Davis Wong. I work with ZBW Radio." His eyes were very warm.

Amah, always cautious of those she didn't know, but extra cautious now because the interaction was so unexpected, pulled at my arm. "Come on, Missy. Can you imagine if the neighbours saw you talking to strange men in the street?" Her disdain and distrust dripped off her like wet paint.

"I'm Tanaka Shigeru," said the pale and slender man. "We want to start a band. We need a singer. You have a beautiful voice."

His words pleased me, but I kept my face straight.

Wong spoke to Tanaka in English. "Maybe we shouldn't have stopped the lady in public."

"Come on, Missy," said Amah.

My legs followed her, but my gaze followed Tanaka Shigeru and Isadore Davis Wong.

"We might never see her again, man," Tanaka said. He hurried after us and switched back to Cantonese. "Isadore plays bass. I play piano. Truly, we mean no harm. Look, here's my card. If you're not interested, you don't need to call me. But if you are, we could meet you, maybe at the Metropole Hotel, to discuss."

I liked the Metropole Hotel. I extended my hand a few inches forward in the direction of the card.

"Missy, come on," said Amah, yanking me back. "You'll make your father very angry."

"I don't think so," I said to Tanaka, though I know he saw the longing in my eyes.

He smiled, his own eyes light and hopeful. "Just think about it." He was still holding out the card.

I managed to snatch it from his hand before Amah pulled me away.

So that was how I became a singer with Isadore Davis Wong and His Cosmopolitan Elites. Izzy had come to Hong Kong from Jamaica five years earlier because his Chinese father wanted him to marry a Chinese girl from the home village. He got a job at the General Post Office and its offshoot, zBW Radio, and ended up staying many years longer than he had intended. Tanaka Shigeru was born in Hong Kong and spoke fluent Japanese, Cantonese, Mandarin, Russian, and English. He worked as a translator, like his father before him. We played Buck Clayton's tunes. We played "Rose, Rose I Love You," "Waiting for You" and "Bei Mir Bist Du Schön." We sang a song that Izzy and Shige wrote themselves called "Moon and Stars over Sai Kung," for which we became just a little bit famous.

High moon
Bright stars
Milky Way's a river
Flowin' to the galax-sea
Just for me and my baby
Just for my baby and me

For a few years, before our world collapsed, I danced on the roof of the Repulse Bay Hotel, and then later at the Gripps in the Hong Kong and Shanghai Hotel and the Rose Room at the Peninsula until my feet were sore. I sang until my throat ached. I laughed and ate Quails Juniper and shrimp salad. I drank as much champagne and oolong tea as my belly could hold. Best of all, the handsome cricket, football, and tennis player Cheung Tak-Wing, secret star of the Hong Kong Cricket Club and golden boy of the Chinese Recreation Club in Tai Hang, whom I'd met at Tiger Balm Gardens, came to see me at the Repulse Bay Hotel whenever he could, in the company of his more progressive cricket playing friends, who loved Isadore Davis Wong and His Cosmopolitan Elites.

Old Mah was horrified, but in those days it was the job of Chinese daughters to horrify their fathers.

"My English friend Hancock says he saw you at the Repulse Bay Hotel. Dancing. Please tell me it that isn't true."

I said nothing.

"Emily would never do such a thing," Violet said.

Father scowled. "You know very well that she would, Violet. Let her speak for herself. Is it true, Emily?"

"It's a little bit true."

"What do you mean a little bit true?"

"Well ..."

"Well, what?"

"I danced a little bit. But mostly I sang."

"You sang?" His face began to flush.

"She's the singer in a band called the Cosmopolitan Elites," Violet explained, helpfully.

"What's wrong with singing?" I said. "Second Mother Polly was a singer."

Father's face turned a very worrisome shade of purple. I fled the room while Violet stayed to receive his wrath.

CHAPTER 4

LETTERS ACROSS OCEANS

164 Water Street
St. John's, Newfoundland

March 11, 1937

Dear Izzy,

Donkey years since I saw you last. When was it you left us? 1932? Isn't five years long enough to get married and come back home? Well, who am I to talk, since I'm not there either. I sure miss those days of eating chow mein, fried vegetables, and roasted pork while we sat on those little stools at the back of your daddy's store. And those little dried plums your mama would give us for a snack later, so salty and so sour—Lord! I know your mama misses you something fierce. She's still mad at your daddy for sending you away. You could have married a nice Jamaican girl instead of some foreigner who doesn't even speak your language. Her words, not mine. Well, I haven't seen her myself for a while, nor my own mama, whom I miss too.

Last year my old man sent me up here to Newfoundland to work for the Baccalieu Company, see if I can get the fishermen drinking more of our good Screech Owl rum. So here I am in the land of salt fish, my cuz, acres of it drying in the fog. You got to hand it to the people for perseverance, trying to dry anything in air so damp it's practically part of the ocean. Can't sell enough of our company's good stuff to please my daddy, though. And honestly, it's a little lonely here. People friendly and all, but close-knit, and I'm a come from away. Whenever that song "Mood Indigo" comes on the radio, I sure do feel homesick. Duke knows what it is. Hey, are you still plucking away on that bass of yours? I sure was envious when you bought that. Now what I wouldn't give to hear you play again in that little band you put together with that skinny, tall kid in Kingston. What was his name again? Martin something. Man, he could fling a lick on them guitar strings. You making music these days?

I been reading the articles of a brother called Du Bois in the *Pittsburgh Courier*. Do you follow him at all? If anyone is going to give us coloured folks a chance, it's him. First American Negro to earn a doctorate—went to Harvard and the University of Berlin. This brother's a real revolutionary and a real intellectual both at the same time. Got a million ideas for how to get us out from under the boot of the white man. He's really something, gives me new faith every time I pick up his words. I get the *Courier* sent all the way up here to the Dominion of Newfoundland just so I can follow this guy's thinking. He says things hopping in Asia. He says the Japanese are going to drive those bastard colonizers out, make Asia for Asian people, just like how our brothers and sisters across the water going to make Africa for Africans again. Du Bois went to Japan and said he was treated with great respect there. He says Japan has discovered the secret of the white man's power, and without violence has changed her whole stance toward the world. Japan has sacrificed nobly and has emerged in the twentieth century as Europe's equal in education, health, industry, and art. He talks about the oil refineries she has built, and the factories, boats, and trains—just everything flourishing. He says the land is beautiful too, tall mountains covered in pine trees. He says Japan wants to share all she has built with her Asian cousins—cousins like you, Izzy! That's what I thought right away when I read that. I thought, hey, my little cousin is half-Asian, lives in Hong Kong. Soon maybe the Japanese come liberate Hong Kong from the British! Well, that would really be something now, something I'd sure like to witness.

Cousin, do the Asians drink rum? I don't mean to sound foolish, but I don't know if they do. 'Cause I'm thinking if Newfoundlanders aren't buying enough, maybe Asia would be a good place to do business. Daddy wants me to go to America now that Prohibition is over, but honestly, I'd like to see that place where Brother Du Bois says the revolution is imminent. And see my little cousin, his new wife, and maybe a couple of pickney too. Isn't Hong Kong some kind of entrepôt? Isn't there a way I could move my stuff there? Maybe you got a contact who can help me out. If you do, I thought I'd come join you and make a go of it. A good idea, do you think? Love to hear your thoughts.

Niceness and love from your big cousin,

Morgan

119 Lai Chi Kok Road
Mong Kok, Hong Kong

April 4, 1937

Dear Morgan,

Thanks for your letter, cousin. It was really great to hear from you. You are my heart ambassador out there in the world. Mama too much, but I love her. And man, you make me all homesick. Ha ha, yeah, I got married to a nice girl from the home village up in the Sai Kung hills. Her Chinese name is Sum-Yin, and her English name is Jane. Her father and my father were childhood chums, catching crickets together in the village lane. He helped me get a job at the General Post Office, where she was already working, so that is how we met. She was the most beautiful girl there, bar none! I told Mama already that she speaks English—no problem, don't fuss. I'm sure Mama laughed. I know she just worries about me, so far away. But we're doing fine. Got one kid already and another on the way. Someday soon I'll take Jane and the little ones back to Kingston, and Mama will get to meet her.

Yes, for sure if you wanted you could come out here, and I'd help you best I could to set up. Lots of business to be done here, you could do pretty well if the war doesn't come. If it does, well, it'll be hard times for all of us, my cuz. There's no certainty in this world anywhere you go. But right now the war's rattling just over the border in China. People are expecting the Japanese to invade Singapore, but they are saying not Hong Kong. It's too small and too useful. My friend, you'd be taking a risk, though, because rumours are just rumours, and the war is a lot closer to Hong Kong than it is to Newfoundland.

I don't know if Brother Du Bois is right, though, about the Japanese liberating anyone. They been doing some stuff in Manchuria that's not so great. I'm more inclined to throw my lot in with the British. Yes, I know they are thieves too, but the life here is not so bad. A man can make a decent living. These days, I'm working for the radio station ZBW. I have a band with my friend Tanaka and this Chinese girl, Emily Mah—she's got a great voice and is a lot of fun. Tanaka is Japanese, and he has no faith in the current Japanese government. He says Asia for Asians is a nice dream, he believed for a bit, seeing as how the British here keep all the good things for themselves— clubs, horses, cricket fields, fancy addresses, that kind of thing. But there are other forces at work. If you want to come, you'd best just come to sell your rum and maybe a few other things for yourself or other folks, and not hold your breath for anything else.

If you want to come, I say give it a try. I'll ask Tanaka to help you. He's a translator and a fixer for a little import/export company called Earnest Trading. Maybe you could be an import/export agent or something at the company, and from there establish your own business. Tanaka knows all about visas and stuff like that. Just let me know.

It'd be great to have you out here. There are opportunities. I think you'd like it. Be warned though, like I said.

Love from your cousin,

Izzy

164 Water Street
St. John's, Newfoundland

April 29, 1937

Dear Iz,

Aren't you selling out a little bit? Apologizing for the British like that after all the evil they done us? Brother Du Bois is leading the charge in America, protesting Jim Crow and insisting on our civil rights. Internationally, he advocates pan-Africanism. He says that China and Japan have to stop fighting and unite in self-defence. Now's their chance to get free of those bloodsucking imperial tyrants. He says for sure there are philanthropists and reformers in Europe and America who care about all mankind, but they don't rule. It's those two-faced ghouls who do, and they want nothing more than Japan and China at each other's throats so they can crush and exploit both. China and Japan got to get together, and seeing as how China doesn't have the strength to drive the Europeans out, she better take Japan's lead. That's what my old pen pal Noma Kennosuke used to say—Lord, more than ten years ago now. I wonder whatever happened to him. Stopped answering my letters just before he entered military college.

Anyway, what those Europeans are doing in Asia is no different from what they're doing in Africa and the South Seas. They just want to dominate the world, those bloodsuckers. As a Negro and as an Asian you have double the reason to want to kick them back to those icy lands that are their rightful home.

I understand, though, that a man's got to live. Do you really think I could make a go of it in Hong Kong?

Love to you,

Morgan

119 Lai Chi Kok Road
Mong Kok, Hong Kong

May 22, 1937

Dear Morgan,

Hey man, I'm not a sellout. Don't you say that. What you're saying might seem perfect from a distance, but you have to live here to really know how it is. Of course I want our people to get out from under the yoke of the white man's imperialism, you know that. I'm not a coward or a fool. I know Brother Du Bois is thinking about African people, Asian people, and all peoples of the world that Europe is trying to control. If Chinese and Japanese could get together in brotherhood, well, that would be great. And if my mama's folks could be friends with my daddy's folks, well, I can't imagine a better thing. We know more about how to get together in Jamaica than anybody, that's a gift we could give this poor suffering world if only folks would give us half a chance. Mama used to say if she could love and marry an old curmudgeon like Daddy, well, anybody in this world could get along if only they would try. Gosh, I sure miss you all so much. Whatever happened to your little sister Hattie and that fella from the mainland, did that ever work out? Or did she break his heart and make him run home crying? She's a beautiful girl, your sister, and a kind person. I hope she got with someone good.

You should come here, keep me company. Come and dance at the Repulse Bay Hotel to the fine sounds of Isadore Davis Wong and His Cosmopolitan Elites. Meet Tanaka and Emily, and of course Janie and the kids. They would all love you, I know. You would get to see how it is on the ground too, and see how Brother Du Bois's fine ideas mesh up with our lives here.

Tanaka says he's more than happy to help set you up. You want me to ask him to arrange passage for you? Bring your dancing shoes.

Ever your best cousin,

Izzy

164 Water Street
St. John's, Newfoundland

June 14, 1937

Dear Iz,

Hum, hum hum. Well, I'm sure I don't know how things are on the ground, as you say. Brother Du Bois does say China is an inconceivable place. And yet he is so full of hope for what is possible over there, and by implication, what might be possible for us too. I admire him so much, but obviously he can't know everything, any more than I can. And you're there and I'm not, after all. Still, though, imagine if Japan really were that great and could put an end to all the arrogance and all the misery, if they could really kill those imperial cockroaches dead. That would be something, man, a real service to all of the exploited and suffering people on earth. Are you sure it isn't possible? When you say it's not, I feel so hopeless. When Brother Du Bois says it is, well, my spirits sure do lift. I gotta get out of the fog here. If things start to go my way, I sure would love a chance to put an oar in, take part in a real revolution instead of languishing in the damp and cold.

In the meantime, what you say about your friend Tanaka and Earnest Trading, that sounds really good. Screech Owl is losing money by the minute here. Getting pretty lonesome too. Be great to have my cousin at my side and to meet Jane and the little ones. And your bandmates too. I wrote to my old man and he says, yeah, go to Hong Kong and be with Cousin Izzy. I think he's excited about Brother Du Bois's messages too.

Why don't you give me your friend Tanaka's address and I'll write to him.

Until soon,

Morgan

CHAPTER 5

MAKE A WISE DECISION

July 8, 1937

A few fishing boats dotted the placid surface of Clearwater Bay. A British launch boat owned by one of the big hongs in town cut leisurely through the water and moved on to the next bay. On shore, it was hot and humid as the inside of rattan steamer over a boiling pot, but out here on Clearwater Bay there was a little sea breeze and the sun was pleasantly warm. True to the name of the bay, the water was so clear you could see straight to the bottom. Cheung Chiu-Wai, head cook at the Hong Kong Cricket Club, and his sworn brother, Captain Lee Cho-Lam, the fisherman, odd-jobber, and occasional smuggler from the village of Chek Keng on the Sai Kung Peninsula, had their feet up on the gunwale of Lee's ever-faithful fishing boat, the *Oolong*, and their fishing rods over the water. They could have used nets, but nets signified work, while rods meant relaxation and leisure, a fashionable concept they seldom had the chance to indulge. Cheung's younger son, the shy, loyal, and hopelessly skinny Tak-Tam, and Lee's brave and capable daughter, Ting-Yan, rounded out their little party. Tak-Tam loved Ting-Yan for her tanned face, strong back, and quiet wisdom, but the feeling was not mutual. Ting-Yan loved Cheung's older son, the handsome and athletic Tak-Wing. That feeling was not mutual either. Tak-Wing loved a vain but beautiful girl called Emily Mah, whom Cheung despised because of who her father was.

The British launch boat returned to the bay, putting through the mild waters in their direction, kicking up a froth. It didn't come too close, but

Cheung could see a woman on the boat looking at them through binoculars. He scowled. Couldn't they mind their own business on his precious day off? With determination, he returned to the thoughts that he didn't have time for during the workweek, while he ran about to serve exactly the kind of people who watched him now from that shiny leisure craft.

If ever a man had two sons as different from one another as rice and fish, it was Cheung Chiu-Wai. His younger son Tak-Tam was bookish, selfless, and practical-minded; his older son Tak-Wing was just the opposite. Like his father, Tak-Wing was broad and tall—very unusual for a Southern Chinese. Like his mother, he was gregarious and outgoing, though perhaps not the brightest bulb in the box. He was too much governed by feeling, and a little self-absorbed too, not pathologically, but in the way that handsome men can sometimes be. Tak-Tam was a better person, but Tak-Wing was Cheung's favourite, though he could barely acknowledge this to himself.

It was probably because Tak-Wing was the source of the family's greatest pride. Along with seven others from the little village of Tai Hang, he had gone to the 1936 Berlin Olympics last summer as a member of the football team representing China. The village had provided eight out of the eleven team members, so it was in essence a Tai Hang team. This mattered a great deal because the village was so modest, a little backwater previously famous for its laundries, fishing, and quarry work, its poverty and labour. Not yet a hundred years old, it had begun at the same time as the British Imperial presence here in Hong Kong, as a site of relocation for people displaced from other villages, like Wong Nai Chung.

Though they were beaten by the British team, the Tai Hang boys came back as heroes. Who would have thought a handful of village boys could take on the world like that? If that wasn't a Hong Kong miracle, Cheung didn't know what was. Sometimes he wondered if the very existence of Hong Kong was nothing but a collective opium dream. Surely, in some more likely parallel universe, China had defeated the British in the Opium Wars and remained sovereign and strong. *Still*, he thought, *if our reality is as it is, then playing at the Berlin Olympics is as good as taking on Reich Chancellor Adolf Hitler himself.*

Tak-Wing had been promised to Ting-Yan since they were little. That was how it was done in the old days. Cheung and Lee were good friends, and their children liked each other and were of comparable age, so they had betrothed them young, with the understanding that the bond between the families would deepen over the years and the generations. As children, playing together aboard the *Oolong*, or on shore at Lee's village of Chek Keng or Cheung's adopted village of Tai Hang, they had been happy. They'd swum and fished together, played Rock Paper Scissors, Finger War, and Paper Fortune Teller. At Chek Keng, they'd harvested vegetables together and waded through the flooded rice paddies in bare feet. They'd sat on the deck of the *Oolong* for hours while it was docked at the Causeway Bay Typhoon Shelter and watched the big freighters lumber by, the red-sailed junks swoop and dip, the fishing boats sway, and the little sampans jog among them. They'd eaten sticky rice wraps together on that deck, held hands and watched the sun go down over Lantau Island in spectacular pinks and purples. Often Tak-Tam was with them, the cute little brother, pestering them to explain a game or share their packet of dried squid more equitably. Tak-Wing had truly adored Ting-Yan, and she had adored him in turn. While he was packing for Berlin, she had hidden a tin windup chicken in his suitcase so he would have something to play with and laugh about while he was away from her.

But when he came back, he was different: prideful, and at the same time, oddly aloof. He didn't tell Ting-Yan to go away, but he didn't treat her as an equal anymore either. She realized pretty quickly that his feelings had changed, and she was hurt, but she still loved him and continued to hang around. It had affected Cheung's relationship with Lee. He thought that maybe, if the children married, things would go back to the way they had been. It was a gamble, though, because while the situation might improve, it might also continue to worsen over the course of a lifetime. And then both lives would be ruined. And now Tak-Wing was infatuated with that awful, spoiled Emily Mah. Surely it would blow over. Surely it would pass. Anyway, according to tradition, it was the father's decision. Though no good father likes to force such a decision against the child's will. Still, Cheung felt responsible for the outcome, and he was concerned about it.

"What are you thinking about?" said Lee, offering a cigarette from a shiny red-and-gold package.

Cheung accepted. Lee struck a match, and Cheung leaned in to catch the flame. "Nothing at all, Brother," he lied.

Lee lit his own cigarette and took a deep, contented inhale.

In the distance, the nosy British boat changed direction and chugged off to the far end of the bay. It rounded the corner and moved up the coast, out of sight. As it disappeared, a sense of relief came over Cheung, deepening his ability to think. But was it really necessary to have the conversation today? There would be no getting around the awkwardness of it. Really, he'd prefer to fish, enjoy the sea breeze, and not think about anything.

Cheung and Tak-Tam, who worked as a helper in Cheung's kitchen at the HKCC, had Wednesday off so they could work the other six days of the week. Though nominally Cheung and Lee were fishing, this was a rare day for just taking it easy and enjoying the gentle waters of the South China Sea on a summer morning. The sea was rich with all kinds of underwater life. They didn't have to try that hard to catch something good. A couple of croakers, three groupers, and a sea bream gazed balefully up at them from the bucket of water that held their live catch for a feast of fresh fish with Cheung's family at Tai Hang Village on Hong Kong Island later in the day.

In the meantime, Tak-Tam and Ting-Yan were steaming a pot of salt fish and rice for their lunch. These days Ting-Yan was often quiet in her sorrowful recognition that Tak-Wing was moving away from her, but she chattered vivaciously about her two favourite village dogs, and Tak-Tam listened attentively, asking the occasional question about cuteness of face, sharpness of teeth, speed of chase.

The men had been doing this since they were teenagers, when the boat was home to Lee and his mother. She'd passed several years ago, but when Lee was young, she had come fishing with them.

The boat had a shallow hull and a green canvas roof that curved over the rear half to shield passengers from the rain, sun, and wind. The deck was covered with planks in the fore and aft, but the low basin of the boat was still accessible in the middle. Under the planks were stored all of Lee's fishing nets and crab traps, as well as rope, a spare anchor, buckets, white glazed tin basins, blankets, towels, various hooks and tools, and an extra canvas tarp. Everything smelled of salt water, sun, and mildew. A little statue of the Virgin Mary sat in a small alcove beneath the tarp, a rosary around her neck. To Cheung, she looked a lot like the sea goddess Tin Hau, who watched over all the junks and fishing boats in this harbour, so he wasn't put off. Unusually, this boat had a motor, Lee's gesture to modernity and convenience bought with the dregs of a fortune he'd made, then lost, long ago in his misbegotten youth. On a regular workday, Lee used the boat for serious net fishing or crab trapping.

The salt fish had been split and dried at Chek Keng, Lee's village on the Sai Kung Peninsula. Because Lee was Tanka and Cheung was Hakka, they would not have been friends a hundred years ago. But the rice under which the salt fish steamed might have come from the Cheung family fields in the village of Wong Nai Chung, Cheung's natal village, where his mother and sister still lived, inland from Victoria Harbour. But those rice fields had been outlawed in 1844, two years after the end of the First Opium War and the signing of the Treaty of Nanking by the British colonial government, who were eager to put the land and the people to some other use.

Cheung's mind raced with all of these things in spite of his wish that it wouldn't. He put down his feet and turned his face toward the warm, placid sun. He breathed in the salty air. Ting-Yan and Tak-Tam kept an eye on the steaming rice and chatted softly. He could not hear what they were saying above the roar of the motor.

"Have you given any thought to our children's futures?" Lee asked. The wind shifted a little, and Lee turned the tiller to adjust the boat's direction.

Well, Lee had broached it. Cheung would have to say something now.

In the distance, the British launch boat careened back into the bay. The voices aboard it were loud and drunk.

"Idiots," said Cheung.

"Too much money, not enough brains," said Lee.

The British boat wobbled and fishtailed, drunk as her passengers. Cheung and Lee tried to ignore it.

Cheung knew Tak-Wing wanted to marry his sweetheart, Emily Mah Wai-Yee. Tak-Wing had met her at the Tiger Balm Gardens, owned by the colony's most famous Singaporean, Aw Boon Haw, famed for his camphoric medicinal ointment, on a Sunday afternoon when both the Mah and Cheung families were there to take in the sights. He'd recognized her as the singer with Isadore Davis Wong's band, and when she stumbled on a rock and dropped her parasol, he'd caught it as it rolled like a cartwheel down the garden path. When he'd returned it to her, their eyes met, and a little flame had flared between them, so Tak-Wing had said.

The drunken launch boat lurched toward them, much closer now than it was the last time Cheung looked. He ignored it.

Tak-Wing had said that Ting-Yan was his friend, but he'd never intended to marry her and didn't know where any of them had gotten such a silly idea. Cheung called him a liar and an ingrate, but it didn't do any good. A further complicating issue was the fact that Lee had no sons, no other children at all except for Ting-Yan, which meant that whoever she married would be expected to move to the village at Chek Keng and eventually take over Lee's boat and the life that went with it. If only Ting-Yan were interested in Cheung's second son, Tak-Tam, everything would have been easy. Tak-Tam would likely take well to a traditional life of fishing, rice-growing, and animal care. He would be happy to go, if only Ting-Yan would have him. But Ting-Yan was still fixated on the spoiled, gregarious Tak-Wing. Tak-Wing would likely botch a traditional life completely, but

Ting-Yan's eyes still followed him as they had all her life, as though he were the sun and she were the moon.

Captain Lee was the closest friend Cheung had. They'd known each other since they were boys, when Lee's father sold fish to Cheung's father down at Victoria Harbour and once gave him a basket of unsold crabs at the end of the day. Cheung wanted his friend's daughter to be happy, even if it would mean sending his favourite son out of the village. Of course, it was unconventional to marry the first son out and keep the second at home. But Tak-Tam would be perfectly capable as head of household at Tai Hang. Though neither a football hero nor a man of the times, he would care for the house as the distinguished scholars of old did, in fine Confucian tradition.

Lee stubbed out his cigarette. "Take your time, Brother. We don't have to talk about it today if you don't want to."

He meant the opposite, of course.

Cheung inhaled the last drag of his own cigarette and then stubbed it out.

He had another motivation for wanting Tak-Wing to marry Ting-Yan. Emily Mah Wai-Yee, the girl Tak-Wing loved, was the daughter of Cheung's mortal enemy. Besides being responsible for the death of Cheung's father, Mah was the descendent of Henry Witt-Weatherall, one of the colony's original taipans, for all intents and purposes a nineteenth-century drug lord. Because Cheung could not afford to hate Witt-Weatherall and Co., which had diversified into so many businesses that it was impossible to live in Hong Kong without being indebted to it in some way, and because he could not afford to hate the toffs who employed him at the Hong Kong Cricket Club, he hated Morris Mah. He owed Mah less than nothing, and so he could hate him without reserve. The possibility of Tak-Wing's marriage to Morris Mah's daughter was the greatest horror that Cheung could imagine.

More of his conversation with Tak-Wing echoed in his head.

"Haven't I taught you not to imagine yourself as one of them? You have two options: marry Emily Wai-Yee and shame your family for eternity, or marry Lee Ting-Yan and inherit her house and boats at Chek Keng and bring honour to both Captain Lee and your venerable father."

"I'd take Ting-Yan and honour," said Tak-Tam.

"I'll take Emily and shame," Tak-Wing said.

"You insolent idiot!" shouted Cheung.

"But you said I had two options."

"Forget it. You have no loyalty and no sense."

Fisherman Lee understood the nature of Cheung's two sons. In all honesty, he preferred the gentle and bookish Tak-Tam. He saw in Tak-Tam a strength and a wisdom that Cheung did not. It was true that Ting-Yan and Tak-Wing were betrothed when they were little. But Lee could see as clearly as anyone that Tak-Wing's feelings had changed. Though he still liked the idea of that union, it had to be a happy one, and he was a little bit afraid that Tak-Wing would make his beloved only daughter suffer. Also, when the children were promised to one another, everyone had assumed that Lee would eventually have a son of his own to inherit the boat and the house at Chek Keng, and that Ting-Yan would move to Tai Hang to be with Tak-Wing. Now it was clear that whoever she married would have to be willing to move to Chek Keng. It would make a lot more sense for her to marry somebody's second son. Tak-Tam fit the bill and was a close substitute for her beloved Tak-Wing. But for reasons Lee didn't fully understand, Cheung seemed to really want Ting-Yan to marry Tak-Wing.

A conversation from another Wednesday fishing with their feet up echoed:

"I'll give you my first son."

"Nonsense. You need your first son to carry on your lineage in your own natal village."

"Tai Hang is not my village. My village was Wong Nai Chung, and it drowned in 1920."

"Doesn't your mother still live there?"

"Yes. With a disordered mind and too many ghosts."

"Tai Hang is your village now. You should honour it."

What man gave his first son to another village? Was there something wrong with Tak-Wing that Lee didn't know about? Tak-Wing was a little full of himself, though Lee had seen worse. Was Cheung trying too hard to be modern, letting the lovestruck girl drive the decision? Or perhaps he was offering Tak-Wing out of true loyalty and a belief that promises, especially those made long ago, must be kept.

Lee decided he would let Cheung, as the father of the sons in question, take the lead.

Cheung wished the final decision of who should marry whom didn't fall upon his shoulders. If it wasn't possible to make everyone happy, he could at least do what was best for the family. Someone would be upset with him no matter what he did. He must think of the future. To hell with everyone's petty desires. They would grow out of them. Finally, he said, "Best if my older son, Tak-Wing, marries your esteemed daughter, Lee Ting-Yan. I'm a modern person. Sometimes a woman must get what she wants."

"Are you sure? Are you asking me to send her to Tai Hang? I would for your sake, Brother."

"No. Tak-Wing will go to Chek Keng, since you so generously offer to make him head of household there. I'll keep Tak-Tam here at Tai Hang. He's young. There's time to find him a bride elsewhere."

"He seems to dote on Ting-Yan, though," said Lee. "And he's a grown man now, no longer a pesky little kid. Are you sure this is the best decision?"

Ting-Yan continued to chatter about dogs, cats, and who knows what else as she and Tak-Tam chopped vegetables to go with the rice and fish. Tak-Tam listened attentively, laughed, and nodded.

"I'm sure," said Cheung. "Ting-Yan should not marry a man she doesn't want. Tak-Wing will do as I say, and his old love for her will return. He's just going through a period of youthful stupidity. Remember what we were like at his age? He will see that this is right."

The more Lee thought about it, the more awkwardly Cheung's decision struck him. Still, it was not Lee's place to call the shots on this one. Aloud he said, "If it's what you want and what Ting-Yan wants, then I am happy."

Cheung said, "We'll celebrate at Tai Hang tonight. And in the morning, I will talk to my wife about the luckiest date for the wedding."

The modest Tanka craft began to rock. Cheung looked up just in time to see that British launch boat roar by, much too fast and much too close. It kicked up a massive wave that rolled over the deck of Lee's fishing boat and put out the small flame over which the young people were cooking.

"Diu!" cursed Lee. "Dead white ghosts."

"Never mind," said Tak-Tam. "The pot is still hot. The rice will cook on the heat that remains."

Cheung shook his fist. "Get away from here! Barmy bastards!" Though he was promoted to head cook only last year, he'd been working at the HKCC since he was a young man, so his English was pretty good thanks to his daily contact with the British club members and the education in curses that accompanied his early lessons in dishwashing, floor scrubbing, mantel dusting, and, later, menu preparation.

The launch boat circled back. The young captain, drunk and in a daredevil mood, cut as close to the modest fishing craft as he could. Another great wave washed over the deck and dumped Tak-Tam, Ting-Yan, their vegetables, and their pot of fish and rice into the ocean. The day's catch followed them. Both young people were good swimmers. Like sleek porpoises, they glided to the starboard side and climbed up the ladder—first Ting-Yan, then Tak-Tam.

But lunch was gone. So were the fish that the friends had spent the morning catching. From the deck of the launch boat came the clamour of drunken young British men laughing and shouting obscenities.

Cheung yelled at the idiot bastards while Lee pulled the green tarp over the boat's roofing frame to create shelter for the kids.

The British men hooted and shouted in response. They swooped around for a third pass, but didn't cut quite so close this time. The little fishing boat rocked, but didn't tip. The drunkards zoomed off into the next cove. Peace returned once more to Clearwater Bay.

"Stupid foreign devils," said Cheung, wiping water from his face.

"Curse their mother's holes," said Lee, wringing water from his soggy singlet.

"Imagine if we hadn't lost the Opium Wars," said Cheung.

"The bay would be so peaceful," Lee said. He had the mop out and busily swabbed down the deck.

Cheung said, "We'd have a good lunch and a decent catch to cook five different ways tonight at Tai Hang."

"I'm sorry, Brother," said Lee. "I was looking forward to your wife's rice noodles with beef." He laid the mop in its special compartment beneath the gunwale.

"Heh," said Cheung, "the beef noodles didn't go overboard! Yim-Fong knows you're coming and will have made them anyway. She doesn't know we lost the catch!"

"My stomach is already growling."

"We wouldn't have lost the Opium Wars if our great-grandfathers didn't get addicted to opium," said Cheung.

"My great-grandfather smoked opium before the Opium War, for the pleasure of it," said Lee. He lifted a floorboard to get at the towels, though they weren't much drier than the four drenched passengers. He tossed one to Cheung, one to each of the kids, and took one himself to dab the water out of his ears, then vigorously dry his soaking hair. "He was a Macau pilot, bringing those big foreign ships to the docks at Whampoa. He only became an addict afterwards because he was so dismayed at having lost the war. My great-uncle smuggled opium to pay for my great-grandfather's habit. If I ever become so useless, Cheung, you have to throw me overboard. Then motor away and don't look back."

"My grandfather became an addict after the Punti–Hakka Wars because he couldn't bear the memory of mother and father gutted before his eyes."

"Too many men shot in front of their families," said Lee. "Too many women raped." Lee's eyes went elsewhere, thinking of his own grandmother and great-aunts. Maybe thinking of things his grandfather or Cheung's might have done.

"Too many villages burned to the ground," Cheung said. "Did they tell you much about it?"

"Nah," said Lee. "The old people don't like to talk. They don't like to pass on the sorrow."

"My parents didn't talk either," Cheung said. "If my aunt weren't such a gossip, I wouldn't know a thing. May we live out our lives in peace so that we can freely tell our children of the sweetness we lived through, all blessings to Tin Hau, the great goddess of the sea."

"I wish you wouldn't invoke her," Lee said. "There is only one God, and that is Our Father who art in Heaven." He crossed himself. "It's not too late to get baptized, you know. There's a priest at my village who will do it for you, any day of the week."

"No, thank you, Brother. Tin Hau is good enough for me."

"Last time, you said you would think about it," Lee said.

Cheung went silent. He loved his friend, but he didn't want to join the white man's strange religion. Cheung's mother was Hakka. Her side of the family was in the Taiping Rebellion, but they had never converted. Cheung blamed the rebellion on the leader Hong Xiuquan's Christianity, though he didn't want to say so to Lee. He cared for Lee, and Lee was devout.

Lee realized he'd overstepped his bounds into a sensitive area and didn't say anything more for a long while. Finally, he asked, "Hungry?"

"Yeah," said Cheung, with a soft chuckle to release the tension. "I'm so ready to eat Yim-Fong's beef with flat noodles."

"Me too," said Ting-Yan.

"Let's get going to Tai Hang, then." Lee pulled up the anchor, the first step in the journey home, but as he did so, there was a ruckus in the harbour. The launch boat with the drunken captain had returned. It veered into the bay at an outrageous speed, on a motor too powerful for an idiot like that to be operating. It swooped in on a little Tanka craft, cutting close at an impossibly tight angle, almost on its side. The Tanka craft went over, tipping an old granny into the sea, along with her small granddaughter. A second later, the British boat went over too, dumping the captain and his half-dozen young, drunk friends.

Lee rolled his eyes. "What a bunch of morons." He yanked the cord to start the motor. Turned the little craft in the direction of the incident.

Cheung shot him a surprised look. "Going to help those devils?"

"Going to help Granny Tang and her granddaughter. And then, yes, going to help those silly devils too. They're dead ghost crazy but they're still human. The Lord says, 'Do unto others as you would have them do unto you.'"

Cheung laughed. "Do what unto others? Even when you are that drunk, you would never try to mow down another boat just for the fun of it."

Granny Tang floated on her back in the water, holding her granddaughter, who wailed as the though the world had ended. While Lee motored in as close as he dared, Ting-Yan threw down lifesavers to them. Granny got the girl to hold on to one and grabbed the other. Ting-Yan and Tak-Tam jumped into the water and pulled them to the starboard ladder while Lee held the boat steady.

The British yahoos were in the water too, yelling and blubbing. None of them knew how to swim. Lee tossed buoys to them, while Ting-Yan and Tak-Tam swam around to help.

A few of the other boats from the area rowed toward the accident scene, shouting and calling to others. By the time they arrived, Cheung and Lee had already got Granny Tang and her granddaughter on board, as well as all six of the British pleasure boaters.

Granny berated the British, mostly in her own Tanka dialect, but with bits of English thrown in. "Stupid eggs ... my whole life on that boat ... you don't respect the people here ..." The little girl wouldn't stop crying. A woman from the British launch boat apologized. "We're sorry. It was really stupid. Selby was so drunk. We were trying to get him to stop. He can be such a lout ..." Everybody was shivering. Because of the soaking that Lee's boat had received earlier, there were no dry blankets or towels for anyone until more of the boats from the area arrived. But eventually they did.

Lee was well known on these waters. He'd grown up playing and fishing on them, and gained and lost a fortune on them too, in his youth. He collaborated with some of the fishers occasionally, purse seining for sea bream. The other fishers and boat people were generous when the saw the two downed craft. They didn't know whose fault it was, and they didn't ask. They gave towels and blankets and hot tea to the wet victims. Under Captain Lee's direction they righted Granny's boat. She was still upset because she lived on that boat, and all her worldly possessions were lost.

The British woman continued to apologize. "I'm sorry. We'll replace everything. Selby, tell the lady you're sorry. What you did wasn't very nice."

The British captain said nothing. He was embarrassed, but he didn't want to make himself small before this low-class Chinese woman.

Cheung recognized him. He was the nephew of the Hong Kong Cricket Club's president, Richard Hancock. This nephew, Selby Hancock, worked as a teller at the Hongkong and Shanghai Banking Corporation. Like many of the expats who worked here, he'd been in Hong Kong for only a couple of years. He didn't seem to recognize Cheung. Or if he did, he didn't let on. Cheung wondered whether he should or shouldn't identify himself.

Selby Hancock drained his teacup. A woman from one of the boats that came to help poured him more tea.

"Mr Hancock," Cheung said, "you know me, I think?"

Selby Hancock wouldn't look at him.

But the British woman said, "Cookie Cheung! It's me, Elizabeth!"

Cheung recognized her too, then. She was Hancock's young wife, who sometimes came with him to the club. "Mrs Hancock," he said.

"I didn't think you would know these kinds of people, Cheung," said Mrs Hancock. She'd never seen him outside the context of the cricket club.

"These kinds of people?" Cheung gave her a quizzical look. "These people are my people. This is Captain Lee. My sworn brother. Brings you the crab you eat at the club on Tuesdays."

"I'm sorry, Cookie," Mrs Hancock said. "I didn't mean it like that."

But she did, and Cheung knew it, and he felt absurdly ashamed, whether for himself or Mrs Hancock, he wasn't sure.

Unlike her husband, who couldn't care less, Mrs Hancock was astute enough, and cared enough, to know that she had hurt his feelings, though she couldn't fully figure out why. "We're sorry, Cookie, truly," she said. "What can we do to make it up to you?"

"You didn't hurt me," said Cheung, automatically saving face for both of them. "But Granny Tang lost everything."

"Ask her what she lost," Mrs Hancock said. "We'll replace it."

Lee's English was pretty good because he'd studied at the floating church when he was younger. But to be thorough, Cheung explained in Hakka what Elizabeth Hancock had said. Then Lee, whose native tongue was Shuilowaa, the language of the Tanka people, explained to Granny Tang what Cheung had said.

In Shuilowaa, Granny Tang said, "All my pots and pans, including the good cast iron wok."

"We'll replace it," said Mrs Hancock, after the translation relay.

"You going to replace my dead husband's photograph?"

Translation relay.

"I'm afraid I can't help with that," Mrs Hancock said, gazing sympathetically at Granny Tang, but also too intensely.

Granny Tang didn't look at her at all, and Cheung found the exaggerated sympathy in Mrs Hancock's eyes irritating, all the more so next to her guilty husband's determined indifference.

"We better right the white man's boat too," said Lee.

Granny Tang responded in her dialect. Cheung didn't understand until she said, in rudimentary Hakka, "Let those dead devils fend for themselves."

Cheung agreed. "It's their fault. Let the British boats come and help them."

"The Bible teaches that all men are brothers," said Lee. He called to the other boats.

They looped all the rope they had among them through the portside railing of the British boat. Then they all lined up alongside it.

"On my signal, row and pull!" Lee shouted. His boat was the only one in the whole harbour with a motor.

The men got into position.

"That is never going to work," said Selby Hancock sullenly. But he didn't try to stop them.

"One, two, three, pull!" Lee shouted. The fishing people dug into the ocean and pulled against it. Cheung gunned the *Oolong*'s motor.

The British boat shuddered, then dropped back into the water.

"One more time!" Lee yelled.

It took all the power of all the boats and the loudest shouting of all the fishing people, but miraculously, they pulled the British craft upright. Some of the Tanka men attempted to climb aboard to check its seaworthiness, but Selby Hancock cursed them. "Get away, you filthy Chinamen!" He abandoned his teacup and climbed aboard himself. "Go on! Get away from there!" He shooed them off as though they were stinking vermin. He restarted the motor, and when all seemed more or less well, he beckoned his compatriots to climb aboard. Mrs Hancock turned to Cheung one last time. "I'm truly sorry, Cookie," she said. "I'll tell his uncle. We'll do something for your granny, I promise."

"Elizabeth, come on!" shouted Selby Hancock.

"She's not my actual granny," Cheung said. "We just call her that out of respect." But Mrs Hancock didn't hear.

"Come on! What's wrong with you!" Selby Hancock again.

"Thank you, Cookie Cheung," said Mrs Hancock, with overwrought sympathy.

Annoyed at the surface, and at a deeper level steaming with shame, rage, and other feelings he couldn't identify, Cheung nodded. Why didn't she say thank you to Captain Lee or the fishers, who had done all the work?

The launch boat motored off with all the fishers' precious rope still tangled in its railing.

"Dead devils," said Granny Tang in the general direction of the departing British boat. "Stupid eggs."

The rescuers hung around Lee's boat a bit longer, talking and laughing about what had happened. Finally, grandmother and granddaughter got back on their boat, and one of the larger Tanka boats towed them back to Aberdeen, where they lived.

"You were kind to them," Cheung said to Lee as he pulled up anchor a second time. "Even though they were not kind. We deserve better masters."

"This is what the Good Book teaches," Lee said. "To treat all men as brothers. If we were all brothers under God, perhaps we would be our own masters."

"Tin Hau teaches people to help one another also. She is the goddess who helps especially ocean-going people when they're in danger of drowning. If any supernatural intervened today, it was her."

"Perhaps. But only the Christian God wants to unite all of the people. Unity among brothers is what we need in order to be free."

"Your brains are scrambled. The Christians wants to unite people under the white man's God. Then the white man will be our master forever."

"Better the white man than a Manchu emperor puppeting for the Japanese," said Lee.

"I don't want either," said Cheung.

"Then we are back where we started," Lee said.

The sunset over Fragrant Harbour was a beautiful misty pink and purple. The men began the long journey back toward the Causeway Bay Typhoon Shelter, trying to forget their differences and dreaming of the feast they would have with Cheung's family at Tai Hang once they got there, even if there would be no fish.

CHAPTER 6

Typhoon Shelter
THE TROUBLES OF CAPTAIN LEE
June 30, 1997

*G*reat-Aunt Violet has been talking so much, she's forgotten to eat. Though it would be more polite to leave some for her, the crabmeat is so sweet, tender, and garlicky that Ophelia can't stop munching. She sucks the meat from the shell and then uses her teeth to scrape the peppery, crunchy deep-fried coating onto her palate. She eats the slivers of fried garlic by themselves as though they were potato chips. The crab's head stares balefully at her, so she picks it up, turns it over, and scoops out its creamy, grey insides. A little bitter, yet redolent of the sea.

You want to be a hero or a zero? If you want to be hero, you should try to be like Captain Lee Cho-Lam. He's the closest thing our family has to a hero. Not a zero like Cheung Chiu-Wai or Cheung Tak-Wing. Or your uncle Raymond. Captain Lee wasn't born a hero, you know. He came from humble beginnings, very humble. He was a boat person, what we call "on-water people" in polite company. But you know, Cantonese people are not very polite. They call them "Tanka" or "sea gypsies." Don't ever say that to your Auntie Ting-Yan. She'll be very upset because she is part Tanka. I don't judge her when I say that. You know me, I treat everyone as equal. And besides, she is very dear to me, my nearest dearest one. But she is one of them. These are the people who used to live on the water in houseboats, fishing boats, and sampans, down in Aberdeen and up on the Sai Kung Peninsula. They've mostly come ashore now, but you might have seen some of their boats when we passed through Aberdeen to visit your Great-Aunt Hok-Yee in her care home last week. There are all kinds of theories about them. Do you know what a theory is? It's when people have an idea about something, but they don't know for sure, so they make their best guess based on intuition and gossip. I know, I know, you've been to university. You have a degree in sociology. Why didn't you study bio-chemistry so you could be a doctor? I guess with sociology you could still go into law. Just don't be a writer, whatever you decide to do.

Oh yeah, so the Tanka, I mean the Sui Seung Yan. Some people say they are descended from the Aboriginal people who lived in South China before the Han people came down from the north. And that they were pushed onto boats when the Han people took all the land. Some say their legs are shorter than most other people's because they lived so many generations on water; they needed a lower centre of gravity to walk on the boats without falling down. Obviously, that is rubbish made up by people who are low and ignorant themselves. Some say they belong to the Yue tribes, that they are the same as the Viet people of Vietnam. Some say that they are the same racial stock as the rest of us, a combination of Yao, Tan, and Tai mixed with Han people. Some say they are Yue people who mixed with the Tan mountain tribes and then were called Tan to distinguish them from the Yue people who are part of the general population. Who knows for sure? There was no such thing as anthropologists or sociologists to keep records back then.

What you need to know is that they live on boats. They were disdained and looked down upon by other Hong Kong people. They had to do all the bad jobs and all the hard jobs. They were the labourers, what we used to call "coolies," and sex workers, what we used to call "flower girls." But primarily they fished. We bought fish from them sometimes. Rumour says they were also smugglers and that long ago when the British forced opium on us, they were the ones who used to run the opium ashore at Whampoa, and bring back tea, silk, and rice for trade. I think this is how Captain

Lee got rich. Not smuggling opium or its modern versions, heroin and morphine. I'm not saying he didn't do that, but I'm not saying he did. But his time was a bit later, when other goods were more important. Ting-Yan told me once he made a fortune in the 1920s, when the new Chinese Nationalist government was trying to make money to keep its hold on power. They hiked up the tariffs on all kinds of goods as a way of raising funds to support the new government. To make it modern, on par with all the European states. But the tariffs were so high, and smuggling was such an old tradition all along the South China coast, so old that you can't even really call it smuggling. It was just trade in the old-fashioned way. But in those years, people could make a lot of money evading the tariffs. They didn't even need a black market. They would just quietly transfer the goods to ordinary shops through family and old business connections and they could make a pile. Ting-Yan thinks that that's what her father, Captain Lee, did.

Captain Lee was a poor Tanka, living on a tiny houseboat with his mother. His father and older brothers were dead. They died in a storm at sea. You know these nasty typhoons we get here. Their little onboard Tin Hau shrine was not enough to save them, and they had no motor in those days either. The storm came up quickly. All the men were at oar, desperately working to keep the little boat upright. It was a wooden fishing boat, you know the kind with the green cover that rolls over top? We call them tang tsai, which just means small boat. The whole family lived on that boat and made their living by it. Well, the winds blew strong and the waves rose to the height of mountains only to collapse a second later. Little Lee and his mother clung to the central mast, each with an old rubber tire around their waist. A big wave came and washed all the men clear off the deck, while Little Lee and his mom cried and wailed. You don't know what life was like back then: it was so hard, the people really suffered.

The men washed right off the deck and into the ocean. They were all drowned. Little Lee and his mom hung on for dear life. Can you imagine? I can hardly imagine. Life was so terrible, ai yah, what a tragedy. Somehow,

Lee and his mom hung on. Ting-Yan says Lee didn't pray to Tin Hau, but cursed her. He prayed to Mary—in those days the Christians proselytized through their floating church down in Aberdeen and up on the Sai Kung Peninsula. He cursed Tin Hau and prayed to Mary and promised her that if he and his mom survived the storm, he would convert to Catholicism. Well, somehow the boat remained upright. Somehow, they clung to the main mast. They survived that storm. The boat was damaged, but it was not smashed to pieces, which is a miracle, don't you think? The next day they were rescued by other Tanka boats in the area, and that afternoon, Little Lee went straight to the priest to get baptized. He didn't remove the Tin Hau shrine from the boat though. He just put a rosary around the little statue's neck and called her Mother Mary or Our Lady of Grace from then on.

Do you want to know the story of how Captain Lee got his wife, your great-great-aunt Siu-Wai, to marry him? She was Hakka from the respected village of Chek Keng. He saw her one day at Sai Kung, which is where the main dock for that area was and is. Wah! He thought she was so beautiful. He saw her, and he was so smitten, even more smitten than Macy is by Sutton Ngai—you saw them together at dinner last night, they couldn't stop staring at each other, so embarrassing, lah. But of course Captain Lee was not rich like his granddaughter Macy. Not yet, anyway. I told you, he was a poor Sui Seung Yan looking after his aged mother, with no father or older brothers to protect him or look after him or give him face. You know in those days no one would marry a Tanka. Not the Punti people, for sure. Not even the Hakka. They were really looked down upon. We really treated them badly, I'm ashamed to say.

What do you mean I put the Hakka down by saying "not even the Hakka"? Don't be such a sociologist. I don't look down on the Hakka. You know me, I treat everyone the same. Ting-Yan is part Hakka and isn't she my nearest and dearest?

Anyway, so Captain Lee saw Siu-Wai, Kwan was her maiden name, at the Sai Kung docks. And he thought to himself, *Wah, that lady is so beautiful. I'm going to marry her for sure. If Our Lady of Grace can save me from certain death in a storm that killed everyone in my family stronger than me, then she can help me marry that beautiful lady.* He burned incense at the little onboard shrine every day, and prayed to Tin Hau with her rosary on. "Mother Mary, I have sinned," he said. "Mother Mary, please make that lady love me." What patience that onboard Tin Hau must have had, to be dressed as some other deity and asked favours in that other goddess's name. Don't tell your aunt Ting-Yan I said that, she really believes in God. I kind of believe, but I believe in Tin Hau too.

What? Yes, I know doctors like me are supposed to believe in reason. I believe in reason! That doesn't mean I have to believe in it to the exclusion of everything else! Lots of Chinese people believe in more than one thing. I'm no different from the rest of my people.

Captain Lee knew that your great-auntie Siu-Wai was not a Sui Seung Yan like him. He knew how impossible it was. And still, he prayed and prayed and prayed. He prayed so hard he started having visions of Tin Hau with her rosary on—I mean, Mary. Sometimes he saw her ahead of him at the prow of the boat with her hands open and down at her sides, in true Catholic style. Sometimes he saw her with the right hand up and the left cupped at the belly in a mudra of courage. But her message was always the same: "Learn English."

How is a poor, fatherless fisherman to learn English? he thought to himself. *I can barely speak my own Shuilowaa dialect! And I certainly can't read or write in any language. I have to make money so that me and my old ma can eat!* But if he could learn English, he could perhaps pose as an overseas Chinese, and in so doing hide his Tanka roots. Then Siu-Wai might be convinced to marry him.

One day, when he was rinsing off the deck after a day of selling fish, a student walked by, and his book blew out of his hands and right onto the deck of the boat. The book had Chinese characters and English lettering in it, but neither did Captain Lee any good, since he couldn't read at all. But what it did do was give him an excuse to go visit Padre Donovan of the Catholic floating church in Aberdeen. Padre Donovan had to get one of his pupils to translate Lee's desires. The good priest thought Captain Lee was a little old, but let him sit in class with the small Sui Seung Yan boys of the floating church for English lessons after mass on Sunday mornings. It was humiliating to be a dim giant among all those snot-nosed little water bugs. But Captain Lee was a humble man and he also really wanted to marry your great-great-auntie Siu-Wai. It took him four years of hard work, humiliation, and eye strain late at night under a kerosene lamp after the fishing and odd jobs were done. But after four years, he could carry on a rudimentary conversation in English. All those four years, he saw her pass by the docks on her way to the Sai Kung market to buy fish for her family. Though she occasionally approached his boat, on days when he had fish to sell, he would make extra sure she didn't see him. He asked his mother to sell her the fish.

He could tell she was wealthy because her clothes were nice. Not city wealthy—not that wealthy. But village wealthy. Her family grew rice and vegetables. They raised chickens and the occasional pig.

As he became more educated, he realized being able to speak English wasn't enough. He would have to be able to bring wealth to her family also, or they would never permit the marriage. They were getting older by then. And he had no idea what plans her family might have for her. In those days, most marriages were arranged. Even if he weren't Sui Seung Yan, a love marriage would have been so unlikely. He had to make money, and he had to make it fast.

He prayed to Tin Hau with her rosary on. He prayed to Mary. He prayed to Our Lady of Grace. This is the part Ting-Yan doesn't like to talk about, so I don't know if it's true. If it is, it makes your great-uncle a crook, but what is a crook in a place where there are old customs and new laws, where the new laws are evolving, and where authority itself is an ever-shifting centre? It was 1928 and the Soong-MacMurray treaty granting China tariff authority and thus a route to modern statehood had just been signed. A guy could make a lot of money selling the kinds of goods that were taxed by evading those taxes through the old business and family connections that joined all the shopkeepers and boat people up and down the South China coast. Lee knew about the old trade routes because his mother knew about them. His mother knew about them because his father knew about them. His father knew about them because he'd travelled those routes like his father and grandfather before him.

I don't know if Lee trafficked in opium or its modern versions, okay? I don't know if he transported arms. He might have. There was a lot of political unrest in those days, a lot to be gained and lost through acts of war. It's just as likely though that he carried cargoes of tungsten, kerosene, rayon, salt, and sugar—all materials that were heavily taxed if imported the way the Nationalist government wanted them imported. But Lee's networks were the other networks. The networks that didn't pay tax. The networks that made money. Having lived all his life on a boat, having survived a storm that killed all the other men in his family, and having the protection of Our Lady of Grace made him both lucky and skilled. Up and down the coast he went for several years, ferrying bolts of cloth and sacks of salt in one direction, and crates of tea and silk in the other. He made a stinking fortune. I'm telling you, a *lot* of money. The kind of fortune that every Hong Konger, Sui Seung Yan or otherwise, dreams of. He bought a flat in Kadoorie Hill. He bought a nice suit. He bought a closet full of nice suits. He invested in real estate, shipping, and casinos. He proved good at investment, and it became his main line of business. He didn't need to smuggle anymore.

Well, rich people in Hong Kong are kind of like celebrities, you know? In making investments, he made name for himself, though he was strategically quiet about his smuggling history. It didn't matter anymore that he was Tanka, because he was so rich. He kept the tang tsai because it was his original home, and he docked it among the yachts at Royal Hong Kong

Yacht Club to show he was proud of his humble beginnings. This was a good thing because, as it turned out, he would need it later on.

He sent a go-between straight to Chek Keng to inquire about a young woman there, none other than Kwan Siu-Wai.

Well, as you can imagine, the rest is history. Her father, Old Kwan, was only too happy for his daughter to marry such a wealthy man. And as for Siu-Wai herself, she knew who he was. She had seen him scurry under the green awning whenever she approached his boat to buy fish from his mother. I think she truly loved him for the clever, humble man he was.

But the sad thing is, they had trouble conceiving children, and trouble being a proper married couple. Captain Lee could not sleep at the house in Chek Keng that he'd inherited through his wife. He could not sleep in his flat at Kadoorie Hill either.

On their wedding night, Siu-Wai woke up to find him out of bed. She searched the village up and down, as quietly as she could so no one would see her. Finally, she found him fast asleep under the green awning in the little tang tsai down at the tiny local dock. She loved him so much, she crawled in beside him, but the rocking of the boat made her nauseous, and she had to return to land. So it was between them their entire lives. They were lucky they had a child at all, my own nearest and dearest Ting-Yan, conceived in a brief undocumented moment on land or on water, where one was comfortable and the other was not. It turned out Old Lee could only sleep in the merciful arms of Tin Hau, the lady he called Mary, who had killed his father and brothers, but afterwards granted him almost everything he could have wished for.

The problem was the "almost." Though he loved his daughter, Captain Lee desperately needed a son to inherit his investments and his growing collection of boats, not to mention the land at Chek Keng he'd inherited through his wife. In the meantime, their nights together became harder and harder. It was as though the minute the sun set, Lee could not remain on land. And Siu-Wai's nausea on boats became so bad that the only way she could come and go from Hong Kong Island was to travel overland as far as Tsim Sha Tsui and take the brief ride on the relatively stable Star Ferry. Even then, her stomach lurched, and she had to spend the whole trip at one railing or the other, leaning over just in case. Lee's wobbly tang tsai was out of the question. She couldn't even stay there for a few minutes.

Lee's businessmen friends encouraged him to take a concubine. They were a hearty party lot of landlubbers with dozens of mistresses and voracious appetites for feasts and drinks. But this wasn't Captain Lee's way. He refused the bevy of lovelies they pushed at him. He even turned down the sorrowful Macanese fado singer Dulce de Melo, whom it was said no man could resist. Lee loved his wife, and even more than his wife, he loved Our Lady of Grace and was true to her edict of purity.

One by one his investments failed, first the real estate, then the shipping, then the casinos upon which he had gambled his fortune. He even had to sell the flat at Kadoorie Hill where his mother was living. There was no such thing as insurance in those days. Many men's fortunes rose and fell like ocean waves. Captain Lee was one of those men. Soon all that remained was Siu-Wai's family property at Chek Keng and the tang tsai he had inherited from his father and brothers. The day he sold his final property to pay his final debt, he brought his mother back to the village to live with Siu-Wai, returned to his boat, and slept as well as he ever had, which is to say quite well, because he still had his mother, his daughter, his beloved, a house with land and a little tang tsai watched over by Our Lady of Grace. That's a lot more than most Hong Kong people had in those days. It's a lot more than most Sui Seung Yan had. He still considered himself a wealthy man.

The crab is gone. Ophelia stares at the giant pile of shells on her plate, and the relatively small pile on Great-Aunt Violet's.

"Oh my gosh, I ate it all."

"Never mind. Not my favourite, anyway. I wanted you to have it. I prefer tang tsai jook. The congee they used to make on their little boats for sale to passersby."

Great-Aunt Violet raises her hand in the air and shakes it furiously to get the server's attention. The server comes, grumpy as ever, to take their order.

Great-Aunt Violet glances at the pink-haired girl on the wall. "1:30. Still time. We eat this, then we go. You can watch Chris Patten leave Government House on TV at Macy's."

"You told me before that Grandmother Emily eloped. I didn't know Chinese girls did that in those days."

"It was a little unusual. But anything a British girl can do, a Chinese girl can do better. Don't you know that by now?"

CHAPTER 7

ELOPE

July 8, 1937

On July 8, 1937, the *South China Morning Post* reported that, the previous night, the Japanese Imperial Army had entered Wanping, a walled city outside Beiping, with the excuse that a Japanese soldier had gone missing inside the city. The soldier returned unharmed to the barracks, but the Japanese had not left Wanping.

Amah was worried, but Father said that Hong Kong was going to be okay. "We're a British colony. Why would they bother with us?"

"Because we're a British colony," I said. "Haven't you heard the slogan 'Asia for Asians'?"

"With the Communists and KMT together, and Stalin backing the Chinese, the Japanese don't stand a chance," Father replied. "We don't need to worry."

"We need to have a plan for all eventualities, Father. No one can say for sure what will happen."

"The Chinese side will win. Then we can have Asia for Asians without the murdering Japanese Imperial Army, without the Manchu, and without the British. We will get free through commerce."

"I don't think that's how it is going to work. There are too many different kinds of political unrest."

"Just you wait and see," Father said.

In the afternoon, Emily came to my door in a simple white dress, beneath which a red slip peeked.

"Come and be witness for my marriage."

"Your what?"

"Tak-Wing and I are eloping." Her makeup was nice—her face carefully powdered, her eyebrows tweezed and pencilled in. She wore lipstick too, but the colour was subtle. No one would be able to tell what she was up to from her makeup.

"You can't do that."

"Why not?"

"Chinese people don't elope."

"Sure they do."

"Respectable ones don't," I said. "I mean, maybe if you were a sampan flower girl you could."

"Is there something wrong with sampan flower girls?"

"No. But—"

"The world is changing, Violet. And haven't we both sworn to become modern Chinese women? That means we can't be classist. And we can elope."

I chewed on what she was saying. "Tak-Wing?"

"Who else?"

"Father is going to be mad as heck."

"The old poop will get over it. He always does."

I scowled, but I went to get my shoes.

Tak-Wing was waiting for us at Statue Square. Neither Tak-Wing nor Emily was particularly unnerved by the statue of Queen Victoria. They had agreed to meet under her watchful eyes. I looked up at her, and she seemed to gaze back sternly. The city of Hong Kong was originally called "Victoria" in her name. What would that distant, dead English queen think of my sister running off with a village boy? I had read *Romeo and Juliet* in my first-year English class, stumbled my way through "Wherefore art thou Romeo?" and many more thees and thous besides. But could Queen Victoria ever have translated the Montague and Capulet feud to make sense of the enmity between the Mahs and the Cheungs? Or did she see us as all alike, as so many her emissaries here did? Of course, we were all subjects of George VI by then. And he'd had to take the throne because his older brother, Edward, had eloped with the American divorcee Wallis Simpson. Who was married when they met and got divorced in order to depose a king so she could marry him. If the English king could give up the throne to marry an already married woman, maybe a couple of Chinese kids eloping across a class divide with the anonymous assistance of the British colonial system was not a terribly great matter. But unlike Edward VIII's father, George V, who was dead, Emily's father and mine, Old Mah, was very much alive, and he was not going to be happy.

My sister linked arms with me and with Tak-Wing also to give herself courage. We hurried toward the Supreme Court Building, passing right under King George V's nose, and that of blindfolded Lady Justice also. I found the myriad statues so creepy, though Queen Victoria was decidedly the worst. I felt as though I were passing through a garden of ghosts.

Noticing my consternation, Tak-Wing said, "Just think of her as Tin Hau for English people."

The idea was so silly that I chuckled, and he chuckled with me.

"My father works at the HKCC," he said, waving his arm to indicate the cricket field behind the Supreme Court. "So I come here all the time. I remember that when I first saw her, I was terrified. But I'm used to her now. Let's go give her a poke for good luck." She was fenced in, but there was an entranceway so one could come inside the enclosure. We ascended the stone steps, and Tak-Wing gave me his umbrella to take a jab at her. I felt ridiculous, but I poked at the base of the statue as though with a rapier.

"En garde!" Tak-Wing shouted.

When the tip of the umbrella touched her foot, a giggle rippled through me—so undignified. This made both Tak-Wing and Emily laugh with delight. I saw the absurdity of both the queen and myself through their eyes and laughed along with them. I didn't need to be so serious all the time!

"The old sow is dead now anyway," Tak-Wing said. "She can't hurt us."

In high spirits, we skipped down the steps and across the walk to the big front doors of the courthouse.

The clerk at the marriage registry was a White Russian with a pointy face and little wire-rimmed glasses. He looked at us as though he could see right through us. My sister didn't blush, but I did. I knew it was ridiculous, but I couldn't help feeling a bit of second-hand shame because of the sacrilege of tradition broken. Emily knew that Father would be angry, but she wouldn't be able to see the sorrow beneath the anger. Whereas I would feel that sorrow with him for weeks, if not years. For me, it would be layered with a simmering sense of guilt at my complicity in this ill-advised project. And yet I couldn't deny Emily, partly for her own sake, and partly because I thought no one would ever love me as much as Tak-Wing loved Emily, and I wanted to be able to experience the thrill of that love, vicariously at least.

"Why are you scowling, Violet?" said Tak-Wing. "This is a happy day!" He turned and grabbed Emily and mussed her hair.

"Tak-Wing! Stop that!" she said, but she was laughing.

I imagined there would be more fanfare. The clerk gave them a yellow form and they filled it out, then signed.

I signed too, as witness.

They held hands and kissed, and we ran out of the Supreme Court singing at the top of our lungs, not "Here Comes the Bride," but absurdly, "Rule, Britannia!" Their glee was so infectious that I felt it too.

But they skipped ahead of me, and I thought of all the things that hadn't happened. No brothers of the groom ritually arguing bride price with the bride's father. No tea service given by the bride to the mother- and father-in-law. No twelve-course feast with shark's fin soup, fried shrimp balls, and roasted capon. Father would be so mad. And Mother, were she still alive, would have been devastated. I tried not to think about my parents, tried to get with the spirit of the new age.

Tak-Wing took us for a ride on the Peak Tram. Unlike the larger but tightly packed red trams in use through the city, the Peak Tram was wide, squat, and green—the same green as the velvet jacket I wore for the special occasion, though it was uncomfortably warm for the muggy Hong Kong summer. Amah said that young ladies should wear dresses, but she wasn't my mother, so she couldn't tell me what to do. Tailor Chang had warned me I would be too hot, and he was right. I loved the jacket anyway.

I watched the leafy trees and many banana palms go by the tram windows. The English didn't really like us to go to the upper levels of Hong Kong Island—they saw it as their domain. But there was one Chinese who lived up there—a wealthy comprador called Sir Robert Ho Tung, who, like us, descended from one of the original taipans. While Chinese were forbidden from renting houses up on the Peak, the British had never supposed that one of us might be rich enough to buy. But Robert Ho Tung was, and he did. And there was nothing the British could do about it. I'd been up here a handful of times with Father, to visit with Robert Ho Tung's daughters while Father visited with Sir Robert himself.

The air was noticeably cooler and greener-smelling up on the Peak than it was down in the city. When we got to the upper station, I took out my camera, a Kodak Brownie my father had given me as a birthday gift the year after my mother died. I'd used it mostly to photograph plants and bugs until I was in my teens, and then I used it mostly to photograph Emily and Father. I'd never had a lot of friends. I took photos of the bride and groom, and they took a few of me in my jaunty but overwarm jacket. We looked down into the city below. We could see the Central Market, the Gloucester Building, the Douglas Steamship Wharf, and the whole built-up city besides. Beyond it lay Victoria Harbour, dotted with big international freighters, regional cargo boats, foreign navy ships docked for R and R, tugboats, walla-wallas, launch boats, yachts, coast guard boats, ferries to various destinations, Chinese junks with their distinctive red sails, and lots of fishing boats and little sampans too. It was very pretty, and the fine sight made me relax, in spite of my worry about what trouble this wedding might bring.

The Peak Hotel had closed last year, but we wandered the grounds and looked in the windows at all the fine furniture made of oak and black leather. In the hall, there was a real grand piano covered in dust. Above it hung a chandelier netted with cobwebs. In one of the upstairs bedroom windows, I thought I saw flames lick the curtains, but when I looked again there was nothing wrong.

Tak-Wing produced a picnic lunch of sticky rice wrapped in bamboo leaves, tea eggs, and a cake box containing pork buns, pineapple buns, and yellow cake. To drink he had brought two bottles of Awakening Lion aerated lemonade, which delighted Emily. We pretended the abandoned hotel was Tak-Wing and Emily's castle, and we were dining at a long table in the main hall rather than out on the crumbling front steps. The air was thick with moisture. It began to rain, and we had to pack up the food and picnic blanket in a hurry and take cover under the hotel's awning. The sun came out and poured its light over us even as the rain continued to descend. I finished the roll of film, and put the camera away. Emily and Tak-Wing kissed and I pretended not to see. To me, the light and mist seemed thick with spirits. Not ancestral ghosts, but mountain spirits breathing their magic into us as we stood there sheltered from the actual rain but not the elemental forces of wind and water.

Then we took the tram back down into the city, and the two of them went off to have dinner with Tak-Wing's family at Tai Hang, while I went to the Kimblewick to inform Father.

"That spoiled brat sent you as her errand girl?" Father was steaming mad, but trying not to take it out on me.

"She had to go meet her new in-laws," I squeaked.

"Why did you let her do this to you?" he said. "You should have more pride. Let Emily do her own dirty work."

"She knew you'd be upset with her."

"And now you've come to take her punishment. You're a fool, Violet. So is your sister, but not in the same way."

I bowed my head.

"Hilda Selwyn-Clarke was here this afternoon with some news. It seems Dr Selwyn-Clarke and Professor Ride think you are talented. They've found a scholarship to cover your dormitory fees at HKU. You'll have to wait for a space to open up, but once it does, you can live there and concentrate on your studies. You can acculturate yourself more deeply into the life of the university as a medical person."

He didn't say, *And get yourself out of that decaying Chinese house where no one knows what time it is. Where no one knows what part of history they are supposed to inhabit.* But I understood him. Perhaps he was right.

"I don't know," I said.

"Think about it, Violet. Only if you decide to go, remember to come to the Kimblewick on the weekends to visit your lonely old father and learn how to run a company. Dream Horse will be yours when I'm gone."

"What? But I'm the second child. And I will be a doctor. You should leave it to the eldest, Emily."

"You think I'm going to leave my estate to the son of Cheung Chiu-Wai? My mortal enemy? Have you lost your mind?"

"Of course not. I—"

"And when you see that traitorous sister of yours, tell her to bring me her shameful news herself."

CHAPTER 8

DINNER AT TAI HANG

July 8, 1937

The water got choppier as they motored in the direction of Tai Hang Village, where Cheung's family had relocated from Wong Nai Chung Village in 1920 after a massive typhoon—all except his mother, who to this day refused to leave, and his sister, who'd stayed behind to look after her. Because the family wouldn't give up the Wong Nai Chung house, Cheung had had to pay for the house at Tai Hang that they otherwise would have been given in compensation by the colonial government. Fortunately, there was the compensation money Old Mah had paid out after Cheung's father's death. It wasn't enough for a very big house, but there was enough space for him, his wife Yim-Fong, and their two sons. There was also enough room for his mother and sister to squeeze in, if only they would come.

In spite of all the mischief that Tak-Wing got up to, Cheung still looked forward to seeing him. It was impossible not to adore the young man, who was congenitally happy and full of stories. It wasn't fair to Tak-Tam, who was more thoughtful, but who worried so much it gave him boils. Tak-Tam's company tended to make a fellow feel a bit depressed, while Tak-Wing's lifted the spirits. If all Chinese people were like Tak-Wing, perhaps they could find their way in the world, slough off the British humiliation and all other external threats too. Cheung thought a lot about politics, but he wasn't sure what to want, so he mostly kept his thoughts to himself. Really all he wanted was for his family to prosper in peace.

The wind picked up a little, and Lee pulled the awning down to shelter them. "Did you hear about the Japanese going in to Beiping this morning, Brother? Chiang is going to have to fight them now."

"I wish he'd put down the Communists before it is too late."

"Don't be a fool, Ah Cheung Goh. Mao Tse-Tung is a kinder and more principled leader, and it's only together they stand a chance of driving out the Japanese scourge. Also, Mao doesn't use Triads to do his dirty work."

Cheung scowled. Why did Lee talk about Triads as though they were a bad thing, when there were Triad members in Lee's own family? It would be rude to ask this question, though, so Cheung didn't. Instead he said, "The Triads are only the inheritors of past dynasties, unjustly displaced. None of us—Tanka, Hakka, or Punti—had any real love for the Qing. Arguably, in ending the Qing, we all became Triad people."

"The world is changing too fast, Brother," said Lee. "But the future belongs to the people. Good, upright people with kind hearts and strong backs. No more banditry."

Cheung knew for a fact that Lee himself had been involved in the smuggling of kerosene and medical supplies from British Hong Kong to mainland China to support the kind and upright Communist efforts there. He suspected, too, that Lee smuggled arms, but didn't know for sure. Wasn't that still banditry? He didn't broach it, but his scowl deepened.

As if reading his mind, Lee said, "I mean no more slaughter. No more rape."

"Sure," said Cheung, sensing that his friend actually wanted to speak of the usually unspoken. "But how are you going to prevent that if you are running British guns over the Chinese border?"

"I don't run guns," said Lee. "What I transport, I transport to ensure a better future for our children. Those monsters who have invaded Manchuria, they are not the same as the Japanese like your son's friend Tanaka, who helped Brother Sun Yat-Sen. Who believed in a better Asia for all of us. These new Japanese think they are better than Chinese people.

They talk about brotherhood, but they mean Japanese imperialism as a replacement for British imperialism."

"But the British give you supplies. And you want the British out."

"At least the British are honest about their intentions. They may not care about us, but they don't actively try to hurt us."

Cheung grunted.

"Who are you to judge?" Lee said. "You work for them."

"I take care of my family."

"There's an art to war, Brother. Us little people have to weather the contradictions."

Speaking of weather, the water had gotten choppier still, and grey clouds hung low overhead. There was a storm coming, if not a full-blown typhoon. Both men recognized this silently together. Lee gunned the motor at full throttle, while Ting-Yan rolled down the canopy roof.

The rains began just as they arrived at the Causeway Bay Typhoon Shelter. It was already packed with boats, mostly little fishing boats like Lee's. Lee found a place to dock—less sheltered than he liked, but probably okay. They had to hop across the whole line of little boats that had arrived earlier to get to the first walkway.

Lee and Ting-Yan, alongside Cheung and Tak-Tam, hurried up Wun Sha Street along the route of the wide nullah from which Tai Hang got its name, "Big Ditch." The whole village smelled of sewage and stale fish, though Cheung was used to it by now. All the hand laundries were closing for the day. Hauling their tattered rattan baskets on long poles slung over the shoulders, exhausted quarry workers—those unsung movers of mountains, fillers of oceans, and makers of land—walked beside Cheung and Lee. Cheung watched them wistfully. His father had been a quarry worker, until he was murdered by that swindler Mah's bogus anti-opium pills. By the side of the road, hawkers sold roasted sweet potatoes, fried turnip cake, tea eggs, and sticky rice steamed in bamboo leaf. Even under threat of rain, people crowded around the noodle stalls hoping to grab a quick bowl before the downpour. The street smelled of all these delicious foods over and through the less pleasant smells of sewage and rot. As they went up the street, the scents of home-cooked family dinners mingled with those of glossy street food. The fragrance of red stick incense wafted up from shrines to the Earth God, who guarded the village flats from his hallowed ground in the portico of each dark front door.

It was starting to rain, but the men didn't want to arrive at the party empty-handed. Ting-Yan, however, was anxious to get to the house because her mother, Siu-Wai, was already there helping Cheung's wife, Yim-Fong, with the cooking. At least, that was what she said. Her eyes glittered with the anxious desire of one who loves too much without any certainty of being loved back. She wanted to see Tak-Wing.

"You go ahead, then," said her father, pausing in front of a sweet potato seller. "I want to talk to Old Cheung anyway."

"I'll come with you," said Tak-Tam.

Though they'd been peaceful and light together on the boat, now she cast him a look of scorn.

Tak-Tam didn't notice, or pretended not to.

The two old fathers watched their children walk up the hill through the mist.

"Are you sure you want Ting-Yan to marry Tak-Wing?" said Lee. "I think that Ting-Yan and Tak-Tam would be just fine together."

"Your daughter is a good woman. She should marry the man she loves. Besides, it's a practical match. My number one son, Tak-Wing, is a little childish. She'll have to take care of him. And I want him to be well taken care of."

"To give your first son to a modest fishing family is to throw away your wealth."

"My family is more humble than yours because we lost our village. Even if my old mother doesn't think so. Whereas you made a fortune."

"And lost it, Brother," said Lee, a little sadly, but without bitterness. The ritual of humility was only meaningful if it was grounded in true feeling. Finally, he asked, "Do you truly wish this?"

"I do," Cheung said. "Truly, my brother, I do."

When they arrived, Lee handed the package of roasted sweet potatoes to Yim-Fong. "We lost the day's catch. I'm sorry."

"Never mind, plenty of food," Yim-Fong said, though this wasn't entirely true. Because of the war in China, she'd encountered shortages at the wet market.

"Is my daughter here?" Lee asked. "She came with Tak-Tam just ahead of us."

Then they heard it: a soft, very high-pitched keening from the back room. Lee recognized the cry. It was his daughter, bawling her eyes out. He rushed to her, past the large round dining table where Cheung Tak-Wing sat beside a beaming Emily Mah Wai-Yee. Through the doorway Cheung could see Lee's wife, Siu-Wai, sitting on the bed beside Ting-Yan, holding the girl as she howled out her grief and disappointment. Tak-Tam sat on the floor at her feet, gripping her clammy hand in his.

Cheung remained in the front room. "What is going on?"

"The fools eloped," said Yim-Fong. "So shameful."

"It was so easy," said Tak-Wing. "We just went to the British magistrate at the Supreme Court across the road from your work. Done! Quick as an onion pancake."

"What onion pancake?" said Cheung.

"They got married, you numbskull!" said Yim-Fong.

"You were struggling so hard to make a decision, Ba," said Tak-Wing, "so I did it for you. Emily's father was going to marry her off to some ugly rich guy from Singapore. It would have been such a waste."

"You're kidding me," said Cheung.

"Do you see me kidding?" said Tak-Wing.

The reality of the situation slowly dawned on Cheung. "You shame me like this in front of my friend? You humiliate his lovely daughter?"

"Aw, Ba, don't be like that. Emily and I are happy! Isn't that what you want for your favourite son?"

"You are *not* my favourite son."

"Ba, come on. It was always going to be Emily and me. Ting-Yan will get over it. You know, Tak-Tam is really into her. You should give him to your friend."

"Please have the humility to remove yourself from my house."

"But I live here."

"You only live here because I bought you this dead ghost house!"

"But—"

"Out!" said Cheung. "Now. I never want to see your dog demon face again."

"You better go," said Yim-Fong to Tak-Wing. "Come back later when your father has calmed down."

"Where am I supposed to go?"

Cheung had a broom in his hand. He raised it above Tak-Wing's head. "The nerve of you!"

"Just go for a walk," said Yim-Fong.

"And don't come back!" Cheung yelled.

Tak-Wing took Emily's hand and they strolled past the main pillars of the house and out into the gathering storm.

Cheung slumped onto one of the chairs that surrounded the old wooden dining table and dropped his head into his hands.

Captain Lee, Siu-Wai, and Ting-Yan came out from the back then. Tak-Tam was with them also.

"Maybe we should just go back to Chek Keng," said Lee.

"Nonsense," said Cheung. "There's a typhoon coming."

"I made a lot of food," said Yim-Fong. "Just stay. We don't have to talk about it. We can sort it out later."

"I've brought you too much hardship already, I think," Lee said.

"Not at all, Brother," Cheung said. "If anything, it's the other way around. My idiot son has brought trouble to you. You can't travel now anyway. You better stay for the night."

True to her word, Yim-Fong had cooked a solid dinner in spite of the shortages. Now, she took the shrimp Granny Tang had given Captain Lee, and fried them typhoon-shelter style, with garlic, ginger, fresh chilies, and Shaoxing wine. She laid out the dishes—two kinds of stir-fried greens, a large steamed rock cod brought down earlier that morning by Siu-Wai, minced pork steamed with salted duck egg, large-head bean sprouts, and a big pan of homemade turnip cake.

The storm broke for real. Water gushed down the nullah on the street outside.

"Maybe you should go look for them," Yim-Fong said.

But Cheung was still seething. "If those two brats are old enough to get married on their own, they're old enough to weather a storm on their own."

"I'll go," Yim-Fong said.

"Don't bother," Cheung said. "You made all this food. Stay and eat it."

The rain came in torrents.

"I can't leave them out there."

She went out into the rain. Tak-Tam followed her, concerned about his brother and his brother's new wife. Everyone else picked at the meal, uncomfortable with the situation and unsure what to do.

They came back an hour later. Yim-Fong was drenched and shivering. Tak-Tam had put his coat over her and was shivering too, in his thin white shirt. They sat under the bare light bulb that hung sadly from the ceiling and ate the now cold food. No one was in the mood to talk.

In the morning, before the Lee family had the chance to take their leave, Emily's younger sister, Violet, showed up wearing a ridiculous green velvet jacket. If Emily was as beautiful as the moon, Violet was ugly as the toad in the old stories, the one that lives on the moon, drooling out its venom. "I'm sorry to be the bearer of bad news," she said. "Father is demanding a bride price for Emily." She named the amount.

"That's exactly the value of this house," muttered Cheung. "Which is, of course, the same as the compensation amount we received from Old Mah after his pills killed Father. He's killing Father all over again."

"I'm sorry to bring you such crummy news," Violet said. "I asked Amah to do it, but she wouldn't."

Cheung had to get back to the cricket club, where the toffs were waiting for their boiled eggs, porridge, toast, and Earl Grey tea. "I'll discuss it with my wife tonight, and we will work something out," he told Violet.

"I'm to tell you that you could go to prison," she said, "for stealing a man's daughter. I didn't want to bring you this news, but Father wants to be sure you know." Her toad face wrinkled unpleasantly—with shame or malice, Cheung couldn't quite tell.

"Okay," said Cheung, "you've told me. Unless you've got more bad news—"

"I'm going," she said. "Don't worry." She turned around and disappeared into soggy mist from which she'd come.

Cheung walked with Lee down to the dock, where he would catch a tram back to the club. He was quiet, not wanting to show his despair. Several paces behind, Tak-Tam accompanied Lee's wife and daughter.

"You know," Lee said, "I think Ting-Yan would be content to marry Tak-Tam, once she's had a little while to recover from the shock. Tak-Tam was always my first choice. Tak-Tam can inherit the house at Chek Keng. And the boats and fields. I think he would be happy. And the God of the Hearth—I mean the Christ—would be content with this order of things also. But if they were to marry, the whole family, including Tak-Wing and Emily, could relocate to Chek Keng. I mean, if you have to ... if ..."

"If I have to sell the Tai Hang house?"

"I didn't want to say it."

"You're a good friend to me, Ah Lee. Give me a day to clear my head?"

And that was how the house at Tai Hang was lost. But as the Christians say, "The Lord giveth and the Lord taketh away." There is also a Taoist moral tale about a man whose son loses his ability to walk when he is thrown from a wild horse. As a consequence, when the army comes recruiting, that man gets to keep his son while all the other villagers lose theirs.

CHAPTER 9

Typhoon Shelter
THE GEOMANTIC FATE OF WONG NAI CHUNG VILLAGE

June 30, 1997

O*ver the tinny sound system blasts an infectious tune that Ophelia recognizes as a Top 40 song popular with tweens in the late 1980s, by the
manufactured British girl band, Cat Call.*

> Woman wanting
> Only daunting
> For a guy that's low

*The music infects the grumpy server, who wiggles a little dance step on her
way to the table. But in the back, someone is irritated. The song comes to a
halt mid-line.*

> Woman wanting
> Don't come haunting
> 'Less you've got some—

*Then a new song rises in Mandarin: "Mei Gui, Mei Gui, Wo Ai Ni," "Rose,
Rose, I Love You." Ophelia's going through a riot grrrl phase and can't be
bothered with any of it, though she has to admit that the rose song is catchy.
The congee arrives in a steaming pot, fragrant and rich with the smells of*

seafood and warm rice. Great-Aunt Violet ladles some out for Ophelia and then for herself. There's lettuce, green onion, cilantro, and peanuts in a little dish on the side to sprinkle over the congee to taste. Great-Aunt Violet takes a sip. "Done right," she says. "The rice was muddled with thousand-year-old egg and left to marinate before boiling. Good quality pork stock." Ophelia likes most of it—the fresh fish, the bean curd skin, the dried squid, the slivered roast pork, and the fish cake. The only thing she's not nuts about is the boiled pig skin, tender-crisp in that way that Chinese people like. "Pah," says Great-Aunt Violet. "Your taste is too Western. You should come back to Hong Kong and live here for a while. You will learn to find different things delicious."

In the old days, that rice would have been grown in our own fields. Did you know that before the British came, Happy Valley was a rice paddy? The British banned rice growing as a first order of business and forbade the people to cultivate it. By the time Yim-Fong came to Wong Nai Chung, the rice paddies were long gone, and horses ran in the valley, as they still do now. I'll take you to the Jockey Club for dim sum next week if you are not too busy.

Marrying into Wong Nai Chung Village must have been quite a shock for Yim-Fong, who was a daughter of the little salt pan village Yim Tin Tsai. Her father had met Cheung and his father when he was selling salt, and the Cheungs—father and son—were doing quarry work up at North Point. Those were the days when the Public Works Department knocked down mountains with impunity and poured the rock into the sea, to take land from Tin Hau and make the new colony prosperous and strong. And also, bigger. There's a land shortage in Hong Kong because it is so small and so mountainous. You know that because you flew in through Kai Tak Airport. Did the wings not shave the mountains? Did the belly not touch the rooftops? The Public Works Department had a few lorries and backhoes to help them with their work, but the main instruments of their work were human. That was the kind of work Cheung's father did as a quarry worker. We used to call them coolies in those days. Any Chinese man who did physical labour was a coolie, though there were almost as many different kinds of labour as there were Chinese men. Anyway, Grandfather Ng was at North Point to sell a shipment of salt. He saw Cheung and his father on their way to work in the morning and thought they looked strong and lucky. He was probably actively on the lookout for a husband for his daughter by then. In those days marriages were arranged, and a lot of responsibility fell on parents to choose the right spouses for their children. When he was young, Cheung was so handsome! Like his son Tak-Wing in the next generation. Imagine Grandfather Ng checking him out. Ha ha, what I wouldn't give to have been a fly on the wall. Or the cliff, heh heh.

Grandfather Cheung was badly injured while drilling a hole at the bottom of a cliff. Part of the cliff collapsed, a boulder rolled down the incline, and his leg was pinned under it. Grandfather Ng had just finished selling his salt and was recruited off the street to help lift the boulder off Grandfather Cheung. His foot was broken. Grandfather Ng helped the younger Cheung carry Grandfather Cheung all the way back to Wong Nai Chung Village. Neither man was wealthy; they had to walk. It took the rest of the day and the better part of the night. It was a very unusual thing to go so far out of one's way to help a stranger. Old Ng said later he felt called upon by Tin Hau to do it, that he wasn't in the habit of such benevolence. The men became fast friends, visiting one another at Chinese New Year and sending parcels of salt or fruit on other special occasions. Since Old Ng had a daughter and Old Cheung had a son and their friendship was so strong, they pledged to bind their children together in marriage.

Yim-Fong and Cheung were introduced and nominally consulted, but in those days, children really had no choice. So they married as strangers, and Yim-Fong came down from her small island home to the big island of Hong Kong, where everything was noisy and boisterous all the time, and the streets were packed with tall, hairy foreigners who smelled of sour milk. Because of the rigours of salt farming at home, she was a sturdy and reliable person. She took good care of Cheung. They were both smart—Tak-Tam inherited his intelligence from them. They studied English together from one of those little phrase books that gives a rough transliteration in Chinese characters.

Usually, Chinese daughters-in-law and mothers-in-law don't get along well, because the mother-in-law likes to oppress the daughter-in-law the way she herself was oppressed by her mother-in-law before. That's Confucian patriarchy for you! But Cheung Wan-See wasn't like that, maybe because, like Ting-Yan, my nearest and dearest, she'd stayed in her natal village and brought a husband in. This was also unusual. Cheung's wife and mother got along like a house on fire, or should I say a flooded house, since that was the fate that bound them. Both were steeped in the culture of geomancy—do you know what that is? It's like what those New Agers these days call feng shui, the orientation of life toward the flows of wind and water. Cheung's sister, your Great-Aunt Hok-Yee, was good at it too, particularly skilled at a kind of fortune-telling called bone-weighing.

In the old days, Wong Nai Chung was perfectly situated at the head of a long and fertile valley with a mountain behind it and the waves of a warm harbour peacefully lapping the shore at the far end. Since the Ming dynasty, the valley was a network of cultivated rice paddies, with just a brief interruption during the Qing clearances, when all inhabitants were cleared from the coast on pain of death. So Wong Nai Chung was a wealthy village—countryside wealthy, I mean, not bank-wealthy stinking rich like the taipans that grew out of the British empire. But when the British came, the first thing they did was outlaw the growing of rice in the valley. The villagers went from being comfortable and content to poor and desperate just like that. Ai yah, those demon bastards, I'm telling you! The three hundred or so villagers complained vociferously, to the point that it was said you could tell a person was from Wong Nai Chung because they complained so much about the loss of the rice fields. To compensate, the government put Wong Nai Chung people first in line for construction and quarry work, which is how Grandfather Cheung ended up in the business even generations later. With paddy work outlawed, the abandoned rice fields soon became a malarial swamp. Lots of people got sick and died, colonists and Chinese alike. To add insult to injury, the British changed the name of Wong Nai Chung Village to Happy Valley, which was their way of saying "Valley of Death." They surrounded the valley with cemeteries and doomed Wong Nai Chung to become just one more burial ground. There was a graveyard for every kind of colonial: a Protestant graveyard that we called the Colonial Cemetery, the Catholic Cemetery, the Muslim Cemetery, the Jewish Cemetery, the Parsee Cemetery. They stuck a fountain in the middle of each and buried all the people who died of the malaria and cholera they'd set off by turning the rice paddies into a swamp. Wong Nai Chung went from being a village that produced rice to a village that produced rocks, mosquitoes, and graves. Talk about curse upon curse! So stupid, lah! Dim dead ghosts! You know that Chinese people are afraid of death the way British people are afraid of sex. It all shows in our curses.

In Grandfather Cheung's time, the Public Works Department got involved and began dredging and digging and building. They drained the water from the swamp and turned it into the Jockey Club. Horse racing, so fantastic! Chinese people love to gamble, you know. But then they put up signs: *No Chinese Allowed!* At least not until 1926, after the floods, after Cheung and his family were relocated. Well, their lucky racecourse was also doomed because of all the ghosts from the cemeteries above wandering through it. But they didn't believe in such things, called it superstition. If it's superstitious to believe in ghosts, why isn't it superstitious to believe in gambling luck? Don't ask me, I'm just one ugly old lady. No one cares what I think.

Well, the three graces, or the three witches, however you want to think about them—Cheung Wan-See, Cheung Hok-Yee, and Ng Yim-Fong—they could see the geomantic trouble coming a mile off. They could see the romantic trouble coming too, but no one asked them like no one asks me. Except you, of course, my darling, but you ask in such a strange way. Ho kei gwai. Very weird. I don't understand you at all.

Public Works would not be daunted! They built roads, they built a sanatorium, they built residences. They knocked down Morrison Hill and used some of it to build up the land and some of it to reclaim ocean. Wong Nai Chung Village, which had once sat on land rising to become hillside at the end of the valley, sank beneath all the new roads and buildings.

Well, the big fight in the family was when Public Works came knocking, looking for workers to build a retaining wall along Stubbs Road. Wan-See, Hok-Yee, and Yim-Fong were against the men going to do that work. But Cheung and his father wanted to go. By then, the family was so poor. Three generations had passed since it was possible to farm rice. Cheung and his father were always looking a job, and construction work close to home paid as well as quarry work farther away. Whether they helped or not, the wall was going to get built. So why not work close to the village and be able to come home for dinner? "Anyway, the wall will protect the village from flood waters by holding them back."

The women wailed and shouted. "The village was fine before any of these construction projects!" They burned incense for the Earth God and laid out precious oranges for him. The men called it superstitious hogwash and reported to the foreman for work. They destroyed the auspicious placement of their own village by moving the landscape around it. Yim-Fong said that Cheung was deranged to the point of death. "Your father doesn't know any better because he's done this all his life. But the world is new now. You have to learn to use your head! If you can't look after your own interests, how do you expect anyone else to?" She was mad as the hot place below because she knew what would happen, while Cheung did not have that foresight. Cheung said, "All you do is complain like all the generations that have gone before. When are you going to stop complaining and start taking responsibility?"

But Yim-Fong was right. When the floods came in '23, all 130 houses in the sunken village were flooded and twenty-six collapsed. Between the reclamation work at the back end of the village and the huge bank of earth thrown up at the front, there was nowhere for the water to go but into the houses. All of the village's pigs and chickens and one little boy who was washing clothes in the nullah when the flood struck were drowned. The waters were so deep people had to swim to safety. They lost all of their belongings—furniture, mattresses, cooking pots, dishes, clothing, everything.

Worse luck hit the family in '25, when robbers came to the house and stabbed Grandfather Cheung. He survived, but between his poorly healed foot from the quarry accident years ago and his poorly healed stab wounds, he was in a lot of pain. Our Dream Horse products, especially Immortal Carp, were a great help to him, at least until they weren't. The robbers took what little money and jewellery the family had saved from the '23 flood. Shortly after that, the typhoon of '25 hit. The retaining wall that the men had helped build collapsed, and mud, debris, and water flooded again into the village. Public Works had mixed the cement with red earth rather than the sand that would have made it strong. Everyone had to flee in a hurry. When they got to higher ground, Cheung Wan-See wasn't with them. It turned out a house had collapsed right on top of her, though miraculously, she was unharmed, in a little pocket of air. The fire brigade had to come and dig her out.

Yim-Fong said, "Through your own actions you brought bad winds and waters onto the family." What's that expression you kids have? Literally! Cheung loved his wife, but he resented her for being too clever. Though they remained married and continued to live together, things were never quite right between them after that. She couldn't forgive him for shitting where he slept. And he couldn't forgive her for pointing it out. It's hard to fight back when your survival depends on the well-being of the one who oppresses you. It's hard to fight back when you hate the one you love.

But on the day of the 1925 flood, one of the fire brigade men saw Cheung with his mother and thought he seemed a sturdy and responsible fellow with a lot of people depending on him. The fire brigade man, Edward Kerrison, went to talk to him and was impressed when Cheung squeezed out a few words of English. He asked Cheung if he'd like to come work at the Hong Kong Cricket Club, and so that is how Cheung got his job, which was how Tak-Wing became friends with the young cricketers, which, in turn, is how Tak-Wing ended up hanging out at the Repulse Bay Hotel, and hearing Emily sing. So, in a way, without those floods, you wouldn't even be here. I can't fully curse the destruction of the rice paddies because without them, I wouldn't have you!

Ophelia has slurped down two bowls of tang tsai jook, even the boiled pork skin. It was delicious after all, with all the elements mixed together and extra lettuce for crunch. As before, Great-Aunt Violet has been talking and forgetting to eat. Ophelia is afraid she will burst while Great-Aunt Violet wastes away before her eyes. She usually has more self-restraint, but it's as though she's been starving for this particular food all her life.

"Gosh, it's getting late," says Great-Aunt Violet. "We better get going."

"But what a happened to poor Ting-Yan and the shy brother, Tak-Tam?"

"I'll tell you that story later. Surely you want to know what the white men at the Hong Kong Cricket Club thought of Emily and Tak-Wing's little ruse?"

CHAPTER 10

RESIDENT ROMEO AND JULIET

July 8, 1937

When young cricketers at the HKCC heard about the unsanctioned marriage, they were scandalized and delighted. It turned out they approved of the King and Mrs Simpson, and they approved of Emily and Tak-Wing too. Elizabeth Hancock, the president's daughter-in-law, thought it so romantic. "Our own resident Romeo and Juliet!" she was reported to have cooed. If she'd seen the play, apparently she hadn't stayed 'til the end.

"They want to have a wedding for me at the club!" Emily told me. After Cheung had chased them from the Tai Hang house, she and Tak-Wing had gone to the Repulse Bay Hotel to shelter from the storm. Emily's friends, Isadore Davis Wong and Tanaka Shigeru, were playing as a duo that night, with an expectation that she might come after dinner if it ended early. They played a fabulous set, danced, and drank champagne. When the storm let up, because they couldn't afford to stay the night at the hotel, they went to visit our old school friend Lai Po-Chuen, who was now studying medicine at HKU and had a dorm room there. This was where I visited them after I had delivered my message to Cheung. I envied Po-Chuen's room mightily because it sheltered her from ridiculous family dramas—those of her own family, at least. I couldn't wait 'til I'd have my own in September. Emily and Tak-Wing crammed together on the narrow bed, while Po-Chuen slept on cushions on the floor. If the prefect caught them, Po-Chuen would be in a lot of trouble, so it wasn't a permanent solution, but it was a solution for now.

Emily was still high from the feat they'd pulled off, and higher still because of the cricket club invitation. "Imagine that! Tak-Wing and I will be the first Chinese people to marry at the HKCC."

"Who marries at a cricket club?" I said. "Chinese or not." My green velvet jacket had been ruined by the rain while I ran her errands. I felt both irritated and scandalized.

"Don't be such a stick in the mud," said Emily. "If Father won't acknowledge us, his betters will."

"Those snooty foreigners are not better than us just because they've come here and taken the best of everything!"

"Of course they are. Why else do Chinese people copy them by setting up clubs that are exactly like the British kind?" Someone had given her a fancy tin of chocolates, and she popped one in her mouth without even offering me one first.

"Uh, because the British won't let us into their clubs?"

"Well, there must be something good about the clubs for us to want to go in! You're just jealous because no one's asked you to have a wedding there. They're pooling funds so Father won't have to pay a thing. Because they respect Head Cook Cheung. They aren't nearly as bad as you say." She took one more chocolate, then held the tin out to me in a desultory fashion.

I ignored it.

She shook the tin, and the chocolates rattled against the sides.

"It's a monkey's wedding, Emily."

"What are you talking about?" She shook the box again.

I waved it away, in spite of the lovely vanilla and caramel scents that wafted up from those delectable confections. "Can't you see they are making fun of us? And pushing their tastes and traditions on us in order to indebt us. It's the Opium War all over again. What is wrong with you?"

"They are just trying to be nice, Violet. Don't be such a sourpuss."

"They undermine our traditions with impunity, then act as though we have none and give us theirs as an act of charity. A monkey's wedding. That makes you the monkey."

"I was going to ask you be bridesmaid."

Old Mah would be furious, not just because the man who killed the Immortal Carp line had stolen his daughter, but because the British colonizers were now also doing so. If the original taipan of this backwater fishing village had accepted Grandfather Mah as his son, we'd be Witt-Weatheralls ourselves. And Emily would have had a proper wedding at the Church of Christ on Bonham Road. This would have been fine with Old Mah. He was a hypocrite like that.

"I wish you'd put more work into finding a place to live and less into these ridiculous schemes of yours," I said. "Father will never forgive you."

"He will," said Emily. "Just you wait and see."

THE WORLD OF EMILY MAH

July 9, 1937

Emily might have been spoiled, but she wasn't incorrigibly so. Early in the morning, while Lai Po-Chuen and Tak-Wing were still asleep, she snuck out of the dorm to get them some breakfast. There was a street vendor in Wan Chai whom Tak-Wing particularly liked. It was a bit ridiculous to go so far, but these were the days of grand gestures. The bus arrived quickly. Emily hopped on. She very seldom went around the city on her own. Usually, she was with someone—Violet, Po-Chuen, Amah, or Tak-Wing. It was exhilarating to board the bus on her own and jostle the other passengers, businessmen and colonial administrators on their way to work, mothers taking young children to school, amahs on their way to do the morning marketing. She wasn't entirely sure she'd be able to find the street vendor. He was, after all, just a man with a cart, who set up in more or less the same location each day, depending on who else got there first and what the rumours were around police raids. Street vending was illegal, but it was also the way a lot of people made their living. There were so many street vendors that the colonial administration couldn't deal with them all, and had to settle for the occasional raid, more as a show that the law existed than as an effective enforcement of it.

Another person was afoot in the district that morning: Lee Ting-Yan. Ting-Yan had also awoken early, to do her dirty deed before her father and mother woke up in the back bedroom at Cheung's Tai Hang house, vacated by Cheung and Siu-Wai to accommodate their esteemed guests. She had come from the opposite direction to find a villain hitter to curse Emily and Tak-Wing, those two petty people who had ruined her life forever. She felt hurt and helpless, and she wanted them to die. There was a granny called Kwok in this neighbourhood, famous for the efficacy of her curses. She worked beneath the Goose Neck Bridge, alongside a dozen other grannies with varying degrees of notoriety. Ting-Yan seldom came to this district. It took an hour of wandering, sweating in her black cotton tunic and wide-legged trousers, to find Granny Kwok's stall. When she got there, there was a long lineup for Granny Kwok, even though it wasn't yet the season when insects awaken. There were other grannies she could approach, but she wanted the curse to be strong, so she waited. No point wasting her money on a charlatan.

Her heart began to pound as her turn came close. Granny Kwok's little red-and-green altar was busy with oranges, wine, and gourds. Amidst these offerings the five deities stood proud in painted porcelain, all lined up in a row. Tin Hau exuded calm and compassion in the middle. To her left, Man Cheong, the God of Literature, gazed seriously inward, scroll in hand, his long black beard and moustache flowing gracefully down his face. And to his left stood the serene, dark-faced god Pak Tai who protects against floods. To the right of Tin Hau, the martial, green-robed Guan Gong, the God of Brotherhood who watched over both police and Triads, raised his sword above his head. And to his right, Wong Tai Sin, the God of Healing, smiled beatifically in blue robes and a high hat. In front of each sat a lucky red packet. Incense smouldered in the large, rectangular incense burner that stood before the altar. And in front of that, a table lay covered in neatly stacked paper charms, coins, dice, a ceramic tiger, and several glass jars half full of ashes. Ting-Yan watched Granny Kwok burn spirit money for the customer ahead of her, and sighed impatiently.

"When will luck come to me?" the customer asked Granny Kwok.

"Perhaps at the next high tide, perhaps at the next new moon," said Granny Kwok. "The gods are not often specific about timing. Know too that the results you wish for can appear in unexpected forms. So you have to be both patient and attentive."

Why does she go on at such length, Ting-Yan wondered. *Is my turn ever going to come?*

"You're the wisest granny under the Goose Neck Bridge," the customer in front said. "Surely you must be able to predict the timing to some degree."

"I've already told you what I can," Granny said patiently.

Come on! said Ting-Yan, inside her head. *Hurry up!*

"What do you mean by unexpected forms?" the customer said.

Ting-Yan rolled her eyes, though no one saw her.

"I hope you made your wishes clearly and without ambiguity," said Granny Kwok. "The gods can be capricious."

Mary, Tin Hau, and God in Heaven! Come on!

"What does that mean, capricious?" said the customer.

Finally, it was Ting-Yan's turn. Her heart raced with excitement and fear.

"General curse or specific curse?" Granny Kwok asked. She wore a pantsuit in brightly patterned fabric, flashier and more contemporary than Ting-Yan's traditional garb. Several of her teeth were missing, though one of ones that remained was capped in gold. Her face was spattered with liver spots. Her eyes shone bright and lively.

"Specific curse," Ting-Yan said.

"It'll cost you more," said Granny Kwok.

"How much?" Ting-Yan asked.

Granny Kwok named an exorbitant amount. Ting-Yan, well raised as a bargainer by her mother, Kwan Siu-Wai, argued and quibbled, but the granny stood her ground. She could smell desperation and determination. And she knew her worth and insisted on her price.

Ting-Yan made to leave.

Granny Kwok said, "Fine, why don't you go to Granny Chan's stall. See if anything works out for you ever!"

Ting-Yan saw that her ruse was not going to work. She sighed. She handed the old woman the sum requested. "You drive a hard bargain, Granny Kwok."

Once she'd been paid, Granny Kwok's demeanour shifted. Her broad face went soft, and a tone that conveyed genuine concern entered her voice. "What sorrow brings you here today, daughter?"

Ting-Yan poured it out, her long and patient love for Tak-Wing since they were little children, the days of kite-flying together, or combing the beach for shells, the sunsets, the hand-holding, the longing gazes. The laughter too, the harmless pranks, the windup tin chicken she had put in his suitcase. And then the trip to Berlin, the sudden coldness, the appearance of that glossy Emily Mah Wai-Yee. By the time she told the tale of last night's dinner and the presence of the newlyweds when she arrived at the Cheungs' house in Tai Hang, she was a bawling, howling mess, drenched in self-pity. Water gushed from her eyes and nose. She horked up a great wad of snot. She coughed, and then she spat on the ground.

"We will fix it, child," Granny Kwok said kindly. "We will fix it."

Ting-Yan mustered a small smile through her tears.

"You have to be sure, though," Granny Kwok said, "because it will require a serious curse." Her eyes grew wide and gentle.

"I'm sure," Ting-Yan sniffled.

"In all honesty, I advise you against it," said Granny Kwok.

"I want them to suffer."

"Okay," said Granny Kwok. Her eyes narrowed. "I'll warn you, though, my curses are very effective."

"Good," said Ting-Yan. "I should hope so."

She wrote her name, animal sign, and birthdate on Granny Kwok's packet of spirit papers. On the boy and girl "petty person" papers, she wrote Tak-Wing and Emily's names, animal signs, and birthdates. She smeared pork grease from a little dish that Granny Kwok provided onto the mouth of the neatly folded three-dimensional paper tiger that Granny also handed her, so that it would be well-disposed toward her as it journeyed through the spirit world.

On a stool in front of her with a brick atop the seat, Granny Kwok beat the effigies of Tak-Wing and Emily with and old shoe and chanted:

Hit your wicked hand
Gain nothing that you planned
Hit your wicked eye
This is how you die
Hit your wicked arm
Open you to harm
Hit your wicked chest
May you never rest
Hit your wicked groin
Demons may you join
Hit your wicked foot
Cover you in soot—

The beating continued until the repetition of curses droned in Ting-Yan's ear and she saw in her mind's eye an army of demons descending on her enemies.

When the paper had been beaten to a pulpy mess, Granny Kwok stuffed it into the belly of the paper tiger, set the tiger alight, and dropped it into the ritual ash basket. Ting-Yan watched its striped face go up in flames. As it burned, Granny fed the flames with the gold- and silver-coloured papers in the stack that Ting-Yan had written her name on. Granny chanted blessings for Ting-Yan. She waved burning spirit money over Ting-Yan's head to chase away the evil spirits. She followed with a thick bunch of smouldering joss sticks. The smoke permeated her skin and Ting-Yan relaxed.

"Nearly done," said Granny Kwok. "We just need to ask the spirits if they've heard your prayers."

She threw a pair of moon blocks and one landed on its side and while the other landed flat against the table. "Yin and yang together," she said. "The world is back in balance. The spirits have heard us."

When the ceremony had finished, Ting-Yan felt a palpable sense of relief and optimism that she might get some vengeance on the man who had betrayed her and the permed and lipsticked hussy who had bewitched him. "Justice at last," she said, as she got up to go.

"My work has great strength," Granny Kwok said. "But if you really want it to work, then you need to back it with your own actions. The next time they get married, you must be there. And you must interrupt. Even if the interruption has no immediate effect, it will have deep long-term ones. That is how you will get your justice. If it is justice you really want."

"What do you mean the next time they get married?"

The old lady beckoned her to lean close. Ting-Yan, already standing, came over and crouched beside Granny Kwok where she sat. Smoke from the still-smouldering spirit papers filled Ting-Yan's nostrils and mingled with the scent of joss sticks that thickly filled the air. She coughed, but repressed the urge to spit again. The old lady whispered something into her ear, so softly that Ting-Yan didn't hear.

"What?" she said.

Granny Kwok scowled.

"I didn't hear you," Ting-Yan said. "Would you mind repeating?"

Granny Kwok leaned close and whispered again, even softer than before.

Ting-Yan still didn't hear, but her eyes glazed over for a brief moment, and then her mouth spread into a wide, toothy grin. Then the glazing passed as clouds moving over the sun do. Her mouth returned to its normal, serious demeanour. She didn't know what she'd received, but she'd received it. Before she stood again, she pressed an extra coin into the old woman's hand. "Thank you, Granny Kwok. You are kind to me."

Also wandering the district at that same hour was Selby Hancock, though for him it was the end of a long night rather than the start of an early morning. He'd been moving from establishment to establishment over the last twelve hours, sampling beer, gin, and a wide range of cocktails made from very different spirits than the kind than Granny Kwok conjured. Now, he was looking for a flower girl, going up and down along the waterfront whistling and catcalling the girls who worked the flower boats. He shouted to them in a manner so annoying and embarrassing that the sailors attempting to enjoy the pleasures of those boats shouted back at him to shut the hell up you stupid fool. Selby responded that the girls were dirty and diseased, and three sailors coming up the dock having had their fun punched him the eye, threw him to the ground, and gave him several good kicks in the ribs. Too drunk to feel the pain yet, Selby wobbled farther into the district.

Edward Kerrison, the health inspector, sent by Selby's very respectable father, Richard Hancock, saw Selby lurch down a lane toward the sellers of pastries and congee. He'd been searching for almost an hour and was glad to see the stupid boy. Why in God's name did he not just stay at home with that nice young wife of his and keep out of trouble? Kerrison understood though—he'd seen it tons of times before. These young men, boys really, coddled in their British prep schools and disciplined within an inch of their lives, came to Hong Kong and imagined it a free-for-all. They struggled with the humidity, the heat, and the mix of cultures that, while far from egalitarian, accommodated a much wider variety of people than boys like Selby Hancock would have encountered at home. Unable to really see what was there, they imagined it a fantasyland where they could do anything they wanted. And so they did. *"I should have brought him out here sooner, blast it," Richard Hancock had said. "Now he's too old to acclimatize and too young to handle a world he doesn't understand. If only that wife of his were not so pious and guilty, so embarrassingly attentive to the Chinese. She'd be much better off paying attention to Selby and keeping him off the streets."*

Emily was managing well—she'd found Tak-Wing's favourite vendor and was getting her tiffin filled with congee, oily stick, shrimp dumplings, and steamed pork buns—when Selby spotted her.

"Hey!" he shouted. "Hey, lady!"

Emily recoiled, aghast. "Do I know you?"

"How would you like some company?"

"No, thank you."

"Come on, don't you recognize a charming fellow when you meet one?" He lurched toward her.

She stepped away. "Please leave me be."

"What's wrong with you?"

"Nothing's wrong with me. What's wrong with you?"

"Stuck-up cow."

She wished now that she hadn't come alone. "Please just go away."

He approached her closely, much much too closely, and towered over her, clearly enjoying his height in relation to hers.

"I don't know you," she said.

"Come on—" He attempted to put his arm around her just as the vendor handed back her tiffin full of hot, delicious food.

As Selby leaned toward her, she skirted away. His lean was a little more aggressive than he intended. He lost his balance, tipped over, and crashed into her, knocking the congee and pastries all over her and the ground. She yelped as hot congee splashed her face.

Ting-Yan and Edward Kerrison simultaneously entered the alley just as Emily fell and cried out, "Oh!"

Without seeing the face of the woman falling, Ting-Yan rushed forward and, miraculously, caught her.

Kerrison rushed to Selby and helped him up. "Come on, old boy. What do you think you're doing?"

"That lady was so rude to me," said Selby.

"Well, you're a bit of a sloppy mess, aren't you? She was probably right to be." Kerrison glanced at the two unimpressed women and nodded apologetically, though he was not the one who had done anything wrong.

Selby continued to whimper. "Speaking to me as though I'm an animal. Doesn't she know who I am?"

"I don't think you know who you are right now, old chap. Come on, if it's girls you want, I'll take you a classy place. Later. When you're a little more attractive. Let's go then." He nodded at Emily and Ting-Yan one more time and urged Selby toward the alley entrance.

"I don't want one of your classy girls," Selby slurred. "I want that one."

"Come on, let's go." Kerrison pulled Selby by the hand as one might a delinquent child.

The two women watched the British men leave. Emily turned to look at her rescuer.

"Oh, golly. Thanks." She paused. "I know you."

"Yes," said Ting-Yan, recognizing Emily in that same instant.

"But from where? Give me a hint."

"Uh ..." What do you say when the person who has ruined your life forever doesn't recognize you? Especially when you just saw them yesterday, and you've just cursed them to the hottest recesses of hell.

"From my volunteer days at Po Leung Kuk? Yes, you're the lady who signs in the new girls, and gets all their details."

"No, I don't think that's it."

But Emily had already forgotten Ting-Yan and returned to her own indignation. "He thinks I'm some dirty flower girl."

"What's wrong with being a flower girl? Two of my cousins are flower girls. People have to make a living." One of those cousins, who had been Ting-Yan's childhood playmate, still worked in the flower boats. The other one had met four rich men in one lucky week, played her cards right, and was now the celebrated star of one of the wealthiest and most popular brothels in the district. But Ting-Yan's world was still a judgmental and shaming one. No one from the village talked to those two cousins except their parents, who loved them and agonizingly repressed their own feelings of shame in order to bring them leftovers on feast days. Emily knew nothing about people like Ting-Yan's cousins and never would. Ting-Yan hated her more than ever and gave her a bitter glare, which Emily didn't notice. "What are you doing here?" Ting-Yan asked. "Tak-Wing abandon you already?"

"I was getting breakfast," said Emily. She still hadn't placed Ting-Yan.

"No breakfast now, I don't think." Ting-Yan helped Emily gather up the pieces of her tiffin.

The vendor, feeling sorry for the pretty lady, called to them to approach, and when they did, he refilled the tiffin. But Ting-Yan knew how hard it was for a street seller to make a living. She didn't have much in her pocket, having already paid a handsome sum to Granny Kwok, but she gave the vendor everything she had left. So she'd both cursed Emily and Tak-Wing and paid for their wedding breakfast in the same morning. She didn't want to think about it. "Where are you staying?"

Someone blew a whistle. Police raid! The vendors slammed down covers and pulled wraps over carts and wheelbarrows and hightailed it out of the alley so fast that Emily and Ting-Yan were left standing there alone when the police rushed past them.

JOLLY GOOD FELLOW

July 9, 1937

When Cheung got to the Hong Kong Cricket Club, the first-floor bar was abuzz with a story that to him already felt like ancient news—the story of Selby Hancock's drunken misbehaviour at Clearwater Bay yesterday and Cheung and Lee's rescue of the entire crew. The news of Selby's further misbehaviour early this morning in Wan Chai was also beginning to trickle in. Vandeleur Grayburn, head of the Hong Kong branch of the Hongkong and Shanghai Banking Corporation, wondered if he should fire Selby. He wondered, too, if they'd done the right thing to elect Richard Hancock as president of the HKCC. Lindsay Ride, physiology professor at the University of Hong Kong, said that it wasn't Hancock's fault, and that the trouble Selby got up to wasn't so unusual for young men new to the colony. He rattled off the names of half a dozen other young cricketers who'd had similar troubles when they first came. Grayburn agreed that there was nothing unusual about Selby, but said that it was embarrassing just the same, and that because of who Selby's father was, it was embarrassing for the club too.

But the bar also buzzed with a second story, which was that of Cheung Tak-Wing's secret marriage to Emily Mah Wai-Yee. But since it was about Cheung in a shameful way, the toffs did not speak this gossip in his presence. It was minor gossip anyway because no actual members of the club were involved.

But there was a third story that developed before Cheung's eyes. The club's chief steward, Martin Colville, was returning to Melbourne. Colville was convinced that the Japanese were going to invade Hong Kong. "I don't know when, mates, but I'm telling you, they are coming. I have a family. I've got to keep them safe."

Colville had a wife and two young daughters who lived with him in the steward's quarters of the HKCC pavilion, the third one built since the club's inception, and the most luxurious, with a full kitchen, two bars, a change room, and plenty of equipment storage.

Dr Percy Selwyn Selwyn-Clarke, director of medical services for the colony, thought it wise for Colville to go. "Who knows what is going to happen here? You should go, and keep your wife and kids safe."

"You don't think I should stay and fight?" Colville asked Selwyn-Clarke. "You're going to, aren't you?"

"I'm too old to fight, but I have duties here that I can't see letting go. Hilda won't leave either, I don't think." Selwyn-Clarke's wife, Hilda, was secretary of the Eugenics League and very passionate about contraception for Chinese women. She was also deeply involved in the China Defense League and committed to her friend, the widow of Dr Sun Yat-Sen, Mme Soong Ching-Ling. It wasn't a matter of guessing. He knew she wouldn't leave. He wouldn't even dare raise it with her. They had a daughter called Mary whom they worried about, but Mary was also committed to humanitarian principles, like her parents. Nevertheless, Colville's station was different, and both men recognized this, though neither of them would state the fact out loud.

"Perhaps I should stay and join the Hong Kong Volunteer Defence Corps," said Colville.

"Perhaps," said Selwyn-Clarke. "Though no one would blame a family man for taking care of his wife and children."

In the end, Colville decided to go. He wasn't a doctor like Selwyn-Clarke, and his wife was not a public figure like Hilda. If he wanted to serve his country, he could enlist when he got home. He took his leave and returned to the kitchen to see about more sandwiches.

Richard Hancock suggested that the HKCC promote Head Cook Cheung to Colville's position. "I'd consider it a personal favour from the membership of the club to me, since it's my nephew he rescued. He's proven himself more than loyal, helping our boys no matter how foolish, even after our boys have done him wrong. If that's not loyalty, I don't know what is. Plus, if the Japanese invade, he can't go back to Melbourne!"

The pith helmets guffawed.

"How about that, Cookie Cheung? Ready for your second promotion of the year? Doing pretty well for a Chinaman, I'd say!"

Cheung smiled. "Certainly, Mr Hancock."

At cocktail hour, there was a small celebration, not in the men-only upstairs bar, which was reserved for presidential speeches and the like, but in the everyday ground-floor bar, still an attractive place with its dark wooden counter, little tables, and red velvet chairs. There, they said farewell and bon voyage to Martin Colville, and sang "For He's a Jolly Good Fellow" to Cheung. They congratulated him on his promotion. Selby Hancock, temporarily sober, even apologized to him for his bad behaviour. Pressured by his wife and uncle, he had to, or else it was a loss of face, something the British cared about too.

"I behaved badly yesterday, Cook Cheung. I'm sorry," he said.

Cheung flushed. "Never mind, never mind. It doesn't matter."

"He really is sorry, Cookie," Elizabeth Hancock said. "He's just not very good at expressing himself."

"I said I was sorry," Selby said to his wife, peeved.

"Stop behaving like such a bore, Selby," said Mrs Hancock. She turned to Cheung. "Congratulations on your promotion."

"Thank you, Mrs Hancock. I'm very happy."

Mrs Hancock brought Cheung a glass of syllabub to celebrate—a frothy white concoction that smelled unpleasantly boozy and animal to

Cheung. He took a sip and made a face before he could stop himself. The drink was creamy and oversweet—not a Chinese taste at all.

The cricketers roared with laughter.

Mrs Hancock laughed too. "I don't like it either, Cookie. Would you prefer a beer?"

Cheung nodded gratefully.

"You'll get Colville's flat too, if you want it," said Richard Hancock. "You'll be the club's first Chinese steward, and the first Chinese person to live in that flat. I hope you'll find it comfortable and to your taste."

This was very welcome news indeed, given the loss of the Tai Hang house to that bastard Mah. The steward's flat had two bedrooms and a parlour.

Talk turned to the recent invasion of Manchuria by the Japanese, and rumours of concentration camps being built in Germany. David Edmonston thought that Colville was a fool to go back to Australia. "There's going to be a war in Europe. You'll be drafted and shot. You'd be much safer staying here in Hong Kong."

"I'm not a coward," said Colville. "It would be an honour to fight for my country. I just don't want the wife and kids caught in the crossfire. Because, mark my words, something terrible is going to happen here in Hong Kong."

The toffs began to argue about the likelihood of the war spilling over from China and forgot about Cookie Cheung.

Cheung backed to the wall, feeling awkward among his masters. There was a series of four paintings on the wall by the Portuguese painter Marciano Antonio Baptista, famous for his paintings of Macau, but known also for his works on Hong Kong. Cheung knew the paintings well because he'd dusted them so many times in his late twenties, after he was promoted from working in the basement kitchen. He liked the one of the temple for Tin Hau, whom the Macanese called A-Ma. But it wasn't his favourite. He gazed now at his most cherished one. It showed another expatriate sports club—the Hong Kong Jockey Club—as a wide expanse of green field. In the foreground stood a lush forest of unidentifiable trees. In the background, on Morrison Hill, stood a posh European settlement, a lost castle from some distant other place. He could see it was meant to make Europeans long for Europe. The light fell on it in such a way that it glowed a warm terracotta. And beyond it in the distance, Victoria Harbour with six ships barely visible in perspective, all of them with tall European style masts. These were the ships that had brought them here, and the ships that could take them home to their real castles far away, except that they didn't own those castles—their fathers, older brothers, masters, and employers did. The harbour water glimmered a pale, mysterious blue. In the far distance lay the Chinese mainland, Kowloon, and the New Territories, not yet ceded to the British at the time of the painting—1846 by the Western calendar. To the left was the old Colonial Cemetery, though you couldn't tell from the painting what it was; you'd only know if you knew a bit of the history.

Cheung understood what was behind those unidentifiable trees in the foreground because his mother still lived in Wong Nai Chung, their natal village. Where once it had sat on high ground above an expanse of rice paddies, it now sat on low ground, all its geomantic advantages destroyed by the unrelenting changes to the land surrounding it.

The half-swallowed village was mostly abandoned after the typhoon of 1923, and more fully abandoned after the typhoon of 1925. But after the flood waters had receded, a handful of stubborn villagers returned, including his mother, dragging his sister, Hok-Yee, with her. When Cheung was a boy, his mother had been powerful there as the village matriarch. Now he visited her when he could, which was not often, because the needs of his masters at the club were so great. And the Hong Kong Cricket Club smelled a lot better.

When Cheung was a boy, Wong Nai Chung Village had smelled of warm mountain, sea air, steamed rice, and incense, and sometimes of salted fish when his cousins from Chek Keng and Wong Mo Ying in the New Territories near the border to the Chinese mainland came down with a freshly prepared batch to exchange for the rice that Cheung's father bought wholesale at the docks in Victoria Harbour. In the old days, the family grew its own rice in the paddies below the village. Now this Portuguese painter Baptista had painted the village out of existence. But Cheung knew that it was still there, under the line of trees. It didn't smell too good anymore, though. These days, the village smelled as though the whole of the filled-in swamp had taken residence there. It reeked of rotten grass and sewage.

He'd long wished his mother would accept that the village was finished and move to Tai Hang with the rest of Wong Nai Chung's former inhabitants. There was really no point staying after his father's death. A move would also be a reprieve for his sister, Hok-Yee, who had stayed only to look after their mother. But now that the Tai Hang house was gone, Cheung didn't know what to wish. Would they come and live with him at the HKCC steward's flat, if he asked?

"There you are, Cheung!" Colville shouted from the far end of the hallway. "Can you get down to the kitchen? The bar wants devilled eggs, and young Nigel doesn't know how to make mayonnaise."

"Of course, sir," said Cheung. What a fool he was to be daydreaming when there was work to be done. He hurried down to the kitchen to give young Nigel Yik-Shun a lesson in sauces and dressings.

The toffs were restless and they drank and laughed and chatted until late at night.

The moon was high and all the trams had stopped running by the time Cheung was finally free to go. He could have hailed a rickshaw, but money was tight, and with everything so uncertain, he decided he'd save his coins and walk. All along Hennessey Road, the little grocers, tea shops, sundry kiosks, money changers, and pawn shops were shuttered. There was no one out except other workers like him returning home exhausted after a late shift. To cheer himself up, he sang a little tune his father had taught him before he died.

Lonely on the mountain path
Through mist and rain
Through rain and mist
I'm searching always searching
Searching for you

Lonely down beside the river
Through mist and rain
Through rain and mist
I'm searching ever searching
Searching for you

Lonely by the ocean too
Through mist and rain
Through rain and mist
Searching still I'm searching
Never finding you

When he got home, Tak-Tam was fast asleep on the front room settee in his singlet and shorts. He looked so thin and pale. Cheung slipped past him into the back bedroom, shed his crumpled day clothes, and crawled into bed beside Yim-Fong.

Up in the mountains above Tai Hang, where Aw Boon Haw, the Tiger Balm magnate, had his beautiful pagoda and gardens, the cicadas scraped their otherworldly tune. Still awake on his plank bed beside his sleeping wife, Cheung tossed and turned. Yim-Fong snored softly. Cheung watched her rib cage rise and fall in the moonlight. He was grateful that there was a solution to his problems, even if it was a modern solution. He was a modern person. He was okay with it. Hadn't he, after all, worked his entire life in the service of a contemporary kung fu, and learned its convoluted rules while serving its red-bearded masters? There was no dishonour in that. Though he had given up his natal village of Wong Nai Chung in order to relocate here to Tai Hang, he could understand Tai Hang as his home village. Didn't all Chinese people have to move house from time to time? Even Wong Nai Chung dated back only to the Ming dynasty. But now he was forced to sell the Tai Hang house, all so his family line could be carried on through the blood of his enemy, Morris Mah, rumoured to be descended from—yet disowned by—one of the British taipans, maybe even the terrible Henry Witt-Weatherall himself. Whatever vestiges of commitment to traditional village ways remained in Cheung's heart dropped to his stomach. He felt nauseous. With Tak-Wing's marriage to Emily, Cheung had lost that last trace of traditional wealth and honour. In exchange, his line was polluted by barbarian blood, while he descended into deeper servitude to them at the Hong Kong Cricket Club. In the meantime, he would likely lose his honest son, Tak-Tam to another village, Chek Keng, if Ting-Yan would agree. And this would be the best of all possible circumstances. Though Tak-Tam would be head of household there, it was not the same as being head of household in a home passed down the father's line. This would not be so bad, if his first son had not dishonoured the family so completely. Now his second son's honour was all he had. It was not enough. And what if Ting-Yan turned Tak-Tam down? Cheung could not bear the thought of more uncertainty.

Of course, being promoted to head steward at the Hong Kong Cricket Club was an honour, even if it was honour tinged with servitude. Cheung's beginnings at Wong Nai Chung gave him a founding place in the new colonial order, in the sense that the village was taken over in the very earliest days of the British occupation. He had worked for the occupation all his life, and now he had been promoted. That was an honour of a kind. But now that the Tai Hang house had to be sold, and Tak-Tam was likely destined for another village, Cheung was truly landless.

Still, it was a piece of luck that the head steward's flat came with the position. He must remember to be grateful to Tin Hau, if not to the white men themselves. The flat offered a solution to the problem created by Tak-Wing's indiscretion. Though it would be painful to share his home with his enemy's daughter, Emily and Tak-Wing could move into to the steward's flat with him. In fact, this seemed to be the only solution. Cheung could not swallow it. This new kung fu was too much. But at least both sons would have wives and there would be descendants. It was a time to be humble and accept fate. He must cultivate honesty and loyalty in situations where these virtues could still be cultivated, and not mind too much about what those situations were. Lying awake in the dark as the cicadas mourned, Cheung tried to draw up the correct attitude, but it would not come.

Cheung wouldn't take over Colville's steward duties for another week. In the morning, there was a full range of menu items to prepare, and stock to inventory. He dashed off a message to Yim-Fong to see if their upstairs neighbour, whose cousin had come from Shanghai and was desperate for housing, would like to buy the Tai Hang house. The cousin said yes, but at the last minute, an anonymous buyer offered a higher price on condition of remaining anonymous. Cheung really needed the extra money, so he rescinded the deal with the cousin and accepted the anonymous buyer's offer. In a few days, the sale would go through. Once the house was sold, Yim-Fong, Tak-Wing, and Emily could come to the cricket club. He dashed off another note to Lee giving his consent to the marriage of Tak-Tam and Ting-Yan, but only if Ting-Yan were truly happy about it.

He considered sending a messenger to his mother at Wong Nai Chung, but decided against it. He didn't want to risk drawing attention to the fact that he came from a family that had opposed the British presence. Though he bore them no great love, they were kind enough to him, so he didn't hate them either. It seemed best not to rock the boat, especially when Tin Hau was in such a capricious mood in her bestowal of fortune. There was spinach cream soup to make, but the spinach supplier still hadn't shown up and Cheung needed to figure out a substitute before lunchtime. There were lots of potatoes left, but he'd served potato cream soup just yesterday. What he wouldn't have given for a good supply of oxtail. He eyed his supplies. There was curry powder, a couple of imported apples, and assorted vegetables both fresh and canned for a reasonable facsimile of mulligatawny. He didn't want to give the cricketers any reason to think him incompetent, especially before he'd taken up stewardship of the club officially. He would go see his mother later.

The week proved a hectic one. In addition to keeping the kitchen running and making the finer dishes, Cheung had to learn everything that Colville wanted to pass on before the old head steward went back to Australia. There were suppliers of sporting goods to meet. There were posh toffs to whom one must learn to speak in the proper way. There was china to inventory, silverware to count, and order forms to master that required the use of English words Cheung didn't yet know. There were uniform standards to understand down to the last buttonhole and eyelet. There were locks, bolts, and keys.

The board of the cricket club promoted Tak-Tam to head cook. But if he was to move to Chek Keng, he would have to leave the club. Cheung wondered if Tak-Wing could rise to the occasion. Or descend to it. Tak-Wing was excellent at cricket and tennis, imagined himself one of the toffs. Though technically Chinese were not permitted to be club members, the young cricketers allowed Tak-Wing to play with them when the older, more conservative ones were not around because he was so good. Even if he did agree to step into his father's shoes, would he have the constancy and perseverance to do it? Probably not, thought Cheung. Still, he would do his best to teach the young man how to make soups and sauces whenever he got the chance.

CHAPTER 13

FRAMED

119 Lai Chi Kok Road
Mong Kok, Hong Kong

July 12, 1937

Dear Morgan,

Tanaka says he got your letter. I told him to hold off spending your
money on that ticket though. Something happened to us recently
that you'll want to think hard on. It might make you change your
mind about coming.

Last week we were at the Repulse Bay Hotel, playing our set after
George Pio-Ulski's Quintette, but before Nick Korin and His Swing
Band. Afterwards there was a girl waiting for me on the dance floor.
I'd seen her at the hotel before and never thought anything of it,
but there was something funny about the sense of purpose she had
about her that night. Tried to get me to dance with her, but I just
wanted to go chill with Tanaka and Emily and our friends. Well,
she got a little aggressive, grabbed my arm, popped a button off my
shirt, and put it in her pocket. Can you imagine? I called her a crazy
mama or something like that, you know, to make her go away, not
to insult her or anything. And I got away from her, though she sure

did give me the stink eye, like every ten minutes, 'til I decided to go home early.

A couple of nights ago, though, I was back at the hotel for our regular gig. I'd forgotten about that girl. Emily had just gotten married a few days before. She snuck off to the registry in the Supreme Court Building with her beau, a young man called Cheung Tak-Wing, the son of a servant at the Hong Kong Cricket Club. Her family was scandalized, as you can imagine, even more scandalized than they were when she joined our band. Rich people the same the world over, cousin, but Emily's a great girl, so full of pluck and determination. We played a fabulous set including "Waiting for You," "Bei Mir Bist Du Schön," and the song me and Tanaka wrote together, "Moon and Stars over Sai Kung." We danced and drank champagne. I noticed that strange girl who took my button was there watching us, but she kept her distance and I thought all would be well.

Well, after Emily and Tak-Wing left, the girl was waiting for me out back with a couple of British guys I recognized from the boxing circuit. One of them called me the N-word, the other called Tanaka the J-word. Dude just kept tapping my face and calling me names, it was impossible not to get mad. I knew he was goading me, but there's only so much a man can take—I have my dignity. I had to punch him. You know me, I'm a little guy, but I'm not soft. Once I got hold of him, well, that was that, the rage took me, I punched and punched and punched. I got on his chest and banged his head against the pavement. I could see the other one was on Tanaka. That crazy girl just stood there on the pavement laughing her foolish head off. I gave as good as I got, but then a whole crew of them came out back to where we were. Well, you wouldn't want to see me now, I got two serious shiners and a broken rib. Tanaka's not going in to work anytime soon either. Emily's spilling with upset, and so is Jane. I mean it's really bad. To top it all off the hotel manager says we started it and now we're banned from the Repulse Bay Hotel, can't ever set foot in there again. And to add insult to injury, I heard they put a new all-white band in our place the very next day, playing all our tunes no less—not just the covers, but also our song "Moon and Stars over Sai Kung." I mean really, cousin, what a total hit and run. What a bunch of greedy cowards. I'm beside myself with rage. I'm going to get even. But I sure as heck don't want you out here in the thick if this. It's not a good time, and Lord only knows what is going to happen next. You best go to the States. Prohibition's just been lifted and there's some serious dough to be made in spirits. You should go to Chicago and make your fortune.

Love from your cousin,

Izzy

CHAPTER 14

Typhoon Shelter
ME AND TING-YAN
June 30, 1997

S *eeing that the congee is almost gone, Great-Aunt Violet waves to the* *grumpy server. She contemplates a dish of running ground chicken with mountain herbs, but decides against it because of the H5N1 bird flu crisis. Instead, she orders a dish of flower conch boiled in spicy wine, specialty of the house. "You won't find these anywhere else," she says to Ophelia. "You should try them."*

Then she glances up at the clock. The pink-haired girl from the future gazes coolly down at them, unconcerned about the time passing over her turquoise face. It's four o'clock.

"You're going to miss Chris Patten's departure from Government House. Ah, never mind. You can just watch it later," Great-Aunt Violet says.

The air conditioner blows so cold that Ophelia rustles around in her bag for a shawl. Outside, it's still raining, and the air is dense with mist that presses against the restaurant windows.

Are you trying to kill me, making me talk about such personal things? I know in your world you let it all hang out—that's emigration for you, empty you of all your natural instincts. They should call it empty-gration! But I'm not dead yet! I saw *Happy Together*. I know about Jenny Shimizu too. And that funny Korean American girl, what's her name, Margaret Cho. Just because I'm quiet doesn't mean I don't know. And don't forget,

I was a doctor throughout my working years. I know about the AIDS crisis and the new antiretroviral cocktails.

Out in the countryside, when women wanted to live together, they had ways of doing so, through a tradition of women's houses. They declared their intentions and had a ceremony for themselves in which they combed their own hair in a single braid. A lot of the cooks who work in Hong Kong come from the county that upholds that tradition.

Anyway, as for me, I just didn't think about it. When I was young, all I thought about was my sister and my father. And my dead mother, of course, whom I missed terribly. It was a full-time job running around after Emily. She was so rebellious and she knew how to rebel. I guess you could say there was a script for her—a very new one, but a script. Whereas for me, not so much. Or not yet. Maybe there is a script for you, Feelie? But who am I to advise you what to do? Things in my time were so different. Hong Kong has changed and keeps changing so fast! Every generation is a new country.

When I met Ting-Yan, I just watched her and didn't know why. I wasn't interested in boys, and boys weren't interested in me. I had enough to do. And then one day, when the worst of the war was over, we were together at Old Mah's house, raising Raymond and Macy. I won't tell you if it was sexy or not, because that's none of your business. I guess there is a bit of the uptight Victorian in me, especially compared to you. I grew up in old Queen Vicky's shadow, after all. What do you want from me? Eat your conchs while they are still hot!

Ophelia thinks she can't eat another thing, but the conchs are so tender and sweet. The taste of the ocean fills her mouth—a little briny, a little boozy, and so spicy she squeals, then grabs her glass of ice water.

CHAPTER 15

MONKEY'S WEDDING

July 14, 1937

Martin Colville's last duty before setting sail for Australia was to organize and oversee my sister's wedding. The hard part would be keeping it secret from Cheung. Colville wasn't at all convinced that it was the right thing to do, but the young cricketers said his name would go down in the annals of Hong Kong Cricket Club shame if he could not achieve this. Their hearts were full of compassion for Edward, Duke of Windsor, and his commoner sweetheart, Wallis Simpson. Just as Edward and Wallis had married in exile, Tak-Wing and Emily would too. But unlike Edward and Wallis, the young cricketers thought, Tak-Wing and Emily would be surrounded by friends. That meant something different to them that it did to the young couple, but the cricketers didn't know that. They put the proscenium right where the near wicket usually went, and festooned it with azaleas, impatiens, irises, and camellias.

Since it was all to be kept secret from Cheung, the food was prepared by the individual cricketers' staff in their grand colonial houses up on the Peak or at the very least the Mid-Levels. Elizabeth Hancock's staff made potato salad with shrimp. Hilda Selwyn-Clarke's staff made spring bean salad and Quails Juniper. Some of the Chinese staff got wind of who they were cooking for and were delighted by the idea of a young Chinese couple getting married at the HKCC. They didn't know or care about church weddings and thought that the HKCC was a romantic and wonderful place to get married. The whole colony blossomed in imagining what was possible and beautiful about taking up the culture of another, without being yoked by the thick braid of power that constituted tradition on both the British and Chinese sides. They cooked fantasy elements into the food—a few dong gu chopped into the cream of mushroom soup, Chinese chestnuts in the stuffing for the roast chicken, a bit of red bean paste between the layers of Victoria sponge. Some sent traditional Chinese treats, also: wife cakes, roasted-pork steamed buns, sticky rice cooked in lotus leaf with chicken, sausage, mushrooms, and mung beans. Emily and Tak-Wing's cricket club wedding became a modern fairy tale for everyone, all the more so because their fathers didn't know about it.

Elizabeth Hancock, née Swire, who had herself only recently gotten married on the Peninsular and Oriental Steam Navigation Company ship as it made its way to Hong Kong via Bombay, Penang, and Singapore, lent Emily her wedding dress. As Emily's sister, I was supposed to play bridesmaid, but I didn't know a thing about a bridesmaid's duties, so Mrs Hancock helped us. She ordered Emily a bouquet from one of the finest florists in the D'Aguilar Street flower market. She did Emily's makeup. She did Emily's hair too. "I'll do it just like Wallis's. You'll be the most fashionable Chinese bride in the city." She helped Emily into the complicated white dress, shortened and tucked by her own seamstress to fit Emily's smaller frame. The dress was very white, and the makeup that Mrs Hancock had applied was too pale for Emily's golden skin. *Is this how things will be from now on?* I wondered. *Do we go into the future as ghosts?*

In my green velvet jacket, thankfully brought back to life under Amah's careful ministrations, I played father and escorted Emily from the ladies' powder room on the second floor (given over to us for the day) to the grand entranceway of the clubhouse. Together, we stood there at the threshold and gazed out over the lawn, all laid out for the ceremony. The guests were seated with their backs to us, row upon row of blond, red, and brown heads, dressed earnestly in their Sunday finest for a ceremony that was both a jest and deadly serious. Resentment welled up in the pit of my stomach about the jesting aspect, but I pushed it down because it didn't serve Emily in any way. I gripped my sister's hand to buoy her up, though she didn't seem to need it ... at first. Her eyes shone, exuding joy. She didn't see the joke—she saw only the romance, and she rode its tender white wings as though on the back of a swan. But Tak-Wing was late. He was supposed to arrive at twelve o'clock sharp, stage left, with his brother Tak-Tam as best man. I heard the noonday gun at Causeway Bay go off, and far across the harbour, the one-ton brass bell of the clock tower at the Kowloon–Canton Railway station faintly rang. Where was he? Had he changed his mind?

Emily's grip on my hand grew tighter. I could feel her imaginary wings drooping, her inner balloon deflating.

"He'll be here any second, Em."

"Where is he?"

"Don't worry, darling, I know he's coming." I knew no such thing, but it wasn't my role to introduce doubt.

"How can you know, ViVi? He's supposed to love me. I'm not supposed to have any cause to worry."

Still he did not come.

She fiddled with the ribbon binding her bouquet.

"I'm sure he's coming, my love."

"What if he's changed his mind?" The fancy bow loosened in her fidgeting hands.

"I know he hasn't. Be careful of your bouquet."

"What?" she said. Then, "Oh!" as the bundle of flowers burst apart and scattered over the floor. She tried to gather them up, darting from one fallen flower to the next and tripping on her train. "What if he doesn't love me and is only after Father's money?"

"What a thing to say, Emily!" I said, moving to help her.

"Greater men have done lesser things."

I bound the scattered blossoms back together into some semblance of a bouquet, not the artful arrangement of a practised flower seller, but passable. Maybe my beautiful sister was smarter than she looked. "You're already legally married to him, so if that's what he's after, he's already got it."

In the steward's quarters belonging to Martin Colville, Tak-Wing adjusted his top hat. He didn't have a clue as to what to do, so a grinning Colville waited on him as though he were a real toff, while Tak-Tam hovered awkwardly. Tak-Wing thought the hat was a bit frumpy, but Colville said that a trilby was too casual for the occasion.

"Edward didn't wear a hat at all," Tak-Wing grumbled.

"Yes," said Colville, "but you're not he, and this is Hong Kong, not the Loire Valley."

Tak-Tam said, "No hat is better, if you ask me." He heard the noonday gun go off. "We're late. We better get going."

"No hat?" said Colville. "Not very dignified." He glanced at his wristwatch, a beautiful if modest Omega 26.5 T2, with a sector dial. Tak-Tam glanced at Coville's wrist too, enviously. He loved watches and studied the advertisements for them in the Chinese papers. Though he didn't expect ever to be able to afford one, he knew all the different makes from Rolex to Audemars Piguet.

The two-tone shoes lent to Tak-Wing by one of the young cricketers were too narrow in the toe. They cut off his circulation so badly that he could hardly walk. His toes felt like the lumps of ice that the toffs put in their glasses to make their water cool. A chill spread through his feet, up his legs, through his belly, and into his heart. He shivered in spite of the good suit of English wool.

What was wrong with him? The hottest day of the year, and yet he'd never felt so cold. Was he making a mistake? Did he not love Emily? Of course he did, but what if he was being a fool, like Edward VIII? Even if his family throne was a smaller one than the throne of England, it was still the place Cheung had made for him. But why should he care about that old poop? Sure, he was Tak-Wing's father, but he was a lackey to the colonizer. He cleaned their floors and wiped their boots. Okay, these days, he made their makeshift mulligatawny and locked their gates, but still, he served them. Whereas Tak-Wing dominated them.

He put the top hat back on.

On the court and on the pitch, he was their better. So what if they wouldn't let him play on their courts and pitches in the sunlight? In the moonlight, when only the young cricketers were out, Tak-Wing was their man. It was only a matter of time before the Chinese got the colony back, and then they won't be able to stop him. Why should he take their charity now? Even in the form of a wedding.

Tak-Tam didn't like the top hat. He frowned and shook his head.

Tak-Wing took it off again.

Did his getting married here make him their servant, their boy, their little Chinaman? Did his love serve their love? Their love of what? Of their own damn empire, of their love of self? Tak-Wing's love for Emily reminded them of their own abdicating king. The one who fell flat on his face for love of the wrong woman. What actual king shirked his duty for the sake of girly romance? Was Tak-Wing like him? Did he love the wrong woman?

He took Colville's trilby and put it on.

Colville shook his head.

Perhaps he was a fool to deny his own poor father, who had never done anything but love him. Maybe he should marry Ting-Yan, like his father wanted, not Emily like these overfed young cricketers wanted.

He took the trilby off.

Was there something wrong with Tak-Wing for wanting what they wanted? Were they playing him as he thought he was playing them? What if his father was right and he only liked Emily for her modern looks? What if he was less like King Edward and more like Emperor Puyi, dethroned by Western-educated republicans and sent into exile in Japanese-occupied Manchuria, then married to some hapless Manchu girl? He imagined his kingdom returned to him by murderers. *Lady Tin Hau, I'm cold, so cold, even in this hot, hot ocean. Is there a storm coming that I do not understand?*

And then, past the window, came an apparition. Ting-Yan in her old-fashioned black village suit, her hair undone and flowing wildly around her, full of rage.

Tak-Wing took a sharp inhale and sat down on the bed, unable to move. His mind rushed back to a memory of her when they were nine years old, rowing her family's sampan among the bigger boats in the Sai Kung Harbour. He was wearing a silly hat she'd folded for him from an old newspaper. A sea eagle had swooped at them, and snatched the hat off his head. He'd been so startled that he'd lost his footing and slipped into the harbour. He hadn't yet known how to swim, and Ting-Yan had dived in after him. Terrified of drowning, he'd clung to her like a life raft as she kicked and paddled. She was a small girl, but she kicked and wriggled with the strength of a sea snake. Somehow, she got them both back to the lip of the boat, and from there he'd been able to pull himself back up on board. If not for her, he might have drowned. Though if not for her, he wouldn't have been wearing that stupid paper hat in the first place.

Now she was at the window, gazing forlornly in. Her brown face was thin and sad.

What dead ghosts was she disturbing? He didn't love her anymore. He waved her away dismissively.

She bared her teeth at him.

At last, almost ten minutes since the firing of the noonday gun at Causeway Bay, the groom arrived with his brother Tak-Tam at his side, as best man. Waiting in the black and white tiled foyer of the clubhouse, I let go of the breath I didn't know I was holding. Emily's hand, gripping mine, relaxed.

The band struck up. Rather than the traditional "Here Comes the Bride," they played the "Free Marriage Song" at the request of the ever-thoughtful Mrs Hancock, under the advice of Hilda Selwyn-Clarke. I had never heard this song before in my life. But Mrs Selwyn-Clarke told me later that it was a song that celebrated true love and choice of beloved against the old traditions of arranged marriage and reverence to ancestors, and that it had been sung at the wedding of Sun Yat-Sen and Soong Ching-Ling, whom she knew personally.

The congregation were mostly young cricketers with a few of the more progressive older generation, including Dr Selwyn Selwyn-Clarke and the astronomer Graham Heywood. Lindsay Ride presided. I played father and walked the bride down the aisle and then I played bridesmaid and stood beside her for the exchange of vows. Tak-Tam stood beside Tak-Wing, and held the plain gold band that the young cricketers had all chipped in to help buy from Chow Sang Sang Jewellers.

I saw a young woman in a traditional black sam foo lurking around the perimeter of the club. I saw Tak-Tam glance over and see her too. I stared too long and she looked back and shot me the evil eye. I tried to stop staring. There was something familiar about her—did I know her from somewhere? She continued to circle the congregation, eventually moving beyond the edge of my peripheral vision. But I could sense her behind us, exuding something unpleasant.

Lindsay Ride didn't seem to notice. He began the ceremony. "Dearly beloved, we are gathered here today ..."

Emily fidgeted with her bouquet, and I was afraid it would come apart again in front of everyone. I touched her wrist discreetly, and she stopped.

Lindsay Ride talked about the meaning of marriage and what it might signify in particular for a young Chinese couple who would witness the growth and changes of a new city coming into its own. "Does anyone here know of any reason why this man and this woman should not be joined in holy matrimony?"

He waited to give the congregation a real chance to answer.

Behind us, the young woman in the traditional black pantsuit took a breath so deep that everyone heard it and turned to look at her.

She spoke.

Her voice was not loud, but it was strangely deep. It came out of her as though from another world beneath her feet. Very slowly, in that other-worldly voice, she said, "A hundred reasons I shall not speak."

She took another deep, croaking breath, like a spirit from the underworld trying to surface, and continued in English that was perfectly clear, though unnaturally low: "But I damn their first-born child to wander the earth for eighty years, lost and confused, without a friend to call his own. May he travel in spirals, never knowing left from right or up from down."

The congregation heard. A few people near the back, close to where she stood, laughed nervously.

Ride heard. He must have. He cast his eyes to the ground for a moment as though some chthonic being were peering up at him through the flimsy platform on which he stood.

A hot wind blew up from nowhere, and everyone began to sweat, even as their fancy jackets and silk dresses rustled in the unnatural movement of air.

Ride closed his eyes and seemed to mutter something, a prayer perhaps. The pause was achingly long, but at last his eyes opened again. "Hearing none, we shall proceed. Emily Mah Wai-Yee and Cheung Tak-Wing have come to enter the holy state of marriage," he said.

Ting-Yan fled the scene, and the hot wind died down.

The congregation murmured, muttered, and whispered. If truth be told, the British are as superstitious as the Chinese. Their fantasy party had been ruined.

Ride, high priest of steady nerves, intoned his way through the ceremony. "Do you, Cheung Tak-Wing, take this woman to be your lawful wedded wife?"

Tak-Wing, in top hat and tails, looked like a nineteenth-century English hero standing on the precipice of a windy cliff. His face was a little pale, but he held his head high and said, "I do."

"And do you, Emily Mah Wai-Yee, take this man to be your husband, to have and to hold, 'til death do you part?"

"I do," said Emily, the beautiful ghost.

She had no idea how death might come to her or to Cheung's handsome if self-centred son.

As for Ting-Yan, she regrets her curse now, just as she regrets the villain hitting ceremony she paid for and enacted with Granny Kwok against Granny's advice by the Goose Neck Bridge. She once said that she'd felt compelled to do it by something deeper than herself, something ancient and primal that could not be stopped. "Don't talk nonsense," I told her. "Jealousy is the most natural emotion in the world. Besides, we are modern women. We know that curses can't come true." Ting-Yan is my nearest and dearest. She is not a bad person. She is one of the best people I know. But she was young and she was hurt and she was angry. Why do we relegate the ones we don't love to realms more distant that those we still hold open for strangers? And even further still if they love us in spite of our neglect. Tak-Wing's disdain for Ting-Yan was more than half the problem, but he would never acknowledge it, not even on his deathbed, not even after all that happened later.

The band played "Land of Hope and Glory." Then there was a party, and Tak-Wing, Emily, and the cricketers danced—first the rumba, then the samba, then the foxtrot and the lindy hop. Tak-Tam and I stood on the sidelines feeling awkward, though the music did make my feet itch. Ferdinand "Sonny" Maria Castro, female impersonator and minor celebrity in the expatriate community sang, and periodically introduced Isadore Davis Wong on bass, Tanaka Shigeru on piano, and on drums, the health inspector Edward Kerrison. A couple of the band members had bruises on their faces, and Isadore winced when it was time for the bass to get fancy. Emily had told me that on the day of the registry wedding, her band had been attacked by a crew of British thugs who had driven them from their most beloved venue, the Repulse Bay Hotel, but they wouldn't miss playing at her cricket club wedding for the world. If the men were in pain, it didn't affect their music. They played with unbelievable skill. They played "It Don't Mean a Thing If It Ain't Got That Swing," "Moonglow," and "Dream a Little Dream." They played "Sweet Leilani," "Sophisticated Lady," and "One O'Clock Jump." They played popular Chinese tunes too:

"Ye Shanghai," "Paris of the East," and "Blooming Flowers, Full Moon." The music was so infectious that eventually Tak-Tam and I also got up and danced and laughed with Tak-Wing, Emily, and the young cricketers. Someone got a cricket ball out and a handful of celebrants played catch over the heads of the dancers. As they tossed and spun the ball, it seemed to dance in the air of its own volition, to do a little cha-cha-cha with the more enthusiastic of the dancers. It was a wonder no one was hurt and nothing was broken. Champagne flowed and everyone ate the shrimp salad and Quails Juniper, and we forgot Ting-Yan's curse and all of our other troubles and differences for those few hours. Maybe this monkey's wedding offered the possibility of a new world after all.

Old Cheung was supposed to be at the Tai Hang house, packing. But he didn't have many possessions, and there really wasn't much to do, so he came down to the club in hopes of getting Colville's key from him directly and saying a last goodbye. He ended up watching the wedding from behind the stands, fuming.

We got bottles of Awakening Lion aerated lemonade from the bartender and sat beneath the wilting proscenium arch while Chinese workers moved chairs and tables all around us.

"Who was that strange girl who croaked like a sea monster?" Emily asked.

"Yes, she very nearly ruined your wedding!" I said. "Thank goodness Lindsay Ride had the forbearance to simply continue."

Tak-Wing didn't say a word.

Instead, Tak-Tam explained, "That was Lee Ting-Yan, the daughter of our father's sworn brother. She's been our friend since we were children. We should have invited her."

Tak-Wing piped up. "We certainly should not have. She's a lunatic."

"Her voice was so strange," I mused.

"I didn't properly hear what she said. Though it sounded ominous," said Emily.

"It was all nonsense," Tak-Wing said, grimacing. "Meaningless gibberish. She's mad."

I had heard her words quite clearly. I opened my mouth to tell them what she'd said, then thought better of it.

"I don't think she's mad," said Tak-Tam. "Sad, maybe. But not mad."

"Let's not talk about it." Emily leaned over and kissed Tak-Wing on the cheek. "It's been a beautiful day. Let's keep it that way."

She snatched his top hat and put it on, then crossed her eyes and stuck out her tongue. We all laughed.

"Where are you going to live?" Tak-Tam asked his brother. "You'll have to find somewhere eventually."

"I was thinking we could return to one of the old village houses at Wong Nai Chung. We could be neighbours with Grandmother Wan-See."

"That haunted old place?" said Tak-Tam.

Tak-Wing nodded but his eyes twinkled. "It floods all the time too, and I've heard rumours that bandits use it to hide out after murders and robberies."

"You didn't think your situation through very thoroughly, did you?" Tak-Tam said.

"We were too romantic," said Emily, with a sigh. "And not very practical-minded."

"And now, a little desperate," said Tak-Wing. "But we have each other." He pulled Emily close and gave her a squeeze.

"Well, we're off to Lai Po-Chuen's dormitory 'til we figure it out," said Emily.

"Or until the prefect catches us," Tak-Wing said with a wink.

They both laughed conspiratorially.

"Where will you go tonight, Tak-Tam?" Emily asked. "I guess your father doesn't take over as steward until tomorrow?"

"I'll go check on my old bean," Tak-Tam said, using the colloquial expression for "father."

"My old man will need attention too," I said.

"At least save it for tomorrow, Violet," said Emily.

I scowled, hating the way she took me for granted. "I intend to do just that."

That night, before I slept, I knelt at my bedside and prayed for my father first, then Tak-Wing and Emily, then the sad brother, Tak-Tam. Then I prayed for Old Cheung and the girl in the black suit too, for much longer than I'd intended.

The next day, I went to the Kimblewick and told Old Mah. He was at his desk, working on his accounts. His office was very warm despite the electric fan blasting at full tilt. His papers, pinned to the table with paperweights, rattled and rustled in the artificial breeze. He looked frustrated and irritable.

"How dare that bastard Cheung arrange a colonial-style wedding for those two spoiled brats behind my back? Colluding with those toffy sahibs at the Hong Kong Cricket Club. Does he think he's better than me because of his connection to those jerks? He's connected to them only because he's their *servant*, for the love of God. A highly placed servant, but a servant nonetheless."

"Steward is a good job," I said. "Old Cheung worked his way up from nothing. We're not all fortunate enough to have been given a head start by a wealthy father."

Old Mah sucked his teeth. "You and Emily are the descendants of a respectable old Hong Kong family. Unlike Old Cheung and his dirty son, you are not riff-raff from the countryside." The papers on his desk rustled louder, as if in agreement.

"Arguably, Old Cheung and his sons are also descendants of an important Hong Kong family. Wong Nai Chung Village was here on the island before the British came. Before Hong Kong was even Hong Kong."

"Don't be insolent, Violet. You have colluded with your sister against me."

"Father," I said, "I may be insolent, but you're an old grump. Didn't you and Mother raise us to be modern Chinese women? We must make our own choices and speak our own minds. That's what you said yourself. Don't be a hypocrite."

He didn't respond because he knew it was true. He was silent for a long time, his brow deeply furrowed. The papers on his desk rattled in the furious breeze. I thought he wanted me to leave, and so I got up to go.

"Violet."

"Yes, Ba?" The familiar Chinese word for "father" slipped from my mouth before I could think.

He cleared his throat. "Tell Emily I want to—"

It came out all squeaky, and I wasn't sure what he said. "Tell Emily?"

"Tell her ... Tell Emily ..."

"Yes?"

He turned off the fan, and at last those clattering papers quietened down. "I want to have ... a Chinese wedding for her. A traditional Chinese wedding."

"But you're against this marriage."

With the fan off, he instantly began to sweat. "Stop arguing with me! If I'm not to be a hypocrite as you say, then I must accept Emily's choice. But I won't have those bloody British pushing their traditions on her."

"What about being modern?"

"I am modern, Violet. But nonetheless, some Chinese traditions must be observed." Water beaded on his forehead.

I could read between the lines. For him, it was a dig at Old Cheung. My father—great-grandson of the old opium taipan Henry Witt-Weatherall—was determined to have the last word.

"Old Cheung had nothing to do with it, you know."

"Pish. Of course he did."

"Father, don't be ridiculous. It was all the young cricketers' doing."

"Enough now. I won't have my last loyal daughter siding against me with my worst enemy." Sweat ran down his cheek. He turned the fan on again, and the papers again began to rattle.

"Pretty and Pineapple are loyal too. Don't be melodramatic."

"Stop behaving like Emily. It doesn't become you." He closed his eyes to signal the end of his patience.

Why did the old poop have to be so stubborn? I walked out, and shut the door hard. I'd had enough of my own entanglement in other people's business. I left him to his grief and consternation, and went back to the Stable.

I went to my own desk and tried to study, but I couldn't concentrate. I thought about the impossibility of being a modern Chinese in the aftermath of the Opium Wars. We didn't play along with the British and their need for Chinese tea, and so they forced opium on us—on our vanity and our need for prestige goods, on our bodies and their need for pleasure, and more deeply than that on our biology and its capacity for addiction. I was learning all about that in Dr Selwyn-Clarke's class on pharmaceuticals.

Most of my classmates thought that to be modern was to be Western— to perm one's hair, to wear rouge and pancake makeup. My English literature professor, Dr Carston Hughes, said that such ideas were pure foolishness. That to be modern was to believe in democracy and freedom, which were the gifts the British could give us as recompense for the scourge of opium. But my Chinese history professor, Kathy Duffy, said no, Hong Kong people had their own traditions of liberty and an open society, but they went back, way back, and we had to look beyond our occupation by the Manchu, that is, the Qing dynasty, which fell in 1911. She said even the Ming, which preceded it, was not so great because it was conservative and militaristic. For cultural openness, one had to look to the Song. But even it was not perfect because, though much was possible for artistic men, and there were many extraordinary poets and painters, that society was not so open for women. To be a free Chinese woman, she said, one had to look to the Tang dynasty. That was why she was a cultural historian of the Tang. I admired her very much and wished I could be like her, but I felt I must do something practical with my life. If I married, perhaps my daughter would be a historian. But in all likelihood I wouldn't marry, so maybe Emily's daughter would be the historian.

Kathy Duffy had told me that there was a burial mound in Kowloon called Sung Wong Toi, and that that last kings of the Song were buried there. "Imagine," she said, "if they had lived. Imagine if the Song dynasty had continued to flourish in Hong Kong for the last eight hundred years. Imagine that they retained their dream of liberty through all that time and into the present. You'd have to imagine that they might at some point have developed freedoms for women. Sometimes that is what I like to dream of—that the Song came here to Hong Kong and flourished. And that it perhaps brought back some of the wonders of the Tang. When I look at your people, sometimes I think that you could carry that in ways that people in other parts of China could not. What do you think, Violet? Would you like to live in such a place?"

I had nodded yes. But now I think it strange that an old Irish lady, educated at Trinity College Dublin, would dream such a dream.

I thought about my old father then, and all the ways that one can be a Hong Kong Chinese. I thought about that creepy old taipan, my great-great-grandfather Henry Witt-Weatherall, and how he made us old Hong Kong Chinese and took our Chineseness away from us at the same time. I thought about how we might be different if he had acknowledged us as family. Would my grandfather have married a Chinese woman? Would my father? Would I then even be here as Violet Mah Wai-Man? I thought about the cricketers at the HKCC, and their lost King Edward VIII, and whether or not their lives would have been any different if he hadn't abdicated.

CHAPTER 16

NOT GOLDEN

July 14, 1937

O ld Cheung was back at the Tai Hang house, and had already done most of the packing. Furniture, clothing, pots, and pans were all stacked up by the window in the front room. He sat on a stool outside, smoking a cigarette, while Yim-Fong washed the floors. Tak-Tam came up the road alongside the big nullah, a wistful look on his face. He handed his father a package of wedding lunch leftovers, though he didn't say where they were from.

"At least one of my sons still comes home," grumbled Old Cheung.

"I've come to help you with the move, Ba," said Tak-Tam, pulling up a stool to sit beside him.

"It's all done, except the beds. I hope you're sleeping here tonight?"

"I hope so too."

"But you won't tell me where you were today, or where your lousy brother has gone."

"Can't. Sworn to secrecy."

"Doesn't matter. I already know where you were. I was there."

Tak-Tam didn't want to admit that he had seen Old Cheung, so he said nothing.

"What I don't know," Cheung said, "is where that idiot Tak-Wing has gone to live. Not that I care."

"Don't worry about him. He's fine." In the presence of Cheung's resentment, Tak-Tam felt his own bubble up. "My brother is always fine."

"How dare Old Mah humiliate me like this!" Cheung demanded. "Is it not enough for that bastard progeny of the invading English to have murdered my father with his filthy pills? A supposed cure for opium that is actually a distilled and concentrated version of it? Now he's taken my oldest son and forced me to sell my house. And he's had a party to celebrate at the very place where I work, behind my back! I should go to his princely palace up there in the Mid-Levels among those bastard usurper English and slit my throat on his green and pleasant lawn!" His eyebrows moved furiously up and down as he raged.

Cheung's agitation would have been comical if it weren't so sad. Tak-Tam felt guilty for his own part in the adventure. "Old Mah had nothing to do with it, Father. The young cricketers were so excited about King Edward and Mrs Simpson. Tak-Wing, Emily, and I all got caught up in their foolish fantasy."

"What about that bastard Colville?"

"He's going to Australia tomorrow."

"Did he have any part in it?"

"Well ..."

"I suppose you all had a great laugh at my expense."

"I'm sorry, Father. I didn't think."

"What times these are," said Old Cheung. "In my day, children never behaved so disrespectfully to their parents. They'd have been shamed for all eternity if they did."

Yim-Fong came out with a pot of tea and some fruit. She had been listening as she mopped. "Well," she said, "on the positive side, Ting-Yan is free."

Tak-Tam sipped from the cup of tea she handed him. Ting-Yan. From his position standing beside his brother earlier that day, he had seen Ting-Yan at the back of the congregation. He had heard her croaking, otherworldly voice as though she were right beside him, and had been horrified by what she said.

But sitting with his poor betrayed parents now, he understood. Like Ting-Yan, Tak-Tam knew what it felt like not to be loved back by the one you loved. His heart, too, was broken. They had that in common, that bottomless feeling in the stomach like one's world was about to end, but not before one shamed oneself one last time through the bowels. For indeed the loss of the thing never possessed did constitute a kind of shame. Ting-Yan had felt it and cursed Tak-Wing and Emily in order to expiate it. But in some ways Tak-Tam was in a worse position. Ting-Yan hadn't gained anything from her rejection of him. Unlike Tak-Wing who gained Emily by rejecting Ting-Yan, Ting-Yan gained no one by rejecting Tak-Tam. She had no golden moment to hold. And because she had none, Tak-Tam couldn't curse her. He had to hold this shivering nausea as something ongoing and continuous, something that would never leave him, something he could never shed. Her curse had entered his ear and made him want to shit.

And yet, because he loved Ting-Yan, he identified with her. He felt for her. When she had fled the club, he had wanted to leave the flowery proscenium and go after her. But loyalty to family must stand above all things. He had glanced at his brother, shining like a golden god beside his beloved on the altar. Tak-Tam loved his brother more than anything on earth. He felt his brother to be a part of him. He couldn't have betrayed Tak-Wing in that moment when Tak-Wing's life was being consolidated by marriage to his soulmate—and by the recognition of the toffs at the HKCC, essentially the princes of the city who held the power of life and death over Hong Kong. Of course, he loved Ting-Yan more than anything on this earth too. So much of what Tak-Tam was existed beyond this world. But his love for Ting-Yan came after his love for his brother, at least in that moment. They were loves of different kinds, and that moment said he had to stay beside Tak-Wing.

But different moments allow for different actions. Now that the wedding was over and Tak-Wing and Emily were safely and publicly married, the duty of that moment was done.

"Will you arrange for me to visit Ting-Yan at Chek Keng? Can I talk to Captain Lee myself?" he asked his mother and father.

"He was here earlier today," Cheung said. "I think he's still docked down at the typhoon shelter. Why don't we go down there and see?"

They locked up the house, then hurried down the road alongside the nullah, past all the sellers of turnip cake, sweet potatoes, tea eggs, and soup noodles. They stopped to buy oranges and wife cakes as gifts for Lee.

Captain Lee had come earlier in the day on the *Oolong* in pursuit of Ting-Yan, who had borrowed her second cousin Ka-Wan's motorboat that morning without asking permission. Second Cousin Ka-Wan had won it the week before in a long-odds bet at a Macau casino, and it was the talk of the village.

When Lee saw them, he knew already what it was about. He stepped up onto the dock, beaming.

Tak-Tam blurted out his desire, awkwardly but clearly.

"Only if your daughter is willing," Cheung said. "I stand by my word."

"Nothing would make me happier," Lee said. "But you will have to ask Ting-Yan, of course."

Cheung said he would stay at the Tai Hang house and take care of what remained to do before the moving van arrived the next day. He wanted to sleep one last night in his adopted village too. Yim-Fong said she would accompany Tak-Tam to Chek Keng. Old Lee offered them tea and a bowl of congee. He laid out the oranges and wife cakes they had brought and sent a messenger boy to buy some dim sum for them to share before the journey. He was very pleased at the prospect of the marriage he had most wanted coming about after all.

When they had eaten and wished one another luck, Cheung left the boat and returned to the Tai Hang house alone. Lee untied the boat, and he, Yim-Fong, and Tak-Tam began the journey up the coast.

At dusk, Ting-Yan was in the chapel at Chek Keng, praying to Mary and begging forgiveness for her sins. The light inside the chapel glowed slightly pink in spite of the fact that outside the sky was deep blue fading to black. The pinkness had no discernable source, not that Ting-Yan noticed as she turned her eyes up to the Mother of God. Actually Ting-Yan believed in Tin Hau, but Lee insisted that she call the goddess Mary, so that was what Ting-Yan did. "Forgive me Mother, for I have sinned."

Though Tak-Wing and Emily had not yet conceived a child, Ting-Yan knew what she had done was wrong. She hadn't planned her actions at the wedding. She had gone on Granny Kwok's prompting, but also out of a feeling of urgent need, a sense that a meeting with fate was inevitable. But she hadn't known beforehand what that fate was. The curse had gushed out of her as many ancient things do, already lying in wait, unbeknownst even to the person who is the conduit.

"Please forgive me. I meant the child no harm. If you see it in the goodness of your heart to lift the curse I did not mean to pronounce, I will remain forever your servant."

When she finished, she was surprised to find Old Lee, Tak-Tam, and Yim-Fong waiting patiently at the back of the chapel. She had been so absorbed in her own remorse, and perhaps a little self-pity too, that she had not even noticed them enter.

"Brother Tak-Tam! Auntie Yim-Fong! Father!"

"Sit down, daughter," Lee said. "You might guess why they are here."

"Oh no," she said.

Tak-Tam's face fell.

"Yes," said Lee. "If you are sorry about what you did to poor Tak-Wing, you'll treat his brother with respect and dignity."

"What I did to Tak-Wing!" The hurt and jealousy had not left her yet. It was too much to ask.

"Weren't you just praying to lift the curse you laid on them?" her father asked.

"No," she lied.

"Sinner."

"Okay, I was." She sighed a long sad sigh, and turned to Tak-Tam. "What is it? Why are you here?"

"Daughter," Lee said, with a tone of reprimand.

"My good friend," she said. "I'm happy to see you."

In truth, she did like Tak-Tam and was happy to see him—it just wasn't the kind of happiness that he wished her to feel.

Poor Tak-Tam! Not only did he have to propose in front of his mother and his beloved's father, but she liked him as a friend only and did not see him as a potential lover or husband. A lesser man would have talked about the weather, fled, or gotten his mother to do the talking. But Tak-Tam, though slender, bookish, and shy, was not without courage.

"Ting-Yan," he said. "I know you know why I am here. I can see as clearly as your esteemed father and my respected mother that you don't feel for me as I feel for you. And yet, as this is my one and only chance to say to you what I need to say, I have to say it. I have loved you since we were little children, playing on the beach down there by the sea below. Then, you were bigger and I was smaller, but now we are equals. Nothing would make me happier than if you would respond positively to my suit." Tak-Tam read books. He knew what to say, and he knew how to say it eloquently. Though he sweated like a demon and his voice was soft, he didn't tremble. He waited for her reply.

She stared at him for a long, cold moment.

Old Lee and Yim-Fong waited too, holding back the urge to push.

Finally, Ting-Yan spoke. "Stay the night in the chapel. I'll give you my answer tomorrow."

In addition to functioning as a place of worship, the chapel at Chek Keng served as a sort of community centre and inn. The priest had his quarters there—a small room where he stayed when he was in town—but there was another small room that contained a couple of beds, a few dishes, a water jug, and some blankets. People from other villages coming to Chek Keng to visit friends or relatives stayed there sometimes. Ting-Yan helped Tak-Tam and Yim-Fong dust off two of the wooden plank beds. She found them each a blanket and a ceramic pillow. Captain Lee invited them around the corner to his modest village house for the supper that Siu-Wai had begun to prepare the minute she'd seen them disembark from the *Oolong*. At dinner, they talked about the abundant rice crop that year and the relative dearth of fish in the ocean. They speculated on the likelihood of the Kuomintang retaining its alliance with the Communists in order to drive out the Japanese over the border in China. Idly, they wondered whether the Japanese would invade Hong Kong. They did not discuss Tak-Tam's suit or Ting-Yan's ambivalent response.

That night was the longest night of Tak-Tam's life. While Yim-Fong snored in her plank bed by the far wall, Tak-Tam lay wide awake in his. He thought of past trips to Chek Keng, which were actually not that many, because everyone was working most of the time. He thought of the way Ting-Yan's eyes followed his brother. He thought of his own eyes, following her as she set crab traps or laid nets, cleaned fish, and bargained with customers on the dock at the Causeway Bay Typhoon Shelter. If she said no, how would he live? If she said yes, would he be able to make her happy? Or would she continue to pine for his golden brother and make him miserable with her pining? If he were to live at Chek Keng, he could make a life for himself here. Himself, Ting-Yan, and their children. He could get out from under Tak-Wing's shadow and be his own person instead of Tak-Wing's skinny brother. He would fish. He would farm. He would love Ting-Yan. He would raise a huge family with many children. Surely everything would be well. But then again, maybe it wouldn't be. Maybe she would hate him for all the ways he reminded her of Tak-Wing, and all the ways he wasn't Tak-Wing. Maybe they would argue and fight. Maybe they wouldn't be able to have children. Maybe his life would pass him by in bitterness and grief in this little backwater village instead of big city Hong Kong where he belonged. It was impossible to see the future—one just couldn't know. In short, Tak-Tam did not sleep a wink.

In the morning, Siu-Wai called everyone to a delicious breakfast of tang tsai jook with side dishes of roasted pork, oily stick, and freshly picked vegetables from the village field.

Ting-Yan came late to the table, looking pale and a little bedraggled. She hadn't slept well either.

Her mother scooped her a bowl of congee and poured her a cup of tea. She ate silently and did not say a word.

Everyone else watched her. No one else could eat.

When she'd finished the first bowl she held it up for another serving.

"Silly child!" snapped Siu-Wai, unable to stand it any longer. She rapped the girl on the head with a chopstick.

"Truly," said Captain Lee.

Both Yim-Fong and Tak-Tam were silent out of politeness, though they both also felt like they might burst at any second.

"Okay," said Ting-Yan.

"Okay, what?" said Siu-Wai.

"Yes," said her father, "okay, what?"

"Okay, yes."

"Yes, what?"

"I'll do it. I'll marry Tak-Tam. Life must go on."

Tak-Tam wasn't sure how to feel. The reply, though affirmative, was hardly a ringing endorsement.

"Child, are you sure?" Yim-Fong asked.

"Yes," said Ting-Yan, a little grimly. "I'm sure."

"If you don't want to marry me, you can say no," Tak-Tam said. "You mustn't sacrifice yourself."

She looked him squarely in the eye. "I'm sure," she said. "What more do you want from me?"

The whole group was quiet for a long moment. Finally, Siu-Wai took the situation in hand. "Well, she's sure. Then it's time to celebrate!" She brought out all the candy and cakes and other gifts that Yim-Fong had brought and a bottle of Yellow Crane Tower rice wine that she had been saving for just this occasion. The parents laughed and told jokes and everybody ate sweet things until their bellies ached and their heads spun. Eventually, Ting-Yan began to smile, and then Tak-Tam could smile too, and so that was that.

CHAPTER 17

POSSESSED BY LAUGHTER

July 15, 1937

Because of her tendency to seasickness, Kwan Siu-Wai was unable to go back to Hong Kong Island with them on the tang tsai. She gave them fried egg sandwiches, a bag of dried squid, some boiled eggs, and a bunch of small heung tsiu bananas to eat on the boat, and an enamelled vacuum flask decorated with peonies, containing tea.

In spite of the nice snacks from Tak-Tam's future mother-in-law, it was an awkward and unpleasant ride. Ting-Yan sat with her father beside the noisy motor at the stern. Tak-Tam sat with Yim-Fong in the bow. No one talked. Tak-Tam replayed the morning's terrible conversation over and over in his head, and grew more and more miserable with each repetition. He loved Ting-Yan, but he had to get out of this wedding. To feel like this for the rest of his life, whether that life were long or short, he couldn't imagine anything worse. And yet the thought of letting her go caused an unbearable pain in his chest that could only be lifted by the thought of keeping her. He was in agony.

His mother watched him, sensing his feelings and wanting to help. But she had no idea what to say. So they both stared at the water, and, as they rounded the bend of the Sai Kung Peninsula, watched the little city of Victoria on Hong Kong Island, tiny at first, grow bigger and bigger as it approached.

At the edge of Clearwater Bay, Captain Lee cut the motor.

"Bream," he said, pointing down into the water.

They all looked down. Beneath them ran a massive school of fish, like a moving, shivering island beneath the boat. Though the water was clear, the fish were so densely packed that Tak-Wing couldn't see the bottom.

"Do you mind if we stop?" the captain said. "There's money for the month swimming beneath us."

"Of course," said Yim-Fong. "Can we help?"

"My daughter will help me," said Captain Lee. "Please, have a sandwich and drink some tea. We'll try to get it done quickly."

The two practised fishers, father and daughter, bustled about the boat, tossed down an anchor, and wound nets into the water.

"What can I do?" said Tak-Tam.

"Just get out of the way," Ting-Yan said, irritably.

She and her father began to reel the net in almost as quickly as they had lowered it, and pull the fish from the nets. They allowed Tak-Tam and Yim-Fong to help. The fish writhed mightily in their hands as they pulled them out and threw them into the hold. As fast as the nets were emptied, Ting-Yan and her father lowered them again. The bream kept coming and coming, and as they did, Tak-Tam's head continued to race with the morning's conversation, which grew uglier yet with each return. Would the fish ever stop?

At last, the hold of the little boat was full. The school still swam beneath them. Captain Lee looked down at all that bounty, wishing he could catch more, but the boat was so heavy with the weight of what they'd already gathered that it sat a full Chinese foot lower in the water.

Tak-Tam knew he'd have to talk to Ting-Yan. He couldn't marry her like this. He had to break it off. Everyone would be so upset with him. He knew Ting-Yan would be mad, even though she didn't want to marry him. To be rejected by the brother she didn't want might be even worse for her than being rejected by the brother she did want. What if she cursed him too? And his mother would be so disappointed. If that weren't enough, Captain Lee would likely feel insulted, and maybe the insult would harm his friendship with Cheung. For all of this, Tak-Tam would be responsible.

But if he didn't break it off, he'd spend his life disdained by the person he loved most in the world. It would not be a livable life. He wished he knew what she was thinking. He had to talk to her.

A cold wind came up from over mainland China. The water grew choppy and the heavy boat rocked and churned. Tak-Tam's stomach churned with it. Would they never make it back to Causeway Bay?

At last, they arrived. It was raining a little and there were no customers down at the dock. The fish had to be sold right away while it was still fresh. All four of them worked to take it up to the causeway, where a few cooks and amahs shopping for the evening's meal were already bargaining with fishers who had landed earlier.

Ting-Yan and Captain Lee coaxed and shouted, haggling with customers, but still giving them good deals in order to move the fish quickly. Tak-Tam and Yim-Fong helped, wrapping fish and taking in payments. There was so much fish! When would it all get sold? Tak-Tam gave the wrong package to a young servant girl, and an older amah from a different family, for whom it was intended, got angry and began to fight with the girl. He had to separate them. Ting-Yan sold a large bream she thought was dead to a quarry worker, but just as she placed the package in his hands, it flipped free of its wrapping and wriggled down the pavement. Tak-Tam kept trying to catch her eye, but she wouldn't look at him. It was evening by the time all the fish were sold.

As soon as it was done, Yim-Fong hurried off to the Tai Hang house, hoping to catch Cheung and help him with the move, though she suspected he'd be long gone by now.

"I need to talk to you," Tak-Tam said to Ting-Yan.

She pretended not to hear, but Captain Lee did.

"Why don't you two go down to the boat and talk," he said. "I don't think Ah Fong is going to catch Cheung at the Tai Hang house. I'm going to the cricket club to look for him."

"I'll come with you," said Ting-Yan.

"Please," said Tak-Tam.

"I think you better let the young man have his say," said Captain Lee.

"If you have something to say, just say it," Ting-Yan said to Tak-Tam.

"Could we go down to the boat?"

"Just say it here," she sat down on a pylon, in the midst of the fish blood and water left from their afternoon's work.

"I'll be back soon," said Captain Lee. He took off in the direction of the HKCC.

Tak-Tam squatted down beside her. There was going to be no getting around the awkwardness—he'd just have to push through it and speak.

She stared at him expectantly, refusing to make it easy.

"I ..." he said. He noticed one fish, maybe the one intended for the quarry worker, still there on the pavement, alive and gasping.

"Yes?"

"Mo mut yeh," he said. Nothing.

"Then what was all that fuss about?"

"If you don't ..." he said. "If you don't ... don't ..." He stopped, took a breath, and started again. "I love you, but I won't marry you unless you really want to marry me."

The gasping fish on the pavement bucked.

"Don't be an idiot," she said. "It's just how things are."

Awful. But at least he was in the conversation now. "Don't be so fatalistic. If you don't love me, your father and mother will arrange for you to marry someone else."

That got her. She was quiet for a moment. Then she said, "I'd rather marry you than anyone else."

"But you don't love me."

"Is love necessary for marriage? It wasn't for so many generations before us. You just got what you got, whether you wanted it or not. Besides, I do love you."

"Not the way you love Tak-Wing."

"I don't love that dead dog anymore."

"Don't call my brother a dead dog."

"He didn't treat me very well."

"You're right. He didn't."

"Now there's no one for me but you."

He turned away from her. Did she not understand how she insulted him? The silence expanded painfully. "I don't want to marry you," he said. "Not like this."

The fish on the pavement gave a mighty heave, but only succeeded in turning itself over.

"I thought you loved me," she said.

"I do."

"Maybe we should just get married and move on to the next stage of our lives. I think I'd be content, you know, once I got used to it. There's just been so much going on lately. Honestly, I can't imagine marrying anyone else but you."

"That's not the same as 'I'll love you 'til the end of time.'"

"It's not. No. But I will love you 'til the end of time."

"How can you say the same words and mean something so utterly different by them?"

"I'm sorry," she said. "I'm trying my best."

"There are different kinds of love."

"Yes, that's right. There are. Could you be content with the kind I have to offer you?" She was finally beginning to see the situation from his point of view and felt bad for him.

"I don't know. All I wanted was for you to love me back. Which now you say you do. It should be enough."

"Well," she said, "I won't force you to marry me if the kind of love I have to offer is not the kind you want. But I thought your love for me was the kind you'd feel no matter what."

"It is."

"Okay," she said, "then, shall we give it a try?"

He reached up and took her hand. But then he let go of it. She reached down and took his hand. He pulled her toward him. She gazed into his brown eyes, so like her own. His lips brushed her cheek and found her mouth. The kiss was a nervy thing for a young man more accustomed to thinking and longing than seeing and acting. He was astonished by how soft she was. As the sun set down the western end of the harbour it poured a pale pink light over them, washing them clean of the day's discomforts.

They pulled apart to watch it descend into the ocean. As they did, that lone fish that had escaped the afternoon's carnage gave a mighty kick, flipped over the edge of the breakwater, and tumbled back into the sea.

At long last she spoke. "I cursed them."

"I was there," he said. "I heard you. It was very bad."

She laughed, a little darkly. "It was, wasn't it?"

"Pretty bad, yeah," he said.

"I don't know what got hold of me," she said. "I was so angry I wasn't myself."

"I understand you," he said.

She looked at him and kissed his cheek softly. "You know, I really believe that you do."

The evening grew darker and the moon began to rise over the Sai Kung hills. A faint star came out, and twinkled at them through the rich, damp sea air. "I should undo the curses. I did more stuff than you witnessed. I should go look for Granny Kwok."

"I'll come with you," he said.

"That would be nice," she said. "But I think I need to do this alone. Besides, didn't your father just move house today? You should go to the clubhouse and help him."

"Are you sure?" he said. "I'd like to come with you."

"I created this trouble on my own. I need to fix it on my own. Don't worry, I'll be all right."

He rode the tram with her right over the Goose Neck Bridge. She alighted at the next stop, while he rode on to the cricket club.

Ting-Yan scurried back to that place beneath the bridge where she'd met Granny Kwok just a week ago. When she got there, she saw two other grannies working, one of whom she recognized as Granny Chan. The other, she'd never seen before.

"Is Granny Kwok still working here?" she asked Granny Chan.

"Not anymore," Granny Chan said.

"You mean not anymore today, or not anymore ever?"

"She's gone," said Granny Chan.

"Do you know where I can find her? I really need to talk to her."

"Gone," Granny Chan repeated.

The other granny joined in. "Went back to China."

"That's right," Granny Chan said. "She went back to her home village."

The other granny said, "Her son and his wife are having their first baby. So she went back for good."

"I really need to see her," Ting-Yan said.

"You have to go to China then," said Granny Chan. "Unless you trust me or Granny Liu here to do your curses for you."

"I don't want to do any more curses," Ting-Yan said.

"We can do blessings too, if you want," said Granny Liu.

"I want to undo the curses I asked of Granny Kwok."

"Undo a curse?" said Granny Chan. She began to laugh. Granny Liu joined her. They giggled, then cackled, then howled with mirth.

Ting-Yan's face fell flat.

But the grannies couldn't stop. They hooted, then shrieked, possessed by laughter.

"Please," said Ting-Yan. "I made a terrible mistake."

"She made a terrible mistake," wailed Granny Liu.

"All curses are terrible mistakes," howled Granny Chan. "Oh my, what a mess."

"Are you sure the curses can't be undone?"

The grannies got hold of themselves. They coughed and choked their laughter back.

"They really can't be," said Granny Chan. "That's why Granny Kwok asked you if you were sure."

"Now all parties concerned just have to live it out," said Granny Liu.

"Oh my, oh dear," said Granny Chan. "I'd help you if I could."

"So would I," said Granny Liu. "But it's too late now."

"Either of us would be happy to take your money," said Granny Chan. "But that would be real dishonesty."

"We do serious work here," Granny Liu said. "There's no overturning a curse. Oh my. Oh dear."

"Oh dear," said Granny Chan. "You'd best do what you can to make it up to the parties concerned. But there's no escape now. Oh my."

"Okay," Ting-Yan said. "All right." She turned to head back to the tram stop. The minute she did, the grannies began to giggle again. She deserved it, no doubt, which did not make her feel any better.

The minute she came up on to the main road, who should she see across the street but the hapless victims of her curses, Tak-Wing and Emily themselves. Did those two laughing grannies conjure them? Of course not. It was a coincidence. She could still hear them under the bridge chuckling.

"Hey," said Emily, "there's the girl who helped me when that drunk man attacked me. The one who paid for our breakfast on our wedding morning, after the first breakfast was ruined. Hey!" She realized she didn't know the girl's name. "Miss!"

Tak-Wing turned. "Oh no. That's Ting-Yan. Don't you recognize the demon that nearly wrecked our wedding? Just keep walking."

But Emily had recognized only her benefactor, and not the demon. "Hey!" she cried. "Siu jie! Miss! Missy Miss!"

Ting-Yan, still not entirely sure their presence was real, had no desire to actually talk to them. But Emily ran up to her and grabbed her arm. "Don't you remember me? I'm the one you helped the other day with breakfast. I'd like to pay you back."

"Please," said Ting-Yan. It had been a day of so many awkward moments. She couldn't handle yet another. "It was nothing. You would have done the same if the shoe were on the other foot."

"I probably wouldn't have had the wits or the generosity," said Emily.

"Hm," said Ting-Yan, wishing herself a thousand miles away.

Tak-Wing crossed the street after Emily, his reluctance palpable.

"Ah Yan," he said. "Lei ho?" How are you.

"Ah Wing," she said.

"Wait," said Emily. "You two know each other?"

"Do you not recognize her?" Tak-Wing said.

"Of course, my love, I told you, she helped me the other day after that drunk man attacked me," Emily said.

"This is the dead demon that nearly ruined our wedding," Tak-Wing said. "Who cursed our first-born child. How can you not recognize her?"

"That was an awful moment," Emily said, "but this not the same girl, not the same at all."

No one spoke for several long seconds.

Then Ting-Yan said, "I'm afraid I am the same girl." She bowed her head.

"Nonsense," said Emily.

"It's true," said Ting-Yan. "I cursed you, then I helped you, then I cursed you again."

Emily stared, taking Ting-Yan's words in. Finally, she said, "Well then you're mad."

"She is," said Tak-Wing. "She's mad."

"Don't you dare judge me," Ting-Yan snarled at Tak-Wing. "Betrayer."

"I don't understand," Emily said.

Tak-Wing and Ting-Yan stood silent, feeling very awkward and not remotely sure where to begin.

"I—" they said, in unison.

There was another long pause.

Tak-Wing waited for Ting-Yan to speak.

Ting-Yan waited for Tak-Wing to speak.

"We—" they said, again in unison.

Then Emily said, "You know each other. There's something between you." She looked at Tak-Wing as though at a stranger. "What is going on? How do you know this girl? Are you already having an affair? We've only been married a week!"

There was no help for it. There on the street above Goose Neck Bridge with the tram roaring by every twenty minutes, the whole sad story came out: the childhood betrothal, the changes of heart, the parental interference, the weddings, the curses, the whole complicated question of who owed what to whom.

"You cursed us?" Emily said, when it was done. "I mean, I kind of understand. Maybe I would even do the same thing. I don't know. But you cursed us?"

"I came here to undo the curse," Ting-Yan said. "But it can't be undone. I'm sorry."

Tak-Wing said, "Never mind, Ah Yan. There's no such thing as curses anyway. So you lost a bit of money to an old charlatan beneath the bridge."

More laughter rushed up from beneath the bridge. Granny Chan and Granny Liu were having the time of their lives.

They all heard the laughter and they all ignored it. Tak-Wing said, "You know, I never meant you any harm. I just wanted to marry Emily. You are still dear to me."

"Do I have to forgive you now?" Ting-Yan said.

"That would be nice," said Tak-Wing. "But obviously, you don't have to do anything you don't want."

"Well," said Ting-Yan. "I'll think about it."

"You cursed us," said Emily, who did believe in such things.

"I'll make it up to you," Ting-Yan said. "What can I do?"

"There is something you can do," said Tak-Wing. "As it turns out, we have no place to go. We were staying with a friend of ours at her university dormitory, but the prefect just found out. I don't suppose the *Oolong* is docked at Causeway Bay?"

CHAPTER 18

CHEUNG'S NEW HOME

July 15, 1937

The light delivery truck that Colville had organized for Cheung came to the Tai Hang house. The driver helped Cheung load it up. "What's the point of having strong sons," Cheung said to him, "if they aren't around to help you when you need them?"

Yim-Fong and Tak-Tam were up at Chek Keng so that Tak-Tam could propose to Ting-Yan while he had a chance. This Cheung could understand and forgive, though he missed them. But where for the love of Tin Hau were Tak-Wing and Emily? Likely living it up with Old Mah in one of his luxurious mansions up in the Mid-Levels. "Young people these days have no sense of duty," the driver said, helping Cheung heave the settee into the back of the truck. Chairs, coffee table, beds, and frames followed, along with half a dozen rattan baskets full of bedding, kitchen implements, and other sundry odds and ends.

Cheung took a last look around the Tai Hang house. Now empty, it seemed much bigger, but also sadder, the sorry shell of his old life already passing into memory. He flicked the switch for the bare bulb that hung over the dining area, though the battered wooden table the family once ate at no longer stood beneath it. He pulled the door shut for the last time and handed the keys to the agent, the only one there to see him off.

"I'm sorry, Mr Cheung," the agent said, while the truck driver gunned the engine impatiently. "It's hard to lose one's home."

"Lost one home already," Cheung grumbled.

"I heard your family is from Wong Nai Chung in Happy Valley. And that you were flooded out in '23. May your luck turn, Older Brother," the agent said.

Cheung grunted. He was grateful that he had a place to offer his children, but what was the point if they didn't appreciate it and were more likely to go live with Mah and Lee than to come live with their own true father in his decent but modest home?

Colville was still at the club when Cheung arrived. There'd been no need to come see him off the day before after all. Cheung was peeved at him for having overseen the wedding, but there was no space to say anything about it, so he greeted him with an expressionless face.

"Here's the keys, old man," said Colville, handing him a massive ring. "I labelled them all for you, so you don't get confused. Upstairs ballroom, downstairs bar, cold storage, equipment room, ladies' powder room, boardroom, billiards room. These are the keys to the steward's flat. The boys gave it a good once-over, so it's clean. I hope you and your family will be happy there."

Colville bade Cheung and the Hong Kong Cricket Club farewell. Servants and president alike paused their early morning labours to sing "Auld Lang Syne." There was much huffing and chuffing and back patting, and then the old steward was off. While workers at the cricket club helped Cheung unload his furniture, Driver Wong took Colville and his family to the docks, where they would board the P&O Strathnaver to Sydney, Australia. From there, they would take a train to their Melbourne home.

In the late afternoon, Lee arrived with a cryptic look on his face. Cheung asked him what was up, but Lee wouldn't talk. "You better let your wife give you the news."

"Where are Tak-Tam and Ting-Yan?"

"Don't ask me."

Cheung showed Lee around the new flat with its modest but comfortable parlour, a master bedroom, and a small second bedroom where

Tak-Tam could live if things with Ting-Yan didn't work out after all. Lee helped him place the settee and coffee table and set up two beds and a simple armoire as well.

An hour later, Yim-Fong showed up, looking exhausted and a little queasy. In addition to enduring two long boat rides and a bad night's sleep, she'd gone to look for Cheung at the old Tai Hang house, not knowing he'd already left. "It seemed so sad and dark without you there," she said. "And with the boys gone too. But I do have good news. Tak-Tam is going to marry Ting-Yan and go live with her at Chek Keng." She smiled as she spoke, but Cheung detected despondency and confusion beneath the surface.

Lee made a face—he wasn't at all confident that the agreement would be fulfilled—but he said nothing.

"Well, that's a wonderful thing to hear," Cheung said, not knowing what else to say.

He showed Yim-Fong around the new flat. She began to clean immediately. It was her way of saying she was pleased they had somewhere nice to live after the loss of the Tai Hang house.

The three of them shared a quick supper of leftover chicken Kiev and day-old wedding cake. Cheung found an unopened bottle of champagne and popped the cork so they could celebrate, but Yim-Fong said that she had drunk too much of Siu-Wai's Yellow Crane Tower wine the night before. She drank hot water to cleanse her system, while Cheung and Lee drank the champagne. It made Cheung feel woozy and a little sick.

A bit later, Tak-Tam arrived and helped them finish the bottle. He was in a surprisingly good mood and told his old mother and father that everything would be all right. Captain Lee nodded and smiled, feeling hopeful that the conversation between the children had gone well. Both Cheung and Yim-Fong smiled and nodded, not wanting to discourage Tak-Tam or Lee, though in their hearts they still felt unsettled. Cheung gave Tak-Tam a plate of day-old potato salad, a few sorry-looking shrimp, and a slightly mangled slice of wedding cake for his supper.

"Where is Ting-Yan?"

"She had some business to take care of without me. She said she'd go back to the *Oolong* after."

"I better go back there myself," said Captain Lee, "to meet her when she returns. It will all work out, and we'll be family! Mother Mary wills it, so it has to be good and right."

That night, long after Lee had left, all the cricketers had gone home, and both Tak-Tam and Yim-Fong were fast asleep, Cheung awoke. He got out of bed and went upstairs to the hallway where the Baptista paintings hung and contemplated the Jockey Club and the invisible village behind the row of trees. Baptista was not English. He'd stood to gain nothing by making Wong Nai Chung disappear. *Why*, thought Cheung, *do we try to forget about the things we've lost?* It only made the sorrow amorphous and continuous. Wouldn't it be better to hang on to the lost object? If he were a painter, he'd paint the village over and over again until it was transformed. But into what? A place of luck and joy. Ha! A jockey club. Maybe Baptista wasn't such a fool after all. Still, Cheung could not shake his sorrow.

He returned to his bedroom and kissed his sleeping wife. Yim-Fong woke up, and smiled at him. Gently, she kissed him back. He fell onto her. But as their bodies moved, he was stirred, then overtaken by heavier emotions—rage and grief. He poured them into her, more violently than he intended.

CHAPTER 19

GO-BETWEEN

July 16, 1937

I'd never liked being the go-between for my father and my sister. But playing mouthpiece for both of them in this battle of weddings was absolute murder. We all knew the bride was no longer a virgin. What in Holy Mary's name was the point? In the meantime, I was the target of rage for each one as proxy for the other.

No one knows more about people than those who serve them. But why should I have had to serve them? Was I not an equal member of this family? I was not a man, like my father. I was not beautiful, like my sister. Did this mean I had to play second fiddle to them both? I gritted my teeth and searched within for what Professor Hughes called "sweetness and light." I remembered that while I was called into the role of messenger, Emily's position as the beautiful but unfortunate woman over whom men staged weddings and wars was only kind of enviable. Professor Hughes had taught us about Helen of Troy. In Helen's shoes, I think I'd have oscillated between ecstasy and resentment over being so much loved and desired, but also so much burdened by familial and national pride and shame. For Emily, there was nothing outside the three nodes of marriage, sex, and death. And me? I ran around the bases of these three poles without ever landing on any of them. I'd die eventually, I guessed. But not having lived, as she was living, would my death count for anything? If not, might I still receive some portion of immortality? For sharing Emily's story with some future descendent? Ha ha! What a laugh.

Ordinarily, if ever I wanted to get in touch with one of my classmates at HKU, I would simply call them on the telephone. Father believed in all the new technologies. We'd gotten a telephone in 1925, when I was ten. But there was no telephone at Lai Po-Chuen's dorm. I wasn't even sure whether Emily was still there.

I wrote her a letter.

Dearest Sister,

Things have taken a turn for the worse in terms of Father's opinion of you and Tak-Wing since your wedding at the cricket club, as I suspected they would. Didn't I tell you it was a bad idea? Father blames Old Cheung and accuses him of the deepest disrespect. I tried to make him see that it was driven by the young cricketers, their romance with Edward, Duke of Windsor, and Mrs Wallis Simpson, as well as their care for Tak-Wing. I promise you that whatever personal misgivings I might have, I did cast the wedding in the best possible light in my conversation with Father. Dearest Emily, he would not be moved. He is furious. He takes it personally, and wants recompense.

The recompense he desires, however, you may find somewhat interesting. He is willing to sanction your marriage to Tak-Wing if you will consent to a traditional Chinese wedding on Father's terms. I know you are at least somewhat familiar with the old traditions because I've heard you talking to Amah about them. The first is the choosing of an auspicious wedding date. We know your birthdate, obviously, but not Tak-Wing's. When you write back, please give us his precious date of birth. By the lunar calendar, if he knows it. Otherwise, Auntie Lim can calculate it from his Western birthday.

Father says he expects the correct betrothal gifts from the groom. If Tak-Wing cannot afford these, I have some personal savings and will lend you the money. Please do not inform Father of this, however, if you decide to take me up on it. I suspect he would not be pleased. These are the items he expects:

- Lai see. (The money from the sale of the Tai Hang house, in the traditional red packet. I understand Old Cheung has already sent this? Custom says you can expect half back. However, I do not know what Father intends. I'm sorry he's being so mean. What a bore.)

- One pair of dragon candles and one pair of phoenix candles. (You'll get one of each back. Have you ever heard the rumour that when the bride's family burns their pair, whichever one burns down first will predict whether the bride [phoenix] or the groom [dragon] dies first? Isn't that morbid? Ha ha. Sorry! You know I'm not superstitious. This is all about Father.)

- Roast pork. (One platter, or two cans of pig's trotters, but I think everyone likes roast pork better. Or a roast suckling pig, but those are expensive. This represents your virginity. Double ha ha! It's supposed to be for the mother-in-law or her proxy, which, I suppose, is me. I'll take the roast pork.)

- Two bottles of wine. (Note that Father wants Yellow Crane Tower rice wine, not European grape wine.)

- Wife cakes. (Those ones with winter melon and sesame paste in flaky pastry with the little red stamp. You know the ones I mean. Mama used to like them before she died.)

- Eight kinds of dried seafood. (Sea cucumber, abalone, shark fin, cuttlefish, dried prawn, dried oyster, dried mushroom, and dried fish maw. I know mushrooms are not seafood, but I guess they were to the ancients?)

- Fruits. (Oranges are traditional. You know that. You probably know all of this already, better than me. You're the one into weddings. I really couldn't care less, except that I love you and I don't want you and Father to be on bad terms.)

- Jewellery. (This is a gift from the groom's family to the bride's, so you will get it back, don't worry. And also, be sure to pick jewellery you like because you'll end up wearing it for the rest of your life.)

I hope you're not offended by this request, dearest Emily. I think that doing the Chinese wedding could be a good thing, if it will reconcile you with father, and perhaps even reconcile the Cheungs and the Mahs. Old Cheung has already had to sell his house, so the worst is already done. What's a couple of bottles of wine, a few shellfish, and a dozen oranges? Since in the eyes of the law, we are family with the Cheungs now, wouldn't it be better if we all made an effort to get along? I think so, and I really hope that you will agree. You know I love you and I only want what is best for you.

Your affectionate sister,

Violet Mah Wai-Man

I asked Amah to take the letter to Lai Po-Chuen's dorm.

If Emily and Tak-Wing weren't there, she was to take it to the HKCC, the next most likely place to find them. I prayed that I had done the right thing and was not making matters worse.

CHAPTER 20

AN UNEXPECTED VISITOR

July 16, 1937

There was a knock at the door. Cheung wasn't expecting anyone. He looked out the back window. There on Jackson Road, between his back door and the side door of the Supreme Court stood Granny Yip, whom he remembered from his youth at Wong Nai Chung Village. His eyes lit up at the sight of a familiar face, then went grim when he remembered who she worked for. She had for the last twenty-five years or so been amah at the house of Cheung's mortal enemy, Morris Mah Chin-Pang. He'd already opened the door. It was too late to do anything different.

She wasn't even looking for him. She was looking for Emily and Tak-Wing. She had a letter for Emily.

"They aren't here."

"Do you know where they are?"

"How on earth should I know? It's not like Tak-Wing is my best and most filial son!"

"I wouldn't trouble you, but it's important."

"Old Mah has already taken my first son. I had to sell my house to pay the bride price. He's already had his stupid wedding, English style. Right here at my place of employment. If that's not adding insult to injury, I don't know what is! What's in that letter?"

"Private letter from Missy Violet to Missy Emily. Not your business."

"Come on, Granny. Haven't you known me since I was a little child running through the village in nothing but diapers?"

"You were a cute child. How did you get so old and ugly?"

"You're one to talk," huffed Old Cheung. "What's in the letter? If it concerns my oldest son, I have a right to know."

Granny Yip sighed. "Chinese wedding."

"Chinese wedding?"

"Old Mah wants to have a Chinese-style wedding for them. Says the English wedding was bad luck."

"I will not pay for a Chinese wedding. I've already lost my house because of that bastard. I've got my other son to think of. The filial one."

"Do you have any idea where I can find them? I have a duty to my mistress to discharge."

"No idea," Cheung said crossly. He slammed the door in her face.

But after she was gone, worry began to set in. A subtle, inconsequential feeling at first. Slowly it grew, like a tickle at the back of the throat that might or might not be a summer cold. By nightfall, he was quite concerned. While the toffs were drinking in the main-floor bar, he called the Stable on the telephone. Granny Yip answered.

"I should have been more concerned when you were here this afternoon."

"Yes, you should have been."

"Have they turned up?"

"They have not. Mr Mah and Missy Violet are quite upset."

"It's getting dark."

"Yes. Any information you might have would be very helpful."

He heard a young woman's voice in the background. "Who is it, Amah? Is it Emily?"

To Violet she said, "No, child. It's just Old Cheung."

"I want to speak to him."

"No, no, no—" Cheung said, but Granny Yip was not listening to him. The next voice he heard was Violet's. "Uncle Cheung?"

"Hello, Miss Violet."

"I'm beside myself, Uncle," she said. "They're not here. They're not at the Tai Hang house. Amah says they're not at the cricket club either. I thought they were moving in with you."

"I thought you were the one hiding them."

"They stayed with a friend of mine at first, but Amah says they aren't there anymore."

"Where are they?"

"I don't know."

"I mean, where could they possibly be?"

"No idea. Uncle, this is a serious matter. Something terrible could have happened. We have to find them."

"I hear your father wants a Chinese wedding for them."

"That is true, but never mind that now."

"I don't want to pay for a Chinese wedding. They already had a wedding."

"Indeed they did, Uncle Cheung," Violet said. "My father thinks you staged it and is not pleased. I tried to explain to him what actually happened, but he doesn't believe me and says I'm covering for you. I really wish the two of you would talk directly. And now Emily and Tak-Wing are missing. We need to find them. We can talk about the wedding later. Why aren't you worried?"

"I am worried," said Cheung. It dawned on him where they might be. "You come to Wong Nai Chung Village with your old father. Your amah knows the way."

"Wong Nai Chung?"

"The village at the foot of the mountain beside the racecourse. You know, where the horses run."

"Oh. Amah's old village." Violet paused. "What does Amah's village have to do Tak-Wing and Emily?"

"Just come," he said. "You will see."

CHAPTER 21

A VISIT TO WONG NAI CHUNG VILLAGE

July 16, 1937

I had an anatomy test the next day. Though I had studied all afternoon, I didn't feel ready. The week before, we had done the respiratory system. This week the test was all about the cardiovascular system. When Cheung's call came, I'd just memorized which veins carried oxygenated blood and which ones carried depleted blood. I'd drawn a heart diagram from memory, but I'd gotten the chambers mixed up. If I flunked this test, I thought, I'd hold Emily fully responsible. Not that she would care. Why did she do these things to me?

Cheung wanted us to go to Amah's village, which was also his mother's and so, ancestrally speaking, his. I'd thought that ghostly place was abandoned. It was hard to imagine anyone still living there. I went to find Father to talk to him about it.

"Why would that brat be hanging out in some ghost village?" he said. "She could be eaten by wild foxes. Or become of one of them. But maybe that's already happened."

"You think they are there?"

"Cheung's mother is the last living resident of Wong Nai Chung, and Tak-Wing has a special bond with her. It's possible."

Amah went to rouse Driver Lim. The lights were already out in the window of his little room above the garage, which he shared with his wife, Auntie Lim, our resident feng shui master. A few minutes later, he stumbled downstairs. His hair was neatly combed, but his uniform was wrinkled. He started the car.

As we drove down Conduit Road it began to rain. Always on this road you could smell the sweet warm smell of jasmine and bauhinia. In the rain, the smell grew deeper, as though the spirits were insisting we take it in. The wind began to blow.

"Typhoon coming," Amah said. "Maybe we should go back. We don't even know for sure that they are there."

"Cheung is expecting us now," I said. "If he knows something about Emily and Tak-Wing, or if they are there, we should find out. What if they are in some kind of danger?"

"Not likely," said Amah. "Those brats are too spoiled."

"I should never have taken a second wife and gotten so distracted by my other family. It was too much to expect Amah to raise two unruly girls," Father said.

"I'm not unruly!"

"You were always the good one," Amah said. "But you are unruly in your own way. You are deeper, so the unruliness will come out later."

"Gee, thanks, Amah."

"I'm an old lady. I know how people are."

The rain intensified as we drove. We parked by the sanatorium, where my mother had died years ago after her long struggle with tuberculosis. The memory of that time, when we'd come to the sanatorium daily to visit her, returned to me as I stepped out of the car and into the cool, steady rain. I shuddered, whether from sudden chill or Mother's ghostly presence I'm not sure. The ground was slick with mud and we had to climb down a wet embankment to get into the village. We skirted through a maze of puddles to get to the house that Amah thought was the right one. A little yellow dog with a black nose met us partway through. She wagged her tail and panted cheerfully, her lively doggy presence breaking through the mist in such a way that made me all too aware of the disorganized army of spirits that began to trail us the minute we stepped down into the mud. All the ghosts of the Qing dynasty clearances, in which people were required to burn their homes and flee inland on pain of death, were layered beneath the traces of the thousands murdered by neighbours during the Punti–Hakka Wars and the Red Turban and Taiping Rebellions. When the people abandoned this village, they had left their memories of starvation and murder in the ruined houses, and it all rushed at us now through the mist. The rain came down even harder, and the wind that followed it rendered our umbrellas useless.

"I'm sure it's this way," said Amah. We followed her, but the path ended at the village wall, and we had to backtrack.

"Must be this one," she said. But the next lane took an unfamiliar curve. Wrong again.

"Sorry," she said. "This is my ancestral village, but I never lived here. I used to visit with my mama before the flood of '23. It's been more than twenty years since I was here. After Mama died, I tried to forget and become a modern person. So I don't remember my way very well."

When she took a left-hand turn, I realized she was grasping at straws. "Amah, do you have any idea at all?"

"I'm sorry, Miss Violet. Familiar feelings return to me, and so I follow. But if I ever had a map in my old brain, it's gone. So spooky, lah, this ancient place. How Cheung's mother can live here, I don't know."

The wind blew harder.

"This was a terrible idea," Father said, "and Cheung is a madman. Let's go back."

The little yellow dog whimpered and licked my hand. "Maybe Ah Wong knows the way." I nodded down at her bright eyes.

The dog trotted forward. "Sometimes the village dogs are smart," said Amah.

"Christ," Father cursed.

"We have nothing to lose," I said and set off after the dog. It was soaking wet, and rainwater poured off its back to its swinging belly and down to the ground, but still it wagged its tail and panted. We followed it down a narrow lane.

"This is stupid," said Father.

"Let's go back, Missy. We'll try tomorrow when the rain has stopped."

"Do you care about Emily or not?" I demanded. The dog turned a corner ahead of us. I ran after it. I could hear Amah behind me. Father's feet hesitated, but then he scuffled reluctantly after us, grumbling under his breath.

Ahead of us, I could see light coming through the crack below a door.

"That must be it." There was no sign of the yellow dog, but we had already forgotten about her.

Cheung answered the door. His mother stood beside him, an ancient lady in an old-style Hakka hat, the kind with the wide brim and black fringe. She wore the traditional blue suit too, with old-style knot buttons high on the shoulders. In her left hand she held a long pipe from which she puffed sweet-smelling tobacco smoke. Mingled with the scent came a floral whiff of our own Dream Horse anti-opium pills, which are popular among the Hakka. I had never met Grandmother Cheung Wan-See before, though Father had during the court case that Cheung and the cricket club toffs had launched against him a decade ago landing him in Victoria Gaol. He nodded a grudging hello.

Inside, Cheung's wife, Yim-Fong, and his sister, Hok-Yee, were preparing tea and laying out snacks.

"We meet again under fresh circumstances, Mr Mah," Cheung said. "Please come in."

Father entered.

"Here's Miss Violet and her amah, Granny Yip," said his wife. "Since we are family now, you can call me Auntie Yim-Fong."

"Auntie Yim-Fong, Uncle Cheung," I said, politely.

Amah followed me. She was the same generation as Cheung and Yim-Fong, though slightly older. But to be polite, she addressed them as Older Brother and Older Sister.

"Are they here?" asked Father.

"Evidently not," said Cheung, "as you can see."

My father did his best not to shoot him the evil eye.

"I'm disappointed too," said Cheung. "I really thought they would be here."

Father's gloves came off then. "What more do you want from me, Old Cheung? You got my money, you got my beautiful daughter, you got the modern wedding you wanted, what more do you think this old horse has to give?"

"I didn't arrange that wedding," Cheung said. "You did."

"I certainly did not," said Father, in English.

"Are you trying to kill me?" Cheung continued. "You took my eldest son and forced me to sell my house. And you staged that dreadful wedding at my place of work."

Outside, the rain descended in sheets.

"I'd never do such a thing," said Mah. "I have much better taste than that."

"The young cricketers at the club did it," I said. "Because they felt sorry for Emily and Tak-Wing, getting married without a party. I told you, Ba."

"Don't undermine me, Violet," he said. "I want them to have a proper wedding, Cheung. With gifts, a tea ceremony, and a feast."

Cheung raised an eyebrow. "You sanction this marriage?"

"No," said Mah. "I don't. But aren't they already married?"

"In the eyes of the British, perhaps," said Cheung. "But not according to Tin Hau."

"No other family is going to want my daughter now," said Old Mah.

"My family doesn't want your daughter either," Cheung said.

"Don't you dare disparage Emily after you've already stolen her from me!" Father shouted. "She could have married any one of a dozen decent men instead of your low-class stinking son!"

"Don't you dare disparage my son!" Cheung yelled. "He could have married any one of a dozen respectable girls if he hadn't been corrupted by your shameless daughter!" He lunged at Father.

Old Mah stepped back in horror. While Cheung had had to defend his honour or that of his family with his fists more than once in his life, Old Mah belonged to another tradition of dignity.

Yim-Fong intervened. "This is no way for family to behave toward one another," she said. "We're all related now, like it or not. And there's a war coming. We'll have to resolve differences deeper than this. The ancestors seem to want our children to be married. We must accept it."

"Well, thank God for the ancestors!" Father shouted.

"I am not a rich man," Cheung said. "If this marriage had truly been arranged, you would have turned me down because I could never afford the bride price."

"But you've already paid it. You sold your Tai Hang house to do so."

"How do you know that?"

"Because," said Old Mah. He was quiet for a long stretch, and I realized that he hadn't intended to disclose what came next. "Because I bought it."

"You bought it? You steal my father's life and then you steal the house I bought with the compensation money? Do you think you own me?"

"I don't own you," Father said. "The toffs at the cricket club own you."

"How dare you!" shouted Cheung, his face flaming.

"Father, Uncle, please stop," I said. "We have to find Tak-Wing and Emily."

"The child is right," said Yim-Fong.

Amah nodded.

Grandma Cheung took a puff from her pipe to signal her exhaustion with the men's belligerence.

"If you agree to the Chinese wedding," Father said, "and carry out the rites that pertain to the groom's family, I will give the Tai Hang house to Emily and Tak-Wing as a wedding gift."

We all stared.

Cheung's speechlessness was palpable.

Finally, Amah said, "You would reward those two spoiled brats for their shocking behaviour?"

"Yes, Amah. They are married in the eyes of the law already. If it would bring peaceful relations to the Cheungs and the Mahs, then yes. I'm tired of fighting with a man who should be my brother. There's a bigger war coming. Chinese people have to try to get along."

"What about poor Violet, who has done nothing wrong. Why doesn't she get a house?" Amah said.

"Pish, Amah," I said.

"Violet is going to be a doctor. She will be all right," said Father.

"Shouldn't we be looking for them instead of trading in their futures as though they were pigs for market?" Grandma Cheung said.

"So true," I agreed.

There was a thump on the door. Auntie Hok-Yee went to open it. There in the pouring rain stood the younger Cheung brother, Tak-Tam, breathless and drenched to the bone. "I found them. Or rather they were never lost. They're with Ting-Yan and Old Lee, on Lee's boat."

We paused together, taking the news in.

"What a relief," said Father.

"My goodness," I said, like an idiot. "Well, let's go get them!"

"They're moored at Causeway Bay. It'll be so late by the time we get there. Better go in the morning."

Father looked at Cheung. "Well, what do you say?"

"You have a deal." Cheung stuck out his right hand.

They shook, like English gentlemen.

After that, the conversation turned. Cheung wanted his old mother to move in with him at the club and finally abandon the drowned village for good. The rain kept coming but it got lighter as the storm moved over us to spend the bulk of its fury somewhere over the border in China. A gibbous moon rose and we ate the snacks and drank the tea that Auntie Yim-Fong and Auntie Hok-Yee had laid out. We said a polite and respectful goodnight, and went back to the car where Driver Lim had been waiting all this time, refusing to come inside despite our entreaties. We rode home in bright moonlight, and went to sleep feeling optimistic now that the runaways had been found.

CHAPTER 22

CHILDHOOD HOME
July 17, 1937

Hok-Yee bustled about in the dark, oily kitchen, making breakfast. There was pork and century egg congee with deep-fried ghosts, purchased at the nearby market before Cheung and Yim-Fong were even awake. She'd already lit incense for Grandfather Cheung at the family altar. She fried eggs with chives too. It gave her pleasure to prepare food for her brother and his wife, whom she hadn't seen in months. The good smells nudged out the swamp smell that had sat with Cheung like a lonely demon the whole night. The chive smell in particular brought him back to his childhood, as this egg and chive dish had been a favourite of his father's. He remembered the conversation from the night before and a warm feeling returned.

Without a car to take them home, Cheung, Yim-Fong, and Tak-Tam had stayed the night at Wong Nai Chung, sleeping up in the loft above the regular bedrooms. Now Cheung climbed down the ladder to the kitchen. "I understand why you want to stay, Ma."

His mother was on to him. "Don't you play white man games with me, clever boy," she said. "I've been studying their methods since before you were born. You can't trick me into leaving my home."

"The village is not as safe as it once was," Yim-Fong said. "There's a war in China. Refugees are coming over the border."

"There are bandits among them," Tak-Tam added. "And you and Auntie Hok-Yee are alone here."

Hok-Yee nodded. She would never abandon her mother, but she'd have been happy to leave this damp and haunted village.

"Clever boy married a clever wife," said Cheung's mother. "But you can't pry me from my home. This is my natal village. My family was strong here. So strong that when your father married me, he came to this village. The usual custom is for the woman to move to the man's village, you know."

"Of course I know!" said Cheung. The food smelled too good not to eat. He dipped his spoon into the bowl and slurped down a first hot, salty sip of congee.

His mother continued as though Tak-Tam were not there. "Tak-Tam is marrying into his wife's family rather than the other way around."

"Ma," said Hok-Yee, "don't embarrass him." She scooped up a large spoonful of egg and plopped it onto Tak-Tam's plate.

"My own father did it," said Cheung, "so it's nothing to be ashamed of."

"That's different," said his mother. "Your father was a refugee. And didn't your old mother give you a good childhood here? Wong Nai Chung was one of the largest and strongest villages on Hong Kong Island before the Qing sold us out. Before those foreign devils came."

"But they did come," said Cheung, digging into the dish of bean thread noodles, white radish, and dried shrimp. "Times have changed. We have to get with the times if we want to live."

"Hmph. My family survived the Punti–Hakka Wars here. We can survive a few stupid ghost people."

"If the village had remained placed as it was and all of the villagers had stayed, then perhaps you could have," said Yim-Fong. "But almost everyone moved to Tai Hang a hundred years ago. How many families remained? Three? And two of those three have since moved to Tai Hang. Now you and Hok-Yee are the last. I know you are attached to your home, but it's not safe anymore."

"I'm attached to this place too, Ma," said Cheung. "But I'm afraid for you. Please come."

"Ungrateful child," said his old mother.

"There's a rumour that the Japanese might invade Hong Kong," he said.

"What do the Japanese know or care about us?" the old lady retorted.

"Where we live now, we get the latest news. All the cricketers are talking about it. They don't all agree, of course, but there's a real chance it could happen."

"I heard that the Japanese are planning to invade Singapore, not Hong Kong," Hok-Yee said.

"Do you want to move somewhere dry or don't you?" Cheung snapped at her.

"I knew you were trying to trick me," said his mother. "I won't leave. Don't ask me again."

"Why do you have to be so stubborn?" Cheung shouted.

"Cheung, don't yell at your mother," said Yim-Fong.

After that, they ate in silence.

Though Cheung was pleased that Tak-Wing would get the family house at Tai Hang back, he was not at all happy about the situation with his mother. He stewed the whole way back to the Happy Valley Terminus. Normally he liked to look through the grate at the Jockey Club on the off chance he might catch a glimpse of a race. Sometimes he stopped at the Chinese bookie across the street to place a bet. He didn't stop this time. When they got to the terminus, he refused to pay for first class, though he had done so on the way out. He made his poor wife and son ride third class with him.

CHAPTER 23

CHINESE WEDDING

July 17, 1937

The telephone rang and the messenger boy arrived, both at the same time. The telephone call was from the prefect in charge of residences at HKU who said that there was a room at St John's College ready for me earlier than expected, all paid for by scholarship.

"Thank you," I said.

"Thank Dr Selwyn-Clarke, Professor Ride, and especially Professor Duffy," said the prefect. "She really believes in you."

The night before, Father had stayed overnight in Mother's room, which was still filled with all her beautiful clothes and cosmetics, as though she might one day recover from death and return to get ready for a party. It was so spooky—I didn't know how he could sleep in there, but then, I didn't know how we lived with her absent presence either.

When the call came, my first thought was, *At last I can get out of this stifling house and away from that creepy room.* But I immediately felt guilty. With Emily married off and me in residence, Father would be all alone with mother's ghost whenever he came to visit the Stable. But maybe he would just stop coming. After all, he had his business, his own house, and the Nest, with Second Mother Polly and her six children, so noisy and boisterous and full of life. But then, who would tend Mother's spirit? She would be all by herself in that empty room without our noise to cheer her up. That house really ought to be sold off, but it was an eventuality no one in the family had the stomach to face.

I felt sad and forlorn on her behalf, and maybe a bit for myself too, which was ridiculous. I knew I couldn't stay. I didn't want to marry, and there was no suitor in sight anyway. This was my chance to get away and lead an independent life. I felt sorry for Father, and I felt sorry for Mother's ghost. For my own part, I tried to feel happy. I went to Father's office to tell him.

"Emily sent a message from Captain Lee's boat at the Causeway Bay Typhoon Shelter," he said. "They're going to Chek Keng this afternoon to make arrangements for the Chinese wedding. She wants to know if we'd like to come."

The thought of that marriage made me feel suddenly wistful, though I couldn't admit the reason, even to myself.

"What has my life come to?" said poor Old Mah. "I'm now related to peasants."

"Don't be classist, Father," I said, practising a word and a concept I'd learned from Professor Duffy. "Weren't we peasants two generations ago?"

"We were gentry in England two generations ago," he muttered.

"Insofar as we are Chinese, we are peasants," I said. "Lucky peasants, to be relatively well-off. Anyway, what does it matter? The world is changing so fast. And Tak-Wing and Tak-Tam are all right."

Driver Lim took us to Causeway Bay. There was a crowd on the boat already: Tak-Wing and Emily, Tak-Tam and Ting-Yan, Captain Lee, Old Cheung, and Emily's bandmates, Isadore Davis Wong and Tanaka Shigeru. Both Wong and Tanaka were a bit older than Emily and Tak-Wing, maybe in their mid-thirties. Emily held Wong's youngest daughter, along for the adventure, in her lap.

Someone had brought a giant bag of lychees and everyone was eating them and arguing about politics.

"Okay, but hear me out," Tanaka said. "You know I was a follower of Shūmei Ōkawa for the longest time. But I just don't think pan-Asianism is a viable concept anymore. I continued to believe after the Japanese invasion of Manchuria. Now there's this incident in Beiping. I hate to say it, but my people are using that missing soldier as a pretext for an invasion. I have true sympathy for my Chinese brothers, as I do for my Negro brothers, Izzy. What the Japanese Imperial Army is doing is not right."

"But Shige, only last month you said that Japan would have to take military control of all of Asia in order to drive the European imperialists out," Izzy Wong said.

"I know, my brother, I know." Tanaka was peeling a particularly juicy lychee and juice splashed onto his white shirt, which was already damp with high summer sweat. He dabbed at it with his handkerchief. "I said that because I was so mad at those bloodsuckers who drove us out of our favourite venue, the Repulse Bay Hotel. I've got a cousin who's really into the idea that the Japanese Imperial Army could drive the colonizer out. But I'm not so sure. Something has gone badly awry in the way it's being done. I just learned about some terrible things about Manchukuo—unspeakable experiments on human beings carried out by the Department of Epidemic Prevention and Water Purification. Don't make me describe what I read."

None of us Chinese liked the Japanese occupation of Manchuria, which we understood to be a Chinese province. We didn't like their renaming it "Manchukuo" either.

"Isn't it true that sometimes smaller injustices are necessary in order to do away with larger ones?" Tak-Wing said.

A sturdy fishing boat with the traditional eyes painted on its bow docked beside us, gunning its motor loudly as it manoeuvred into place. Men shouted from the dock to the deck. "Kill the engine! Use poles! Throw me the rope!"

"Maybe," said Tanaka, loudly, so his listeners could hear him above the noise. "I don't know. Not these kinds of injustices. I wouldn't, for instance, consider cutting you open without anaesthetic as a small injustice worth inflicting to understand the larger injustice of human pain. To me that is sick."

"But if they are cutting imperialists open," said Tak-Wing, "wouldn't that be some kind of justice for the way the white man has cut China open?"

"Pole broken!" came a shout from deck to dock.

"Cut the motor! Use the rudder!"

All of us on Captain Lee's boat were distracted by the harbour action. But Tanaka kept talking. "They are not cutting imperialists open. They are cutting innocent Chinese civilians open. If I laid you out on Old Lee's fish-gutting table to see how loud you scream, would that count as getting back at the British for their subjugation of Hong Kong?"

Two tang tsai a row away angled for the same mooring and their pilots shouted obscenities at one another in Tanka. A group of drunk Dutch sailors stumbled down the dock looking for flower girls.

"Of course not," said Tak-Wing.

"I've seen people hurting their own folks," Wong said, "tearing down their communities in every place I've ever lived. Thinking they were going to get something out of it."

"Did they? Was the violence emancipating in any way?" Tanaka asked.

"No. Just senseless. People in pain don't have the best sense, sometimes. And sometimes too, it is more about choosing the lesser of two evils."

"Hi," I said. "I thought we were here to talk about weddings."

"Better have these weddings quick as possible and then hide out at home," said Tanaka. "The Japanese Imperial Army could invade Hong Kong."

"That will never happen," said Old Mah. "We're too small to be worth the trouble."

"We're a symbol of British imperialism," said Captain Lee, spitting a lychee seed across the deck and overboard. It hit the now-docked fishing boat right in its freshly painted eye.

"I agree with Old Mah," Cheung said. "Why would they bother with us?"

"If I were you, I'd support Mao Tse-Tung," said Tanaka. "I think he has a good heart and a good tactical mind. I think he truly loves the people."

"I can see that," said Wong. "I heard there's a group somewhere on the mainland called the East River Column. I don't know if they support Mao or not, but they believe in the power and rights of ordinary people. They're not for the Japanese, but they're not for Chiang Kai-Shek and his corrupt generals either. Have any of you heard of them? What I wouldn't give to make contact."

Captain Lee and his daughter glanced at each other in a strange way I didn't know how to interpret.

"I've heard of the East River Column," said Tanaka. "Supposed to operate in the Sai Kung hills—where Captain Lee and his daughter Ting-Yan are from. Do you know anything about it, Old Lee?"

"Nothing at all." Captain Lee worked a toothpick through the gaps between his teeth to get some strands of lychee fibre out. "I'm not interested in politics. Trying to make a living is hard enough."

"Now that everyone's here," Ting-Yan said, "shall we get to Chek Keng and start the ceremonies?"

"What?" I said.

"Didn't you get the message, ViVi?" asked Emily. "We're going to Chek Keng for a double wedding: Tak-Tam and Ting-Yan plus Tak-Wing and me!" She beamed with a self-satisfaction that was at once cute and annoying.

Tak-Tam looked at Ting-Yan, but she was busy untying the boat from its mooring.

"I thought we were going there to begin making arrangements. You didn't say it was all planned and under way already."

"Of course I did. But that messenger boy I sent did not look too bright."

"Chinese wedding?" said Old Mah, wanting to be certain.

"What other kind is there?" said Captain Lee.

"There's a registry wedding and an English wedding with only toffs to watch," said Old Mah, resentment puffing out of his ears. "For a real Chinese wedding you have to consult the father of the bride when making arrangements and get his genuine consent."

Ting-Yan pushed the boat off the pier with a long pole, and started the motor.

"You must get over it, Father," said Emily. "You already said yes to us getting married. There's no point getting wound up about the little details."

We stayed in Chek Keng for a week. Old Mah was happy because his daughter and son-in-law served him tea in a proper ceremony. Since my mother was dead, I sat beside him in her place and received tea from my older sister as though she were my daughter. The only disappointment for me was that I was not allowed to comb Emily's hair. It seemed to me that that would be a good sisterly ritual, but tradition said the hair-combing ceremony was reserved for a woman who had lived a lucky life. In traditional terms this meant she must be married, wealthy, and the mother of many children. I was none of those things.

I told Kathy Duffy about it afterwards.

"Remember I told you that in your mother's home county of Shunde, women can comb their own hair in a ceremony of independence and self-sufficiency?" she said. "The ceremony is still alive. You could do it, if you want."

"Why do you care so much about us Chinese people, and so little about your own people?"

She laughed. "I care about Irish people! Maybe too much! But when I was young, I was afraid to, because all my professors at Trinity College Dublin were pro-British and I was afraid to say I admired Sinn Fein. I studied Chinese people, I suppose, as a kind of proxy for Republican Irish. By the time I was self-assured enough to stand up for what I believed in, I was old, and knew a lot about China and very little about Ireland. So here I am."

"If you don't mind my saying, that seems very sad to me," I said.

She smiled a small smile. "I suppose it is, child. If I were in Ireland and had a daughter, I'd encourage her to study Irish history. But I'm not and I don't. However, I am in Hong Kong and I do have a student—you. I'm trying to give you back what the English took from me—that is, your own history."

"Huh," I said. "I guess that makes some kind of sense."

"Don't you sometimes feel like a fish out of water?" she asked.

"Yes, of course," I said. "But I think that all Hong Kong people feel that way, to some extent."

"I can't give you everything you need," she said. "Because I don't have the particularity of your experience. But I'll give you what I can. The rest, I'm afraid, is up to you."

CHAPTER 24

HORACE'S LEAP

164 Water Street
St. John's, Newfoundland

August 2, 1937

Dear Iz,

Well, if your story doesn't make me want to kill those cockroaches,
I don't know what will. Don't you dare leave. I'm coming out there,
and we are going to fight those entitled, arrogant bloodsuckers. I'm
gonna do more than put my oar in, I promise you that. I think the
Japanese are really coming. That's Tanaka's people, right? You tell
him to go ahead and fill my order for passage, pronto, and don't you
dare protest. I want the next passage out. How long does the journey take? Three weeks? A month? Tell him to book me the absolute
quickest passage he can get.

I love you, my cuz. Never stop fighting.

Revolution!

Morgan

1941

CHAPTER 25

STUFFED CRAB

December 25, 1941

It was Christmas Day, but no one was celebrating. Hong Kong was under siege by the Japanese Imperial Army, and had been for the past three weeks. All the cricketers had joined the Hong Kong Volunteer Defence Corps, and were out in the territory now, doing their damned best to protect it, along with the 5/7th Battalion, Rajput Regiment; the 2/14th Battalion, Punjab Regiment; the Winnipeg Grenadiers; the Royal Rifles of Canada; the Hong Kong and Singapore Royal Artillery; the 2nd Battalion, Royal Scots; and others Cheung didn't know about. But the small assortment of British planes at the Kai Tak Airfield had been flattened on the first day of the invasion, along with its two flying boats and three outdated torpedo bombers. Fifth columnists, mostly Triad members cultivated by the Japanese, had cut barbed wire and telephone lines, led the Japanese Army through perilous mountain paths to the city, and hoisted a Japanese flag atop the Peninsula Hotel, tricking the Winnipeg Grenadiers into thinking they'd been caught in a pincer movement and laying down their arms before the Japanese army had even arrived. Rapidly and utterly routed, the British had abandoned Kowloon without informing the Chinese populace, and as a result the people understandably ceased to see the war as theirs and abandoned their support positions as amahs, drivers, clerks, and workers. Hong Kong was mercilessly shelled and bombed. Japanese soldiers and Triads alike rampaged, looted, burned, and raped. In the harbour, three bombed-out oil tankers smouldered.

Cheung was left in charge of the cricket club. He felt a duty to be there, but he sent Yim-Fong back to Tai Hang to stay with her parents as a precaution. It was only a twenty-minute tram ride away, or an hour's walk. He could visit any time. But it was better that she wasn't actually living at the club. Tak-Tam and Ting-Yan were up in Chek Keng. Tak-Wing and Emily were at the old Tai Hang house. It was so hard to know whether any one place was safer than the other. Nowhere seemed safe, but concrete information about what was actually going on was scarce. The only news Cheung had access to was through rumour. In the meantime, gas lines had been cut and sewage mains destroyed. The Japanese army had taken control of the reservoir at Shing Mun, which up 'til then had provided most of the city's drinkable water. There was no building in the city that did not reek of shit, piss, and sweat, including the battered HKCC. Cheung, like every other inhabitant of the city, choked daily on the vile stink of despair.

Footsteps sounded on the tile floor upstairs. They didn't sound military. They were the footsteps of just one person, a familiar shuffle, but out of place. Cheung rushed upstairs.

"Lee!"

The old fisher stood gawping in the foyer, a pole balanced across his narrow back. On either end hung a rattan basket of blue-black crabs, still dripping sea water onto the polished black and white tile floor.

"What are you doing here? Don't you know the city is under siege?"

"It's Tuesday," said Lee. "Stuffed crab night. You taught my lazy nephew how to cook it just right. Where is that pea brain?"

"How on earth did you get across the harbour? How did you get across the city? No one made it to work today, except young Yan, who sleeps in the kitchen." Cheung himself was only present because he lived there.

"You owe me forty dollars."

"Your mind's deranged!" said the head steward, reaching into his pockets. "Those Japanese demons could have killed you. Don't you know that under the circumstances, the order is cancelled? There are no ghost devils left in this pathetic cricket club to eat them."

"I tried to come around back, but the door was locked. Why did you leave the front door open?"

"Put the load down, fool," said Cheung, handing the money to the fisher. "Haven't you carried it far enough?"

Lee shifted the load on his back in order to reach out and take the crumpled bills. "On this nice clean floor that the English step on in their white shoes? Why did you lock the back?"

"Because I don't want stupid eggs like you sneaking up on me in my private domain! Put your load down."

At last Lee did. "Why did you leave the front open?"

"Because," said Cheung. "Because Colonel Noma of the Kempeitai himself is coming. If I lock it, the soldiers will break down those beautiful oak doors. Why let them be ruined? The club is already defenceless. You should go, unless you want to become part of the permanent Chinese staff."

"You should go yourself," said Lee. "The British have surrendered and the invader is merciless. I've seen them down at the docks. They load Chinese people onto boats, shoot them down for target practice, then sink the boats. They've been beheading people on the wharves. Just hope they don't come here to rape your wife."

"So it's true then," said Cheung, casting his eyes to the floor. "I have heard the stories of this happening in Nanking. I sent Yim-Fong home to her parents to keep her safe. Did you see anybody we know?"

"I didn't get too close," said Lee. "I value my own life."

"You want to stay and have a shot of brandy?" said Cheung. "No cricketers around today to stop you from sitting at the bar."

"Nah," said Lee. "I should get back to Chek Keng before things get any worse. And also to stop that crazy son of yours from joining the Kuomintang. If he wants to join the army, that's not the one. You want to come with me? It might be safer, though I can't offer you any guarantees."

"No guarantees anywhere in Hong Kong. I think I'll stay here in case any of the other workers come back. This club is the only home I've got, and someone's got to take care of it. Are Tak-Tam and Ting-Yan doing okay?"

"They're both full of fighting spirit," said Lee. A glimmer of light flashed up in his eyes. "Are you sure you won't come to Chek Keng? I heard the Kempeitai are going to use the Supreme Court Building for interrogations. This place might not be the safest."

"I'm sure," Cheung said.

"Okay. I've given you my best intelligence. See you next Tuesday."

"Don't risk your life. I told you, there's no cricketers to eat your crab anyway."

"I'm leaving the baskets with you. I'll pick them up when I drop off the new batch."

"Be careful, Brother."

The crabs writhed unpleasantly in the battered baskets. Cheung picked them up, one in each hand. They were heavy. How could that skinny Lee be so strong? He lurched downstairs on unsteady feet.

At the bottom of the stairs, young Yan was already mopping.

"You might want to get the foyer first, just in case the colonel arrives."

It had been several hours already since the British surrender, but the Japanese Imperial Army was too busy looting and pillaging to bother to claim the cricket club. Cheung suspected they wouldn't be long, though. The Hong Kong Cricket Club was an emblem of British colonial presence, and the Japanese Imperial Army would want to show Asian mastery soon. His diligent and careful stewardship wouldn't count for much.

Yan rushed past him up the stairs to render the foyer spotless.

Cheung took the crabs to his old domain, the kitchen. Tin-Lok, Lee's nephew from Chek Keng and Cheung's assistant of eleven months, had slipped away again. Cheung didn't know where and wouldn't ask. In their battered rattan cages, the crabs wriggled. The reddish black tips of their claws caught the artificial fluorescent light of the kitchen. There was no point letting the creatures suffer, and there was no point wasting food. Cheung filled a large pot with water. Though the gas lines were cut, he'd had the foresight to purchase a couple of portable kerosene burners before the invasion. He lit one now. He got onions from the icebox and started chopping. When the water came to a boil, he opened a basket and picked up the first writhing creature. Dropped it into the boiling water and attended to its silent scream.

CHAPTER 26

ST STEPHEN'S COLLEGE

December 25, 1941

I was tending a man who had been bayonetted in the belly on Christmas Day, 1941, the day the Japanese Imperial Army took the city. I was a volunteer at St Stephen's College, which had been converted into a field hospital. Emily was with me on the same ward, working as a nurse. There were about twenty doctors and nurses working there—British, Canadian, and Chinese—caring for the wounded and dying. The sound of gunfire had been steady outside the windows for the last two days. Bombs periodically exploded, far away at first, then closer and closer as the battle wore on. My nerves were frayed, but like all the other medical staff at the college I kept going out of necessity.

The man I was tending was a soldier in a plain British Army uniform, with an embroidered patch on the shoulder that said CANADA. When I first saw him, his teeth were gritted bravely, but his eyes streamed tears. I could tell he was in a lot of pain. Who would not be, gashed in the gut like that? I gave him a morphine injection. Once he'd relaxed a bit, I noticed that his face was a bit like mine. How odd.

On my way to the supply closet to get sutures, I saw them through the hallway window: a contingent of soldiers and their general, crossing the yard in formation. Alongside them ran a handful of men wearing the white armbands of the Kempeitai, the dreaded military police. The one who led the Kempeitai was taller and better fed than the others and wore his pride so palpably that I could feel it from where I stood.

There was a ruckus at the main door. Shouting and gunshots.

I heard Dr Oliviera yell, "This is a hospital! You have no business here!"

There was a gunshot, and screams.

There were boots on the stairs.

After that, I can't tell you what I heard.

I heard nothing.

I heard everything.

I wasn't there.

I am always there.

Men barked. I didn't know the language but the epithets were racial.

Patients screamed.

I heard pleading and crying.

Grunts. Insults in another language.

Please no please sir please I'm a nurse please no please no no no no no no no no no no

I truly can't hear and I can't see. Not the sound of gunshots. Not the sound of wounded soldiers stabbed in their beds. Not the sound of doctors begging for their lives. Not the sound of nurses raped atop the dead and dying. Not the repetitive judder of hips, not the grunts, not the animal screams.

I look through a crack in the door. I see nothing. My retinas burn.

This is a fire that will never go out.

I stay in the supply closet for an hour, two hours, three. I stay in the closet for a year, a decade, a century. I will never leave this closet. The closet is full of packages. I take inventory in an attempt to neither see nor hear: field dressings, shell dressings, morphine tartrate, morphine syrettes, tubunic ampoules, anti-tetanus serum, anti-gangrene serum, needles, iodine swabs, adhesive tape, eye dressings, tourniquets, linen ligature thread, scissors, safety pins, boric acid ointment, Dettol, cotton wool, instrument rolls, and tablet tins. At the start of each shift, the doctors and nurses hang their civilian clothes on hooks along the wall, and put on scrubs. Here's Doctor

Wong's overcoat. Here's Nurse Petrov's pretty scarf. Doctor Oliviera's belt is very worn. The floral pattern on Nurse Eagleton's blouse is too busy for my taste. Nurse Chan's simple dress is exquisitely cut. My mother was a seamstress before she died. Not out of necessity, but she liked to make her own cheung sams. She'd used to take me with her to the fabric shop to choose cottons for summer, silks for winter. The shopkeeper, a handsome Chinese man who wore Western suits and put Brylcreem in his hair loved my mother, would keep her chatting as long as possible. Have you eaten rice yet? How is your sister in Guangzhou? I think the monsoon rains will come early this year.

I stay in the closet. The century flows by.

I try to remember more of the things the Brylcreem man said to my mother. All the fashionable ladies in Shanghai are wearing two-toned silk this year. Organza is cool in summer. Have you seen the new rayon fabrics, strong and delicate as silk but much cheaper?

She'd used to make our clothes herself, but later, after she got sick, she started sending us to the tailor. I think about all the little backstreet shops. We chose one that had piles of fashion books from England, France, and America to study. There were so many lovely drawings of ladies in cloche hats, coats in elegant grey or flashy green and black with fur collars. There were ladies in drop-waisted dresses. They wore pointy-toed shoes with straps across the tops of their feet and mink stoles draped over their shoulders. They pointed discreetly at the ground in kid leather gloves.

There was a book on ribbon art that Emily particularly loved. It showed all the things you could make with ribbon: elaborate hat decorations that looked like fans or cummerbunds, elaborate bows to decorate babies' blankets or baskets, garters in frilly pink and black or ruched blue and tan, decorations for negligees to make them seem longer and more fluttery than they already were, lampshades and flowery wall hangings, headbands decorated with leaves and flowers that were all the rage when we were girls.

In the back of that tailor shop you could hear the whirr of sewing machines and the chatter of the tailor's assistants. We would hand over the fabric we'd bought from the Brylcreem man and the tailor would come and take our measurements, and in ten days Emily and Mama would have smart dresses and I'd have a pantsuit or whatever it was I wanted—Mama was indulgent and Father's business was doing well.

On our way home we would walk through the flower market and admire all the open-air flower stalls. You could buy any kind of flower you wanted, loose or in bunches with leaves and baby's breath, all firmly tied together with a piece of hardy grass. You had to be careful, though. The flower sellers were tricky—they'd wire fast-fading blooms to stalks of split bamboo. Mama loved those flower stalls. She loved to chat and bargain with the sellers.

Sometimes she would take us to the department stores. She was more comfortable at the Chinese-run Sincere and Wing On, but sometimes we would go to Lane Crawford or Whiteaway, Laidlaw & Co. just to marvel at the wide array of goods, some made in Chinese factories across the border but many imported from Britain, Australia, Japan, and even Canada. She took us to the Swatow lace shops that sold fabulously embroidered tablecloths, Swatow drawnwork, filet lace, and silk shawls decorated with birds, flowers, and dragons.

These are the things I think about in the closet. I can't be where I am.

I still can't hear the screaming, the pleading, the grunting, the shouting, the human teeth tearing human flesh

There are smells. Of gunpowder blood shit fire vomit. My nostrils burn.

I focus on a bird on Nurse Petrov's pretty scarf—its bright eye, its curved yellow beak. Its blue feathers flutter in the light breeze that blows in the scarf's imagination. The pretty pink flowers surrounding it rustle, and a lovely, delicate scent of roses wafts off them. The leaves that surround them clatter softly against one another. The scarf's breeze is so cool I can feel it on my face. The bird's beak opens, and a pretty song warbles from its throat, which quavers, soft and fragile. The breeze blows harder, becomes a wind that scatters rose petals to the supply closet floor. I hear her voice. "Violet."

"Mama?"

Her hand is on my head. She strokes my head, begins to brush my hair as she used to do for both me and Emily at night when we were little. Where did she get the brush? Is she really there? It's not possible. I know where I am. I know what's going on outside. But if I turn around and she is not there, that would be the absolute worst thing in the world. I can't lose her, I can't lose her, I can't lose her again. Mama, please don't leave me, I can't bear it, I just can't. She brushes and brushes, and all the time, that soft wind blows. The little bird sits beside the boxes of morphine syrettes and sings. More flower petals rush from the folds of the scarf, now flapping and blowing as the wind grows stronger. The floor is littered with petals, an inch of pink snow covering the ground. She brushes and brushes and brushes my hair. The wind grows stronger, colder, no longer entirely pleasant. She brushes harder. She's pulling my hair. Ow, Mama, stop, that hurts.

I pull away.

I turn.

There's no one there.

Of course there's no one there. What was I thinking? When I turn again there is no wind, no birds, no flower petals. Nurse Petrov's scarf hangs on its hook beside her coat where she left it before this whole ordeal began.

Another century passes. It is a quieter century than the centuries previous. I leave the closet.

I cannot describe the ward in which I sutured ordinary wounds just yesterday.

I heard groaning. "Help me."

It was coming from a body beneath two other bodies, those of a dead naked nurse still bleeding from down there and a dead soldier without eyes. I stood for a long moment and looked at them, seeing without seeing.

Tenderly, I moved them to empty beds. How did I get so strong? Beneath them, a man was alive. Miraculously, it was the soldier I'd been tending before the attack. He was holding in his guts with his hands.

I went back to the closet to get ligature thread, morphine syrettes, and iodine. I was still stitching the way Professor Ride had taught me when a British captain came to tell me that all the soldiers who hadn't been killed were to be interned.

"Since you're Chinese, you're still free. You should go home to your mother."

"My mother is dead."

"I'm sorry."

"It was a long time ago."

The man in the bed groaned softly.

"He's Chinese too," I said, on impulse. He looked enough like me that he could be.

The captain scowled. "Looks like a soldier. He's wearing a soldier's uniform." He examined the man's face. "A Chinese soldier? It doesn't make sense ..."

"Chinese enough," I said.

"Okay," said the captain, though he probably knew better. "I leave him to your care. I'm just a messenger boy now anyway, since the British have surrendered."

I finished stitching. To the patient I said, "Can you walk?"

"Courchene," he said.

"What?"

"Courchene. My name. William Courchene."

I didn't know how to respond.

He waited.

"Pleased to meet you," I said, like an idiot. "I'm Violet. Dr Violet Mah Wai-Man. Can you walk?" I'd shoved a handful of morphine ampoules in my pocket, but if I gave him one, he'd likely fall asleep, and then he'd be done for.

Emily was beside me then. Her hair was dishevelled, her face haggard, her eyes empty as a hungry rice pot. "Let's get out of here, Vi."

"The British are letting us go, but will the Japanese?"

"They are letting the Chinese at St Stephen's go, but they are still murdering us in the street. We need to get back to the Stable."

"Okay. I'm taking this one."

"A half-dead British soldier? Why?"

"He's Canadian. Maybe Canadian Chinese? Look at his face."

She looked. "He's handsome."

"I suppose he is, yes."

I took some of the clothes from the closet and dressed Courchene as a civilian. The doctor to whom the clothes belonged didn't need them anymore.

There were mutilated bodies in the hallway. A woman with her head hacked almost, but not completely, off. A man without eyes, ears, nose, or mouth. We tried not to look. We passed survivors scrubbing blood from the stairwell as Japanese soldiers shouted orders. We scurried past them dragging our groaning patient with us. By the mercy of Mary we made it to the door. When we stepped out we saw half a dozen mutilated bodies laid out on the lawn, all without heads. I averted my gaze, but the sight had already cut my eyes as though with a knife.

We made our way past Ng Wah Hall toward Tung Tau Wan Road where the bus stop was. Other Chinese workers from the field hospital hurried past us.

Emily walked with a limp.

Had she—

I didn't want to think about it.

Her face was fierce, trying to push down the pain.

"Emily."

She ignored me, and continued to stumble forward.

"Emily."

"Don't ask me, Violet."

"Did they—"

"I told you not to ask me."

So I didn't ask her. The three of us pushed onward, away away away from the scene behind us, what had just happened, what we'd seen and not seen, heard and not heard, smelled and not smelled. I'd walked this moist path to the bus stop on Tung Tau Wan Road a dozen times before, since the field hospital was set up earlier that month, always with the anticipation of home warming my belly. I had moved back to the Stable shortly before the invasion, to be better prepared for trouble, though not necessarily the trouble we had just gone through. But I couldn't put today's events behind me, and because I couldn't, I couldn't anticipate home either. I lurched in its direction like an animal, on instinct, because I couldn't go back and I couldn't think what else to do.

Courchene said, "Her leg."

"What?"

"Her leg," he repeated.

There was blood trickling down Emily's leg.

"Em."

"Don't talk to me Violet. I can't talk. I just want to go home."

"You're bleeding."

Once I said it a switch turned in her. She stopped, and sat down on the side of the road. She didn't cry. Her face was white as salt, that is to say a bit grey, a bit yellow—pale.

"Can I see?"

"Of course not. Don't talk to me."

I tore off the bottom third of my lab coat and gave it to her to clean herself. She turned away from me and cleaned. She didn't cry. Her elbow moved mechanically. I could have given her morphine but then we would never get out of here.

Tung Tau Wan Road was pure chaos. Japanese soldiers were everywhere. There were very few civilians, and those who were there were ran along the ditches trying to get away from the soldiers, who bayonetted them indiscriminately as they moved in our direction, toward the field hospital. I pulled Emily and Courchene into the ditch, and we scrambled through fields, angling away from Tung Tau Wan Road now, back past St Stephen's chapel toward the beach, roughly in the direction of Stanley village. Emily was bleeding badly and moved slowly. She was in rough shape, though also numb with shock. Courchene, too, bayonetted in the gut and newly stitched up, could not move very fast. I had to get them somewhere safe soon.

Along the beach was a little row of huts. I knew that to enter one might present dangers, but we couldn't stay out in the open. I approached the nearest one and stepped onto the porch, which still had chairs and a fold-out bed on it from a happier moment days earlier. Bamboo blinds were rolled down to cover the single window. I tried the door, but it was locked. I shook it and thought I heard a whimper. Was there someone inside?

Out of the corner of my eye, I saw soldiers crossing the field. I had no other choice. With my sturdy foot in its thick Mary Jane, I kicked the flimsy door, once, twice, and then the lock broke and we were in.

There were people there. "I'm sorry," I said. "I don't mean any harm. There are wounded among us." As my eyes adjusted to the dark I saw there were two Sikh children, a very young British couple, and a Chinese teenager. They were all hiding too, and I had just broken the door. They cowered away from us.

I felt bad for them, but my first concern was Emily. I helped her sit down on a dilapidated rattan couch. Courchene sat down on the floor and leaned his back against one of its arms. I gave him an ampoule, which he took, gratefully. He groaned softly and closed his eyes. It was amazing he had made it this far. I wondered if he would last the night.

I turned to Emily, my poor sister, who had been so joyous and self-absorbed, fun-loving and desperate for love in spite of all the love she was given. She had sunken into a hole so dark that no light could ever enter again. What I knew that she didn't was that things could get so much worse. I had the power to stop it, but it wouldn't be easy. Someone had to take care of her. Judge me if you want. Maybe I judge myself, but in the moment, there seemed only one thing to do. And I had to do something. I had to move toward the future, because I couldn't stay in the present, and I couldn't leave her there either.

"You can't tell Old Mah," I said. "He wouldn't be able to handle it. His world—our world—would fall apart."

She looked at me as though I were a foreigner from another country.

"Old Mah. Remember? Your father."

Was she so far away she had forgotten her family? Her head slumped.

"Em. Things could get so much worse. You can't tell Tak-Wing either. Men cannot understand these things."

She didn't answer.

There was nothing more I could do in the present, so I was trying to fix the future. Not that it did any good. I put my arm around her. She leaned into me. Her body was so cold, like a block of ice, even though it was a warm day.

Finally, she whispered, "Whatever you say, Violet. I don't care."

Well, it was wrong of me to ask her to keep it from Tak-Wing and Father. I see that now. I thought I was protecting her. I thought I was protecting them. I don't know what I thought. When the past comes back in the light of day, it feels so impossible to make sense of it, even of my own logic and my own actions.

After a while, she turned toward me again.

"We can tell them you hid in the supply closet with me, and that we heard a lot of screaming. But we'll tell them we're okay."

"Okay, Violet," she said. "You're right, they won't be able to handle it."

My beautiful, clever, mischievous sister was gone, replaced by this pale, cold ghost. The lively young woman never came back, but somehow Emily went on living.

We were so exhausted that we fell asleep on that battered rattan couch. We were so distraught, though, that we didn't sleep for long.

When we woke up, the young British couple told us that Hong Kong had surrendered. They had a radio, which made it possible for us to get the news. Masaichi Niimi and Takashi Sakai were named co-governors of the Japanese Occupation Administration.

CHAPTER 27

WHEN IS A FISH NOT A FISH?

December 25, 1941

When is a fish not a fish? It's a fish once it's hatched from its tiny, glossy egg. It's a fish when it is swimming in the ocean in a school of other fish. It's a fish as it darts through the coral reef, or rides a current down to the lip of another continent. It's fish when it's entranced by a scrap of flesh dangling in the water, and it remains a fish when it's hooked through the mouth. It's still a fish when it's reeled aboard the fisherman's boat. It's a fish when it flaps on a wooden plank in the open air, gasping for water. It's a fish even if it's slapped to death with another plank. It remains a fish when the cleaner slices its belly open and drags the guts out, tosses them back into the water for other fish to eat. It remains a fish when a knife is run against the grain of its shiny, protective scales, dislodging them in long strokes from the follicles until its flesh is naked as a human baby's. It's still a fish when it's tossed into a wok with peanut oil, garlic, and shallots, or steamed in plain water, or dipped in batter and deep-fried. It's fish if it's eaten raw too, as the Japanese do, dipped in shoyu mixed with wasabi. It's fish if it's torn from bone by knives or human teeth, fish as it's swallowed, fish even as stomach acids go to work digesting it. Only when its fibres are torn down to proteins, when the eating body incorporates into it eating muscle, does it cease being fish and become human.

If you want to know what happened. That's what happened. How we became ourselves. Finding differences to eat. Eating. Changing. Finding fault in the mirror. Eating again.

CHAPTER 28

Typhoon Shelter
THE CHINESE COOPERATIVE COUNCIL
June 30, 1997

The teapot is empty. Neither Great-Aunt Violet nor Ophelia can eat during the telling of this tale, but Ophelia has been nervously sipping tea. "Did Old Mah ever find out? He must have been devastated."

He never asked. Maybe he knew—in the old days we shared as much knowledge by not speaking as we did by speaking. It's different from how Westerners like to confess every little thing and imagine that doing so heals them. He probably knew. I suspect so because he sent Second Mother Polly to visit us at the Stable, where I'd returned when the invasion started and where Emily often visited, though her official residence was Cheung's old house in Tai Hang. Second Mother Polly came to the Stable in a floral-patterned suit, her stick out in front of her, feeling her way forward. Her daughter Pineapple kept trying to take her arm, but, ever stubborn and independent, Second Mother Polly pushed her away. As I told you, we weren't close with her. She had her own family to take care of, and we, as the daughters of the first wife, posed a minor threat within the logic of Chinese family politics. But still she came with our half-sister Pineapple, and she brought us half a dozen pork buns, a rare treat that was very hard to get in a time of such scarcity. She didn't ask us what had happened. She just came, sat with us, and spoke kindly. That was how she showed care, and how Old Mah showed his care for us through her. We were lucky. Lots of women committed suicide after such atrocities. Some were disowned by their families. Emily did not commit suicide and Old Mah did not disown us. He showed love through a judiciously pitched kind of silence. We didn't speak of the events, just as many Chinese women did not, all driven by the powerful and intractable value of saving face.

But in fact, we didn't see Old Mah at all for the next couple of months. Right at the hour when Second Mother Polly and Pineapple were visiting us, the Kempeitai went to the Kimblewick and took him away. We didn't find out where until much later. He was kept incommunicado at the Hong Kong Hotel, one of the many once-glorious establishments where Emily used to sing with Izzy Davis Wong and His Cosmopolitan Elites. There Mah was pressured, in every way you can imagine and some I'm sure you can't, to "voluntarily" support the new government and Japan's project in Asia.

He was forced to attend Governor Sakai's speech at the Peninsula Hotel, where Sakai told 133 prominent Chinese, who had been rounded up just like Old Mah, that his quarrel had never been with the Chinese people, and that his objective was "co-prosperity for all the races of Great East Asia." The men were encouraged to slough off their European masters who, Sakai said, had used Chinese volunteers, as well as Canadian and Indian battalions, on the front lines in order to preserve their own lives. He invited the business leaders to form a committee to assist the new pro-Asian government in bringing about a new prosperous peace. Of course, it was not actually an invitation. Anyone who did not comply would be interned and executed. Old Mah had no choice.

It wasn't a good time for him. He wasn't a traitor. How could he be, since Hong Kong was not a nation? We were a new people—a people who had followed the malaria, cholera, dysentery, and ghosts out of the stagnant swamp that Happy Valley became after rice growing was banned. We weren't British, we weren't Japanese, and we certainly weren't the kind of pan-Asian that Governor Sakai dreamt of. We remained Chinese, but

Chinese on a path of our own, different from the Chinese of mainland China, who crossed one set of thresholds while we crossed another.

Don't you read your history books, Feelie? Nations themselves have not been around for very long. Britain only had a nation because it had an empire; it had the likes of us, who didn't have a nation to prove to them that they did. And Japan and China soaked the land in blood trying to forge nations of their own. It wasn't that there were no national ideals to be loyal to, it was more that there were too many incomplete ones, all of which looked wonderful on the surface but none of which looked good when you dug deeper. You could be pro-democracy, but the possibility of being pro-democracy without being pro-British and therefore in favour of European colonialism, was not yet available. You could be pan-Asian and anti-colonial, but then you'd find yourself supporting Japanese fascism. You could be a Chinese Nationalist, but the Kuomintang leadership was notoriously corrupt and actively employed Nazi Brownshirts to train its own Blueshirts. You could be pro-Communist like Captain Lee and Kwan Siu-Wai, which, in those days, was probably the most noble option, but look at how many millions of people were murdered by the Communists later in the Great Leap Forward and the Cultural Revolution! In the moment, we had no nation, so there was nothing for Old Mah to betray. Old Mah did not want to work for the government that had violated his daughter, but he did what was pragmatic because pragmatism was all he had.

By the time the Kempeitai released him, a lot of Chinese had fled, either to Macau, like Mah's old friend Robert Ho Tung, who was tipped off by the Japanese consul, or else inland to China. The new Japanese administration was encouraging ordinary people to leave. The city was already crowded. There were the people who had been here since before the British came. There were the many who came in the early colonial years seeking work and seeking to escape the wars and feuds that plagued South China through the late 1800s and early 1900s. And there were thousands of new refugees fleeing the current war in China that had started in 1937, while Hong Kong was still free and relatively peaceful. There were

Sikhs, Gurkhas, and other South Asians who had followed the British from India to Hong Kong and worked mostly as policemen and security guards, though they did other kinds of work too, like any other Hong Kong person. The famous Harilelas were tailors. Some other South Asians threw their lot in with the Japanese during the war because they saw the pan-Asian project as compatible with Indian independence. There were Portuguese who worked as clerks and administrators. There were people from Jamaica who had come to do administrative work, or who were the children of Chinese workers and shopkeepers in Jamaica, sent back to the home village to marry in that old Confucian way, like our friend Isadore Davis Wong. There were Japanese people too, who worked for Japanese branch companies in Hong Kong, or as journalists and translators, like our friend Tanaka Shigeru. Some, like the Japanese barber at the Peninsula Hotel, were spies, but a lot were just ordinary people like you and me. Generally, the occupation government wanted everyone out. They were not well prepared for civilian administration, and the fewer people there were in the territory, the fewer they would have to look after. Plus, food was in short supply and getting scarcer by the day. The Japanese Army raided the godowns and took control of the warehouses. They confiscated cars and held them at the Hong Kong Cricket Club until there were ships available to take them to Japan. They gathered up everything that might be useful—most of it was sent back to the motherland to support the Japanese war effort, leaving very little for use here. There were rumours of mass shootings to reduce the population. Diseases, primarily cholera, diphtheria, and dysentery, were becoming a serious problem, affecting enemy and ally alike.

The only people Sakai didn't want to get rid of were a handful of British bankers whom they required to oversee the transfer of economic control, a handful of medical people to help manage the deteriorating health of the city, and so-called Chinese "justices of the peace" like Old Mah, whom they needed to help administer the colony by exercising influence on the general populace. They preferred to put Chinese people, rather than British, into positions of responsibility.

Not all anti-colonial things are good, Ophelia—think about it! It matters how you get there! And it matters what you put in place after the Europeans are gone.

There were two committees—the Chinese Cooperative Council led by Shouson Chow, and the Chinese Representative Council lead by Lo Kuk-Wo, also known as Robert Kotewall. Mah was placed on the Chinese Cooperative Council. His job, along with that of thirty other men, was to convey the needs of the people to the Chinese Representative Council, who in turn consulted with the Japanese leadership, who brought directives back down to the Chinese Representative Council, who passed them on to the Chinese Cooperative Council. Both the Representative Council and the Cooperative Council then did their best to lay out those directives to the people.

Old Mah's political sympathies, such as they were, lay with Dr Sun Yat-Sen, and after Dr Sun died, with his successor, Generalissimo Chiang Kai-Shek and the Kuomintang. Old Mah knew vaguely that Chiang was a very different kind of man from Sun, but he believed in Chiang's ability to carry Sun's republican project forward. Though Mah had no interest in serving the occupation government, he was also a shrewd businessman. There was no such thing in Hong Kong as a businessman who wasn't shrewd, because, if you weren't, you didn't survive. So Mah did what he could to protect himself, his family, and the Hong Kong people, in that order. He assisted in the devising of a workable rice rationing scheme. He worked with Shouson Chow to put an end to the rape epidemic that plagued the city by setting up military brothels—a far from perfect solution that really only protected women from gentry families. Like all the other so-called "justices of the peace," he was good at protecting those close to him, but bad at protecting ordinary people.

As the rumours and stories of the massacre at St Stephen's and many other places all over the territory came out, he thought all the more about

Emily. Though no one directly told him what had happened, he knew. He thought about revenge. Second Mother Polly told me he slept badly and smoked too much Dream Horse White in order to relax. But he also did what he had to do and bided his time, as so many of us do, even now, much to the detriment of our children and their futures, if you ask me. I wish he had fought back though. I wish they all had, those grand old men of the city. Do you suppose the tide of history might have turned if they had?

As for me, I was beside myself with a furious restlessness, a need to act. We were thwarted at every turn. My mind spun hourly from the grim contradictory position my father was in to the horrors that had befallen my sister to all the unspeakable things I myself had seen and not seen at St Stephen's. When Dr Selwyn-Clarke asked me come work for his humanitarian mission, I jumped at the chance. I had graduated with my medical degree from HKU earlier that year, rushed through by Professor Ride and the university administration in anticipation of the likelihood that I and my fellow graduates would be called upon to do exactly this kind of work. It was how I'd ended up working at St Stephen's on that fateful Christmas Day. And now it would give me something meaningful to occupy my mind. There would be some action I could take to mitigate my overwhelming feeling of helplessness.

Emily wanted to help too. She took every chance she could to get away from Tak-Wing, who had grown rageful and quarrelsome, perhaps suspecting what had happened to her, perhaps just full of general pent-up rage and grief like the rest of us. Courchene, trained by the Canadian Army as medic, joined us after he had recovered from his stomach wound.

The fluorescent lights at the Typhoon Shelter flicker. Great-Aunt Violet looks up at the turquoise girl. "It's 5:20! You better get going!"

"But what happened to Emily? Was she pregnant with Uncle Raymond?"

"You'll miss the arrival of President Jiang Zemin and Premier Li Peng!"

"I don't care about President Jiang Zemin and Premier Li Peng. Tell me how Emily made it through."

CHAPTER 29

STUBBORN

Undisclosed Village

New Territories

December 25, 1941

Dear Morgan,

Well cousin, it sure was hard to leave you in Hong Kong all on your own. Though you've got Tanaka, who is a good man, albeit one in a tight spot. Why do you have to be so stubborn? I'm sure you're right that all the news coming out of China is propaganda, but I promise you the basic reporting is correct. I'm not a radio man for nothing, you know. I managed to drag my radio set into these hills, so I'm one of very few folks up here who knows what's going on. Six days already since Kowloon fell to the Japanese Army. The New Territories are overrun. Chinese people here are feeling pretty abandoned by the British, who didn't even have to courtesy to let them know the state of affairs, but left them here to die, just so their own lives would be easier in retreat on the Hong Kong side. I won't describe to you the scenes of murder and looting I've seen, though if I did, I know you would change your mind about Asia for Asians. I'm sure Brother Du Bois would too. He's a good man and an intelligent man. His only fault, as far as I'm concerned, is that he is not here. The Japanese are brutal. Their Taiwanese allies are even more so. But our people—Triads, fifth columnists, and bandits from our own hills, are some of the very worst.

The news just came through that Hong Kong Island has surrendered, and that all the British have laid down their arms. If it means the pillage can stop, that would be a blessing. If it were only soldiers who were being killed, that would be awful enough, but I've heard tales of women and girls rounded up into houses and systematically raped. I've heard stories of crowds of refugees loaded onto boats that are then sunk. These murderers like to behead people. Every house in Kowloon has been stripped of its contents, and any inhabitants that didn't go into hiding quick enough were killed. These hills are thick with refugees, upon whom the lawless prey. If someone doesn't impose some kind of order soon, the same horrors are going to spread to Hong Kong Island. I'm worried about you.

So far, I've been all right. My little village is so remote that the Japanese haven't found it yet. My people aren't beyond a little banditry—no one in these hills has yet recovered from the Clan Wars. If you haven't ever had fairness, how can you know what it is? But my cousins here are at least not fifth columnists, and we have banded together with a few other villages to begin a bit of resistance work. If you could see what we are doing, I think you would see that our work is more in the spirit of what Brother Du Bois dreams of than what the cursed children of Hirohito have put into motion. It might not be as beautiful as he dreams, but at the very least, it's better than all the demon activity happening around us.

I'm not sure how you feel, so I won't tell you where I am. But if you decide to dream a different dream, or the same dream with different Negro and Asian heroes, and come fight by my side, you could give a note to the messenger who bears this letter. Our network is safe. Won't you consider it—if not for my sake, then for the sake of your own immortal soul?

I love you, cousin. I breaks my heart to think of you on the other side of the harbour, facing so much danger to your life and spirit all alone. If it weren't for Jane and the kids, I wouldn't have left you, you know that. Even though you're so stubborn. Please change your mind and come. I've started a little vegetable garden in anticipation of shortages. I'm growing some of those white radishes you like, and a few different kinds of greens too. Remember how my mama used to do that back home? She used to grow lo bak right alongside the collards. No one got green thumbs like her. If I've inherited a fraction of her knowledge, we might eat okay up here. Please tell me you'll come.

I trust you care for me enough to keep this letter to yourself, regardless of what you decide.

Love and niceness from your cousin,

Izzy

CHAPTER 30

LOOTED

December 26, 1941

The baby was already crawling. She had a huge head, and large round eyes like the water buffalo that ploughed the village fields. She crawled across the floor of the *Oolong* like a fish, on her elbows, dragging the rest of her body across the floor. As she crawled, she gurgled, delighted with her own movement and the sweet, warm stink of the village: vegetables growing in human manure, salt air, drying fish. Ting-Yan watched her with one wary eye while the other focused on the painstaking work of mending a fishing net. Out of the corner of the eye that watched the baby, Ting-Yan saw a tall tree fall in the distance, by the next village over. That was the sign that the Japanese were coming. Kowloon had fallen two weeks earlier, when the 5/7th Rajputs were forced to withdraw at Ma Yau Tong. Rumour said that Hong Kong Island itself had fallen. The Sai Kung hills had become a free-for-all, overrun by Triads, bandits, and the conquering Japanese Army all running through the territory looting and pillaging. The Nationalists, on their way to Hong Kong when it fell, might have had an advance guard in these hills. There was a Communist presence too, that some of the villagers were sympathetic to.

Ting-Yan's cousin Ka-Wan—the one she'd borrowed the motorboat from four years earlier—came down to the dock to make sure they knew.

"Hurry, hurry! Japanese soldiers coming!" he shouted. Before she could acknowledge his words, he was halfway back up the path to the village to warn others. Ka-Wan was part of a guerrilla force that had been preparing, keeping abreast of what was happening in the city and what was needed by friends and extended family. They had a patchy network from Kowloon stretching through the New Territories and over the border through the network of roads, boats, and villages as far as Waichow. They called themselves the Hong Kong and Kowloon Independent Brigade, and distinguished themselves from the ordinary bandits who roamed the Sai Kung hills harassing anyone who passed through, and the pro-Japanese supporters of the puppet government in Nanking who functioned as a fifth column, preparing the way for the Japanese invasion. The Hong Kong and Kowloon Independent Brigade had been running a regular patrol along the perimeter of the village in light of reports that the Japanese Army was on the march through the villages.

Ting-Yan snatched up baby Macy Koon-Ying and slung the girl on her back. Her mother, Siu-Wai, who had been sitting on the dock cleaning fish, got up and scurried after her. Captain Lee, though reluctant to leave his beloved boat, followed. The bombing of Hong Kong Harbour had been intense for the last several days and he wasn't a fool. Though Chek Keng Harbour and Mirs Bay were less central and had yet to be touched, if the Japanese were going back over already conquered territory, the chances of something happening on these waters was high. Mirs Bay was a major route to mainland China. They'd be safer in the trees.

They hurried up to the edge of the village and along the outer path that ran parallel to the shoreline for a while before moving up into tree-covered hills. They had already plotted out a spot, a natural dip in the ground below a stony bluff, well away from both the lower and upper paths that led into the village. They all rolled into it now, and pulled over their heads the extra leaves and branches they'd prepared several days earlier. Within minutes they could hear the shrieks and cries of fellow villagers caught unawares. Ting-Yan tried not to envision who was getting raped, shot, or bayonetted. She was related to them all—it would be a beloved auntie, uncle, or cousin. She burrowed deeper into the leaves and twigs and stroked Macy's soft, downy head. Macy gurgled and sighed as Ting-Yan soothed her.

When Macy began to cry, Ting-Yan offered her breast.

Macy wouldn't take it. She fussed and muttered.

"Please, little one," Ting-Yan said. "Come on." She pressed her nipple toward the baby's soggy mouth.

Macy refused it. She chittered and drooled.

"You have to relax or you'll get us killed."

Macy shrieked.

"You have to relax yourself," Siu-Wai said. "She picks up on your feelings and feels the same way as you."

Ting-Yan took a deep breath. "Please, my sweet child, my most beautiful little one."

Macy coughed and grunted. She growled, then roared. She spat. She shrieked again.

Captain Lee lay on his stomach, looking up at the village path. "You've got to find a way to get her quiet," he hissed anxiously.

Ting-Yan felt his irritation and fear, and couldn't stop herself from passing it on to the baby, who wailed. Though it was disrespectful, she said, "Be quiet yourself, Ba."

She stroked the baby's head and softly hummed a few lines of that infectious tune she'd heard Emily singing on the *Oolong*, that long ago day of the double wedding. It was the song Emily's friends Tanaka Shigeru and Izzy Davis Wong had written called "Moon and Stars over Sai Kung."

High moon
Bright stars
Milky Way's a river
Flowin' to the galax-sea
Just for me and my baby
Just for my baby and me

Little Macy hummed with her, took her breast, and finally settled down.

Tak-Tam also knew of this spot. It was understood that in the event of a Japanese attack or a bandit one, they would all meet here. The family had survived the initial invasion on account of their village being so remote that the Japanese Army had not passed through. But they had heard the stories of other villages closer to the market towns of Sheung Shui, Fanling, Tai Po, and Shatin that had not been so lucky. They knew what had happened to the people in those places.

The cries coming from the village were agonizing. Ting-Yan heard the wails and shouts of both women and men. She couldn't tell whose voices they were specifically, though. The feelings those voices now carried were not the feelings of the village's daily life in the vegetable and rice fields or out on the water, and so they were all unfamiliar. She heard a man cry out and thought it could be Tak-Tam, but it could equally be her cousin Ka-Wan, or one of her mother's brothers. She wished Tak-Tam would come.

But the day wore on, and still he didn't. She soothed the baby and tried not to worry, though as the afternoon progressed, the screams and gunshots became unbearable.

Just after sunset the scent of smoke wafted through the trees. Was the village on fire?

Cooking smells drifted out to them on tendrils of smoke. The invaders weren't burning the village. They had decided to stay the night. The aroma of roasting meat made her stomach rumble, though it also likely meant that one of the village's precious pigs had been butchered. Going back to protest would only get them killed. Even moving a limb was out of the question, since the soldiers had probably posted sentries around the village. She held Macy tight and kept as still as possible.

Why didn't Tak-Tam come? As the night wore on, she began to resign herself to the likely fact of his death. She thought about that day on the boat four years ago, and the conversation about her favourite village dog. She thought about the simple pleasure of making that pot of salted fish and rice on the deck, the one they'd never gotten to eat because their cooking had been disrupted by a careening British launch boat. She thought about Tak-Tam's awkward marriage proposal the day after Tak-Wing and Emily's cricket club wedding and how rageful and mean she'd been. She still couldn't believe he'd still wanted to go through with it. She thought about the red dress she'd worn here in Chek Keng on the day of the double wedding, and the innocent, happy face Tak-Tam had put on, she knew, to mask other, more complicated feelings. He must have had misgivings about her, given how she'd treated him. Though he'd never said so.

Why didn't he come? And image of him lying dead in their ancient village home, torched by the Japanese soldiers, caused tears to come. They dripped onto the baby's quiet, round head. Macy Koon-Ying looked up at her, gurgled, then returned to suckling. Her last conversation with Tak-Tam had been about getting more firewood and whether to partake of a stash of looted furniture that Cousin Ka-Wan said came from a rich house on Argyle Street in Kowloon. The whole Sai Kung Peninsula was awash in looted goods, and it was hard to say no to them without seeming like you thought yourself better than the people who had taken them, who had risked getting shot by the Kempeitai or the lingering remnants of the Hong Kong police or rival Triads. Tak-Tam, ever principled, had said they shouldn't. Ting-Yan said they should—she was pragmatic like her mother who had lived the ups and downs of these hills all her life. They had bickered about it, and in the end Tak-Tam had given in, and they had taken the furniture, some clothes, and a large box of canned bully beef. She felt bad about it now. He had probably been right. For the sake of a few earthly goods, there was likely an unfathomable spiritual payment the family would have to make now. The Christian God wouldn't like what they'd done any more than Tin Hau would.

Why didn't he come? Ting-Yan realized how fond she'd become of Tak-Tam in their four years of marriage, and how much happier she was than Emily, who still didn't have a child, and who bore Tak-Wing's wandering eye with a stoicism no one could have foreseen. Tak-Tam on the other hand remained shy but warm. Working the fields and the boat day and night, he'd grown stronger and sturdier too. She'd married a kind person and grown to love him. She hated to admit it, but her father's judgment had been correct.

Why didn't he come? The village grew quiet as the moon rose across the water. The fragrances of food and smoke dissipated. He must be dead in the burnt-out family house, or out in the fields, or somewhere in the trees that surrounded the village. He was a good man. Why hadn't she treated him better?

From the pocket of her light summer jacket, Siu-Wai produced a tin. "I don't know what it is," she said. "I brought it down to the pier to ask one of you. But we can eat it now!"

The tin had a white label, and a picture on it of little round green balls. Ting-Yan, who could read a bit of English, sounded out the words. "*Fresh ... Garden ... Peas!*"

"What are garden peas?" said Siu-Wai.

"A kind of English vegetable," said Ting-Yan, laughing. "Not very tasty, but food is food!"

Captain Lee produced a knife. He drove it into the lid and carefully worked the can open. "Must have come from one of those English houses in Kowloon," he said. "Poor dead devils." They each had a couple of mouthfuls. The peas were hardly satisfying, but they were better than no dinner. They burrowed further down into the leaves and tried, unsuccessfully, to sleep.

Early in the morning, Ting-Yan heard the Japanese soldiers marching along the upper trail out of the village. She, her parents, and her little daughter remained in hiding until they'd heard the last footsteps echo in the distance. Then, stiff and hungry, they stood up, shook off the leaves and twigs that had covered them, and returned, trepidatiously, to the village.

It was more or less still standing, for which they were thankful. Back in the family's lane house, they found Tak-Tam, grey as a ghost, but otherwise all right. Fourteen women had been raped. Eleven men had been shot. The recent rice harvest had been taken, as well as the water buffalo and all the pigs and chickens. All the village's watches, fountain pens, and jewellery were also gone, as was all the food, furniture, and clothing that she and Tak-Tam had fought about just the day before, and all the other shares of loot from Kowloon that the villagers had divided among themselves.

They soldiers had looted and sacked, but really they had been looking for guerrillas. They had lined all the men up against the village wall and examined their hands for calluses. Tak-Tam had many, but they were as much from the work of farming as from handling guns. He had said as much to them in a few words of rudimentary Japanese picked up a hundred years ago, it seemed, in his studies. Those eleven dead cousins hadn't been so lucky.

"We'll avenge them," Tak-Tam said, his throat phlegmy with determination and grief. "And we will get back everything that's been taken."

Some of the men were going up into the hills to search abandoned British pillboxes for weapons caches. Tak-Tam said he was going to go with them. Ting-Yan wanted to go too, but Siu-Wai said she had to take care of the baby. Macy began to cry. Ting-Yan took her into the bedroom she shared with Tak-Tam to feed her, though her nipples were sore from all the feeding she'd offered through the night. Now she had no milk. She was dried out and exhausted. Macy's whimper gave way to a whine, and the whine gave way to a wail. She bawled and howled the way everyone in the house felt like doing.

When she quieted a bit, Ting-Yan could hear her parents and Tak-Tam in the main room making a plan.

"Food is more important than weapons," said Lee. "If Ting-Yan doesn't eat, Macy doesn't eat."

"Cousin Ka-Wan says there's money to be made ferrying people from Sai Kung town to Kat O and Tung Ping Chau," said Tak-Tam. "There's tons of people fleeing the city, now that it's under Japanese control. The Japanese are driving them out because they don't have the resources to keep order. And there's not enough food. He says you could even stay here in Chek Keng. The people are so desperate they would eventually find you. But there's immediate work in Sai Kung."

Macy just whimpered now. Ting-Yan went out to join them in the main room.

"You go, husband," said Siu-Wai. "Mrs Tan and two of her daughters were ... you know ... I don't need to say. I'm going to go see if I can help them. Ting-Yan, you come with me. Sum-Sum has been your friend since you were little, and she really needs you now. I know you love your father but the kind of work he has to do now is no good for a woman with a baby."

Unlike her mother, Ting-Yan loved working on the boat. She gave Captain Lee a wistful look. The prospect of adventure was infinitely more attractive than having to confront what had happened to her friend. But she knew Sum-Sum needed her, and that she had a duty.

"Never mind, daughter," Lee said. "Your old man is still a mighty pirate." He struck a pose to make her laugh.

Ting-Yan gave him a half-hearted smile. She had no laughter in her right now. They had entered into a new kind of time, the kind where anyone could die at any minute, and any time you saw someone you loved might be the last.

"I better get going," Tak-Tam said. "The Independent Brigade needs to get to those pillboxes before the Japanese do."

Ting-Yan cast him a look of dismay. If only she didn't have to look after her friend Sum-Sum and baby Macy. Then, if she couldn't help her father on the boat, she could be up in the hills looking for cached weapons in British pillboxes and making sure no harm came to Tak-Tam.

"Don't worry, Ah Yan ahh. We will all be back together soon. I'm only going for a couple of days, and if your old father's going to be a ferryman between Sai Kung and Tung Ping Chau, well, Chek Keng is a stop along the way. We will all come home soon."

"I'm not worried for me," she said. "I'm worried for you. I wish I could come."

"Another time, daughter," Siu-Wai said. "You're needed here now."

The child had finally settled. Ting-Yan stroked the downy hair on Macy's giant head. "Poor little girl," she said. "What a time you've been born into."

1942

CHAPTER 31

NOMA WANTS A PARTY

August 26, 1942

The Festival of Hungry Ghosts was more subdued than usual because of the occupation, but there were still some families on the street burning spirit money for their ancestors and for the ghosts who wandered. The scent of smoke and joss swirled through the city. Hong Kong had been occupied for eight months and a day. Emily Mah Wai-Yee had been pregnant for exactly that long, and her belly was out to here. Her father-in-law, Old Steward Cheung, tended the bar at the Hong Kong Cricket Club because that was what he'd been asked to do by Colonel Noma, head of the Kempeitai, housed in the daytime with his men in the Supreme Court Building, which was located behind the clubhouse, on the other side of Jackson Road. Noma's men were thirsty at the end of a long day, and the colonel had taken a shine to the old steward. It was Cheung's red face, brimming with its peculiarly pan-Asian sorrow, that Noma wanted to see at the end of each workday. Noma liked Cheung so much that he'd assigned the translator Tanaka Shigeru to stay with him all day, every day, so that he'd be there if Cheung ever needed translation services.

Noma's English was actually pretty good, but he didn't like to let on because he thought these blasted colonials should speak Japanese. He didn't really need Tanaka's services, but the other Japanese officers and interrogators did. Of course, there were lots of other interpreters in the Supreme Court during the day, and some of them came to the cricket club at night to drink. But still, it was good to have Tanaka on hand. While

Cheung polished glasses, Tanaka sat at the end of the bar sipping beer. Beside him, Morgan Horace, sole proprietor of Screech Owl Fine Liquors and ambivalent pan-Africanist, sipped a rum and Coke.

It wasn't as hot at the end of August as it had been at the end of July, but it was still hot. Though he had every fan in the bar going, Cheung sweated profusely. This bar, with its dark wood tables and its red velvet chairs would have been cozy and pleasant in old England. In humid Hong Kong, it was a strange hothouse where no one who used it could feel quite at home, not even Cheung, who had worked here for most of his adult life. Wiser colonials would have decorated with white paint and rattan. Whoever had built this place must have been terribly homesick. Cheung was a stout, strong man, but he couldn't take the heat. Tanaka sweated too. Volunteered in English, "Christ, it's hot." And swore in Cantonese. "Diu!"

When Cheung saw Noma enter the room, he mopped his brow discreetly one last time with a yellowed handkerchief.

The colonel plunked his skinny ass down at the bar. In spite of the heat, he looked cool. "Syllabub," he said.

Cheung moved to the bar and measured out a half a shot of rum. The portrait of Emperor Hirohito gazed sternly down at him, looking regal and Asian in King George's former place. If either the colonel or Horace ordered another rum-based drink, the last of the rum would be gone. Cheung glanced involuntarily in the direction of the Supreme Court, then pushed from his mind the thought of death by beheading. He poured the rum into a metal bowl and measured half a shot of Madeira. Added sugar, lemon juice, and an ounce and a half of heavy cream. He took out a whisk and began to beat the drink into a froth. Noma talked to his back.

"All over the city many families are expecting first-born sons next month! What a lucky occasion! But my good servant Cheung, of all these children of a new and prosperous Asia, your grandson is the one I want to honour! What say we have a cricket match and a garden party a month today? All this war is getting to me. Let's have a real celebration!"

Cheung could hardly hear him for the regular beat of the whisk against the sides of the bowl. How had all of his hard work and good fortune come to this? He whisked, tuning the colonel out. He wished he could whisk away the whole war, but the weapon was so insubstantial. He whisked and whisked. The drink would solidify if he whisked it any more. He poured it. Grated a little nutmeg over top. Turned and placed it in front of the man who held the absolute power of life and death over him. "I'm not following you, sir."

Noma's eyes gleamed bright. "Isn't your son about to have a son?"

"My daughter-in-law is giving birth, sir, yes."

"What's her name?"

"Emily Cheung Wai-Yee."

"What will you call your grandson?"

"I'm not sure yet. I don't know for sure it will be a boy."

"But if it is?"

"I was thinking Raymond Duk-Ming, sir."

Noma turned the glass to admire its frothy beauty.

"I think you should give the kid a Japanese name."

"Sir?"

He turned the glass again and jostled it a little to see how stable the bubbles were. "My name for instance."

"The honour would be too great."

Finally, he took a sip. "Delicious. A bit less sugar next time, maybe." He took another. "Do you know what my personal name is?"

"No, sir."

"Kennosuke. I'm Noma Kennosuke. Your grandson could be Cheung Kennosuke. A fine pan-Asian name!"

"I wouldn't presume to give my humble grandson your illustrious personal name," said Cheung. He was taken aback and frightened by the colonel's familiarity with him. To say nothing of this bizarre proposal.

"Are you sure your grandson is yours?"

Cheung was not. Not at all. But he couldn't afford to say so. "I am, sir." He spoke as firmly as he could.

"There are stupid Chinese men all over this blasted ex-colony who are as sure as you are that their grandsons are their own," said Noma. "Nine months after the liberation. Do you know what my men did the day we set you free? And in the weeks after?"

Cheung knew. With glassy eyes, he stared at the colonel.

"You say you're sure because you've been so colonized by those toffy white-skinned devils you've lost your ability to speak the truth. Do you know what my men do in the Supreme Court of Justice to liars like you?"

Cheung knew perfectly well. But with the wisdom of the doubly colonized, he shook his head.

"Lying again?"

"Please, sir."

"For the love of Kannon, don't beg!"

Cheung gulped. Discreetly wiped his brow with the handkerchief that was beginning to smell. He'd heard the screams coming from the basement of the Supreme Court Building these last nine months. He'd seen buckets of clear water being carried in. He'd seen buckets of flesh being carried out. He knew he was being threatened. To say what he really thought could place him in that basement within the hour.

Noma's thin lips spread over his large mouth. "Come on now, my little Asian brother," he said, though Cheung was clearly a decade older than him, if not more. "Why do you look so frightened? Do you think I would harm my dearest little brother, the best friend I have on this cursed island of white-man-loving sheep?"

"Of course not," breathed Cheung, mustering the greatest cheer he could draw up from his queasy stomach.

"We'll have a timeless Test match! However many days it takes! With lunch on the lawn! And tea! And cocktail hour! Won't that be grand?"

"But who will be the players?" Cheung hadn't seen any of his former masters since February when the last of them had been interned at Stanley or Sham Shui Po depending on whether they were civilian or military.

"We haven't locked up all of those barmy bastards, you know," said Noma. "There are a few at large. Medical men to take care of the sick. Bankers to liquidate the banks. A baker. They can all be one team. They are all staying at the Sun Wah Hotel, living among the prostitutes like the pimps they really are. We'll put my officers on the other. Give them a break from the hard work of interrogation. What say?"

Cheung tried not to grimace. The old, snobby masters versus the new, murderous ones. Then he registered: timeless Test match. Never before had a timeless Test match been held at the Hong Kong Cricket Club. They were International Cricket Conference certified. That meant they played Twenty20 International. Test cricket was only for professionals, which meant only teams from England, Australia, New Zealand, South Africa, India, and the West Indies. Timeless Test cricket ... Cheung racked his brain for the rules. The old club president, Richard Hancock, had explained them to him a lifetime ago. A timeless Test meant four overs, but no time limit. The timeless Test matches he'd heard of had gone on for days. Theoretically they could go on for years, decades, centuries. If only this cricket match could go on forever and so put a stop to this mother-cursed war. At the very least, it would be a pause in the murder of civilians all over this ruined city. A blessed respite.

"Come on now. I'll give you the honour of deciding who to put on the British team and who to put on the Japanese one."

There had to be a catch. The first-floor bar at the Hong Kong Cricket Club had become a hangout for third nationals with nowhere else to go— Portuguese, Eurasians, Irish, White Russians, and anyone else unlucky enough to find themselves still in Hong Kong for whatever reason, whether because they habitually conducted business here, lived here permanently, were escaping China, or were heading into it. Until now, they had been oddly safe in the first-floor bar, right next door to the Kempeitai's major interrogation site for British nationals and their Chinese collaborators.

Within Noma's simple request, Cheung detected a demand to rat out the sympathies of the nominally neutral. So he was silent for a long moment, contemplating his options. Then he said, "I'd rather not, sir. If it's all the same to you."

"He voices an opinion!" shouted Noma, mock triumphant. "Did you hear that, Horace?"

Horace took a sip of his rum and Coke and nodded, but didn't say anything. He had come to Hong Kong looking for his cousin Isadore Davis Wong, and his boyhood pen pal, Noma Kennosuke, from whom he hadn't heard for over a decade. They had corresponded for a few years when they were teenagers, since around the time of the Conference of Asian Peoples in Nagasaki in 1926, which the precocious fifteen-year-old Horace had read about in Kingston, Jamaica's *Daily Gleaner*, leading him to seek out a pen pal in Japan.

High on the ideas of Brother Du Bois, he had come wanting to witness triumphant Japan taking Asia back from the white oppressor, hoping that a strong Asia might show the coloured peoples of the world a way out of the scourge of European imperialism. He still dreamt such a dream, but as the horrors of the occupation unfolded, his fascination with the Japanese project was waning. He had seen the ditches and hillsides spilling with desperate refugees. He'd seen the ways Japanese soldiers and military police abused and killed them without compunction. He was shocked and dismayed by the way Japanese soldiers stopped people in the street just to take their fountain pens and watches, how they beat people for sport, and how they knocked on people's doors at night to demand the sexual use of their wives and daughters. The Japanese empire had twisted the anti-colonial dream to the edge of recognizability. This wasn't a bit of benign, close-knit imperialism. It was something quite else that he didn't feel ready to name, but didn't want to get behind either. It was certainly nothing like what he wanted for his own people, or for his beloved cousin. He felt as though his heart were drying out, and growing brittle as a wedge of hardtack. He'd made a mistake in coming, but he was here now. And he couldn't express his doubts to anybody because to do so could cost him his life. He watched his erstwhile pen pal torment the barman.

"He'd rather not, Horace," Noma said. "Is his preference sensible, do you think?"

"He should have the right to do what he wants. If you really believe in pan-Asianism, like we used to talk about ..."

But Noma wasn't listening, he was staring at Cheung—a cold hard stare. He waited for the old steward to squirm.

To Cheung's credit, he made Noma wait a long time.

But Noma had the power. He stared.

Cheung squirmed.

"Do you want me to tell you my favourite way of getting a Chinaman to talk?" said Noma.

Involuntarily, Cheung caught Noma's direct gaze with his own. Held it for just a fraction of a second, but that was already too long. He looked at the ground.

"So," said the colonel, "you'll do as I say." After a long pause he added, "And there will be syllabub. Lots of it. I don't know why those barmy bastards love their gin and tonics so much."

He finished his drink in silence. Horace asked for another rum and Coke. Tanaka pointed to his empty beer glass. Cheung fetched their drinks. Threw the empty rum bottle into the bin. He wiped down the counter and tried not to catch anybody's gaze.

When the colonel left for his residence in the Mid-Levels, Tanaka spoke to Cheung in affectionate language, calling him "Big Brother." "You'll put me on the Japanese team, please, Ah Cheung Goh. And Horace too. We don't want him to get sent to Stanley." He glanced in the direction of the Supreme Court. "Or worse."

Cheung nodded. Anyone whom he put on the British team could be doomed to death by water torture or beaten lifeless with a lead pipe. He began to polish glasses.

Those two had been sitting at the end of the bar every night since Christmas 1941, when it had first become acceptable, thanks to Noma, for non-whites to sit at the end of the bar in a white man's club. Though he knew Tanaka as Tak-Wing and Emily's friend, it was hard right now for Cheung to know how much he could trust him. He trusted Tanaka's heart, but the man's political interests were now different from his own. He didn't know what Tanaka might do when the going got rough. Perhaps Tanaka himself didn't know. Better to just keep quiet. Play it safe and bide his time.

"Your labour is like one of Psyche's," Horace said. "In order to be reunited with her true love, she has to do a superhuman task—separate a bushel of mixed grains into individual types before the night is out. You have to separate Japanese from British. But there are no Japanese or British in your bushel, unless you count Tanaka here, who is as Chinese and British as he is Japanese. And of course, Noma will kill you if you do it wrong! It's a task that no human can possibly do. Only the superhuman are worthy of love. And life. Ha ha, what a laugh!" He rumbled out a soft baritone chuckle. Then caught himself. "Oh, I'm sorry, Cheung. It's not funny at all. But please put me on the Japanese team, Brother."

Cheung arched an eyebrow ever so slightly, but didn't look up from his work.

"I saw you empty that bottle of rum," Horace said. Do you have any more?"

What is this Japan-loving coloured man getting at? Cheung wondered. Did he really believe the slogan "Asia for Asians" would be of any use to oppressed Negroes in America? Or was he spying for Noma out of some unknown self-interest and trying to get rid of Cheung? Did he want to tend the bar in Cheung's place? Cheung decided he'd better not reveal anything.

"I'm pretty sure I do," he said. "You want another rum and Coke?"

In the cupboard, Cheung had an old rum bottle he'd filled with gin. He'd mixed the gin with a few drops of Angostura bitters to give it a pale golden colour. This was the ammunition he'd prepared against Noma's next syllabub order, but he could use it on Horace if he needed to. Horace looked like a man who would be able to tell the difference, but Cheung had already thought of an excuse for the foul taste. He'd blame the Bacardi supplier, who was already imprisoned at Stanley. They were unlikely to fetch him and kill him for the sake of a bad bottle of rum. *If they do, well, too bad for him and bully for me. I'll live to mix another crummy drink.*

"Nah, I'm good," Horace said. "But if you need more, I've got a supply I'd be happy to part with for a fair price."

"You have a supply? Of rum?"

"I do indeed. That's my gig!" said Horace, laughing. "I'd sure be happy to have a little business in these lean times."

If he wasn't bluffing, this was a godsend. "I'd be very happy to buy from you," said Cheung.

"It ain't Bacardi, mind," said Horace. "But I think it's better!"

From his bag under the counter, Horace pulled out a full bottle of glossy liquid the colour of sunshine. There was a red and orange label on it that read *Screech Owl.*

Cheung hoped his eyes didn't betray his desperation. "I've never heard of that brand."

"It's a Newfoundland and Jamaica company. We were just getting a footing in the industry when the war broke out. You wanna try?"

Cheung nodded. "I do." He put a shot glass up on the counter.

Horace cracked the cap and filled the glass.

"Enough, enough!" said Cheung. "Just a taste."

Horace kept filling until the luscious golden liquid spilled over the lip of the glass and onto the counter.

"Don't waste it!" said Cheung. He lifted it and examined the warm light that poured through the precious water. He took a small sip. Closed his eyes. Ambrosial salvation.

"I'll put you on the Japanese team," he told Horace.

Tanaka, quiet until now, looked up at Cheung. He was afraid of Noma too.

"Brother Tanaka, I won't forget you either," Cheung said.

Horace pulled an envelope out of his pocket then. "Have you ever seen writing like this?" He took a letter out of the envelope, but it was written in a strange code consisting of *P*s, *U*s, *Q*s, and *V*s in a variety of orientations to the page.

Cheung shook his head.

"Ever heard of a guy called 'Ga-chan'? Or something close?"

"I'm sorry," said Cheung.

"Please tell me if you ever do," said Horace. "The kid who brought me these said 'Ga-Chan,' or something like that. It was hard to make out."

Cheung nodded.

"And thanks for putting me on the Japanese team."

Cheung quipped an English expression he remembered from before the occupation: "All in a good day's work."

CHAPTER 32

BURN THIS LETTER

Undisclosed Location
New Territories

August 28, 1942

Dear Morgan,

I haven't heard from you in all these months. I'm so worried. Did you get the letter I sent you last Christmas? I sure hope so, and I hope you're not lying dead in a ditch somewhere. I hope you haven't been rounded up by the Kempeitai. I cannot repeat the stories of what they do to people in their prisons. Maybe my letter just got lost. I know the messenger would have had the good sense to destroy it if he got caught in a tight spot.

It broke my heart to leave without you, as I wrote before. As you know, I have Jane and the kids to think about. Better for you and better for me if you don't know where I am.

Since those early days of the occupation, things have calmed down a little. How safe the situation is for a guy like you, I can't say. It can't possibly be that you still think Brother Du Bois's ideas could still play out in the real world, can it? He is a smart man surrounded by propagandists. Surely you know that now? I bet you he's changed his mind himself, or he would if he could see how things are here.

The Japanese governor is encouraging everyone who can to leave. You must be feeling the food shortages. Me and my cousins up here, we been helping a lot of people escape to Free China. Lots of refugees. Maybe a couple of escapees from the concentration camps too, who's to say? Why don't you come up and put your oar in here. Or if you wanted to go to Free China yourself, we could help you.

Jane and the kids miss you, as do I. Please send me word by the messenger who gave this to you. Even if it's just a scrawl. I'd really like to know what you intend to do.

Though you'll receive it encoded, I know you'll have the good sense to burn this letter once you've read it.

Love from your cousin,

Izzy

CHAPTER 33

VERY PREGNANT
August 30, 1942

Emily was all belly, and sweating in the muggy August heat. I felt positive that the pregnancy was a result of the rape at St Stephen's last Christmas, although she insisted it wasn't. "I was pregnant before that, Vi," she said again. "It's Tak-Wing's kid. Why won't you believe me?"

"How could it possibly be, Sis? The timing is perfect for it to have been St Stephen's." We sat at the wooden dining table that had been with the Cheung family since they left Wong Nai Chung Village decades ago. Because Colville had left his old table in the steward's flat for Cheung to use, Cheung had given this one to Emily and Tak-Wing to return to its old position under the bare, yellow light bulb which surely must have been changed from time to time, though it seemed to me that it had been hanging there for a hundred years.

"Please don't speak as though I was visited by a holy person." Her body weighed heavily on the ancient kitchen chair. She leaned back, trying to get comfortable. The chair creaked.

"I'm sorry ... I ..." I struggled for language. I wanted to help her, but I didn't have a clue what to say.

"Christ, Violet," she said. "I don't how to talk about it either. But it wasn't Saint Stephen, or good King Wenceslas either, I promise you that." She tried to get up. "Do you want some tea?"

"I'll get it." Someone had made tea that morning. It was cold now, but still drinkable. I poured us each a cup. "I just don't see how you can be so sure."

"I was attacked by only one of them. That vicious one that murders people in the Supreme Court."

"Just one?"

"Isn't one enough?"

"That came out wrong. I didn't mean ..." I took a sip of the tea. It was unpleasantly bitter.

"Never mind. I know what you mean."

"I wish I could have protected you."

"Sometimes I feel guilty. Most of the nurses there were raped by at least a dozen, and several were murdered." She shifted again on the flimsy chair, but could not get comfortable. Her face was flushed and hot.

"Guilty? You shouldn't feel guilty."

"He took me into a separate room. And left me there afterwards. I hid beneath a big oak desk until the rampage was over."

"It would be tempting fate to call that luck."

"It was a roll of the dice. But the baby is Tak-Wing's. I just know it is. He's kicking. Want to feel?"

I came around the table and put my hand on her stomach. "He's moving!"

She smiled weakly. "A new life, Violet. It must count for something good."

Up close, I noticed the bruise on her throat, which began with a thumbprint midneck and snaked like a river down beneath her blouse. She didn't have to tell me it extended to her breasts and farther down. Though I had never seen him hit her, the way the bruises moved over her face, hands, and neck, like different clouds on different days, made it obvious. I never heard him speak of it, but he must have had his suspicions about what had happened at St Stephen's on that terrible Christmas Day, and he must have blamed her for it. This was the only explanation for the vast shift in his attitude toward her.

"You have to get out of here before you miscarry." I knew that beatings could cause such things, and Emily had clearly endured many.

"Where would I go?" she said.

"Just come home. Come back to the Stable."

"What would Father say? I married Tak-Wing three times, ViVi. Three times. And I've consorted with the enemy. I can't come home. It's too humiliating."

"Father is a kind man. Under the circumstances, he would forgive you." While she'd deliberately orchestrated her marriage to Tak-Wing, what had happened at St Stephen's could hardly be construed as her fault, if the men thought to make a distinction. But of course, they couldn't handle it, so they didn't think. They knew, but they pretended not to know, and in their pretense, they forgot, or they relegated the knowledge to some other part of their being, a part that generated shame without language. Their unknowing knowledge was a machine that poured shame over all the women of the city like a coating of glue that wouldn't wash off.

"I don't think he would. Maybe he would pretend to, but in his heart, he wouldn't. How can I come back? I married Father's mortal enemy and got pregnant, either by that enemy or by an enemy of our people."

"He did send Second Mother Polly."

"Who gave us pork buns, but didn't say a word about what happened. If I had any sense, I'd ask you to help me get rid of it. But I can't do that either. It's still my child. And beyond that, it's a life amid so much death."

"Are you saying it is the soldier's?"

"No. Definitely not. It's Tak-Wing's."

"It's too late for an abortion anyway," I said. "At this late stage it could kill you."

"I'm tired, Vi," she said. "So tired. Will you help me to bed?" I led her to the backroom of the Tai Hang house, the bed she shared with the man who beat her. I wished with all my heart that she did not need to lie down there, but she had nowhere else to lie.

"Hold my hand, ViVi," she said. "And tell me a story until I fall asleep."

I started telling her a story about when our mother was alive and we went to Tiger Balm Gardens and had our photo taken in front of the tall pagoda. Our mother wore a bright yellow cheung sam with orange fish on it, and Emily had on a child's version in the same fabric. She'd loved that dress, had worn it until she hit a growth spurt and popped the seams. I'd never liked to wear dresses. But I'd worn an outfit that I was fond of that day as well, a sailor suit with shorts that I had whined and pleaded with my mother to make. As we walked through the gardens, all the statues of gods and goddesses and the magic birds and fish seemed to admire us and speak to us. We met the Tiger Balm prince Aw Boon Haw himself, just in the process of setting up an orphanage for children less fortunate than us. We didn't know then that Mother would die of TB, or that Father, on his way to jail for the poisoning of Grandfather Cheung, would consider sending us to Aw Boon Haw's orphanage. We only escaped that fate because Dream Horse White, the anti-opium pills he invented after marrying Second Mother Polly, made Father a fortune, which allowed him to keep the Stable, as well as the services of Amah, Driver Lim, and Auntie Lim. My story devolved into a contemplation of the range of possible fates Emily and I could have lived out. If Mother had not died, if Old Cheung's father had not died from the Immortal Carp pills, if British forensics had not traced his death back to our product, if the Immortal Carp pills did actually bestow immortality, if the Japanese had invaded Singapore but not Hong Kong, if Chiang Kai-Shek had sided with the Japanese instead of the Communists as he'd originally planned, if the KMT-Communist alliance were able to drive the Japanese out, if the Japanese were actually as benevolent as they'd pretended to be before the war, if there were no war in Asia, if the British had lost the Opium War in the nineteenth century, if Mongols had never invaded in the thirteenth century, if the Song had never fallen to them, or even better, if the Tang had never fallen in the tenth century. My mind reeled with the possibilities of the present we might have inhabited, and with the future that might have come. But then, if anyone had inherited the beauty of the Tang and carried it into the present, it was the Japanese who occupied us now. Though we were most certainly not experiencing anything of Tang beauty. Thankfully, Emily was asleep by the time I began to speak of such things.

When I came out to the front step, Tak-Wing was there, back from the cricket club where he'd been helping his father cook for the Kempeitai. They were using the HKCC as their own recreation club now. He was sitting on a stool smoking a cigarette.

I gave him the evil eye and would have left without saying a word to him, but he called out to me. "Vi."

"What do you want from me, Ah Wing?"

"Can't you take her home?" His eyes, which usually blazed with rage these days, were sad and forlorn.

"This is her home."

"It's my home," he said. "I grew up here."

"It's Emily's home. If our father had not given it back, you would be living on the street. You should go to the street, where you belong." Old Mah had indeed kept his word after the Chinese wedding and given the house to them, though with only Emily's name on the deed.

"I don't love her anymore," he said. "I want to, but I can't."

"You have a responsibility to love her."

"You think I don't know that?" he said. "But hate does not know responsibility."

"Well," I said, "hate will have to learn. You married her three times, Ah Wing. Where did that sweet boy who married my poor innocent sister three times go?"

"That boy is long gone," said Tak-Wing. "He died when his beautiful wife was soiled by that Japanese soldier. Please, Violet. I'm afraid of who that boy has become." I caught a glimpse then of the Tak-Wing

I knew before the invasion, the one who had given me his umbrella to jab at Queen Victoria's feet, the one who had taken us for baked Alaska at Jimmy's Kitchen, the one who had celebrated his registry marriage to Emily with bamboo-wrapped sticky rice and a bottle of Awakening Lion aerated lemonade on the steps of the abandoned Peak Hotel.

"Did she tell you what happened?" I asked.

"She told me enough."

"You have a responsibility," I repeated. "To love her and care for her and have a big Chinese family with her, for the sake of your father and mine."

Later, at home on my own, I wondered if that had been the right thing to say. Though, in our family, the brunt of the Japanese Imperial Army's hatred for us Hong Kong Chinese had fallen on Emily, we had all been soiled by the Japanese soldiers. I remembered something else I'd heard shouted in English as I hid in that supply closet. "We'll stop raping Chinese women when Hong Kong stops supporting the British and joins the Asian brotherhood. Who is so stupid as to use their women to protect their colonizer?" I had never loved the British, but I didn't hate them either. They had never used us as this infernal Japanese army was using us. It was hard to understand what to want, politically, and I had the benefit of my HKU education. No wonder Tak-Wing, once so beloved and so sweet, was confused. But it was impossible to think of him now as sweet. It was impossible to love him. Humiliation had descended upon him through the body of his wife, and he had become a monster, while Emily and other Hong Kong Chinese women like her were forced to absorb without acknowledgment or recompense Japanese disdain, British indifference-turned-helplessness, and the Confucian despair and self-loathing of Hong Kong Chinese men like Tak-Wing. Maybe I should try to drag Emily back here to Old Mah's house before it really was too late.

The next day, I went back to the Tai Hang house to get Emily. Despite her black eye and her pregnant belly, she still wanted to go to St Paul's, the

French hospital, to help Dr Selwyn-Clarke. The car had been confiscated by the Japanese and sent to Japan to support their war effort, and Driver and Auntie Lim had fled in the first days of the occupation, so I went to the house on foot, and we took a streetcar from there.

Dr Selwyn-Clarke, chief medical officer of Hong Kong, had been permitted by Colonel Eguchi to keep running medical services for the city. Eguchi was a civilian administrator, not military police like Noma. He had known Selwyn-Clarke before the war and respected him. He knew, too, that if no one took responsibility for public health, Japanese soldiers and civilians would die of diphtheria and dysentery along with the general population.

Selwyn-Clarke had convinced the new governor replacing Sakai, Governor Rensuke Isogai, not to put him in the civilian internment camp at Stanley for humanitarian reasons. True to his word, Selwyn-Clarke had avoided the underground resistance work of the partisan British Army Aid Group. Working with the compassionate Christian interpreter Kiyoshi "Uncle John" Watanabe, he'd smuggled anti-diphtheria serum into the POW camp at Sham Shui Po and brought it to the civilian POW camp at Stanley, along with food, bandages, vitamins, and medical instruments. He'd helped Isogai control the cholera outbreak in the city, so Isogai had grudgingly let him operate and turned a blind eye to the less legal parts of his operation.

Emily and I had both been working with him since February under the supervision my old friend, Dr Lai Po-Chuen, who had graduated a year ahead of me. We helped Selwyn-Clarke gather medicines from stashes hidden before the invasion, as well drugs provided by friendly Chinese chemists, and distributed the aid to patients throughout the city. The brave among our humanitarian group, including William Courchene, took them even to the gates of the internment camps at Stanley and Sham Shui Po and placed them in the hands of interned doctors and nurses to administer to the gaunt and ragged prisoners. Sometimes, too, we helped the refugees from mainland China who lived in the ditches and in squatter villages on the hillsides and were slowly dying of starvation, dysentery, cholera, and abuse. Their lives were wretched beyond my powers of description. I saw an old woman on the street once, tormented by Japanese soldiers. In front of her, they burned the meagre bundle of sticks she'd spent the whole day gathering. She berated them for it, and they beat her to death.

More than medicine, the people needed food. We did what we could. I tried to see the people beyond their numbers and their suffering, but my heart was not big enough. I moved through the streets and did my work. I would come back home, try to eat supper, and then vomit the few bites I'd been able to choke down. Kathy Duffy, also working for Selwyn-Clarke, told me I had to separate my feelings from my work or I would go mad, like Edward Kerrison, the health officer charged with disposing of all the bodies of the dead.

Emily, though she had no medical training, had proven an able nurse, even after her attack at St Stephen's. Now, though, her pregnancy was so advanced that she couldn't do much, and Selwyn-Clarke had told her numerous times to stay home.

"What would I do there, Doc?" she said, smiling past the lipstick she applied daily to keep her spirits up. "I'd be bored silly."

I was sure Selwyn-Clarke had noticed the shifting cloud pattern of her bruises and knew what they signified, because he didn't press her. He gave her ledgers to work on so she wouldn't have to stand or move around.

Tonight, Emily wanted to sleep on the cot at medical HQ. "I'm so tired, I can't walk back," she told Lai Po-Chuen.

The young woman doctor gave me a helpless look.

I shrugged. "It's safe enough here. I'll stay with her. Old Mah is getting on my nerves anyway." Himself distraught, he had begun sleeping at the Stable in my dead mother's bed again. It seemed to comfort him. He talked to me too, more than he ever had in his entire life up 'til now. So, while Emily suffered from too much hate, I suffered from too much love, in a strange reversal of how things had been before the war. "There is no need for you to risk your life in the way you do, Violet. I didn't work so hard for you to suffer in ditches and doorways with those dirty coolies!" he would say. And Amah would back him up. "Listen to your father, ViVi! You can play doctor when peace comes again! Why risk your life when there is no need?" War surely turns the order of things upside down.

Courchene, the soldier I had pulled from the horror at St Stephen's, said he would stay and protect us. With his black hair and high cheekbones, he'd been passing as Eurasian these past several months, and continued to move through the city in civilian garb, making secret medical deliveries to his fellow Winnipeg Grenadiers interned at Sham Shui Po. He always knew exactly what was needed, and he never forgot a thing. I could see from the start that he was sweet on Emily, and remained so even as her pregnancy became obvious.

Dr Lai rolled her eyes. She could see it too. She also knew that I was a better shot than Courchene, because she'd seen us practising. If there was any protecting to be done, I would be the one doing it. Not that either Courchene or I stood much of a chance in the face of the Kempeitai's numbers and organized ruthlessness. "Please yourself," she said. "You know where to hide if the gendarmes show up." We had built several hiding places: one under floorboards in the clinic, and one through the false back of an armoire, which led to a hiding place behind the wall. These would serve us far better than Courchene's bravado or my shooting skill. "Violet, you have to pick up potassium permanganate at Chemist Chang's in the morning, so don't stay up too late."

It was good that we stayed, because toward midnight, who should appear at the gates but Emily's brother- and sister-in-law, Tak-Tam and Ting-Yan. The sentry alerted us and we let them in. We took them into the staff kitchen.

"Is there a guy called Courchene with you?"

I went to his room to get him.

"This is for you," Tak-Tam said. He handed Courchene an envelope, the kind messengers used. Courchene took it, looked at us nervously.

"Should we leave?" I said.

"It's okay," he said. "It's okay. I trust you." He cut the envelope open with a dinner knife.

The paper was covered in tiny writing, but it wasn't any language I recognized. There were little triangles, some upside down, some right side up, some on their sides. Little *V*s, *U*s, *P*s, *Q*s, *J*s, *L*s, and *Z*s—at least that was what they looked like to me—ran along the page, also in various orientations. Some kind of code? After the war Emily told me that Courchene was trained as a Cree code talker, but he'd missed the call-up to go to the Western Front. She couldn't explain that little note, though, or others like it that we found later among the things he'd left behind.

"The Kempeitai are going to raid the clinic," said Courchene. "They are after Selwyn-Clarke, but they know you associate with him. If they catch you, you could suffer the same fate as him." We didn't know at the time what his fate was. We hadn't seen him since that afternoon. If the Kempeitai were looking for him, he might already be dead. Or he could be held at the Supreme Court, suffering indignities we didn't want to envision, yet couldn't stop guessing at.

"Why don't you come to Chek Keng, where you'll be safe," Ting-Yan said. "Emily, you can have your baby there."

"I don't want to get involved with the East River Column," she said. We knew that Tak-Tam and Ting-Yan were members of the communist guerrilla group based in the Sai Kung hills because Cheung had whispered the news to us. It had once been called the Hong Kong and Kowloon Independent Brigade, but in recent days it had been verified by Communist leadership in China as part of its army. "And I don't want Violet involved. I have a baby coming. I need to stay neutral."

"We came all this way to rescue you," said Tak-Tam. "The raid could happen anytime."

"You shouldn't have risked your lives," said Emily.

"We've become good at safe passage," said Ting-Yan. Her face was brown from the sun and her eyes were bright. "But the Japanese are getting wiser to us every day. This is your chance. You should take it."

"If Selwyn-Clarke is taken, the medical people will need us more than ever," Courchene said.

"Do you want some supper?" I asked everyone.

We made a pot of rice and shared a can of chicken curry. Tak-Tam and Ting-Yan continued to cajole us. I began to feel convinced, and if the other two had agreed, I would have gone, but Emily and Courchene stood firm. "Selwyn-Clarke needs us. We can't afford to be partisan."

We invited them to stay the night in the clinic, but they wanted to leave right away so that they could travel while it was still dark. After they'd gone, I lay on my cot and wondered how things might be different if Ting-Yan had married Tak-Wing instead of Tak-Tam. Whether Tak-Wing would have beaten her as he beats Emily. Not that I wished such a thing on that beautiful, sensible woman. It was more that I wondered whether she was the kind of person Tak-Wing would feel he could hit. What a stupid thing to think about. I went to sleep.

CHAPTER 34

GET OUT WHILE YOU CAN

Undisclosed Location
New Territories

September 2, 1942

Dear Morgan,

Well cousin, I don't know if you got my last letter or not, though I'm sending this to you through the same network of messengers, whom I trust. My contact says you received it. I have half a mind to come back to Hong Kong Island myself to get you. It's a bit dangerous for me to do so, but it would be worth it if I could get you out of there. I still haven't heard from you, though you could easily have given the messenger who brought my letter a missive of your own in return. Why didn't you? It can't possibly be that you think what the Japanese are doing is good and right? Not still?

It is possible to get out. The Japanese administration is encouraging it. You might need to swim a bit, and you'll for sure have to climb a couple of hills. But didn't we used to ramble through the Blue Mountains all the time at home? Remember our trip to Nanny Falls and how we met that Maroon couple up there? We sat on that rock talking to them for hours. That was really something, man, to meet those folks. Well, the people I've met up here aren't exactly Maroons, but I've assisted in the movements of hundreds of refugees and escapees. Hundreds, cousin, do you understand me? I know you're a brave man, and the travel is easier than you think, especially for a young fella like you with no injuries and no encumbrances.

Not that things don't happen, of course. Things happen.

In the meantime, it gets more dangerous for you every day you stay down there. And even if it weren't dangerous, surely you must be getting very hungry. Stop dreaming, please, my cuz. I'm only saying this because I love you and want you to live.

Please burn this letter after you read it, for obvious reasons. And for God's sake, give the messenger something for me in return, even if it's just a few scribbled words. I miss you, and I'm worried.

Love as always from your cousin,

Izzy

CHAPTER 35

SCAR

September 5, 1942

Courchene's scar had healed without infection, a testament to Violet's impeccable surgery skills. She removed the sutures for him one night in the surgery at St Paul's. She should have done it months ago, but with all that had been going on, normal follow-up procedures had fallen by the wayside. The scar ran the length of his belly diagonally, a long mouth cut for him by a man in a different uniform, eyes blazing rage at what the century had offered him, a man who looked but didn't act like a brother. It was a miracle his gut wasn't punctured. The slash followed its outer contours identically, an exquisite brushstroke the length of half an intestinal convolution. He ran his fingers along the ridge that was left after the stitches were gone. It was bumpy and coarse. Though the pain was no longer stabbing, it ached in a cold, bony sort of way. His was the last surgery that Violet had done before fleeing the horror of St Stephen's. He watched her now at the sink, a seamstress of human flesh. She carefully washed her tools, her face folded in determination and sorrow. Her unkempt black hair was already tinged with white. Had she sewn her own grief into his belly, to join all the sad spirits already swimming there? Mother Mary knew that he had enough of his own grief without taking on hers. Or Emily's, for that matter, though Emily's was clearer, less amorphous, sharper, and more vivid in its lines. Courchene had had plenty enough of his own grief before he even came to this steaming jungle, packed wall to wall with starving cousins hell-bent on destroying each other. He'd come trying to escape his own frustration and rage. He had no desire to take on someone else's. He really did not want to stuff it into his belly.

He'd come fleeing his father, who'd made him go trapping when he wanted to read, and his mother, a midwife who, like Violet, had poured her lifeblood into fixing a community beside itself with loss for a hundred years, ever since the white men came with their Christianity, their laws, their cattle, and their trains. He'd come fleeing the school at Beauval in faraway northern Saskatchewan, the twisted priests and their wandering hands, the other boys, devastated and violent, the mouths that opened inside all of them hungering for a clean return of what had been taken, though the law and the priests transmuted what they took as fast as they could so they would never have to give it back. He'd been given a place at the school as though it were a gift, because they had places to take on a few Métis boys after those provided for by the Indian Act were already placed. They said "gift," they said "charity," and then took you far far from home, from the rich urban community of Saint-Boniface to this tiny rural place where you didn't know anyone, and stuffed your mouth with things you didn't want to swallow and then held your nose until you did. He'd joined the army to flee those memories. The last thing he needed was another mouth.

"That's a nasty scar," said Violet. "It's turned keloid. You have to massage the lumpy bits, and help them smooth out." She tried to show him, but his fists were up in her face before he even knew what he was doing. She gasped.

"I'm sorry," he whispered.

"I didn't mean—"

"It's okay."

"I'm sorry," she said.

"I said it's okay."

"None of us is okay," she said. She gave him a drink of water, put her instruments in the autoclave, and went off to do her rounds.

Courchene wished he'd gone to Europe to fight fascist white men instead of fascist Asians. At least then the enemy would look like the enemy. Though there were people in his family who looked white but were not the enemy, people whom he loved. But still, he would have preferred it. He had enlisted early and begun to train as a code talker. If he'd completed training, he'd have been out on the Western Front, defeating the Germans by speaking Cree. Suddenly the language they'd been beaten and punished for speaking was working to help the Allies. He wondered sometimes what the heck was the point of committing to anything if the world and its rules could flip like a pancake at the merest hint of self-interest for those in power. He didn't blame anyone who got confused, like that Japanese Canadian guy working as a guard for the Japanese army at Sham Shui Po, whom his fellow Grenadiers had told him about when he went to drop off medicine.

Anyway, he hadn't completed because the commanding officer had wanted to pair him with his greatest enemy in this world, Thomas McMahon, who had married Estelle LaVallee, Courchene's childhood sweetheart from before he was sent away to Beauval. He still loved Estelle desperately. So he had quit, and fallen into a depression, and begun to get into fights. He'd enlisted with the Winnipeg Grenadiers a year later to save himself from himself, in the hopes that loyalty to a cause would help him forget all the things he wanted to forget. But now Emily reminded him of Estelle. Still, if he could protect Emily, that was something pure and clean that made sense and didn't have to be complicated.

CHAPTER 36

THE NEWS ABOUT TAK-TAM

September 8, 1942

"Hello, Big Brother," said Lee. "How are things? Have you eaten yet?" "Not yet," said Cheung. "I was going to warm up some baked spaghetti, whatever's left that those murderers did not eat last night." They spoke the old Hakka dialect, so it was easier to be frank. "You want some?"

"Sure," said Lee. "If you'll take these." Grinning, he placed a can of bully beef, a small jug of cooking oil, and a basket holding six eggs on the counter. "Share these with your family, not those marauders."

"Where on earth did you get these things?"

Lee just smiled.

Cheung poured Lee a cup of tea to drink while he fried leftovers on the portable kerosene burner. "I guess I'm lucky to have all these things—leftovers, a stove, hot tea. And a friend who knows how to find things."

"Have you been to Tai Hang lately to check on Yim-Fong?" Lee asked. "How is she doing?"

"There's been too much to do here. But I've had messages. She's as well as anyone can be given the times. I'm just glad she's there and not here. This vipers' nest is no place for women."

"Safer," said Lee.

"Yeah," said Cheung. "The big demon is really sick in the head." He was referring to Noma, of course. "So are all the interrogators and most of the interpreters too. They drown men in buckets of water. They pull out their fingernails with pliers. If they are still alive after that, the interrogators cut their heads off with those absurd traditional swords of theirs, as though they are medieval knights fighting devils at the gates of hell. As though these are feudal times. Maybe they are, after all." His own face was red and hectic, as though he himself were one of those hell demons. "But you know what the worst thing is? Some of those torturers in there are Chinese guys. Like us."

"Traitors will get what's coming to them," said Lee. Both men knew that for some, it was more important to be anti-colonial than it was to be pro-democracy. After all, Hong Kong was not a democracy and might never be. Perhaps they themselves were fools for supporting the Allies more than the Axis, as though the Allies might ever help them to democracy and independence. They held these things out, half-spoken, as tantalizing ideals. Some Hong Kong people followed the Japanese for anti-colonial reasons, reluctantly or enthusiastically. Some of the Chinese gentry were coerced. A few found zeal in it. It was the zeal that neither Lee nor Cheung could stomach, though they could still perceive both rhyme and reason in those people. They understood, too, that their own differences—Lee's commitment to the East River communists, Cheung's sympathies for the nationalist Kuomintang—might come between them, though they pushed the thought from their minds.

The leftovers were hot. Cheung dished them up. "Without the things you bring me, I have to eat from the same trough as them if I want to eat at all."

Lee was famished. "It smells great, Brother. Food is food. I'm just glad this is spaghetti and not people. There's rumours of cannibalism in the ditches."

"Don't think about that now," said Cheung. "Eat up! Enjoy your food while you can."

Lee ate. When he'd cleared his plate, Cheung filled it again, even though Lee shook his head no. Cheung poured him more tea.

"You are too good to me, Brother. Much too good."

"Never mind," said Cheung. "It's just leftovers."

When he'd finished eating, Lee broached the subject he'd been wanting to broach. "Your son Tak-Tam has not been to Chek Keng in a week."

"Ting-Yan must be very upset."

"She's beside herself."

"We made a good match for them then, Brother."

"It didn't look that way at first. But sometimes the old folks know what's best."

Another long silence.

"I sent him to Sham Shui Po to deliver a message to a British corporal."

"You what?"

"I should have sent some other man's son."

Redness bloomed on Cheung's placid face. He flushed redder and redder until he glowed as red as the statue of Duke Guan at the Tin Hau temple.

"Have you ..." Lee struggled to ask the question.

Cheung's mouth opened but nothing came out.

Lee took a deep breath and spoke the question fully. "Has he been here?"

Cheung's stomach dropped. Lee's face blanched.

"I came to see you, but I also came to look for him. You haven't seen him ..."

"I saw them take a man who looked very much like my son into the basement of the Supreme Court. But I didn't think it was actually him, because—because—"

"Because you thought he was safe with me."

They were both silent for a long moment.

Then the truth of what had happened to Tak-Tam dawned on them simultaneously, in a single bolt of horror. Neither knew what to say. The silence expanded, ugly and pitiful.

Finally, Lee found a few banal words. "Brother, I'm truly sorry."

Cheung spoke slowly, as though through a cloud of dry dust. "It might not have been him."

"He hasn't come home."

"You ..." Cheung coughed.

Lee opened his mouth, but nothing came out. Cheung cleared his throat.

"I might have lost your son."

Again, that raspy whisper. "I'm sure it wasn't him."

They were both silent for a long time.

"Brother Cheung, you have to believe me, the last thing in the world I wanted to do was lose my best friend's son, who is also my daughter's husband. I was asked to do it by one of the generals. As proof of my loyalty. Tak-Tam was—is—smart. I thought the risk was small and the payoff would bring peace in our ranks. It was stupid. I should have lied, said yes, then sent another man."

The redness in Cheung's broad face did not dissipate. Impossibly, it intensified. He tried to speak again, but only air and spit came out of his mouth.

"Brother, please say something. Punch me, kill me, I don't care. Just don't look at me like that."

"My son." Cheung said. His mind's eye burned with what he'd seen—a garrison of Kempeitai marching a broken group of Chinese men into the basement of the Supreme Court. The men had already been beaten, and they descended into that terrible basement to experience the darkest horrors Noma could devise before dying a terrible death. He'd seen bodies come out in pieces before. This time wouldn't be—couldn't be—any different.

And he really had seen a man who looked like his own son among them. But Tak-Tam, he'd thought then, was safe at Chek Keng.

He saw that he'd assumed wrongly. It was Tak-Tam he'd seen—shy, loyal Tak-Tam, the slender, bookish one with an internal fortitude Cheung recognized too late. Always he'd thought of Tak-Wing as the strong one, but that strength was external and superficial, whereas Tak-Tam's was infinitely deep and essential. Why hadn't he seen this until now? Unknowingly, he had watched the military police march his beautiful son into that dreadful basement, as one of half a dozen men who would share the same terrible fate. Afterwards their bodies, whole or in pieces, would be thrown to the starving dogs, the ones that roamed feral and desperate through the streets, gobbling down anything they could find that was already dead and made of flesh.

Now, in this moment of true awareness, Cheung wanted to hurl his own body at the Kempeitai. He wished he had a submachine gun so he could mow them down, or if not that, a samurai sword like the one Noma sported. He would run at them, behead them on the spot, without a moment's mercy, watch blood spurt from their aortas and squirt high into the light of the setting sun, feeling nothing but satisfaction at their deaths.

But he had no submachine gun, no samurai sword.

"Cheung."

Cheung was lost in murderous fantasy.

"Brother."

He looked at Lee, but his eyes were far away. He said nothing.

"Cheung. Come on, Brother. Snap out of it."

"They took him. You let them take him. My beautiful son." He lunged at Lee, grabbed him by the throat. But Lee was not without resources. He threw his arms up between Cheung's and pressed down to break his hold. Then slapped him to bring him to his senses.

Cheung came back to the light, saw his beloved brother before him again. "I—"

"I know it's my fault. I was prideful. I thought he would be fine. I risked his life to secure my own position in the East River Column. I understand if you blame me. I should never have sent him to deliver that message." What neither of them said was that it was Cheung's Kuomintang sympathies that had made both Lee and Tak-Tam vulnerable with the East River guerrillas, who leaned toward the Communists as the occupation progressed.

Cheung flushed red again, but got hold of himself. "You were trying to secure Tak-Tam's position too. It's not your fault. It was the Kempeitai. The East River Column is our only hope." While Cheung was not particularly partial to the Communists, he loved his friend, who was one. And the East River Column was the only group Cheung knew of here in Hong Kong that was resisting this new, brutal occupier. "We have to get those Red Sun bastards. Every last one of them."

But because he had no choice, by nightfall, Cheung was back at the bar, whipping up a frothy glass of syllabub for Noma.

CHAPTER 37

WHAT CHILD IS THIS?

September 8, 1942

It was barely dark when Ting-Yan arrived again at the clinic. I was there on my own. Tak-Wing had promised to be good and Emily had gone back to Tai Hang. The senior staff had all returned to their billets for the evening, except those who had rooms at the hospital, and they had turned in for the night. I was busy cleaning all the surfaces and making sure that supplies were in place for the next day. We hadn't seen Selwyn-Clarke for over a week, and we were all very worried about him. We worried about each other too, but no one wanted to give up the work of our humanitarian project, which Selwyn-Clarke had dubbed the Informal Welfare Committee.

I was surprised to see Ting-Yan again so soon.

"Have you seen Tak-Tam?" Ting-Yan's brown skin was smooth as ever but her usually bright eyes were dull with worry.

"Not since you were here with him last week."

"He's been gone almost that long."

"Oh?"

"I'm afraid the worst has happened. Old Lee sent him on an errand, and he hasn't come back. It's not like him."

"I'm sure he'll come back," I said, continuing to wipe down the counters.

"There are rumours of a Japanese ambush along the route he took." Her eyes had a flat, dead look. The muscles around her mouth twitched.

This wasn't a routine visit. She was really distressed.

I pulled her into my arms and hugged her tight.

She released a single sob. "Do you know what they do to them, Violet, when they catch them?"

"I have some idea," I said.

There was commotion at the gate. Tak-Wing and Emily staggered into the clinic with a bang and clatter. Emily had a black eye and a bloody nose. She could barely walk. She blubbered uncontrollably as Tak-Wing did his best to hold her upright and keep her moving forward.

"What did you do to her, you monster?" I didn't raise my voice. The words came out dead cold.

Emily got hold of herself with a massive gasp. "Violet—" She hiccupped.

"I barely touched her," said Tak-Wing.

I ignored him. "Come on, Em, come sit down."

Tak-Wing helped her into our most comfortable chair, a battered wingback from before the Christmas 1941 invasion.

Ting-Yan stared at Tak-Wing's red, hectic face. "You need to get it together, Brother."

Emily huffed and coughed. "The—baby—"

"The baby?"

She choked.

"He's coming, for better or worse," Tak-Wing said. "The little demon."

Emily's whole body convulsed.

Tak-Wing said, "A lot of water came out of her about an hour ago. I wasn't sure what it meant, but I figured I ought to bring her here."

"Oh my God—" Where were Doctors Selwyn-Clarke, Lai, or Ho when I really needed them? I'd never delivered a baby before.

She gagged and puffed and gasped.

Ting-Yan and Tak-Wing helped me get her onto the table. Sweat poured from her flushed face and her whole body heaved.

Courchene came back from his rounds then. "What is going on?"

"Baby coming!" I shouted, though shouting was not at all necessary.

"Oh," he said. "You need help? My ma's a midwife back in Saint-Boniface. I've helped her deliver dozens. What happened to Emily's eye?" He saw Tak-Wing, who was holding Emily's hand as she wailed, and glared at him hard enough to kill. Tak-Wing stared back, stony faced, sensing Courchene's attachment to his wife. Gentle, sensitive Courchene saw that Tak-Wing registered his attachment and stopped breathing for a second.

"You've done this before?" I said. "Come on, then, because I don't have a clue. Help me."

"Breathe, Emily," Courchene said, and began to breathe himself. "That's it, darling, just breathe and let the contractions come."

"I can't!" Emily howled.

Courchene took her hand. "It's going to be okay."

"Don't you dare touch my wife," Tak-Wing said. "You fake Chinese."

"Otipemisiwak," said Courchene.

"What?"

"Otipemisiwak. I'm not a fake Chinese. I'm Métis, me."

"I don't care what you are. Don't you dare touch my wife, I'll kill you dead."

"Tak-Wing," I said, "don't be an idiot. Courchene is the only one it this room with experience delivering a baby."

"Aren't you a doctor?" he demanded.

"Technically yes. Professor Ride rushed a handful of us through early because of the invasion. I've read about how to deliver a baby." In my mind's eye, I saw a drawing of a child hanging upside down in a textbook womb, like a textbook fruit about to drop from a textbook tree. "But I've never actually done it."

"I don't care. I don't want that foreign ghost touching my wife," said Tak-Wing. "If you were a real man, you'd be interned at Sham Shui Po with the other military gweilo."

"The Canadians came to help us," I said, popping a shot of morphine into Emily's arm. If I could have gotten Tak-Wing still, I'd have given him one too.

"I don't really think of myself as Canadian," said Courchene. "I just joined the army to get away."

"They came to help the British," Tak-Wing said. "They are the British. We don't need them."

"I'm not British!" said Courchene, indignant.

"So you love the Japanese now?" I said to Tak-Wing.

"I ain't no Jap lover!" Tak-Wing yelled. I realized he was drunk. Not that it was an excuse for anything he did.

Emily screamed as a violent contraction rolled through her. "Bill!"

"I'm right here, my sweet," Courchene said.

"I'll kill you!" Tak-Wing shouted. He charged Courchene.

I cast Ting-Yan a pleading look.

She grabbed Tak-Wing by the shoulders and yanked. "Come on, Brother-in-law. Let's get you out of here."

"Get your filthy hands off me!" he yelled. "You think I have any interest in you? I never liked you, not even a little bit! Just because your father and my father are friends doesn't mean I have to give a hoot about you. It was always only ever Emily."

"Whatever interest I had in you is long over, you stupid fool." Ting-Yan had pried him off Courchene and now had a firm hold of his arm. He tried to shake her off, but she wasn't having any of it. "Come on, let's go."

By now, Emily was howling like a wild dog in the hills.

"Breathe, breathe, breathe now, darling," Courchene said, mopping her brow with his left hand, as she clutched his right, so hard that someone's blood oozed red and steaming through both his fingers and hers. Tak-Wing wrenched out of Ting-Yan's grasp and tried to pull Courchene off Emily but they had one another in a death grip. I went over to help Ting-Yan pull Tak-Wing away. It was like trying to get a grandpa barnacle off an old rock, but finger by finger we got him loose. Though he was already filthy drunk, Ting-Yan gave him a shot of brandy. "Let's go for a little walk, shall we?"

"You're the ugliest girl I ever saw," he told her.

She just smiled at him and patted his hand as though he were an idiot child. "That's right," she said. "The ugliest girl ever. Let's get out of here, okay?"

Where she found the fortitude, I didn't know. I wondered how she felt, disillusioned by Tak-Wing, but not necessarily any more attached to Tak-Tam, the bookish brother she hadn't wanted to marry in the first place. Or maybe she had become attached to him. They had been married for five years, after all, and they had a little girl. And now he might be dead. Or he might still be alive. Or somewhere in between, on another bloody table in another part of the city, under the ministrations of the twisted Colonel Noma and his merry band of nail pullers. But in this moment, somehow, she managed not to think of him so she could mesmerize this fool Tak-Wing enough to get him away from Emily. As they left, I watched Ting-Yan go with more than a little admiration.

"I need your help, Violet," said Courchene. I snapped back to the task before me. Emily wouldn't let go of him. Wise enough to understand the comfort function he filled, and genuinely fond of her, he stood behind her, and held her by the shoulders as she gripped his arms and pressed her head back into his stomach. It must have made his scar ache, because he grimaced, though he didn't let go. "It's gotta be you, Vi," he said. "Every doctor has a first birth."

The contractions were stronger than Emily was, and she writhed on the table like a woman possessed.

"Get her still," said Courchene. "Get her legs into the stirrups, if you can." A river of sweat ran from his hair into his eye, but he couldn't wipe it away because Emily had a death grip on both of his arms. "Not the easiest birth, this. And I've seen a few."

"Come on, Em, old girl. You've got to get a grip," I said. I pulled her legs up into the stirrups as she cursed me.

"I hate you, Violet. I hate that bastard Tak-Wing more, though. Hate you, and hate him. You're a lousy sister. He's a worse husband, the biggest disappointment of my life. Why did you help me marry him? You should have protected me from that dead demon. What kind of sister are you? Aaaaaaaaggggggggggghhhhhhh!"

"Hate me all you want," I said. "But on the next exhale, you gotta push. Okay?"

"That's it," said Courchene. "Try to get your breath steady—it will really help. Deep breath in now."

She obeyed him and took that breath in.

"Now out," he said. "Come on, sweetheart, that's it. Steady as she goes."

A slender, boat-shaped sliver of baby skull appeared, slimy red between her legs. "I see him!" I shouted. The skull expanded, then contracted again. "You have to push, Em!"

"I'm pushing!" she yelled.

"Breathe in," said Courchene. "Attagirl. Breathe out. Push."

She pushed, but the baby wouldn't budge.

"Again," he said. The wet wedge of skull grew, then shrank once more.

Blood and water gushed out of her, but still the baby refused any real movement.

"Inhale," he said. "And exhale. Push, push, push."

Her belly seemed to grow impossibly huge as she heaved. Still the baby did not move.

"Holy Mary, Mother of God," said Courchene.

Emily pushed and screamed. Still the child would not come.

More breath, more hours, more blood, more water. Emily seemed to vanish, so that there was nothing on the table but a bloody vagina and a stuck head.

"Keep breathing," said the ever-patient Courchene.

"Hate you," wept Emily. "Hate that dead dog Tak-Wing. Hate those murdering Japanese soldiers. Death to Japan. Death to Britannia rules the waves. Death to opium. Death to tea. Death to the Hongkong and Shanghai Banking Corporation and the Bank of China too. Death to the KMT. Death to the Qing. Why was I ever born into this painful, fleeting life?"

At last, the baby crowned between her legs. Its head was enormous, like a giant pumpkin, covered in blood and mucus. What if it wasn't human? What if it was some kind of monster? It seemed to be twice as big as she was. After all Emily had been through, after all her crying and wailing, what if the child had transformed into a demon in her belly? I thought of Ting-Yan's curse at the cricket club wedding. What if it was materializing now? I knew this was ridiculous, superstitious, no way to think, but the thought possessed me like an evil spirit.

"Violet!" Courchene shouted. "Ding, ding! Wake up! See if you can help the baby out. Gently, gently, easy does it. This is the most delicate moment when the brain can get damaged or the neck can get twisted or caught in the umbilical cord. After all this, it wouldn't do for the baby to die by hanging."

I laid my hands on the bloody pumpkin and pulled gently.

Emily took a croaking gasp inward.

"Now exhale, and push again," Courchene said. "Long and slow. Come on, sweetheart, nearly there. It's going to be okay."

She screamed like a demon scything murder through a whole village. The shoulders emerged. Arms, a body, little kicking legs followed. A boy. I pulled him to me, and cradled him against my chest. He was slimy and stank of blood and iron, but his wriggly warmth infused me with a strange joy. On the giant head, a giant mouth opened. The universe howled out, pursued by a trail of sparkling stars.

And so, in a bath of blood, war, and family dysfunction, little Raymond Duk-Ming was born. Praise Mary and the Son of God, Jesus Christ Our Lord.

CHAPTER 38

MOON AND STARS OVER SAI KUNG

Undisclosed Location
New Territories

September 12, 1942

Dear Morgan,

I can only think that you are not receiving my messages, or else that I am somehow not getting yours. Surely you would write me back if you knew how terribly worried I am. I really hope you are alive and well and still at large, my dearest cousin. I'm sick with worry that something has happened to you. I should never have invited you out here to this godforsaken outpost where justice is a distant dream and human life counts for less than nothing.

I did discourage you, remember? I did try, though I curse myself every day for not trying harder. Where are you? If you don't want to leave Hong Kong Island, you don't have to, you know. Of course I want you to join me, though you did say no a hundred times in the days Jane and I were getting ready to leave. If you don't want to come, that is fine, but could you at least let me know you're alive? I can't bear the thought that you're out here because of me, and now you're dead by the side of the road, or in the torturing hands of the

Kempeitai. I just can't bear it. I blame myself. Lord, what I fool I was to ever suggest to you to come.

But maybe you've already gone to heaven and I'm writing this letter to thin air. Is that maudlin? Of course it is. Cousin, where are you?

I believe you are alive, and I hope the war will end quickly, so Isadore Davis Wong and His Cosmopolitan Elites can play "Moon and Stars over Sai Kung" again at the Hotel Metropole, if not the Repulse Bay Hotel. And Morgan Horace can dance the hop, and drink rum and Cokes, and maybe even come up to the mic to sing a little duet with the beautiful Emily Cheung. Wouldn't that be something? I'll be praying every night for that shining day to come soon.

And if it doesn't, well, my cuz, we had a good run, didn't we? But let me not venture further into that line of thought. If you've received this note, it's been passed to you by someone who cares for us both. Please give them something for me in return.

My love always,

Izzy

CHAPTER 39

TIMELESS TEST MATCH

September 15, 1942

It was the morning of the garden party and the cricket match. Governor Isogai was delighted about the event because it offered an opportunity to entertain the constituencies he needed on his side to keep the city going. A large part of his work since taking control of the city had been in devis-ing means to get the majority of the population on his side, and the match presented an opportunity that required little of him. Packing the stands were some former members of the Rajput and Punjabi regiments who felt anti-colonial sympathies with the occupying Japanese, as well as many Sikh policemen who continued the same duties they'd carried out under the British. They had been lifted by the Japanese administration into posi-tions of power over the Chinese policemen, reversing the British racial order. Some Chinese policemen also were present, though in fewer num-bers. Many Eurasians were present; the Japanese administration needed them to continue clerical and secretarial duties in banks, post offices, and private firms. Middle-class local Chinese, as well as overseas Chinese, particularly those with connections to Australia, were also present, being courted as potential allies. Triad members, too, who had prepared the way for the occupation and continued in service to the Japanese administra-tion, were there beside Japanese military police, ordinary soldiers, civilian Japanese administrators, and members of both the Chinese Representative Council, including Robert Kotewall and Shouson Chow, and the Chinese Cooperative Council, including Old Mah, who was accompanied by

Second Mother Polly, in turn attended by Pineapple, who helped her up into the stands. Aw Boon Haw, the Singaporean Tiger Balm magnate was also present, genuinely hopeful that the Japanese project in Asia might work out. Governor Isogai himself sat in the seat of honour, musing with pleasure on the possibility that Hong Kong might one day become an ordinary Japanese city.

Yim-Fong came from Tai Hang for the day, and sat in a special section close to the pitch that Cheung had arranged for her and the rest of his family. Cheung sat with her—it was so seldom these days that they got to visit. But eventually, he and Noma would be out on the pitch, as umpires.

Cheung heard the child screaming before he saw it. It sounded like the ghost of an ancestor improperly mourned. Emily stepped onto the pitch. She held a tiny bundle in her arms—it was from that bundle that the howling poured. Yim-Fong stood and Cheung rose with her, startled at how unwell Emily looked. Nowhere in her being was there a sign of the beautiful woman Tak-Wing had married five years ago. Her back hunched, and her body seemed to have collapsed from the inside, as though none of its internal structures had the strength to fully hold her up. Her hair had been neatly pressed in soft waves, but as she came closer, Cheung could see it was streaked with grey. Her skin sagged and there were dark circles beneath her vacant eyes. This woman was only twenty-four years old, but she looked fifty-four. The unearthly demon in her arms shrieked, and Cheung shuddered. It was as though time were running in the wrong direction. As though, instead of looking at his daughter-in-law holding his grandson, he was gazing back into the past at his grandmother holding his father in her arms. For a moment, he longed for Wong Nai Chung Village.

Tak-Wing rushed up and put his arm around her. Cheung had been reluctant to place his son on the British team, but Noma had expressly asked, "What about that sportsman son of yours, the pan-Asian hero who showed up all the white men on the pitch and the court? The Asian star of all the British games?"

One of the bankers must have told him of Tak-Wing's reputation. Cheung had had no choice but to put Tak-Wing on the British team, though he feared desperately for his son. Cheung grimaced when he saw Tak-Wing, so handsome and neat in his cricket whites. The thought of losing his only remaining son was unbearable, yet he had to bear it.

Together, Tak-Wing and Emily approached the stand and bowed. Emily held the child out toward Cheung. This modern woman whom his son had insisted on marrying spoke in the most old-fashioned way: "Honoured Father-in-Law, honoured Mother-in-Law, I have had the good fortune to have borne you your first grandson."

Still the child bawled.

"Raymond Duk-Ming, as you wished to name him," croaked Emily, joyless but polite. "Shh, little one, hush," she whispered.

The child did anything but. He kicked and wailed, as though furious to have been born into the world when it was in such a sorry state.

At least he is strong, thought Cheung.

Emily bowed again. Tak-Wing smiled, though there was something grim behind the smile.

Yim-Fong didn't notice. Her eyes glowed with eagerness. A grandson at last! She knew nothing of the ways Colonel Noma tormented Cheung about the child's parentage because Cheung was too ashamed to tell her, though in a moment of weakness he had told Tak-Wing. Yim-Fong knew nothing of Emily's rape either. Cheung thought it better to spare her. So she reached out for Raymond as a creature of pure joy.

Emily gently placed the writhing, howling little worm into her arms.

In Yim-Fong's arms, the child calmed a little. She hadn't birthed as many children as Cheung's sisters-in-law still up in the village at Tai Hang—nevertheless, with two children, both boys, she had done her duty. And she knew how to soothe a baby. She jostled Raymond Duk-Ming and cooed. "Hush now, little one, Grandmother is here. Don't you want to be quiet and good when all these guests have come to see you?"

Tak-Wing and Emily sat down beside her as she rocked the baby. Tak-Wing tried to take Emily's hand, but she pushed it away. Yim-Fong, preoccupied with the child, didn't notice, but old Cheung did, and wondered what was going on.

Raymond fell asleep in Yim-Fong's arms, and when he was snoring as loudly as an old man, Emily took him back and brought him over to meet Old Mah and Second Mother Polly. Tak-Wing came with her to pay his respects to his in-laws. Old Mah, Second Mother Polly, and Pineapple were sitting up in the stands several rows behind Yim-Fong. Since the Chinese wedding at Chek Keng five years ago, the Cheungs and the Mahs had reached a kind of détente, a tentative peace that did not constitute love exactly, but did comprise a kind of willingness to go on living in the same city together with the familiarity that family brings.

The British bankers, including Vandeleur Grayburn, Charles Hyde, Richard Hancock, and his son, Selby Hancock, were already on the pitch in their cricket whites, sipping tea and puffing as though their empire weren't over, as though their luck and privilege had not run out. It was all bravado. The bankers, Cheung knew, were being compelled to liquidate the Hongkong and Shanghai Banking Corporation and transfer all funds to the Yokohama Specie Bank and the Japanese-run Bank of Taipei. The medical men were there too, including Selwyn Selwyn-Clarke. The Kempeitai had picked him up at St Paul's Hospital two weeks earlier. There had been a lot of escapes from the military internment camp at Sham Shui Po, including that of Lindsay Ride, and the Kempeitai suspected Selwyn-Clarke of aiding and abetting the escapees. They'd been holding him for interrogation for the past two weeks, and thought Noma a fool to release him just to play in this ridiculous cricket match, but Noma was their commanding officer and they had to obey.

Though the bankers and medical people in positions of authority were British, not all those who did the work of banking and medicine were. In their midst, Chinese, Eurasians, Portuguese, Irish, and White Russians worked in these same two fields. The Chinese and so-called "third nationals" on the team were all of Cheung's choosing at Noma's command. Cheung had selected them by profession, in hopes that their profession would stand as cover for them. He hoped he had not given anyone away and doomed them to the basement of the Supreme Court in so doing.

The Japanese interrogators and interpreters, eyes blazing with war fury, stood in orderly rows, awaiting instruction. To Cheung, whose mother had taught him about traditional Chinese medicine, including how the organs influenced temperaments, they had a heart illness—not an innate one, but one that came from too much military training. In this, they were unlike Tanaka and Horace. Though those two were not without troubles, their hearts were better balanced. Tanaka and Horace stood with them, but off to one side and at a slight distance from the rest. For their sake, Cheung hoped that Noma didn't notice. Cheung had also included on this team Chinese policemen already under Noma's command, including Chan, a Chinese interrogator whose eyes had the orange fire of bloodlust in them. Chan had a reputation of doing terrible things to his own countrymen, mutilating people from his own neighbourhood the worst. There was a rumour that he'd blinded his own brother with a machete before beheading him. Though it had happened right next door, Cheung didn't want to think about it.

Noma approached now. "There he is, my little namesake! How are you, little Raymond Kennosuke? An exemplary citizen of the New Asia. We will get there very soon, Mrs Cheung," he said, addressing Emily to show he knew who she was. "Very soon. Just you watch."

Emily looked up into the eyes of her tormenter from the Christmas Day massacre. Sitting beside her, Tak-Wing saw her blanch and raised an eyebrow. What did Noma mean by "Raymond Kennosuke"? He scowled, darkly.

Raymond, who until that point had been asleep in Second Mother Polly's arms, gurgled, then hissed at Noma and began to cry. From down on the pitch, where he was inspecting the placement of the wickets one last time, Cheung looked up, saw what was unfolding and prayed silently that nobody would die today.

The British were up to bat in the first innings.

Cheung wanted Tak-Wing to be first up to bat, so that the young man could show off, as he was wont to do, while the Japanese were at their most hopeful.

Tak-Wing refused. "You should save me for the middle of the lineup, when I can do the most good."

"Absolutely not," Cheung said. "That's the most dangerous spot. Don't you know this game is not about winning?"

"What do you mean? It's always about winning!"

"Not this time," Cheung said.

"This is our chance to show those Japanese bastards who the real boss is around here!"

"Don't be stupid," said Cheung. "This is the time to lose strategically, so that we live to fight a real battle when the odds are more in our favour."

"The odds are in our favour now!"

"Sure, for something that matters only as an exercise to stay in the good graces of the Japanese. Sometimes you need to think, my son."

"I always think. Cricket is a thinking man's game! Anyway, it's up to the team captain to decide, not the umpire," Tak-Wing said, and stormed off to talk to Richard Hancock.

Cheng shot Hancock a desperate look. Hancock had no reason, however, to protect Tak-Wing in particular from Noma's wrath. Still, Cheung's piqued red face was so sad that Hancock put Tak-Wing in the normally low-value nightwatchman position.

Tak-Wing pouted.

In the end, the opening batsman was Vandeleur Grayburn, the chief manager of the Hongkong and Shanghai Banking Corporation. At the other end was Charles Hyde, Grayburn's counterpart at the Kowloon branch of the HSBC. The opening bowler was Harada Goro, of the Yokohama Specie Bank. Before the war he had been a pitcher for the Osaka Tigers baseball team and still played a bit of baseball with a wartime league here in Hong Kong. Though the techniques for baseball and cricket were not identical, he had an arm that was well-practised at propelling balls.

Now at the edge of the pitch in his role as the second umpire, Colonel Noma chuckled, pleased with the little drama he'd staged for himself.

Grayburn, under detention at the Sun Wah Hotel, was gaunt and thin. Day in and day out for the last four weeks, he signed massive stacks of unbacked banknotes that he and his compatriots hadn't had time to burn before the invasion. The currency was not legal, but Hong Kong was already an extra-legal place, doubly so since December 25, 1941. Grayburn put on a fierce, brave face. But he was unsteady on his legs. Harada bowled low and fast.

As umpire, Cheung saw Harada's foot move out too far. Grayburn tapped the ball, and it flew high into the sky, then dove in a steep arc onto the field. An easy catch for the outfielder.

Cheung contemplated what to do. The Supreme Court was mercifully quiet today because all the interrogators and interpreters were out here. Their buckets were empty and their swords, machetes, and pliers lay quiet on the bloody tables inside. But Harada's foot really had moved out too far.

"No ball!" Cheung shouted.

"What?" shouted Noma.

"His foot went over the line."

Noma grunted.

"One run for Britain," said Cheung. The scorekeeper put it up on the board.

"I like you, Cheung," Noma yelled across the field, "but don't get cocky."

"It was a fair call," Cheung said. He had worked here all his life. He knew the game. He shot Noma the subtlest of stink eyes, which, thanks be to Tin Hau, Noma did not see.

Grayburn raised his bat again. Tried not to grimace. These Japanese bastards had sucked up all the proper Hong Kong currency in the colony and replaced it with bunkum military yen. They'd instituted exorbitant taxes of thirty percent on all business over five thousand military yen. They funnelled currency out of the colony in every way they could imagine to fund the torture and murder of his friends and employees and, more broadly, the war in China, in order to drive the Europeans out.

Harada bowled the next ball with a spin, but Grayburn saw the flick of his wrist. He hit the ball with all his once considerable might, which was still sufficient to send it sailing over the spectators' heads and out onto Chater Road.

Cheung pointed to the ground with his forefinger to signal a boundary. This gave the British team six runs.

One of the Japanese fielders ran out to the road to retrieve the ball and send it back to Harada. Colonel Noma made a face. He didn't like to see a Japanese reduced to petty labour, but the local ground rules said the fielder had to get the ball back to the bowler to end the play.

Cheung signalled, honest as ever, to the scorekeeper, who posted *Britain 7*.

The fielder threw the ball to a furious Harada. Really in a snit, Harada glared at Grayburn so hard that Cheung thought he saw light pouring from Harada's eyes. Grayburn spit. As he did so, Harada hurled the ball and hit the wicket hard.

"How's that?" said Noma, threat in his voice.

What Harada had done was completely illegal, but Cheung knew that Noma could call a halt to the game at any time, and carry out repercussions for anything that made him unhappy.

He hesitated.

Noma glared.

Reluctantly, Cheung raised his right hand and pointed his forefinger into the air. Out.

Grayburn gawped at Cheung, as though to say *traitor*.

Cheung shrugged.

Grayburn considered approaching him to have a word, but Cheung gave him an anxious, real-world look. Grayburn hesitated, then turned around and left the field.

The next batter on the pitch was Hilda Selwyn-Clarke, a known communist. And a woman to boot. Noma's eyebrow arched.

"Don't underestimate me, boys," said Red Hilda. "If I can get birth control for Hong Kong women, I can damn well bat at cricket."

"What kind of cricket team is this?" said Noma.

"You asked me to choose," said Cheung.

"This woman," Noma said, "this woman is one of the founders of the China Defense League. In cahoots with Soong Ching-Ling herself. Remind me to have her imprisoned when the match is over."

"Okay," said Cheung. "But it's a timeless Test. You said so yourself. And it has just begun." He wished the match would go on forever, so that they would never have to get back to the march of history and horror as usual.

Harada bowled. Red Hilda hit the ball straight down the line to practically whack the Supreme Court in the rear door. Red Hilda and Charles Hyde ran while the Japanese fielder chased the ball. The rest of the fielders crowded to the wicket.

Red Hilda's husband, Selwyn Selwyn-Clarke, the humanitarian doctor and former chief medical officer of the colony, was up to bat after his wife. Weak from the rigours of questioning, he did not have very good focus. Harada bowled low and hit him right in the shins.

"How's that?" called Noma.

"LBW," said Cheung. "Out."

Cheung could have put Selwyn-Clarke's humanitarian partner Francis Lee on the team. He was not an East River man as such, but he was close enough to them that Cheung had decided against it. Francis Lee had been part of the team that had helped Lindsay Ride escape to Free China. Selwyn-Clarke didn't even know about that—perhaps Noma didn't either.

Cheung knew only because of the snippets of information that Lee shared with him when he delivered seafood. Best keep it a solid secret and let Francis Lee continue his work, especially now, during the cricket match, when the Japanese leadership was momentarily distracted.

Next, Edward Kerrison went up to bat. Health inspector in charge of cremating all the bodies the Japanese Army had shot for target practice or beheaded simply to reduce the population, he was already half-mad and wouldn't be long for this world, Cheung thought. His heart filled with pity. In better days, Kerrison had been a healthy, jovial colonial who had given red packets—Chinese-style—to Cheung on both Chinese and Western holidays. He had played the drums sometimes with Izzy Davis Wong and His Cosmopolitan Elites. He had been a strong batsman. But now, the man neither batted well nor ran well, and was soon bowled out.

When lunchtime came, the first innings was still under way and there were still eight undismissed players on the British team. They understood what a boon this match was for their friends in the outside world. It was more important to stay in play than it was to score runs, but even so, they weren't doing badly with a score of 56.

Returning to his duty as steward, Cheung called to his helpers. They brought out long tables with white cloths. They brought chairs and umbrellas. Though there were food shortages in Hong Kong, Noma had spared no effort to ensure a handsome luncheon of cold consommé, chicken livers in bacon blankets, cucumber sandwiches, shrimp cocktail, jellied springtime veal, and chicory salad with eggs.

By teatime there were seven undismissed players on the British team. Gráyburn sent Tak-Wing to bat opposite Selby Hancock between teatime and cocktail hour, that dead period in the afternoon when everyone was tired and no one was paying much attention. This was a great relief to Cheung, who did not want Noma to notice his only remaining son. But this slight really bugged Tak-Wing. He played like a fiend, batting into the most unexpected places, way out in third-man space for one play, and then barely onto the pitch the next. He and Selby were still accumulating runs when cocktail hour hit, and everyone was restless, except the Japanese bowler, Harada Goro, who was just irritated.

Noma approached Cheung. "Do you think you could convince your show-off son to lighten up a bit? He's becoming a bit of a pill."

So much for evading Noma's notice.

In the end, the Japanese team switched bowlers, putting Tanaka, formerly one of Izzy Davis Wong's Cosmopolitan Elites, into the position.

Unnerved at having to face one of his wife's dearest friends, Tak-Wing was soon bowled out.

Finally, everyone could leave the stands to drink Colonel Noma's syllabub, though most were grateful when Cheung began to offer gin and tonic, fruit punch, and EWO beer in addition.

It took the whole of the first day, and half the next for the Japanese team to bowl the British team out.

The Japanese team did well in its first innings, which took the rest of the second day and most of the third. More cucumber sandwiches and shrimp cocktail were devoured. Thanks to Horace, the syllabub flowed. Everyone got into it, remarking that the rum was unusually good, and asking how Cheung had managed to procure Madeira under the current conditions. At the end of the Japanese team's first innings, the score was Japan 256, Britain 254. The teams were practically neck and neck.

When the fourth day arrived, a restless anxiety came over the British team. Each team got only two innings each, which meant that, while their first-time batting gave them a sense of hope and freedom because the game was just beginning, they were despondent and nervous the second time, because it was to be their last. But the most important thing was to stay in play as long as possible in order to keep the Kempeitai off the streets and away from the people and to give the Allied troops the maximum possible time to gather out there in the storm of war where the clock kept ticking forward. Their strategy was pure, brazen Scheherazade. Some of the Winnipeg Grenadiers, released from the camp at Sham Shui Po for the duration of the match, had brought instruments with them from the internment barracks. Whenever there was a break they took out their trumpets and clarinets and played the most infectious tunes they could remember, each one rolling into the next. They had makeshift instruments too—a double bass made from an oil drum, a guitar fashioned from a broken chair and an old tennis racquet. When they were up to bat they batted like actors, performing snippets of *A Midsummer Night's Dream* between the wickets. "Ill met by moonlight, Proud Titania!" and "Lord, what fools these mortals be!" they shouted. They sang "Show Me the Way to Go Home" and "Rose Marie." They did Fred Allen impressions. When it was their turn to bowl, they square danced while the bowler fiddled. This was something the Winnipeg Grenadiers and the Royal Rifles particularly liked to do. The Royal Scots played along. The 5/7th Rajputs and the 2/14th Punjabs were happy to learn, as long as they got to teach bagaa when Mengha Singh went up to pitch. They played cricket as slowly as they could, and got up to as many shenanigans as possible. Noma grumbled, "Soon the childish races will be ruled by a dignified, adult one, as it should be." But he didn't put a stop to their games.

CHAPTER 40

A CUP OF SALT
September 18, 1942

Early in the afternoon on the fourth day, the air began to grow more humid and damp than it had been the previous three days. Cheung knew what was happening. "Smells like a typhoon is coming."

Sure enough, by late afternoon, the first few drops of rain began to fall. By cocktail hour it was coming down in sheets. Everyone rushed into the first-floor bar to have their syllabub and snack on bar peanuts. Cheung and his men poured whisked cream and rum as though the Beelzebub of the Christian Hell himself were after them, until a messenger boy appeared at the door, drenched to the bone. He called for Cheung, and when the chief steward came he said, "Please Boss, your mother and sister at Wong Nai Chung are calling for you."

Cheung's heart flooded with worry. "What's wrong? Are they okay?" But the messenger boy had already fled into the downpour.

Cheung cast his gaze back into the bar. Noma was engrossed in conversation with Vandeleur Grayburn, discussing the best way to structure currency when the war was finally over. Tak-Wing and Emily sat with Yim-Fong at the back of the room. Emily held Raymond, and Tak-Wing leaned over the baby, cooing. Cheung was a little surprised by his son's tender posture; Tak-Wing had been suspicious and volatile throughout the pregnancy. For a moment Cheung considered asking Tak-Wing to come with him, but decided against it. He didn't want to disturb their rare moment of peace. It was more important to just go. He snatched up an umbrella from the stand, not caring whose it was, and rushed out into the rain.

He hurried to the tram stop in front of the Hongkong and Shanghai Banking Corporation. It took forever to come, though he couldn't have said how long he waited. On the second day of the occupation, the watch that the toffs had given him upon his promotion to steward had been taken from him at gunpoint by a Japanese soldier already wearing a wristful of looted watches. Worry gripped Cheung and his heart raced. Maybe it would be better to walk. But he didn't want to risk making the decision and then seeing the tram go by minutes later, so he waited a bit longer. The wait was too much. He took a step in the direction of the village, then two, then three.

The tram came around the corner.

He scurried back, and boarded. The tram was in rough shape. The Japanese army had stripped it of everything that could serve the war effort. But it was good to be out of the rain and moving. Outside the windows of the tram, devastated people huddled in doorways against the deluge, those who were still alive. There were bodies in the streets and the wet stench that poured in through any crack in the window was unbelievable. Or maybe it was the tram itself that stank. He saw a naked body on the sidewalk. It was hard to make out details through the rivulets of water that poured down the window, but it looked like the body's calves and buttocks had been cut away. For what, he didn't want to think about. He shuddered.

He got out at the Happy Valley stop and hurried past the racecourse, as the wind picked up. It smelled pleasantly of grass and horse manure. He thought he heard the thunder of hooves, though it might just have been the rain coming down even harder. Ahead of him through the rain and mist Wong Nai Chung Gap spilled between Jardine's Lookout and Mount Cameron, the hills that had protected him throughout his village childhood. There were buildings all around the village now—the sanatorium and many apartment blocks—extending up into the hills to look down on the racecourse. It was through Wong Nai Chung Gap that the Japanese army had entered Hong Kong and wrought such devastation. Fifteen years earlier, flood waters had poured through the gap, as they were pouring again today. As he drew closer, he could hear those waters rushing.

The sunken village was a swimming pool. Winds whipped around the trees on the bank in front of it. Across the windblown pool, Cheung could see the roof and the upper third of his childhood home. The whole village was submerged.

There was no help for it. He closed the umbrella and wedged it between two large rocks. He took off his coat and laid it on the bank. Put a rock on it so it wouldn't blow away. It would get drenched regardless, but at least it wouldn't encumber him in his next move.

He dove into the pool, and began to swim down the alley he'd grown up playing in. Typhoon winds howled over the surface. A big wave smashed him in the face. He inhaled water, coughed, pushed forward again. Somehow, through the murky, swirling water, he reached his childhood house. He tucked his head beneath his armpit to protect his mouth, took a deep breath, and plunged down into the whirling dark. Underwater all he could see was the churning mud before his eyes. So he closed them and kicked downward. Felt for the doorway. It had already been pushed open by the force of the water. Inside the house, but still underwater, he opened his eyes again. The water still turned and churned, but he could make out a rectangular shadow above him. A pair of legs kicked absurdly above his head. His sister's? He glided up to the surface.

"Ah Goh," his sister Hok-Yee sputtered. "Big Brother. Thank the Goddess of the Sea you made it."

Their mother lay atop the kitchen table, which floated thanks to his sister's kicking. Old Cheung Wan-See's eyes were only barely open, her grey lashes brushing grey, damp cheeks. "My son. Tin Hau be blessed."

"She tripped and broke her leg this afternoon, when the water first started coming. Now we're trapped. There's no way out." Hok-Yee had been keeping the table afloat for hours. Her face was gaunt with fear and exhaustion.

The water kept rising and the ceiling seemed to descend on them even as they talked.

"The only way out is the way I came in," Cheung said, looking down into the murky water. It was so thick and brown he couldn't see the door through it.

"I thought about swimming with her down there, but I don't think it's possible," Hok-Yee said. "There's got to be another way."

"Through the roof?" said Cheung. "Even if I could smash a hole in it, outside there's only more water."

"Maybe together we could guide her out?" Hok-Yee said. She was so pale. She didn't complain, but it was clear that even if the ceiling weren't rapidly closing in on them, she wouldn't be able to keep the table and her mother afloat much longer. They had no choice.

"Can you hold your breath for two minutes, Ma?" said Cheung.

The old lady nodded, but the nod was slight.

"Can you, Ma?" Cheung repeated. What if she drowned? His stomach churned. He didn't want to be the one to lead her to a watery death.

His mother opened her eyes fully. "Yes, my son. Only because I know you will safely guide me through." The old fighting spirit was still present in her open eyes, which reassured Cheung.

"Okay, then," he said. "Okay."

"Follow me," he said to his sister. To his mother, he said, "Arms on my shoulders, all right, Mama?" He turned his back to the table and kicked hard to stay afloat.

The old lady rolled over and climbed onto his back.

"Big breath," Cheung said to both of them, repeating what his mother used to say to him when he was little and she was teaching him to swim at Blue Pool, the swimming hole at the edge of the village.

The three of them inhaled in unison. He slid down into the cold, dark water and felt his way toward the floor. It seemed to take forever, like they would never reach the ground. Then he touched it. He groped against the inrushing current toward the dark shape of the door. He could feel his mother's grip on his shoulders, but it was weakening. He kicked with all his might. Together, they glided through the door. Then upward. The water seemed to press down on them in a spiralling fashion that forced him to flail. His breath was running out and her grip was growing fainter. *Hang on, Mama*, he said with his mind. *Hang on. Not much longer.* He kicked hard with legs that were accustomed to standing twelve hours a day or more. They popped up to the surface and took a long gasp more of wind than of air. His sister popped up beside them. *Thank you, Tin Hau. Thank you, great Goddess of Compassion.* They frog stroked along the surface to the bank where Cheung had left his coat. Like three poorly formed fish, they crawled up onto the shore.

Miraculously, the coat and umbrella were still there, wet, but not as drenched as Cheung and the two women. He handed the umbrella to his sister, draped the soggy coat over his mother's shoulders, then hoisted her onto his back once more, being careful of her broken leg. Her bones were so light it was like carrying a bird. Shivering, he walked away from the drowned village, and behind him, Wong Nai Chung Gap seemed to exhale a long sigh, propelling them forward into an unknown future.

It took an hour for the tram to arrive. In that time, the wind and rain ate at his mother, as she sat on the bench, her face stoic but grey. As the minutes ticked by, she became greyer and greyer. Finally, the tram arrived, but it was full of Japanese soldiers. They had no other option. They boarded.

"Dirty Chinaman, you smell like a sewer," said one soldier.

"How dare you soil this good Asian tram with your filthy white-man-loving presence?" said another.

"Traitorous vermin!" Two soldiers rushed at them and pushed. With his mother on his back, her arms around his neck, Cheung stumbled backward onto his sister as the tram began to move forward. They fell to the street, Hok-Yee on the bottom, their mother in the middle, and heavy, burly Cheung on top. He heard his mother gasp once.

"Mama!"

He could no longer feel her breath on his neck. He rolled off her as fast as he could. "Ma!"

His sister rolled out from under her. But his mother did not move. "Mama!" Cheung put his thumb on her wrist. He choked in a desperate inhale. There was no pulse. He waved his hand beneath her nose. No breath. Water rushed over her grey skin and the wind blew her wet white hair so that it seemed to writhe on the sidewalk. He put his hand over her heart. Nothing. Cheung opened his mouth and released a deep, low bellow of pure unearthly grief.

They decided to walk rather than wait for the next tram, which could take another hour, and off which they might be pushed again. The rain came in torrents as Cheung and Hok-Yee stumbled back toward the Cricket Club. The wind blew tiles off the roofs of buildings, and lifeless signs from their fronts. Cheung carried the body of his old mother down the long route of Hennessey Road, with his sister staggering behind him, struggling to remain upright. She'd long since given up on the umbrella. Debris blew down the street—a scraping piece of steel sheeting, a large tree branch still covered in leaves, the corpse of some unfortunate beaten to death by the Kempeitai last week. The sorrow that had gripped Cheung at the moment of his mother's death began to change its tenor. With each step he took, grief dripped out of him and anger entered. Wong Nai Chung was his village. He stepped over a fallen tree branch. Hong Kong was his town. He stepped around a wide puddle in the road. All these rampaging usurpers had pushed their way in, first the British, now the Japanese. He scurried past a family of refugees from the mainland huddling in a doorway. They reached pitifully toward him with their skeletal hands. He didn't look at them until they were safely behind him, and then he glanced back at them with a complicated mix of guilt and·horror. He would make the usurpers pay.

The rage became sorrow again. Though his mother's body was not heavy, the sorrow weighed on his back like a quarry worker's pole with a basket full of rocks on either end. The wind came harder. His back doubled over. His knees bent and wouldn't fully straighten again. He staggered forward like an old man.

"Do you want me to carry her for a while?" Hok-Yee said.

"No, Sister, you go on ahead."

"I'm not going to leave you walking along this deathly road by yourself," she said. "Are you sure I can't carry her? I'm stronger than I look."

"It's fine," he said. "I can manage."

"You don't look like you're managing. Don't be so stubborn."

"Leave me be," he said. "I don't want to have to carry two dead women!" he laughed at his own grim joke, which made him feel just a little lighter.

Hok-Yee laughed too—thinly, but she laughed. Her eyes remained dark with grief.

At last they were back at the cricket club. Cheung staggered up the front steps with his mother in his arms, went straight to the first-floor bar, and laid her on the counter, at which Noma, Tanaka, and Horace sat, nursing their drinks. All the astonished players and fans in the first-floor bar, including Yim-Fong, Tak-Wing, and Emily, stared, unsure whether Cheung and Hok-Yee were alive or dead. Even little Raymond stopped his howling and gawped in amazement.

"How has my life and the life of this poor fishing village come to this?" wailed Cheung. "Curse you Japanese devils and curse you vile British. Down with Englishmen and their damn superiority complexes! Down with pith helmets, bureaucracy, and cricket! Down with the opium trade that brought this evil upon us! Down with tea! Down with silk and porcelain, down with the hard work and genius of my people that caused us to make things you vile devils wanted! Down with our capacity for hard work and suffering! Down with junks and clipper ships, down with indentured labour, down with coolies, their long poles and strong backs. Down with our beautiful women for bearing children for you demons to exploit. Down with the Manchu who have not cared for us poor southerners for centuries. Downs with the queues of our servitude! Down with bound feet, down with nimble fingers! Down with you arrogant Japanese and your fascist emperor! Down with your army, your brutal and brutalized young men, your bayonets and penises! Down with the Kempeitai, your samurai swords, your beheadings and executions! Down with the pan-Asianism! All Asians are clearly not brothers! Come on, Colonel Noma, I know you've got a pistol in your pocket."

He raised his arms, staggered like a drunk toward the demonic head of the Kempeitai. "I don't care anymore. Everything has been taken." He thumped his chest. "Go ahead. I know you want to. Shoot me."

All of the bar's drinkers, with their own weary and bloodshot eyes, looked on, amazed. Stoic, sturdy Cheung was not supposed to crack.

Finally, Tanaka said, "Come on, old man. Let's get you to bed. Your mother will still be dead in the morning."

Exhausted from his ordeal, Cheung slept, but not for long. He woke with the sun, his mind racing. His uniform was still wet from the day before, so he put on an ordinary white shirt and black pants. In the foyer outside the bar, Horace and Tanaka struggled with four Kempeitai, who were attempting to carry his mother's body downstairs.

"Where are you taking her?" Cheung said.

"Disposing of the body," said one of them, whom Cheung recognized as an interpreter.

"They are taking her to the dogs," said Horace.

The interpreter shot him the stink eye.

"You will not!" Cheung rushed the men, tried to pry his mother's body from their arms. "Give her back to me!" he roared. His large body swelled with rage to twice its normal size. In the ex-colony's only instance when one of the occupied was able to intimidate four of his occupiers through the sheer force of grief and anger, Cheung wrenched the body from the arms of the policemen. With Tanaka and Horace's help, he carried his mother back into the bar, where Noma slept on the same stool he had occupied while drinking the night before.

"How dare you!" Cheung snarled, waking Noma.

Tanaka and Horace laid the body out on the counter, as it had been last night.

"The old witch was giving me nightmares."

"Stinking dead man!" Cheung grabbed Noma, threw him to the ground. The bar came awake with other Kempeitai asleep at the tables. It took eight men to pull the raging hulk of the normally compliant chief steward off the kicking colonel, and even then, not before Cheung had landed his massive fist in the monster's left eye.

The eight men yanked him upright.

Noma's chief executioner had his sword drawn, ready to sheer Cheung's head off right there in the jovial first-floor bar.

Noma stood, spat out a tooth. Grinned a bloody grin, then began to laugh. Said something in Japanese.

Tanaka whispered a translation: "Don't kill him, Daichi. Don't you know Cheung is my favorite Chinaman?"

To Cheung, Noma said, in English, "If I let you go, will you promise not to hit me again? My eye kind of hurts."

Cheung grunted like an animal.

"Speak English, man."

The executioner ran his sword across Cheung's chest, slicing a clean gash in his fresh white shirt without even grazing skin.

"I want a proper funeral for my mother."

"Proper Chinese funeral, or proper Japanese funeral?"

"Chinese funeral. She wanted to be buried at the Colonial Cemetery in Happy Valley so she could watch her natal village for eternity."

"Japanese funeral," said Noma. "And it's a deal."

The swordsman slashed. A thin line of blood opened at the level of Cheung's heart.

"Chinese funeral. Buddhist style. With mourners in white hoods and real crying."

The swordsman directed his sword at Cheung's solar plexus, as though readying to disembowel him. Pressed it into the white shirt.

"We will cremate her here at the cricket club," said Noma. "Ashes to be guarded by whichever team wins this infernal test match. If the British team wins, you can bury her urn at Happy Valley. If the Japanese team wins, we will cherish her ashes as those of the first citizen of New Asia."

The sword pressed in, and the shirt tore again.

"Cheung," said Horace. "The man could kill you. If you die now, what will happen to your mother's spirit?"

Blood appeared at the tip of the sword and seeped into the white cloth around the hole in Cheung's shirt. Cheung didn't care. He wanted to die.

"Come on," Tanaka said. "The storm is over. Let's return to the match."

"Save yourself and save us all," Yim-Fong said.

"Please, Brother," said Hok-Yee.

Cheung hadn't noticed his wife and his sister approach closer.

The pain intensified as the sword probed deeper into his flesh.

Yim-Fong said, "Think about your sons."

Cheung shot Noma one last vicious glare, then drew on all the martial calm his father had trained him how to will. He nodded his head. "All right. Deal."

No coffin was possible given the circumstances. But in the storage room, the Japanese soldiers found the perfect shroud—the Union Jack that used to sail from the rooftop of the club, until it was replaced on Christmas Day 1941 by the Rising Sun. They found it as they'd left it, respectfully folded and placed on a high shelf along the with the spare uniforms for the HKCC's international tournaments. True to their word, with the respect and care they'd normally reserve for one of their own, the Kempeitai wrapped the last inhabitant of Wong Nai Chung Village in the British flag.

Out on the cricket pitch they built a pyre consisting mostly of wickets and bats, preserving only the ones in play for Noma's timeless Test match and one set of spares. To it, they added an old sofa and half a dozen chairs from the first-floor bar. For a platform, two bar tables were made to serve, set atop the pyre like an arrangement for a party of eight. Cheung, Tanaka, and Horace laid the venerable old lady atop this heap. A couple of bottles of good English gin served as lighter fluid. Tak-Wing and Richard Hancock did the honours of setting the pyre alight.

In the thick mist that had engulfed the city after yesterday's storm, they gathered around the pyre and solemnly watched Cheung Wan-See burn. Because the air was wet, it smoked prodigiously at first. Tanaka poured on two more bottles of gin—there was lots available because the British had left a lot (it had been the substance that allowed them to turn unseeing eyes to whatever they didn't want to acknowledge), and the Japanese didn't much care for it. Still, it burned wet. Horace contributed a single bottle of Screech Owl rum, all the more precious because of the peculiar taste for syllabub that all the Test match players and guests had developed. Miraculously, this made the fire burn with a clean blue flame, even when a strong wind brought them steady rain to remind them of the power of the storm the day before. It burned so cleanly that the wickets, bats, sofa, chairs, tables, and one old Chinese lady were all burnt down to a cup of fine salt, transparent as pure quartz crystal. When it was cool enough, they swept it into a soup tureen of fine English bone china, the closest thing they had to an urn.

And at the end of the day, they were rewarded by a clearing of the skies and the unexpected sight of the sun as it set behind Victoria Peak and sank into the South China Sea. They all felt very small but strangely grateful for their lives in this little trading entrepôt at the edge of the once and future British Empire.

CHAPTER 41

ENDGAME

September 20, 1942

Japan was down, 332 to 364 in the fourth and final innings. She still had a chance, a pretty good one. The last three batsmen in play were Morgan Horace, star member of the West Indies Cricket Team and veteran of twenty-two Test matches, albeit in his youth; Tanaka Shigeru, the second-best batsman through forms five and six on the Whitsunday Boys' School cricket team across the water in Kowloon; and Colonel's Noma's chief interrogator, Ishiyama Hinata, who'd been a decent baseball player all the way through military college in his day. Though the rules of cricket were different, he was very good at hitting a ball across a field.

Governor Isogai watched intently and the Japanese soldiers in the stands cheered Horace on. Horace was not sure how to feel. These past nine months he'd been hanging out at Cheung's polished wood bar in the Hong Kong Cricket Club. He knew what went on in the basement of the Supreme Court Building. He was not excited to be part of this strange cricket match. At home in St. John's, in the tiny Water Street headquarters of the Baccalieu Company, he thought Brother Du Bois was right about "Asia for Asians." And maybe he was back in Sun Yat-Sen's day, but it had clearly become something else now. Horace felt sick. Noma and Isogai would know if Horace didn't play his best. But if he helped the Japanese win, he would be at least symbolically complicit in the murder of innocents. He didn't care that much about symbols, but he was fully aware that the British, Japanese, and Chinese all did. If he didn't help the Japanese win, they would know that his heart was no longer with them, and he would be in danger of getting marched off to the basement of the Supreme Court. If he did help the Japanese win, his friend Cheung would feel betrayed, though Cheung must also understand that the Japanese were in charge and one must do what had to in order to survive. But what he really wanted was the help of Cheung and his friend, Captain Lee, to get out of this carnival city turned upside down and back to front. Left to right could only follow. If Horace helped the Japanese win, Cheung might be ill disposed to help him get to the Sai Kung hills, where his cousin Isadore Davis Wong had wisely gone before the invasion. He'd received letters he was pretty sure were from Izzy, but he couldn't decipher them. Perhaps someone at the club today would know where he could find "Ga-Chan," if only he knew who to ask.

Horace knew that many of the British had been playing not so much to win, but to draw the timeless Test match out as long as possible in order to suspend the horrors and to give the Allied forces time to gather. Should he, or shouldn't he, support them? W.E.B. Du Bois said the only way to bring an end to the white man's rule was to sabotage them from within. But Du Bois also believed Imperial Japan would lead the charge against all things European and raise up the coloured peoples of the world. Imperial Japan was most certainly *not* doing this in Hong Kong. As long as the cricket game went on, nobody was being beaten or murdered, at least not by the Kempeitai on the Japanese Imperial cricket team. He decided that drawing out the play was the best and most honourable strategy, though he must not make it obvious, lest he himself become the gendarmerie's next victim.

Bowling for the British team was female impersonator Ferdinand "Sonny" Maria Castro, known across the island for his Carmen Miranda impressions. He had been released for the duration of the match from the Sham Shui Po POW camp, where he was housed with the other Portuguese prisoners who'd participated in the Hong Kong Volunteer Defence Corps against the invading Japanese. He wore an elaborate fruit hat for luck, and bowled like a boss. Though the Japanese team was good, the reason they couldn't get ahead was all Sonny Maria, master and mistress in one of knocking the bails off the wicket regardless of who or what was in front of it. Or that was the case until he faced Horace.

Sonny Maria bowled. The ball danced from his hand in a dizzying spiral. Horace thought he heard it singing "Chica Chica Boom Chic." But Horace had studied every bowl there was, and Sonny Maria's bowl, though perfectly executed, was not entirely original, though he had put such a powerful spin on it that it drifted unpredictably in the air, first a little to the right, then a little to the left, then unexpectedly up, then suddenly down and a little to the left at the same time, all within the space of a thousandth of a second. Horace's eye, though not as fast as it had been at twenty-two, was still pretty fast. He followed the ball's every twist and turn, its every rhyme and reason. The ball danced a clever dance, a little merengue, a little bossa nova, but it couldn't quite escape the brunt of Horace's bat. He hit it hard, but not squarely. It flew off in a direction he hadn't expected, behind him to the right, into third-man space. Two fielders—astronomer Graham Heywood and Red Hilda Selwyn-Clarke—both took off after it. Though they were both excellent in their own professions, they were amateur cricketers, and clumsy. They slammed into each other and both blacked out for a second. A third fielder, that young fool Selby Hancock, ran in, snatched up the ball, and hurled it to the wicket keeper, second in command at the Hongkong and Shanghai Banking Corporation, Charles Hyde. Ball in hand, Hyde knocked over the wicket, but Horace was already safe at the crease. While the fielders retrieved the ball, Horace and Tanaka scored four runs for the Japanese team. They could have got six, but it was more important to stay in play.

Sonny Maria bowled again. His spin was fantastic. The ball drifted and danced, seemed actually to speed up and slow down along an arc of such astonishing irregularity that Horace was mesmerized and almost forgot to swing. But he was an old pro, and instinct kicked in. He swung the bat and the ball flew up, high over the stands and right over Des Voeux Road.

It sailed so straight that it looked like it would smack the Hongkong and Shanghai Banking Corporation right in the crack between the left and right sides of the double door, albeit at an interesting angle. Just at that the point, a debtor, going in to pay what he owed at Governor Isogai's order on pain of death pushed both door panels open. The ball sailed into the bank and bopped Teller Number 7 in the forehead.

From the British team, Alfred Steele-Perkins and Mimi Lau, subjects of an embarrassing romantic scandal before the war, chased after it. But the ball was well over the boundary, so Tanaka and Horace had their six runs. They did a few steps of the lindy hop while Steele-Perkins and Lau scrambled.

So the play continued. Horace played as slow and easy as he could without seeming to do so—stopping to drink water, wipe his brow, change his bat. Still, he couldn't seem to stop winning. Before he knew it the score was 359 to 364. The Japanese team was six runs short of taking the match. It looked like it was in the bag. Sonny Maria sweated in the muggy summer heat. He backed away from the crease, did a little cha-cha-cha and then ran toward it at such a fearsome speed that he seemed all fruit and no Carmen. He hurled the ball. It tore toward the striker's wicket like a B-52 bomber from the future. Horace steeled himself, then swung with all his might. But the ball was not there. It hovered two feet out of reach, dancing in the air as though the life of the colony depended on it, which, in a way, it did. When his stroke was complete, out of the way of the ball, it resumed its magical motion and slammed into the wicket, sending both bails flying and laying all three stumps dead flat on the ground.

Horace's jaw dropped in utter disbelief. In fact, the jaws of all on the field and in the stands dropped, absolutely astonished.

Sonny Maria danced a little rumba and sang, "I, Yi, Yi, Yi, Yi (I Like You Very Much)." All the British POWs on the field hooted and whistled their appreciation.

"Out," shouted Umpire Cheung.

So now it was all on Tanaka and Ishiyama, with Tanaka as striker and Ishiyama as nonstriker. They took their positions across from one another on the pitch. Ishiyama, one of Noma's most vicious interrogators, glared at Tanaka as if to say, *You'd better get this done or else.* Tanaka tried his best not to meet Ishiyama's eye. He could not bear the thought that he had anything in common with this murderer, and yet, they were both Japanese. Though required to hang out at Cheung's first-floor bar, Tanaka had been doing everything in his power over the past nine months of the occupation to avoid both Noma and Ishiyama. Of course, they could not be entirely avoided. Tanaka had been to the basement of the Supreme Court. He had translated the words of the doomed Chinese and British prisoners. He had translated the words of their killers too. But when asked to do so, he had refused to raise a hand against his fellow Hong Kongers, the ones he'd gone to school with, the ones he'd sat beside on trams and buses, the ones he'd elbowed or exchanged brief small talk with in department stores and noodle shops. To Noma and his henchmen, he had said, "I can't. I'll translate for you because that is my profession. But I won't hurt them. Kill me if you must." As yet, they had not, though they disdained him as a coward and traitor. Tanaka knew that his death could come suddenly, at any time.

Sonny Maria knew none of Tanaka's thoughts. He didn't even know who Tanaka was. In pre-war Hong Kong, Sonny had worked for his family's shipping company Shun Hing, moving goods in both directions between China and the Latin world. He spoke Chinese, English, Portuguese, some Russian, and enough Spanish for work. There was little back-and-forth between Shun Hing and Japan, though the family's business contacts did include shipping families who concentrated on inter-Asian trade. Sonny and Tanaka's paths could have crossed in the old days, but if they ever did, the crossing was brief and incidental. Sonny didn't remember.

He knew, however, that Ishiyama was an interrogator for the hated Kempeitai. And all the POWs at Sham Shui Po knew what happened to people who fell into the hands of the military police. Since Tanaka was Japanese and was up to bat with Ishiyama, Sonny assumed he was one of them. He whipped the ball at Tanaka with the considerable pent-up hatred that had accumulated as a consequence of all the brutal deaths of his friends, comrades, and lovers.

Expecting the playful kind of bowl that had been thrown for his good friend Horace, Tanaka was astonished. Tanaka had been a good secondary school cricketer, but he didn't have Horace's professional skill. And Sonny's bowl was straight and fast. Somehow, Tanaka stonewalled the ball, but it didn't go far, rolling infield toward the White Russian artist and architect Yuri "George" Vitalievitch Smirnoff, known for his caricatures of Imperial Japanese officials surreptitiously left at cafés and posted on street corners all over the city. Smirnoff had never played this absurd game in his entire life. The closest kind of game he knew was hockey, which he hadn't played since he was a boy in Vladivostok. He fumbled and dropped the ball. Enrico Valtorta, Vicar Apostolic of Hong Kong, scooped it up and threw it underhanded to Vandeleur Grayburn. Tanaka and Ishiyama scored three runs before Grayburn hurled the ball to the catcher at the striker's wicket, Edward Kerrison.

Horace had set the Japanese up well in spite of himself. Tanaka and Ishiyama needed just two more runs for a tie, three more to win. Ishiyama gave Tanaka his fiercest stare. Tanaka gazed back. It was not brotherhood, but it was acknowledgment. Sonny Maria hurled the ball, so hard and fast the air smoked in its wake. Miraculously, Tanaka hit it. A bright flame flared at the point of contact. Both bat and ball sizzled, and the smell of burnt wood and burnt leather assailed the nostrils of the fans. The ball sailed into the sky behind him, square leg, but unfortunately for Japan, Subadar Mengha Singh, Sikh fusilier with the 2/14th Punjab Regiment and top all-rounder for India against Lord Tennyson's XI on their tour of India in 1937 and 1938, stood right in its path. He leapt up and whipped it out of the air in his wide, strong palm. The ball was still scorching hot, but Mengha Singh wasn't a fusilier for nothing. He rolled to the ground and did a double somersault over his large left shoulder, but he did not let go of the burning ball.

The British fans went wild.

Noma was furious. Isogai was outraged. There was going to be hell to pay. Cheung tallied the score and called it: "362 for Japan, 364 for Britain. Britain takes it."

The teams burst from their cages. The players shook hands. When Horace greeted Sonny Maria, he asked, "Ever heard of a guy called 'Ga-Chan'?"

Sonny beamed and winked at him, reached into his fruit hat, and plucked a plaster apple from it, which he placed in Horace's hand. "Never, belo. But come look for me when this infernal war is over, if you want."

Cheung did not want to offer the trophy of his mother's ashes in the fine English china soup tureen to the winning team. Of course, it was better than having his mother's body thrown to the dogs, but it was hardly dignified. Then Noma appeared beside him. "You have to heed the call of duty," he said, in perfect Cantonese. "None of us likes what we have to do, but we don't always have a choice."

Afterwards, the victors shouted, "Huzzah!" Everyone laughed and chatted and shouted some more. Everyone expected tea and cucumber sandwiches.

Noma scowled. "The game might be over but the party is not. Bring on the dancing horses."

He gave a signal, and Emily Mah Wai-Yee walked out onto the green, followed by a parade of Chinese women all carrying babies, which begin to wail in unison. The spectators in the stands collectively inhaled, so loud it was audible above the crying. The women kept coming. There were twenty, then fifty, then a hundred. Still they came. More than a thousand women poured onto the green, each one holding a newborn child in her arms. None of them looked happy. All were pale and grim-faced, their eyes without light. And yet still they came, until there was not a spare inch of cricket green for the women to stand on, and they had to stand on the road. Chinese women with Japanese babies, every woman the subject of rape. Unit 731 in Manchuria could not have done better.

"This!" shouted Noma. "This is the true prize! I give you the mothers and the children of the New Asia!"

Tak-Wing, standing with the young cricketers, stuck his hands in his pockets and clenched his teeth.

Cheung flushed with the incandescent twin emotions of rage and humiliation.

"How do you like that, Cheung?" said Noma in English. "Huh? Your first-born grandson, a child of the new empire. You are free from those barmy British bastards at last."

CHAPTER 42

THIS FISH

September 20, 1942

How many times can a fish be eaten before it ceases to exist? Surely only once. You can only catch it once. You can only kill it once. You can only season and fry it once. You can only serve it once.

Even a fried fish is better off than me, used and reused in every way one might imagine, for what I look like, what I'm worth, what I desire, how I feel, what I can do with my body, what I represent, what I can say, what I can sing, how I can dance, who I can love, what I can bear, what my biology can bear, how I can reproduce, what my reproduction signifies, what it means to different people, how I can be punished for being one thing to one person and something entirely different to someone else.

Well, this fish is sick of it. If only I could be fully eaten. If only I could leave my body. Though even if I could, my death would continue to signify, on and on and on, until the end of women, until the end of fish.

This century was supposed to bring me what I wanted. It was supposed to make real the dreams I dreamt. I was the one who was supposed to step out of the chaotic past, with the sun shining on my face and moonlight spilling from my hair. I was supposed to sing "Moon and Stars over Sai Kung" at the Repulse Bay Hotel. I was supposed to drink champagne at the high table with laughing friends from all over the world. I was supposed to walk hand in hand on a shimmering beach with my beloved.

How did all these monsters come and take it from me? How did they make monsters of the ones I loved? This is not what was supposed to happen.

Not this.

How did it come to this? I'm so angry I could murder the entire Japanese Imperial Army with my bare hands, tear their flesh from their bones 'til my fingernails run with blood. I'm so ashamed, I want to disappear into ether, become mountain mist and forest rain, never be seen or heard from again.

But if I disappear, who will carry forward my beautiful dreams? Will anyone else dream them? Make them grow to encompass my sister, my father, my two mothers, my half-siblings, Courchene, Wong, Tanaka, Horace, Old Cheung, Captain Lee, Ting-Yan, Tak-Tam, the British, the Chinese, the third nationals, and even that miserable devil Tak-Wing until the whole city is dancing, until the whole city is bright and singing?

I don't want to disappear. I wish I had gone to university like my sister Violet so I could speak my dreams better. When I was young I wanted to dance, and I learned how to sing. If I survive this war, I'll sing. I'll sing my dreams and make them real. I'll find the words. Izzy and Shige will help me, and they'll find their words too. If governments and armies won't think about us, we'll think for ourselves. We'll make a new world for ourselves and the ones we love, dance and sing it into being.

I have to live so I can pass it on.

CHAPTER 43

EMILY FLEES

September 21, 1942

I don't know if there was ever a man as helpless as Cheung Tak-Wing. His wife was raped by the invading Japanese. His younger brother was tortured and murdered by them. His wife loved another man—not a Japanese soldier, thank God, but a Canadian one. He had a child who might be his, or might be the child of the raping invader. After Colonel Noma's gruesome parade of women, Tak-Wing lost his last scrap of conviction that Raymond Duk-Ming was his and began to call him Raymond Kennosuke. To me, Tak-Wing was first and foremost the unrepentant batterer of my spirited and beautiful sister, the woman he'd sworn three times in three different ways to love and cherish. What made it all so sad was that the sweet and charming boy my sister had married was still under there, somewhere. That boy had brought Emily to St Paul's so that Courchene and I could deliver her baby. But the monster within had quickly overtaken him. I pitied the sweet boy, but I hated the monster. I had to put Emily before the drowning boy, however sad he might be under his demonic shell. At that age, in that complicated time, I wouldn't have known how to help him anyway.

I worried about Emily staying with Tak-Wing at the Tai Hang house as she nursed little Raymond Duk-Ming, innocent of the sins of his father, whoever that might be. But the needs of the city were also terrible and great. I did my rounds of the doorways and gutters, the hotels and POW camps, administered the meagre medicines we had, the inadequate care we were able to dispense. I saw horrors I can't tell you about, because Professor Duffy encouraged me to push them out of my mind. She said my own psychological well-being was at stake. Because I didn't think about them, I forgot them. I became an automaton for the revolution yet to come, the one that might free my people from a suffering so deep I could not afford to fully see it. Had the people I helped done worse things than my beastly brother-in-law? I didn't know that they hadn't. The misery of this poor city was so deep that surely some of the men must have beaten their wives. But I didn't know about it, and I didn't know about any of the other things they had or hadn't done before I came upon them in the ditches, and so I didn't think about it. They were still human. That meant that Tak-Wing was still human too.

"Stay focused, dear Violet," Professor Duffy said. She worked as a volunteer at Selwyn-Clarke's clinic too. Though she didn't have my training, she had the wisdom of age, books, and travel. Because she was European, however, her look would have attracted attention on the streets, so she mostly stayed in the clinic and helped with the patients Dr Selwyn-Clarke or Dr Lai Po-Chuen had brought there. "Your people need you," she said.

Had I been thinking aloud?

"I want to help Emily, but I don't know how."

"Why do you look after her the way you do?"

What kind of question was that? "I don't know."

"Isn't she older than you?"

"Yes."

"In most Chinese families, isn't it the custom for the older sister to take care of the younger one?"

"Well," I said, like a stunned rabbit, "yes."

"So why is it upside-down in your family?"

Lots of things in my family are upside-down, I thought. But aloud, I said, "I don't know. That's just how it is. Everyone in my family has always taken care of Emily. Mother, before she died. Father too. Because of her beauty, I suppose."

Professor Duffy raised an eyebrow. "But Violet, you are also beautiful."

"Huh?"

"You are also beautiful."

"I'm not. I'm the ugly clever one. Emily is the beautiful helpless one."

"What utter nonsense. Is that how your family talks? You and Emily are both beautiful. You look very much alike. Both clever too, I suspect."

I stared at her like she had lost her last marble.

"You couldn't be more different in spirit," she said. "But in appearance you are clearly sisters."

"Well," I said, "that's the looniest thing I've ever heard. But it doesn't matter. If I don't help Emily now, she and Raymond could die."

Professor Duffy reached into the folds of her jacket and pulled out a book. She handed it to me. *Nightwood*, by Djuna Barnes.

"That's a funny name, Djuna Barnes," I said.

"Up-to-date stuff. When this war ends, the world will become a bigger place. You might use some of the time you now spend worrying thinking about who you want to become."

Emily came to me before I could get to her. Little Raymond lay bawling in her arms. She had her best dress on, light blue speckled with little white flowers, and a pair of stockings from before the war, but the stockings were torn and the left leg was wet with something dark and oily. She had made the mistake of going home after that infernal cricket match.

"Blood?" I asked her. Tak-Wing was not human. Any last vestiges of pity I felt for him evaporated.

"I hit him back this time."

"Will you let me examine you?"

"No, Violet. What's to see?"

I gave her morphine to calm her nerves. She flinched when I touched her, but she let me look. Her body was a mass of bruises. No part of it was sacred anymore to that animal. Grimly, I cleaned what had been soiled and stitched what had been torn.

"Don't go back," I said when I'd done what I could. "Stay here."

"I have to go back," she said.

"Please don't."

"He'll come looking for me. He's in such a rage. You have no idea what he's capable of."

"I have some idea."

"He's gone all vigilante, but who he wants to kill changes every thirty seconds. First, it's the Japanese. Then, it's the British. Then it's Old Mah. Then it's his own father. Then it's me. It could just as easily be you, Violet."

"He's a monster and a fool."

"He's not himself."

"Please don't make excuses for him. And please don't go back."

I had to do my rounds, but Professor Duffy said she would stay with Emily.

It was a miserable day on the streets. It started with rain, and then the swirling typhoon winds kicked in. Water poured like a river from the sky, warm as blood. The bodies of the dead washed down the street. I spent the morning trying to talk one of the missions into accepting the remnants of an extended family from the countryside, grandmother and children alike thin as chopsticks, with sores on their feet and faces. The mission was already overcrowded and the sisters were beside themselves trying to find beds, dry clothes, and water for the sick, bleeding, traumatized denizens. "Tell Dr Selwyn-Clarke we could use more blankets," said the sister in charge. "And if there's any chance of more medicine against dysentery, we could save hundreds of lives."

I had a small supply on me. I went through the mission, injecting those most likely to survive and, because I had to triage, leaving the nearly dead to die.

When I came back at the end of the day Emily wasn't there, and neither was Professor Duffy. I banged on the door of everyone who lived in the compound. Edward Kerrison wasn't in. Nor was Dr Graham-Cumming. Ellen Field was in, but had not seen my sister. I woke Dr Lai Po-Chuen from a heavy sleep. She had not seen my sister either. I woke a lot of patients too, who were not happy to be disturbed.

Eventually I found them both, and little Raymond too, in Courchene's room. Ting-Yan was also there delivering a supply of bandages and vitamin C tablets smuggled down from Free China.

"Tak-Wing came looking for them at the clinic," Professor Duffy said. "I didn't know where else to take them."

"Christ on the Cross," I said. "Could matters get any worse?"

"Well, he didn't find us," she said. "So yes, I suppose they could."

"Did he leave the clinic?"

"I don't know."

"Better stay here for a bit," Courchene said. He went to the hospital canteen to get us a bit of supper. There wasn't much. Watery soup, a small bowl of rice each, Chinese cabbage fried with a few thin strips of meat that we hoped was pork. Courchene had a deck of cards and we played whist to take our minds off the horrors that would otherwise have occupied us as the rain poured down in the darkness outside.

It was after midnight when I heard someone coming down the hall, pounding on doors as he went. I heard the inhabitants of our residential wing coming out of their rooms, one by one. Dr Lai was furious about being wakened again. Someone thumped on Courchene's door. None of us went to open it. The thumping came again, louder. Emily swallowed a hiccup. More thumping. Feeling our anxiety, little Raymond began to cry.

A gunshot sounded at the level of the lock.

"Holy Mary," Professor Duffy whispered.

"We're in for it now," Courchene said. "Hide."

But there was no time.

The door opened and into the room stepped Cheung Tak-Wing, the Angel of Vengeance himself, face as red as a wound, eyes blazing. "Now," he said to Emily. "Get."

Emily shook so hard she could barely stand. She tried to hand Raymond to me.

"The baby too," he said. "Didn't you swear it was mine?"

She paused, then nodded.

He grabbed her and Raymond, keeping the gun pointed at Courchene, Duffy, and me as they left so we wouldn't get up to follow.

I didn't realize I'd stopped breathing until I started again. "He'll kill her. We have to get her back." In my mind's eye, I saw him, dragging her by the hair across the city as the Japanese patrols stared. My mind's ear heard Raymond wailing. I said, "Where did that shape-shifting devil get a gun?"

I noticed Ting-Yan had a guilty look.

"Did you give it to him?"

"Why would I do such a thing?" Her face was pale as a bowl of congee.

"Mother of God," I said. "It wasn't you." Still, she was quiet. But I put two and two together. "It was his dead ghost brother, Tak-Tam."

"Don't call my lost husband a ghost. He wanted Tak-Wing to have some protection against the Japanese."

"You East River people have been smuggling arms."

She didn't deny it, so I knew it was true.

CHAPTER 44

ESCAPE

September 21, 1942

Tak-Wing's ocean of love for Emily had drained out of him completely. He was so possessed by his hatred for the Japanese that there was no room for anything else. As his once beautiful wife had been made a conduit of their hatred for him, or at least, for men like him—Chinese men who worked for and looked to the British colonizer—so she had become a conduit for the hatred he returned to them. He would rather not have been under the thumb of the British, but what choice had he had 'til now? He buried the thought that he was somehow less of a man because he knew their ways and games. He was way too good a cricketer, tennis player, and footballer to be any less than a man. He returned his conscious mind instead to imagining Emily's degradation. As far as he was concerned, the woman he loved was dead, replaced by a fox demon who, horribly, still had her eyes. Even worse was her monster child, the one he felt certain was fathered by the murderer Noma, the sadistic head of the Kempeitai who beat men to the brink of death before beheading them, in spite of all her protest that the child was Tak-Wing's. His once-upon-a-time love for Emily backwashed into him as pure vengeance. And because he was so diminished by his hate, vengeance overflowed from his being like the putrid blood of the dead.

He had willingly accompanied her to the cricket match in the hope that the game he'd once played joyfully might return him to his old self. But since Noma's awful display on the field where Tak-Wing had once been the hero of so many secret cricket matches, he could not bear of the sight of her. His love for Emily and his love for the game had been destroyed in one fell swoop. He should kill both her and the child. And himself too, perhaps. He thought about his grandmother, laid out on that ridiculous makeshift pyre, and the final loss of his natal village that went with her death. He thought of his father's grim face, spilling with rage and grief. And Emily just sitting there in the warmth of that fire, while the monster's child slept against her breast. The remnants of the typhoon that had blown through the city two days ago returned. It began to rain. Though the wind whipped the water around, the water was clear. Something stirred, not exactly in his heart, but in his groin. He felt sick, afraid of himself and his own hatred.

Emily sat in the corner of the room, sobbing as she cradled Raymond in her arms. The little demon bawled its ugly Japanese head off.

Tak-Wing went to them, grabbed them, and hurled them into the backroom before he did something worse to them. He locked the door with an outside padlock, then buried the key in the bottom of the family's dwindling sack of rice, hiding it from himself so that if a murderous impulse he couldn't repress struck him later, he'd have to dig and search to get it out.

When they were as safe as he could make them, he ran out into the rain and vomited.

As the Japanese held the British prisoner at Stanley and Sham Shui Po, Tak-Wing held Emily and Raymond prisoner. She didn't show up at the hospital for work the next morning, so when I set out on my rounds, the first place I went was the Tai Hang house. I stood on tiptoe to look in the window and saw him sitting at the dining table, head slumped forward in his hands. After a minute, he got up, rustled around in a half-full sack of rice that leaned against the wall and then stepped toward the backroom. I saw the lock on the door. He moved to open it, changed his mind, returned to the rice sack and buried what could only have been the key inside. Then he went back to the table and dropped his head back into his hands. What was he doing to her in there?

I had to finish my rounds for the day. There were so many people in the missions and on the street waiting for me. The others would all be out on their rounds too, so there would be no one to plan with until evening.

But that night, while Duffy, Courchene, Ting-Yan, and I shared a pot of rice, a can of beans, and a few wilted vegetables, I told them what I had seen.

"That can't be good," Courchene said. "I've met men like Tak-Wing before and seen what they do. Nothing good ever happens with guys like that." He ate slowly, though he was clearly hungry. We all were. Selwyn-Clarke made sure we had food, but there was no such thing as plenty. He had just come back from three weeks in detention and what he described as the weirdest cricket game in history. Being held by the Kempeitai, he said, was not an experience he'd wish on anyone. And the cricket match had been an utter waste of time when he could have been out there doing his humanitarian work. What on earth did the city's new masters intend for the city, and how were they going to govern it? His wife, Hilda, came in a car to pick him up, and he went back with her to their home in the Mid-Levels to recover.

"Tak-Wing seems unstable." Professor Duffy said. "Still, one hates to invade a couple's privacy." Clearly, she had not been looking very closely at Emily.

"Lots of Chinese men treat their wives badly," said Ting-Yan, nibbling on a leaf of bok choy as though it were fatty pork. "But Tak-Wing is taking it too far."

"Lots of men treat their wives badly, Chinese or not," Professor Duffy said.

"Emily is in a dangerous situation," I said. "This is not the normal bickering that occurs in married life."

Courchene, who'd fallen quiet in the corner, said, "Let's storm the house."

"Maybe we should just go there and try to reason with him. He was a sweet boy once," Ting-Yan said.

"He was. Once." I scarfed my last bite, a forkful of rice with a last lonely bean on it. "But I think he's past reason now. Though the problem with storming the house is that he knows we know."

"We'll have to do something he really doesn't expect," said Courchene.

"If he's already feeling edgy, it'll be impossible to surprise him," said Professor Duffy, scraping her plate.

"He's got her locked in a room," said Courchene. His plate was empty too. I saw him glance hungrily at the rice pot, but we all knew it was empty. None of us complained aloud because we didn't want to make anyone else feel bad for eating. "All over this godforsaken city," he continued, "there are squadrons of marauders banging on the doors of houses trying to get at the women inside. We'd be the only ones doing it for a good reason."

"You have a point," Professor Duffy said.

"We need to get my poor sister away from that monster, however we do it."

"I could train you," Courchene said. "We'd need guns." He looked at Ting-Yan, who looked back but offered nothing.

He waited.

Finally, Ting-Yan spoke. "When you use guns, people die. I don't want to die, and I don't want to kill the brother of my late husband either."

I wondered if she still had feelings for Tak-Wing, though I didn't say so out loud.

As if reading my thoughts, she said, "That was a million years ago, Violet."

"Chinese women deserve more," Professor Duffy muttered, "so much more than they are given."

"Bill can't do this on his own," I said. "I'll go with him."

"I'm not against working with a woman. But Emily is your sister. A deep attachment adds a risk factor."

I snorted. "Then I'll be someone else on the day. I'll be a soldier, like you."

A gift came in the form of two men looking for someone called "Ga-Chan." Old Cheung had sent them over from the cricket club. One of them was Emily's former bandmate Tanaka, the other a rum importer called Morgan Horace. Horace told us that Cheung didn't seem well, but he'd encouraged them to look for me and Emily while it was still possible to do so.

"Horace is my good friend," Tanaka said. "He's Isadore's cousin."

"Isadore Davis Wong is now living in a small village known for its lychees," Ting-Yan said, "but he grows a lot of things—bok choy, gai lan, sweet potatoes, a bit of rice. He's famous for his green thumb. He helps the East River Column move goods and people sometimes."

"You've seen him? He's alive? Praise heaven!" said Horace. "I have some letters. I think they're from Iz, but they're coded." He reached into his pocket and pulled out three envelopes. From each he pulled out a letter in funny writing—all *P*s, *U*s, *V*s, and *Q*s right side up, upside down, and sideways. "I can't make head or tail of these, but they can't be from anyone but Izzy. The kid who gave them to me told me to find someone called 'Ga-Chan.' Have you ever heard of such a person?"

I'd seen this script before. Courchene. Ga-Chan. I went to his room to get him.

"I can translate," Courchene said, once he'd come and looked over the letters. "If you'll help us first. You'll probably want to anyway. It's about Emily."

"I haven't seen her since before the war," Tanaka said. "Is she okay?"

"Not really. Not at all, actually."

"Of course we'll help," Tanaka said. "Won't we, Morgan?"

The rum seller nodded his head. "Of course we will. And afterwards, you'll translate these?"

"Once Emily is safe with us again."

Ting-Yan had a brilliant plan for the men to pose as Kempeitai in order to rescue Emily and Raymond from Tak-Wing. Tanaka would be able to help with his fluent Japanese. Afterwards we could all go to Chek Keng, safe from the monster Tak-Wing had become.

"Won't Tak-Wing recognize Tanaka?" I asked.

"I've grown a moustache since the last time I saw him," said Tanaka. "And lost a bit of weight. I could grow a beard as well."

"It doesn't matter," said Ting-Yan. "He'll recognize all of us. But any element of surprise and authority we can bring to the raid will give us an advantage."

"I would like to come to Chek Keng too," said Professor Duffy. "I've heard there's a route to Free China, and that the East River Column is escorting people there. Is that true?"

Ting-Yan sighed. "Try not to spread that information too freely. It's getting our people killed." She didn't say anything about Tak-Tam, but she didn't have to.

We made a plan. Courchene, Horace, and Tanaka would pose as Kempeitai, storm the door of the Tai Hang house, and rescue Emily and Raymond. Ting-Yan would supply guns. My job would be to steal Kempeitai uniforms. We had a long, absurd conversation about racial types and whose looks would fool which lookers, about whether Courchene could pass as Asian and, if so, whether he looked more Chinese or Japanese, about whether Tak-Wing would be suspicious of Horace as a Negro Kempeitai, and about whether a Japanese of Tanaka's cosmopolitan demeanour would be convincing as military police even if Tak-Wing didn't recognize him as Emily's friend.

"I'm coming too," I said.

Courchene gave me a skeptical look. "It's dangerous, Violet."

"I know. It's dangerous for all of us."

"No more dangerous than sending me," said Horace.

"You have your bona fides as a committed anti-colonial," Tanaka said.

"No one's going to know that by looking at me," Horace said. "Bona fides and membership are not the same thing. Just try living in America for a day or two."

"So that settles it," I said. "I'm coming."

"How does it settle it?" said Courchene.

"If only Tanaka and Courchene go, it'll cut the risk in half," Ting-Yan said.

"It will also cut your strength in half at a time when you may really need it," said Professor Duffy.

"She's his sister-in-law!" shouted Courchene.

"She'll be a small Asian man."

"The Kempeitai recruit so many local auxiliaries," Horace said. "Even you could join, Professor Duffy, and as long as you were in uniform, no one would bat an eyelash."

I still had the job of posing as a laundry worker to steal uniforms. The Kempeitai left their soiled police uniforms at the Hong Kong Cricket Club, to be taken away by the same laundry that used to wash the cricket uniforms.

"Is it truly necessary?" I asked. "I mean, if we have East River guns and Bill teaches us how to storm a fortress, isn't that good enough?"

"You'll need more than East River guns if you don't want anyone to get shot," said Ting-Yan. "Tak-Wing has a gun too. But we want him to give up without a fight, because we don't want to hurt him. That means he needs to be truly and completely afraid. He won't be afraid of a ragtag crew of soft civilians. Especially not if he recognizes you, Violet."

"Hmph," I said.

"I'm not soft," said Horace.

"Me neither," said Tanaka.

"You know what I mean," Ting-Yan said.

"Those uniforms better be clean," Horace said.

"How come you guys don't already have uniforms?" I asked.

"We're auxiliary forces," said Tanaka, "and Colonel Noma's guests. So our armbands are enough." He turned to show us more clearly the words *law* and *soldier* in Chinese characters on his arm.

"All of this is so risky," Professor Duffy said. "How did our little backwater Fragrant Harbour become so frightening and complicated?"

Plan under way, we all went back to our rooms, billets, and homes to bide our time until everything was in place.

From their months at the HKCC helping the Kempeitai and drinking at Cheung's bar, Tanaka and Horace were sure that the regular laundry day was Thursday. So they were surprised when the white truck appeared out back on Wednesday instead.

And then on Monday, unexpectedly, two coolies came, each with a pair of rattan baskets on a long pole, to pick up anything soiled over the weekend and urgently in need of a wash. Everything came back the next day. Were they on to us? Or was this week an anomaly?

In the meantime, Noma had started joshing them in new ways. "How did you miss that strike, Horace? How can you be a real Japanese soldier if you give up your wicket so easily?" Did he suspect Horace's change of heart, or was he just disappointed that Horace didn't seem to be as good a cricket player as he'd hoped?

He also began taking Tanaka into the more brutal interrogation rooms. "Too much blood for a gentle civilian, Tanaka? You have to get tough if you want to be a real soldier." Noma pressured Tanaka to beat an old friend from school, and forced him to break the man's hand. Tanaka felt sure that next time Noma would make him kill the man.

"We've got to get out of here," Tanaka said when I stopped by to find out what they'd learned about the laundry. "It's only a matter of time before we're executed in that basement ourselves, or sent to Canton to be executed there."

On Wednesday, I went to the club dressed as a coolie so that if Cheung was around, he wouldn't recognize me. I skulked around the delivery door at Jackson Road, where both the kitchen of the Cricket Club and the side door of the Supreme Court were. All day I loitered, but no laundry truck came.

On Thursday, I went back, and spent a long morning waiting. At last, in the early afternoon, when my stomach was grumbling with hunger, I saw the truck round the corner and pull up to the door. I watched the workers come and go, and waited for an opening when they were dropping things off inside. But they'd posted a guard by the rear of the truck. They must have a system to guard against thieves and looters.

When they were gone, I tried the kitchen door. I didn't expect it to open, but miraculously, it did. They had forgotten to lock it. I rushed toward the hall, only to see Cheung coming down it, carrying a massive and bloody side of pork. I ducked into a storage cupboard and waited for him to leave, then dashed down the hall to the equipment room.

All the uniforms were laid out on the benches. There were two Chinese maids, sorting them. Awkwardly, they read the names that were inked into the backs of collars and waistbands, or at least those parts of the names that resolved into Chinese characters. They placed the clean uniforms in the lockers of the soldiers to whom they belonged. From the doorway, I watched and listened to them chatting about food shortages, lost family members, and whether it was worth becoming the girlfriend of a Japanese soldier in order to care for their own children as the food shortages got worse. They could try to meet some right here, if they would dare be lovers with members of the dreaded Kempeitai. Ordinary soldiers would be safer, but where would they meet those? Their jobs were here. And the Kempeitai, because they were elite gendarmes, had access to more and better food and drink. Of course, if the Allies were to win the war and find out they'd comforted Japanese soldiers, they'd be branded as traitors, but on the other hand, if they died of starvation before the Allies won, what would that matter? The women were extremely thin.

"The war is men's business," one of them said. "Love, family, and survival is our business."

They compared the sizes of the uniforms, which ones were well-kept and which ones were wearing out. They talked about the individual Kempeitai too.

"The shorter one is better looking."

"The tall one is likely to have a sadistic streak."

"The skinny one has a kind face."

"The one with glasses looks like he's Kempeitai against his will."

They pondered the circumstances that might have brought these men to become military police. Love of uniform? Love of emperor? A taste for violence? Good detective skills? A sense of duty? Hatred of the European presence in Asia? Maybe, too, some of them had been coerced.

When someone came down the hallway, I ducked inside the door, and pressed up against a wall of lockers, out of the women's sight. I peeked out from time to time and watched the stack of uniforms dwindle as each was locked away, one by one.

I had to skulk away, empty-handed.

On Friday, Noma asked Horace to come help with the interrogations. "One of my best men has been relocated to Shanghai. It's time for you to step in."

"What for, man? I don't speak of word of Chinese."

"But you've got Japanese and English. Good enough."

When we gathered again to refine our plan, Horace wouldn't talk about what Noma had made him do. "We've got to get out of here, Miss Violet."

On Monday, early in the morning, I dressed again as a coolie and knocked on the kitchen door, bold as you please. Cheung let me in. He gave me a funny look, like he was trying to place me, but he didn't actually recognize me. I went down the hall to the equipment room and helped myself to the reeking hamper of soiled clothes, making sure to pick out four of the cleaner ones in roughly the right sizes. I piled whatever else was there on top, but left some behind for the real laundry workers to collect later.

Tanaka and Horace put in a full day at the Supreme Court, interrogating prisoners. They came to Courchene's room at the French Hospital in the evening, wearing soiled civvies and armbands. They looked weary and heartsick.

"Are you sure you are up for this?" said Ting-Yan.

"We have to be," Tanaka said. "Cheung remarked this afternoon that the laundry people came twice today. If he hasn't already figured out what's going on, he will soon."

"Noma asked me to do something today," Horace said. "I couldn't. I refused. He made me watch him do it, and told me my turn is tomorrow. I'm not sure if he meant I'd be on the giving or receiving end."

No one was happy about the soiled uniforms in which unspeakable activities had been carried out. But we put them on. Our skins touched the skins of murderers.

Over the last couple of days of surreptitious activity, I had been tucking my hair under my cap. But now, I asked Ting-Yan to cut it. With an eyeliner pencil, she drew a little moustache on my upper lip too. "Too much?" she asked.

I looked in the mirror. "I like it."

Ready as we would ever be, we stepped out into the warm, still night.

When I looked up past the battered bamboo shutter into the open ground floor window of the Tai Hang house, I saw Tak-Wing stumbling around like a confused animal. Given the extreme shortages across the city, I couldn't fathom where he was getting booze. Perhaps from his father, Cheung, whose bar at the old cricket club had become a popular drinking spot for the Japanese military. There was no sign of Emily or Raymond, but the door to the backroom was still closed and locked. I prayed he'd been giving them food and water these last ten days.

We sidled up to the door as Courchene had taught us.

Courchene banged on it with his big fist.

In Japanese, Tanaka shouted, "Kempeitai! Open up!"

"Up your mother!" shouted drunk Tak-Wing.

"Open up or we'll break the lock!" Tanaka yelled.

"Get out of here! Don't you demons do enough damage in the daytime?"

Courchene looked me in the eye. "Here goes." He fired into the lock, and the door swung open.

Tak-Wing had a gun on him, but Courchene didn't bat an eyelash. He fired before Tak-Wing even knew his intentions. The bullet grazed Tak-Wing's shoulder.

"Missed me, big man," said Tak-Wing in Cantonese. He reeked so badly of liquor I could smell him from my position outside the window. Greasy, overgrown hair stuck out from his head in so many dishevelled directions.

"On purpose, fool. Drop the gun." Courchene had picked up a bit of the local tongue.

Beside him, Tanaka trained his pistol on Tak-Wing's heart. He couldn't have shot him if his life depended on it, but Tak-Wing didn't know that. In Japanese Tanaka said, "Drop it. Now."

Hatred blazed from Tak-Wing's eyes and a bullet blazed from his pistol. Blood gushed from Tanaka's neck. Courchene fired at Tak-Wing, but missed. I stepped in behind him, aimed, and shot his hand.

Tak-Wing dropped the gun.

Courchene rushed him and kicked it out of the way.

As they scuffled, Horace and I ran to the back. I smashed the flimsy lock with the butt of my pistol. Emily trembled behind the door, her hand over Raymond's howling mouth.

"Em, it's me," I whispered. "Come on. We're busting you out."

Her eyes went wide with surprise. She noticed my moustache, and began to laugh.

"Shh!" I said. "Don't. It's not safe. Come on."

In the main room, Tanaka lay slumped on the floor. Tak-Wing's bullet had hit a vein. I examined him quickly. Though there was a lot of blood, the bullet had just grazed him. I tore off a piece of my shirt and tied it around his neck to staunch the bleeding.

All the while, Tak-Wing shouted at Courchene. "Are you going to kill me? If you're going to kill me, just do it and get it over with." He clearly recognized Courchene now, though it had completely ceased to matter. They scuffled and danced. Courchene shot again, this time at his foot.

"Death to your mother!" Tak-Wing howled.

Horace and I hustled Emily and Raymond out the gaping door. Courchene and Tanaka covered us. Once we were out, Courchene fired one last shot, nowhere fatal, I hoped. I heard Tak-Wing drop to the floor. He moaned and whimpered, still alive. Professor Duffy was right. This was cursed, awful business. We ran out into the night, not back to St Paul's but down to the Causeway Bay Typhoon Shelter where Captain Lee, Professor Duffy, and Ting-Yan were waiting on the *Oolong*.

On the boat, Courchene looked at Morgan's letters and patiently translated. "I wonder who wrote these for him. Only a handful of Cree speakers in my battalion. There's one guy besides me working on Hong Kong Island. I wonder who's there with Isadore Davis Wong in Sai Kung?"

CHAPTER 45

NOT A DREAM

October 12, 1942

Dear Izzy,

My poor cousin, I got a letter from you dated September 12, put in my hand on September 13 by a skinny Chinese kid with eyes like an old man. He said he was a "little devil," whatever that means, and told me to look for a guy called "Ga-Chan." That's what took so long. I had no idea who this person was. Well, I finally found him, or I wouldn't be writing to you. Though you may see me before you get this letter. We had a little adventure together to rescue that girl who used to sing with your band, Emily Mah, from her mad-dog husband. And then "Ga-Chan" kindly translated your letters back into English for me. His actual name is William Courchene, and he's a Métis guy from Canada. He fought here with the Winnipeg Grenadiers, who were in Jamaica right before the war. It's a small world!

What risks you take, dear fool, to write to me in such times. You should stay in hiding and stay safe. I can't imagine what the military police would do to you if they found you.

I been a fool myself. Well, not a fool—Brother Du Bois's dream is a dream of freedom and love. But I got eyes in my head. I can see that what's been happening on this poor, cursed island is not the unfolding of a beautiful dream.

I'm with your bandmates, Tanaka and Emily. Emily's not doing so good, but Tanaka's fine. We're coming up to look for you, along with Emily's sister and some other expats. I won't say more, as I don't think these notes are the safest way to communicate, even coded. But you sound so desperate, cousin, and I don't want you to worry. Unless of course you get this letter, but don't see me before or shortly after it arrives. Then you'll know something's happened. If that's the case, please don't come looking for me. Don't risk yourself.

But I think we'll be together under the moon and stars again, my cuz.

Love from your cousin,

Morgan

CHAPTER 46

CHEUNG PLOTS REVENGE

October 13, 1942

Ever since Colonel Noma's cruel parade of Chinese women with Japanese babies more than three weeks ago, Cheung had been stewing. He'd been yelling at his wife, Yim-Fong. He'd been slamming doors. He'd been spitting in the soup. He'd been speaking of murder to anyone who would listen. Today, it was Captain Lee, who came with a load of crab for stuffed crab night.

"The least we can do is get rid of the babies. Prevent a Japanese colony from being born in the ruin of the British one," said Cheung. "When will we be free? If my line is cut off, theirs will not be perpetuated."

"That is what Noma is banking on, you fool," Lee said. "If you murder the babies, you become no better than him. And then he has every reason to say Hong Kong is in just as good hands with the Japanese. If the Chinese are baby killers anyway."

"Emily's baby was supposed to be my first grandson."

"He might indeed be," said Lee. "Perhaps Noma was bluffing when he taunted you about Raymond being his. Maybe he is setting you up to lose your mind over it."

"But all those Chinese women with Japanese babies. The message is clear as day."

"Message and truth are not necessarily the same thing," Lee said.

"I can't bear it, Brother."

"Then we have to fight those bastards and hit them where it counts."

"But this is ground zero."

"So you would gamble on killing your own grandson for the possibility of getting revenge on a monster?"

"I would, yes."

"You would murder an innocent child to make a point."

"Yes. To allow the humiliation to stand is unbearable."

"I'd advise you to sleep on it, Brother. Truly. Cool your head. It's a terrible idea. You'll regret it for the rest of your life."

There was a knock at the door. It was one of Noma's men. "Have you seen that devil bastard Morgan Horace?"

"Who?" said Cheung.

"Noma wants him to do some interrogation work today."

"I don't know who you are talking about."

"Don't be coy," said the gendarme. "I'll take you too."

"I'm not afraid. And I don't care."

The policeman laughed.

"Take me. Kill me and save me the trouble."

"Nah. Not today anyway. My orders are to find Morgan Horace."

"Take me instead. I'm planning to kill Noma's baby."

The policeman laughed harder.

"I'm planning to kill Noma himself."

The policeman cackled with pure, twisted glee. *Stupid fool Chinaman.* And he took off up the stairs to look for Horace.

"What were you doing, inviting your own death? Your poor mother would not like that at all," Lee said.

"Well, she's dead," said Cheung, rudely. "And her spirit lives in an English soup tureen."

Lee's sympathetic look made Cheung want to punch him.

"I've known you all my life, Cheung. What can I do to help you?"

Cheung was silent for a long stretch. Finally, he said, "You know that opium paste you bring in sometimes?"

"How did you know about that?"

"I've got eyes."

"My family have worked for the trade since the British first came. It's hard to stop, even when supplies are drying up. You want to smoke? I thought you disapproved. After what happened to your father."

"He died from smoking anti-opium. Not opium."

"Don't be an idiot," said Lee. "You know they are the same thing."

"Anti-opium's more potent, actually. Made with scientific distillation methods and additives directed at Asian tastes."

"As the anti-British Japanese are the same as the British, only more potent," said Lee. "And yet they think they speak to pan-Asian feelings."

"I'll take either."

"What? British or Japanese? I thought you hated the Japanese."

"Either opium or anti-opium."

"There's a traditional opium paste that's very mild and relaxing," Lee said. "I've got a little bit right here." He produced a small cylindrical box made of buffalo horn carved with bamboo leaves. "If you like it, I can bring you more, Brother. No problem."

"I don't want mild and relaxing," Cheung said. He pushed the box back with such force it nearly rolled off the table.

"What are you talking about?"

"I want potent and deadly."

"One can die of opium addiction, but it takes a long time, and you have to smoke it every day," said Lee. "You know that. And also, I'm not going to help you kill yourself."

"I don't want to kill myself, you dumb ox."

Lee was silent for a long moment.

Cheung glared at him as though he were a dim-witted child.

Finally, Lee said, "You want to—" He coughed. "I can't help you with that, my friend. It won't help matters. Why don't you go back to your flat for a bit. Go back to your wife. Rest. You're overwrought. Smoke a bit of this and have a sleep. You'll feel differently when you wake up." He opened the box to reveal a sweet-smelling black paste inside. "Medicine," he said. "Not poison. Ask your wife to prepare it for you the old-fashioned way."

"Get that father-killing filth away from me," said Cheung. "I'd rather have my head sliced from my body by those devil samurai."

"Come with me to Chek Keng, then," said Lee. "I have to go to the boat now to meet my daughter. I'm afraid for you if you stay here."

"Go meet your daughter. Get away from here!"

"Come with me."

"Leave me alone."

"I'm begging you, Brother. You don't seem well."

"I'm fine."

Lee slid off his stool. He gave his friend one last, long, concerned look.

"I'm not dead yet! Go!"

The nightly song of the cicadas was approaching its crescendo when the knock came. Cheung woke from a heavy, sickening sleep. "Are you here for me, you murderers?" he shouted.

The knock came louder.

"Have the courtesy to kill me in the morning." He dropped back into a nauseous doze.

Still the knocking continued.

"Are you so bloodthirsty that you must drink in the middle of the night?"

He went down to the door and opened it.

Who should be standing there but his own beloved son, the only one that remained, hair wild, eyes bloodshot, skin white as the scum on a barrel of soy milk. He limped, and a bloody bandage bound his right hand. "Tak-Wing."

The young man smiled at him, all teeth. He slammed a battered leather briefcase on the foyer table.

"What do you have in there?"

"Let's go to the parlour."

"What are you up to, son of mine?"

They went into the parlour, and Cheung cleared the coffee table. "What is it?"

Tak-Wing put the bag on the table and opened it.

The case was full of little boxes of Immortal Carp, the Carp's Eye type, precisely the variety of anti-opium pill that had killed Cheung's father and been banned from the market forty years ago.

"Where did you get those?"

"The court ordered Old Mah to destroy them when you won the case against him. But he couldn't bring himself to do it, because of all the thought and labour he'd put into developing the product. So he gave them to his daughters to dispose of. Violet did as she was told and had her portion incinerated at the dump. But Emily kept hers. She's kind of sentimental, you know? She was attached to the memory of her father's joy when the pills first hit the market. But she left them when she fled the house." Tak-Wing's toothy smile widened and grew gleeful.

"How did you know I wanted them?"

"Lee came to me, worried about you. He should have worried about me too."

Cheung looked at his once beautiful son. Something noble dug at it his heart, but he willed it away. "Do you understand my plan?"

"Lee told me about it."

"I want to get rid of the monster babies," said Cheung.

"The only monster baby we know is Raymond. The sight of him makes me sick, Father."

"I thought Emily would give me my first grandson."

"The sight of her makes me sick too."

"I told you not to marry her."

"You were right, my dearest father. You were right. Not only have I married a whore, I've married the whore of my worst enemy. And she has borne his child. Now she's running off with one of his henchmen, some stinky hole translator. If I kill her, does that make me a murderer?"

Cheung jolted for a minute into his old, kind self. "My son."

"Does it?"

"It does. It makes you a murderer. If you kill Raymond, you'll be a baby killer too."

"I don't care. I hate them."

"I hate them too. If there's anything more despicable than a woman who sleeps with the enemy, it's a woman who has a child with him."

"Such a woman is worse than the enemy himself. The enemy is standing up for his country. While the woman has betrayed hers," said Tak-Wing, eyes blazing with fervour.

"We have no country," Cheung said.

"And because we have none, our women are not our own either," said Tak-Wing.

"What horror are we speaking of, my son?"

"A horror deeper than the deepest hole. A shame heavier than the heaviest rock."

"I'm sick with hatred and shame."

"Me too, Father."

"I hear that the torments that the Kempeitai lay on Chinese prisoners in the basement of the Supreme Court are such that the prisoners no longer want to live."

"We are not in that basement, but we are being tortured in the same way."

"Give me those pills," Cheung said. "I will poison the Kempeitai if you will poison Emily and Raymond."

The two once good, kind men looked at each other.

"Pact," said Tak-Wing.

"Pact," said his father.

"Those pills are forty years old, and were designed to give pleasure, not to kill. Maybe we should make sure that they work."

"They'll work. They killed your grandfather."

"Old Mah is the world's worst pharmacist. Just because one batch was deadly doesn't mean this batch is."

"Should we try them out on someone?"

"Yes. Let's try them out on someone."

CHAPTER 47

Typhoon Shelter
LET'S GO HOME

June 30, 1997

O phelia stares at the fish tank, dazed. A wise old fish with long whiskers stares back, while above it, smaller fish dart back and forth, confused as to why the ocean has shrunk so small.

Are you shocked, Feelie? That men would blame women for their own violation? That's how men thought in those days. That women were an extension of the nation to which they belonged, to be held up or torn down, depending on which side you were on. Once a woman had had relations with a man from the other side, voluntarily or not, she became a traitor. Their feelings were complicated by the fact that we had no nation and two nations: we were British and not British, we were Chinese and not Chinese. This only it made it worse for them. Because both England and China wanted loyalty from them without expecting such loyalty to be singular or deep, Hong Kong men had to assert the tentative loyalties they felt harder than they would have had they felt secure in their commitments. Treated all their lives as second-class subjects by the British, in a city where some Chinese people had gone over to the Japanese side as fifth columnists against British imperialism, they had to convince themselves that they never would join that Asian nation that now murdered Chinese people with such cruelty and impunity. The slightest intimation that they might, brought on by sexual relations between a Japanese soldier and a woman close to them, however involuntary, sent them into paroxysms of shame. This shame that they felt was unbearable. It wasn't rational. It went straight to the heart of the hate that war creates. It doesn't excuse what they did, though. Not in any way.

Would you like a baked tapioca pudding to calm your nerves? It's custardy on top and has red bean paste at the bottom. Remember how I didn't want to tell you this story? Most old ladies would refuse outright. But I can see that your psyche is different from mine. You need the truth to move on. Whereas my generation thought it was healthier to forget. We think that the worse the events that befall you, the more deeply you ought to bury them, so as not to burden the next generation. We are a people who love our children! I hope I haven't hurt you by telling you this story. Maybe my old form three teacher was right: silence is golden.

Well, everybody lived at the furthest extreme of their worst selves in those days. Okay, maybe not everybody. But during the war, if a person carried ghosts, those ghosts were likely to wake whether the person actively chose to disturb them or not. You could say the war brought to the surface the histories of suffering that they were already carrying. Remember, our forebears lived through enough displacement and violence to make your head spin—the Qing clearances, the Taiping Rebellion, the Red Turban Rebellion, the Punti–Hakka Clan Wars, where neighbour attacked neighbour and unspeakable things were done to women and children.

The other thing that was important was saving face. In those days, men took care of their own pride and prestige above all things and gave very little thought to women's suffering.

Yes, Miss Sociology, I can see that saving face and forgetting might bring about contradictory actions sometimes. Well, that explains the way many people went down, doesn't it?

You don't want to live through times like they had to live through. You don't want to live through a time like we had to live through either. When you live through such times, you find things out about the seemingly ordinary people around you that you don't want to know. Tak-Wing and Old

Cheung were so far down the rabbit hole it seemed unlikely they would ever come out. How could Tak-Wing, who had loved Emily so much, have had such a violent change of heart? In his youthful arrogance, he had thought that modern romance was enough to escape the damage of centuries of pillage and retribution. But in the occupation he discovered all those demons and more residing in his liver. Cheung, who was, after all, just an ordinary village boy with no education, was just as lost, though as the grown-up in the room, he should have known better. But it wasn't about knowing. It was about feeling. It was about spirits they were carrying unbeknownst to themselves. Spirits who were starved and vengeful. It was the way that men drowned. Always taking women with them. I would have beaten sense into them with a broom handle if I had been there with them. I do believe, though, that even as Cheung and Tak-Wing made their plans, they knew what they were doing wasn't right.

What about the way women drowned, you ask? Emily and I fought back in our own ways. Elliptically or belatedly. We weren't raised to give as good as we got. We had to find our own paths in everything. But maybe I shouldn't talk about these horrors anymore. Maybe we should just quit the story here? And you can go join Macy at the waterfront for all the speeches. It's five o'clock. Time to get with the times! Macy gets so mad at me for dwelling in the past. Why don't we eat something sweet and then go down to the waterfront to see if we can catch the farewell ceremony of the British Hong Kong troops?

Great-Aunt Violet flags down the grumpy server.
   "Chung yiu mut yeh?"
   She orders baked tapioca pudding.
   "Twenty minutes, okay?" the server says.
   "Okay," says Great-Aunt Violet. "More tea too, please."
   Ophelia is quiet as they wait for the tapioca pudding. It hits the table twenty minutes later, by the pink-haired girl's clock. Aunt Violet scoops a large serving onto a plate for Ophelia.

Ophelia isn't sure she can eat. She eyes the pudding with suspicion.

"Hong Kong invention," says Great-Aunt Violet. "Neither traditionally Chinese nor traditionally British. And yet so very delicious. Come on, try it."

Ophelia takes a small bite. The combination of creamy tapioca and rich red bean paste sends straight-up bliss to her taste buds. She swallows and asks, "Were Emily and Raymond okay in the end? Did you and the others manage to get her to Chek Keng?"

CHAPTER 48

THE SEA AT NIGHT

October 13, 1942

Captain Lee was waiting for us at the *Oolong* in the Causeway Bay Typhoon Shelter. Ting-Yan and Professor Duffy had arrived ahead of us and explained Emily's rescue and the need to depart as soon as everyone was aboard. We scrambled onto the boat: Tanaka, Courchene, me, Emily, and little Raymond, strapped to Emily's back in the sling she'd grabbed as she fled the Tai Hang house. Ting-Yan untied the boat from the jetty and Old Lee started the motor. We cut onto the dark, frothy waves as the moon rose over the Kowloon hills. The harbour was full of watercraft. I had no idea which were loyal to whom. We had to assume they were all at least nominally loyal to the Japanese, or they wouldn't be out here. Lee's boat was loyal to the Japanese on paper too. As a seafood supplier for the Japanese Recreation Club (what the Japanese called the Hong Kong Cricket Club), he had a permit from the Kempeitai to continue operating on these waters. Still, I wasn't entirely comfortable out there. There were so many dead in these waters. But that night, the harbour was quiet. The *Oolong's* motor, though neither large nor powerful, seemed to roar in our ears.

All of the passengers looked a little grim and a little scared.

Bruised, skinny Emily cradled Raymond in her arms. He didn't cry, but gurgled and muttered like an old man. Courchene sat beside her, too close yet not close enough. Though they tried to hide it, their attachment to each to each other was obvious.

Tanaka and Horace sat opposite them. Courchene had helped Horace to scribble a quick letter to Isadore Davis Wong, encode it, and place it in a messenger's hand before we pushed off, even though it might well be that Horace got to Wong before the letter did. The *Oolong* was going to Chek Keng first though, so maybe the letter would get to Wong first. Old Lee told them that Wong's village was called Tai Kang, and knowing the name seemed to cheer them up.

Kathy Duffy wanted to go on to Free China; she planned go to Tai Kang village with them because an escape party from Sham Shui Po was meant to pass through there in a few days en route to Chungking.

Only Lee and Ting-Yan seem relaxed. They were more at home on these waters than they were on land, having lived on boats for generations.

"I do this once a week," Lee said. "There's no need to worry."

We rounded North Point, which had been one of the main landing points for the Japanese in the original invasion in December 1941.

I had the idea that once we passed through Lei Yue Mun Strait, we'd be home free. Lei Yue Mun was a narrow passage out of Victoria Harbour, which led into Junk Bay and the open sea. Above us lay the barracks where the British had trained in preparation for the Japanese invasion. Up there Royal Rajputs, Winnipeg Grenadiers, and Hong Kong Volunteers had been bayonetted and beheaded on that terrible Christmas Day. Up there still were captured gun batteries and a redoubt. There could easily be Japanese gunners with their sights trained on us from their perches in the dark.

"Can't you go faster?" I said to Ting-Yan.

"I don't want to arouse suspicion," she said.

Out in Junk Bay they cast a fishing net, and shone a bright light into the water to draw the fish.

"Have you lost your mind?" I said. "Fishing? At a time like this?"

"Do you want to get there safely or not, Miss Violet?" said Old Lee.

"Our lights and our fishing nets are our cloaks of invisibility," Ting-Yan explained. "My family has survived for centuries both because we fish to eat, and because we use small fish to capture big ones." She laughed, a tinkling, fairy laugh.

I waited for her to say more, but she didn't. I was meant to put two and two together. I thought about my great-grandfather, the taipan Henry Witt-Weatherall, who had made a great fortune for his paler descendants by selling opium to China, even after the drug was outlawed. My father told me once that the local fisher people used to help bring the opium ashore. It would make sense that Ting-Yan's family were among those fisher people. Maybe even back before the Opium Wars. I thought about the name of this boat, the *Oolong*, and how smugglers would use rice, and sometimes tea, as a cover for their smuggling and also to make additional profits. Of course, it wasn't legal. All of us South Chinese fell between the lines of the law and lived our lives out there. I thought of how the Japanese, the British, the KMT, and probably the Communists too, all used the junks, tang tsai, and sampans for their own purposes: landing troops, smuggling arms, drowning refugees, escaping POW camps. The boat people had their own interests too, of course, to which others could be instrumental or detrimental. All through the occupation, there had been tales of widespread looting. Why not? Who did the local people really have to be loyal to? Me, I felt some loyalty to the British, because, working with Selwyn-Clarke, I could see how he risked his life to help the wounded, the sick, and the starving, and I admired that. But I didn't blame those who weren't loyal. The British, after all, had commandeered this colony in the interests of their own wealth, against the interests of Chinese people here and on the mainland. All that opium. The anti-opium pills my father made were just opium in disguise, so my well-being came from it also. But it did bring people pleasure. It relieved pain. Once, opium-smoking had been the pastime of cultured, gentle folk. Now, coolies and ordinary workers smoked my father's Dream Horse pills so their backs would hurt less. What was so wrong with that? I thought of all the coolies who made this once and future colony run, their strong backs twisted by the long poles they balanced over one shoulder or the other, carrying baskets or buckets of anything from vegetables to live chickens to rocks to night soil. Father used to say that any coolie who lived past forty must be superhuman.

"Give us a hand, will you?" shouted Captain Lee.

I snapped out of my reverie. Tanaka, Horace, and Courchene were helping Lee and Ting-Yan pull a laden net out of the water.

"No food shortages in the ocean," Horace muttered.

I rushed over to help. The net was full of fat, flapping fish.

Ting-Yan lifted the floorboards of the boat to reveal a spacious hold. It smelled of salt and stale water. We poured the fish into it.

Ting-Yan and Lee reeled the net back into the water to try for a second catch.

"You're kidding me," I said.

"Shouldn't we get going?" Professor Duffy asked.

"Mother Mary is generous tonight," said Old Lee.

"He means Tin Hau," said Ting-Yan. "The Japanese destroyers in the harbour have been disturbing the fish. If the sea is generous tonight, we can't afford to turn our back on her."

"Do you want more money?" said Horace. "I'll pay you to start the engine now."

"Good fish, good cover," said Captain Lee, waving away Horace's cash.

"Jesus, Son of God," Courchene grumbled. Emily and Raymond sat in the corner, watching wide-eyed.

The net went down, and the light went on.

Lee and Ting-Yan lived on these waters, and had done so all through-out the occupation. Through poor dead Tak-Tam and that psychopath Tak-Wing, Emily and I were related to them. Watching their expert cast-ing of the net, I felt pride in kinship.

"You're not selling us out, are you?" said Tanaka. "You're not using that light to signal the Japanese? I've been a good friend to you all through this vile occupation."

"You accuse me?" Captain Lee said.

"Of course not," Tanaka said.

Lee muttered something racist under his breath.

In perfect Cantonese, Tanaka said, "I'm sorry, Uncle Lee. I didn't mean disrespect."

"Can we get going?" Horace said again.

As formerly pro-Japanese, Horace and Tanaka had both the most and the least to be worried about. If we got boarded, they could have said that Lee was kidnapping them. There was a fifty-fifty chance that Noma would vouch for them. On the other hand, they could have been apprehended and executed on the spot as traitors to Emperor Hirohito, which of course they were.

The second net filled more slowly than the first, but it filled. Everyone helped haul the catch on board and empty it into the hold. Now the hold was full.

"Crab traps," said Old Lee.

"You've got to be joking," said Courchene.

"Joking," said Old Lee. He fell into a fit of laughter. Tears of mirth spilled down his cheeks. Out of sheer relief, we all laughed with him, except his daughter Ting-Yan, who rolled her eyes. She put out the fishing lights and started the motor.

Lee said he'd take us around Nam Tong Island to avoid Fat Tong Mun, a narrow straight where, if there were Japanese patrols, they could corner us.

"No one prone to seasickness, I hope," he said.

I looked around at the other passengers.

"All ocean-going people here one way or the other," said Kathy Duffy.

"Except me," said Courchene. "At least in part. The landlocked Cree in me might puke, but the French in me has good sea legs."

Unexpectedly, out on the open water, Professor Duffy was sick. She vomited quietly overboard. "My sailor father would be ashamed," she muttered, once she was feeling a bit better, and was seated again. "It's the smell of all that fish in the hold."

We rounded Nam Tong Island without incident. It was only when we turned toward Clearwater Bay that we got surprised. They sprayed us with bullets first. No one was hit, but new holes sprouted in the boat's canvas roof. Suddenly, there was a Japanese patrol boat gunning toward us.

"Into the hold, quick!" shouted Ting-Yan. She lifted the floorboard.

"It's full of fish," Professor Duffy complained.

"Yes," said Ting-Yan. "You get under the fish."

Courchene went down first and helped Emily and Raymond in. Horace, Tanaka, and Duffy followed. I was last. "Must I?"

"Hurry, or they'll see you."

It was dark and smelly under there. The boat seemed to sway more vigorously than it had been a moment ago. We all gagged and choked, but tried to do it quietly. We heard the patrol come up alongside, and stern, rapid-fire Japanese.

Ting-Yan responded with a few Japanese words, awkwardly pronounced. Lee chimed in, even more awkwardly.

There were footsteps above.

"Floor," said the water policeman, in English. With the clicking toe of his boot, he tapped the ceiling above our heads. We all dived under the mass of fish. One, still alive, flapped in my face. I wanted to yelp, but I managed to stay still and quiet. The hatch opened. We lay beneath the catch, not daring to breathe.

There was another mostly inaudible exchange. The floorboard fell again, and we heard the patrol men disembark.

"Don't come out yet," Ting-Yan whispered. "They can still see us. I'll tell you when it's safe."

We lay there choking for what felt like an hour. Finally, the floorboard lifted. "Safe now."

One by one we climbed out of the wet, stinking hold, each of us half human, half fish. Ting-Yan and Old Lee laughed at our sorry state, our bedraggled hair and clothes. But Ting-Yan fired up a little charcoal brazier to make tea. We imagined ourselves home free.

We were not home free. We passed between Tiu Chung Chau and Bluff Island, also known as Sha Tong Hau Shan. For the second time that night, a hail of bullets descended on us, but this time it kept coming. The canvas roof of the *Oolong* was shot to tatters, and it became clear that we would be too, if we stayed aboard. They were shooting at us from Tiu Chung Chau on the port side. A mortar round went into the hull of the boat. It began to take on water.

"Diu!" cursed old Lee. "Not tonight. Did that patrol know about our passengers and send a message ahead?"

"Time to swim," said Ting-Yan. She tossed everyone a buoy. "You know how, right?"

Courchene took Raymond from Emily and used her sling to tie the child to his back. He glided along the dark surface, kicking hard so as to keep the baby's head from going underwater. Emily followed. I went after them. Behind me, I heard the others slip into the water on the starboard side. The bullets keep coming as we swam toward Bluff Island, a rocky, hilly shape far away in the dark.

I looked behind me and saw the *Oolong* tilt and slip beneath the waves. In the distance, someone called for help, and then went silent.

The shooting stopped. I guess they thought they'd gotten us all.

My shoes felt like stones on my feet. I kicked them off. Still, I was impeded by my good denim pants, my grey Peter Pan–collared shirt. I wriggled out of my clothes, down to my underwear, and let them drift to the bottom. I became a small frog in the massive sea. Waves broke over my head and I choked. I kept kicking. I tried to find the pattern of the waves and snatch breath between them. Beneath me, water creatures writhed and turned. I saw a man o' war jellyfish down there, massive, translucent, and pulsing. It was twice my size, and ascending to the surface. I stroked away, as hard and fast as I could. My arms and legs ached, but I kept going. After what seemed like half the night, I reached a flat face of brown rock, covered in barnacles. I swam a little to the right and found a low ledge

I could hoist myself up onto. From there, I found small toeholds in the rock to get myself up onto a higher ledge.

Courchene, Raymond, and Emily were there two rocks over. I couldn't see any of the others. Through the channel where the *Oolong* had gone down, a patrol went by to inspect the damage.

We lay flat on our bellies until the patrol sputtered away.

"We can't stay here," Courchene said.

I nodded to my left. "A sea cave. We could hide in there."

"We could get trapped in there by the tide," said Courchene.

"It goes all the way through to the other side," Emily said.

"How do you know?" I asked.

"I came here once, with Tak-Wing and some of his cricket club friends, for a launch boat picnic before the occupation. We had egg sandwiches and English cucumbers."

"Those days belong to another planet," I said.

"I wonder if the Japanese know," said Courchene.

"It's too narrow for a boat to go through anyway," said Emily. "We could hide on the other side."

Though it was the last thing I wanted to do, I slipped back down in the dark, silky water and kicked toward the cave with the others. It was a narrow slit in a high cliff face of columnar rocks. Was Emily sure this was safe? It seemed so dark inside. I paused, treaded water, caught my breath. In the distance, I heard the sound of a boat, friend or foe, I didn't know. More likely to be foe. I glided into the slit. The walls around me were high and dark. The whole island was made of these tall columns. I hoped there were no jellyfish in there. The centre of the cave formed a dome, which I could barely make out from the reflected moonlight that somehow slanted its way in. I flipped up onto my back for the briefest moment, to admire the beauty. Then cold and fear got the better of me, and I rolled to my stomach again and swam forward. I'd always liked to swim. It turned out I was the strongest swimmer of the four of us. Emily and Courchene, with little Raymond on his back, paddled behind me. It amazed me that Raymond hadn't drowned. When I came up for air, I could hear him squealing, though whether with delight or fear I couldn't quite tell.

On the east side of the island, those strange basalt cliffs loomed twice as high. But jutting out toward the next island over were more of those flat rocks, wide enough to sit on. We clambered onto them.

I caught my breath, exhausted. I wouldn't have been able to go any farther. I was so tired, and wanted to sleep, but I was too cold, soaking wet and wearing nothing but a soggy bra, an undershirt, and underpants. I dozed for a few minutes.

I woke up shivering in the dawn light, alone on the cold rock. "Emily? Bill?"

No sign of them.

I climbed over two more flat rocks. My foot slipped and scraped against a jagged edge. I'd cut it. A thin stream of blood ran over the small toe. I checked to make sure it wasn't serious, then pulled myself up onto a taller rock. There they were, several stones over, still asleep. I scrambled over to them. "Have you seen anyone else?"

Bleary-eyed, Courchene opened his eyes. He nudged Emily. Raymond began to cry. "No, I haven't," he said.

I bit my lip.

"It's incredible that we didn't drown," Emily said. "We're probably the only ones who made it."

I couldn't stop shivering. Emily and Courchene shivered too, and little Raymond, cradled in his shaking mother's arms, wailed himself blue. We'd come this far, but we might still die of exposure out here, unless a Japanese patrol boat put an end to us some other way. My stomach grumbled with hunger.

"You want some seaweed?" Emily said. She reached into the water and pulled up a handful of slimy green stuff.

"Ugh. Maybe later. Do you think we're really the only ones who made it? We should look for the others."

Courchene put Raymond on his back, and we clambered over the wet rocks. We saw no one.

But then we heard shouting.

"Hey!"

We got ourselves to a taller boulder.

From a rock not too far away, Tanaka and Duffy waved.

My heart filled with more joy that I'd thought I would ever feel again. Had they followed us into the cave last night?

They had come through. That was so lucky. Captain Lee, who'd lived on these waters all his life, would surely be here too, or maybe still on the other side of the island. But what about Ting-Yan and Horace? There was no way we all could have survived—it was too much to ask of Tin Hau or any other god, even at their most benevolent.

Duffy pointed upward. I looked. At the top of the cliff stood Ting-Yan and Horace. They shouted and waved and pointed toward the east side of the Island.

Duffy translated what she heard. "Boat. On the other side."

"Friend or foe?" I asked.

Ting-Yan and Horace's voices echoed down the steep cliff face. "Swim! Other side!"

Though we were stiff and cold and hungry, we got back into the water one more time. Ting-Yan and Horace seemed happy about the boat, so maybe it was a friendly one. And if not, well, at least we wouldn't die of exposure. We swam again through the cave. In daylight, the rocks were a pale tan colour. How had they seemed so dark at night? The cave too seemed shorter, and the swim not so hard. On the other side a little Tanka boat bobbed. We were helped aboard by an ancient fisher lady and a very strong little girl, who couldn't have been more than five. They gave us tea, congee with dried scallops in it, and blankets. I didn't think I'd ever eaten such a delicious breakfast. We sipped in silence and watched Ting-Yan and Horace descend the rock face down to where we were.

"Granny Tang," said Ting-Yan, as she stepped aboard. "I can't imagine better luck than this."

"Where is Captain Lee?" I asked her, as she accepted a cup of tea from the little girl.

Her look of elation became a look of deep grief. "Old Lee couldn't swim," she said. "And he didn't want to leave his boat. He went down with the *Oolong*."

"He couldn't swim?"

"It's not so uncommon, for that generation," she said. She sipped her tea to show she wasn't ready to say more.

CHAPTER 49

CARP'S EYE

October 14, 1942

C heung opened one of the packages. Rolled a pill out onto his hand. It was astonishingly white, with a little black dot on it, so that, with the exercise of a little imagination, it looked like a real fish eye.

"Are you ready to do this?" said Tak-Wing, his last living son.

"I'd take it myself, but if they work, my ghost will have to do the poisoning."

Tak-Wing nodded toward the Supreme Court. At its back door the torturers threw their victims' remains to the city's ravenous dogs, who made them disappear.

Cheung shuddered. "I don't want to go there."

"I'll go. I'll lure one."

"With what? A choice leaf of baby bok choy? Those dogs are the only ones in this cursed city who are not hungry."

Tak-Wing asked Cheung to give him a small piece of pork sausage, which the steward did only reluctantly. Meat these days was more precious than gold. Tak-Wing opened the back door and called to one of the skinnier dogs, one of the last in line for the human sacrifice for which those unfortunate beasts gathered daily. This one was scrawny and young. A pale tan colour with an upturned tail. Cute.

"Come, little dog," called Tak-Wing. "Gow tsai. Come, puppy."

While the others clamoured at the side door of the Supreme Court, the little dog crossed the street to Tak-Wing. It sniffed around his legs and

The Lost Century

feet. Its brown eyes shone bright and its ears perked, sensitive to the men's every movement.

Tak-Wing gave it the sausage with the Carp's Eye poked into it. The dog gobbled it down, joyful and grateful, as though happy to be eating something other than human flesh. It wagged its upturned tail.

The last humanitarian creature on this cursed island, Cheung thought bitterly.

Before long, the dog lay down on the back step, curled into a furry ball, and went to sleep. The two men smoked cigarettes and watched the dog rest, peaceful and soft.

Cheung went back inside. Tak-Wing followed. They watched from the kitchen window while Cheung chopped leeks and potatoes to make vichyssoise for the club's evening meal in the first-floor bar.

"Seems like a good immortality pill," he said. "See how relaxed its face is?"

But then its body twitched. They rushed back outside to watch.

Cheung's eyes widened with a twisted combination of hope and horror.

It came to nothing. The dog was still and peaceful again.

Then, another twitch.

A little yelp.

The yelp stirred in Cheung a feeling of pleasure, but it was pleasure of a diabolical kind, not the easy pleasure of spending time with his family, or enjoying a beer after work with co-workers. This pleasure was sleepy and smoky and hungry for someone else's suffering as an antidote to his own. Was this the feeling that those twisted military police had become addicted to?

The little dog dreamt peacefully on. There was no more yelping. In its sleep it wagged a lively tail. Cheung grunted, his dark enjoyment frustrated.

"This Carp's Eye seems like a good anti-opium pill," Tak-Wing said. "I should take them myself."

"Curse your dead mother," Cheung hissed. "Find me something else, son."

351

But then the little dog twitched again. Released a long and troubled whine. It arched its back unnaturally, then began to shake. It vibrated uncontrollably, more machine than animal. The whining grew intense, and unbearably pitiful. A bolus of white foam oozed past its black lips. It whimpered.

Cheung stared, fascinated.

The little dog released a last thin wail, then shuddered. Finally, it went still.

Tak-Wing touched its neck. "Dead," he said. "Quick, easy, and almost painless."

The old steward got hold of his former, human self. "This is devilish business."

"Did you imagine it to be otherwise?" said Tak-Wing.

He took one box of pills, which he figured would be enough to dispatch Emily and Raymond, the monster's child. The rest he left for Cheung to do his work.

"To the victors!" Cheung shouted. He placed on the counter the largest punch bowl in the club, filled to the brim with syllabub, or his own variation of it: Horace's rum, good Portuguese Madeira, fresh Dairy Farm cream, lemon juice, ground carp's eyes, and a splash of Russian vodka for good measure. He grated nutmeg generously over the top.

The Kempeitai were still in a good mood that day because of some success in the torture chamber or on the streets, Cheung didn't know and didn't ask. When they looked in Cheung's eyes they saw a fool and a chump. They felt the power of their supremacy. It would not be long now before Emperor Hirohito drove the white man and his Chinese lackeys from Asia forever. They sipped the syllabub. One glass. Then another. "It's really delicious tonight, Old Cheung!" The concoction seemed to give them real pleasure. "Ha ha, what secret ingredient did you add? Vodka? Oh, the nectar of the White Russians, hey? Or no—the Communists!" They chatted and laughed and patted each other, and Cheung too, on the back. The punch was really good. Each of them took a third glass, then a fourth. "Very good, very good, when the war is over we'll buy you your own bar, and this can be your signature drink! What will you call it? You should change the name to make it yours, but something related to the original." Their faces contorted with thought. They giggled and muttered. "Syllable? Syllabus? Sybillant? Silly babble? Sober sybil? Sybil bubble? Cello blubber? Babble blooper? Bible looper? Sub slubba blub blub blub blub blu—blue—" Their faces grew gentle.

Soon the dark wood first floor bar was like Sleeping Beauty's castle. Over the club chairs and fine oaken tables they lay, all sweetly dreaming their fondest dreams. Some of tortures, blood, and victory. Some of an end to the war and a great New Asia under Japanese leadership. Some of large factories, personal success, and massive wealth. And some simply of wives, mothers, children, or lovers, and their own natal villages by the sea or in the hills, not so different from the villages they had plundered and torched these the last five years. Still others, soaked in horror and their own culpability, though they couldn't admit it on pain of death and dishonour, dreamt of emigration to Canada, Australia, or the United States. They dreamt of becoming someone else someday, somewhere else.

Cheung watched them as he'd watched the little tan-coloured dog with the curly tail. He watched them dreaming, watched their peaceful faces. He became a twisted guide to the underworld, a dreadful shepherd, a broken boatman. They swam the waters he controlled, and he guided them through visions of their own horrors, paddled beside them as they gasped and drowned. He was a frightful alchemist, a blue shaman, walking beside them through fires that scalded and burned, that recriminated without end. Every fingernail remover felt his own nails painstakingly peeled off one by one. Every water torturer drowned, gasped, was revived, and drowned again. Every swordsman felt his own head sliced off, and the blood gush skyward from his aorta. The sleepers twitched. They slept and dreamt some more. They twitched again. They writhed. When the first one arched his back, Cheung breathed a sigh of relief. The medicine was working.

But some of the Kempeitai men were stronger than the little tan-coloured dog. They grunted. They cried out. They fought the air, punching and dodging. One of them, still asleep, got up and walked across the room to another table, sat down, and returned to snoring. One of them sat up and spoke, a long monologue in his mother tongue. Cheung didn't understand a word. Eventually, the speaker drooped forward in his chair, until his forehead touched the table again. Cheung watched them, mesmerized. To ease them on their way, he sang to them, his favourite mountain song:

Lonely on the mountain path
Through mist and rain
Through rain and mist
I'm searching always searching
Searching for you

Lonely down beside the river
Through mist and rain
Through rain and mist
I'm searching ever searching
Searching for you

Lonely by the ocean too
Through mist and rain
Through rain and mist
Searching still I'm searching
Never finding you

It took them the whole night to dream, squirm, arch, and die. But die they did, first one, then ten, then thirty. When morning arrived over a hundred men were dead in the red velvet chairs of the first-floor bar.

But then, to Cheung's horror, one of them opened his eyes. Blinked. Looked around. "What happened here?"

Another blinked awake. And then another.

Colonel Noma's eyes slammed open.

Cheung gasped.

He ran out of the bar, down the stairs, toward the kitchen's back door. He should not have stayed to witness. What had he been thinking? He should have fled to Chek Keng to hide out with Lee until more serious massacres rendered his own forgettable. The military police ran after him, caught him before he could even make it to the kitchen. They hauled him out the back door themselves. But instead of taking him to the Causeway Bay Typhoon Shelter, they pulled him across the road to where the hungry dogs clamoured. The side door of the Supreme Court opened. Two Kempeitai came out, escorting a third, ragged man. A young man. It couldn't be—

"Tak-Tam?"

The Kempeitai were leading him away from the Supreme Court in the direction of freedom. "Father?"

"I thought you were dead." The Kempeitai were leading Cheung toward the Supreme Court in the direction of torture.

"I'm alive. It hasn't been the best time, but I'm still here."

The Kempeitai escorting Cheung to the basement shook their heads at the ones escorting the young man to freedom. Pointed them back inside.

"Father?"

"Tak-Tam! I did a very stupid thing."

"They're letting me go. Noma was in a good mood."

"Not anymore, pretty boy," said the one of the policemen gripping Cheung's arms. "Too bad. He could have told your other son that his child is his own."

"You don't know that."

"I do know," Tak-Tam said. "Noma used to come talk to me at night. He'd tell me everything because I was such a good listener. He told me his greatest shame. When he rapes he can't finish. He fakes it every time for the sake of his men. Who know. And laugh. And fuel his rage. But the child can't be his."

"No!" Cheung cried.

The two military police dragged the young man back inside. "So much for the colonel's special favour. You'll have to keep his secrets now." Cheung understood the Japanese word for "execute."

His own escorts didn't have to push him into the basement behind his son.

CHAPTER 50

IN THE CHAPEL

October 14, 1942

If I could live my life again, I would have been there. Ting-Yan and I were in the rice fields when it happened, harvesting the last of the late season planting, up to our ankles in water, our backs stooped, our heads unwisely bare in the October sun. Courchene was with us too. He'd have preferred to have stayed in the village with Emily, but with both Tak-Tam and Old Lee gone, Auntie Siu-Wai was in pressing need of help.

"Of course, stay with her if you must," she'd said. But her eyes had been pleading. The food shortages were intense, and she'd lost the last rice harvest to a raid by desperate refugees from the mainland. This season's crop was ready and the typhoons were early this year. Tanaka, Horace, and Duffy would have helped, had they remained at Chek Keng, but guided by one of the village boys, they'd gone straight on to Tai Kang to be with Isadore Davis Wong and the mountain guerrillas.

"Why don't you spend the day in the chapel?" Auntie Siu-Wai had said to Emily. "It's the nicest building in the town, and Padre Arcuri might come by later, if you want to have the baby baptized." Most of the villagers at Chek Keng were Catholic, converted by the Italian missionaries who first came in the 1860s.

"Poor Raymond," Emily said. "He's had such a rough start. Maybe the protection of the One God would give him a little advantage?"

"Macy was baptized by Padre Arcuri two weeks after she was born," Ting-Yan said, stroking the thick hair of the little girl who clung to her leg, her daughter with Tak-Tam. "I'm not devout and I don't really care about it one way or the other but Mother and Father wanted it done. I'm glad now that I could give that to Old Lee." Her eyes brimmed. She sucked back a wad of snot.

"May he rest in peace," I said. It was obvious what a loss Captain Lee's death was to this little fishing village.

So Courchene followed us into the fields, though he looked back over his shoulder more times than I could count. I'd like to think I was as worried about my sister as he was, but in all honesty, I was happy to follow Ting-Yan and watch the autumn sun fall on her strong back as she walked the worn path to the rice paddies, as she'd done since she was a child. Macy walked with her, clutching her hand. She was nearly five, and full of beans.

This is how I imagine them.

Tak-Wing motors up the coast in a hired launch boat. The Japanese patrol boats could interfere, but they don't. He makes good time and arrives at Chek Keng in the early afternoon. The Holy Family Chapel is the most obvious building in the village, and Tak-Wing makes straight for it.

Tak-Wing finds her sitting with her back toward the alcove in the second chamber. The altar behind her houses a large porcelain statue of Mary with a Chinese face, who looks quite unambiguously like Tin Hau, the Goddess of the Sea. Emily is breastfeeding Raymond, who gurgles contentedly. They've already been through so much. Why can't Tak-Wing leave her in peace?

But he can't. His red eyes blaze with war-sickness. "You thought you could escape me? Abandon me after you swore you'd stay with me 'til death do us part?"

Emily looks up, shocked. "Tak-Wing? What are you doing here?"

"I loved you. You ruined me."

She scowls. "I was attacked by soldiers."

"If you weren't a hussy you would have fought them off."

"They had pistols and bayonets. No one they accosted could fight them off. Many of the doctors and nurses died horrible deaths."

"Where is the pure beauty I married?"

"Don't be an idiot."

"An idiot? Don't call me an idiot. I won't take that from you."

Raymond howls.

"Can't you shut that brat up?" He grabs the child, moves to hurl it against the sacred chapel wall, but she throws herself at him and wrenches Raymond back. "What are you doing? This is your son!"

"Don't lie. I know the truth."

"What truth, you dead, stupid ghost?"

"Raymond is the son of that murdering devil, the head of the Kempeitai, Noma Kennosuke."

"Raymond is your son, and no one else's. Look at his eyes." She holds Raymond up to the level of Tak-Wing's face. The baby writhes and howls.

Tak-Wing gets a hold of himself. He doesn't need to beat them to death. He's got the anti-opium pills. He looks into the screaming child's eyes. There is indeed a spirit there, connected to his own, but he is too war-sick to see it, so he just pretends. "He looks a little like me."

"Yes," Emily says, "because he is your child."

"I don't believe it," Tak-Wing mutters, more to himself than her. "I don't believe it."

"The child is yours. Many women were raped that day. Almost all of the nurses. It's not our fault. It's a war. I'm the same Emily you married at the Supreme Court five years ago. The one you loved, remember? The one you drank Awakening Lion aerated lemonade with on the steps of the Peak Hotel?"

He stares at her, not comprehending. "Awakening Lion aerated lemonade?"

"We drank it with my sister, Violet, who came as witness."

"Awaking Lion lemonade ... your sister, Violet ..." He's in a daze.

Tin Hau gazes down on them.

"You loved me very much that day."

"Loved you ..."

Tin Hau's gaze bathes them in a pink glow.

"And I loved you. Remember?"

"Loved me ..."

The glow suffuses the room. It reflects off the wall and the pink light pours into them. In the distance, they can hear the ocean, lapping against the pier.

The air seems full of ghosts—all doubles of himself and Emily in better times. But he came so full of hate. And committed to his hate. He digs for it now.

"I can't stay," he says. "But I brought you something." He hands her a pork bun for herself, and some milk for the baby.

"It's not too late, husband," Emily says, though until this moment, she'd thought it was—much, much, much too late. "It's not too late. Stay in Chek Keng and rest. Violet and Ting-Yan are here. You're sick. The three of us will help you get better. Stay."

"Stay?" he says. He feels very warm, and a little sweaty. The sea air is getting to him. "Eat the pork bun. Give the baby some milk. I have to go."

He flees the chapel and rushes back to the waiting boat.

Emily, astonished by the visit, astonished by the conversation, stares after him for a long time.

The boat departs the harbour and goes out to the open sea.

When the afternoon grows late and the chapel begins to get cool, Emily realizes she is hungry. She gives some of the milk to the baby. She eats the pork bun. She closes her eyes.

That is how I imagine them, and that was how we found them, eyes closed, mouths foaming.

"Em, Em! Wake up!" I was beside myself with panic.

"What's wrong with them?" said Auntie Siu-Wai.

I checked Emily's pulse. She still had one, thank goodness. It was very slow and thick, but it was still there. I checked Raymond's. The same.

"Poison," said Auntie Siu-Wai.

With thumb and index finger, I forced one of Emily's eyes open. Her pupil was dilated wide. "Morphine poisoning," I said. "Maybe strychnine too. How could that happen?"

"I saw a boat dock," Courchene said. "And then depart a short while later."

"Tak-Wing," I said. I remembered then the case that nearly bankrupted my father, years ago, when I was a little girl. Old Cheung's father had died like this. In my doctor's bag, I'd had the antidote, but it had gone down with the *Oolong*. "Ting-Yan, do you have any potassium permanganate?"

"What's that?"

"A white powder—" I began to explain. "No pharmacist at Chek Keng, I suppose. No medical supplies?"

"The chapel might have something," she said. "Maybe in the priest's room."

She opened the door to the little private space where Padre Arcuri stayed when he was visiting Chek Keng. There was a small cabinet against the wall. I opened it. It was pretty bare—a little tooth powder, a rusty razor, a bottle of iodine.

"What about here?" There was a chest of drawers beside the bed. We went through the drawers one by one. In the first, a clean but worn singlet, and a spare collar. In the second, two well-thumbed bibles printed on cheap paper, one in English and one in Latin. In the bottom drawer, shell dressings, Dettol, some cotton wool. A small first-aid kit that didn't look at all promising. I opened it anyway. Inside, a roll of gauze, some tape, a few morphine syrettes, and a small jar of potassium permanganate salts. *Praise Mary, or whoever watches over this little chapel!* It would be even better if the padre had a stomach pump kit like the one in the day clinic at St Paul's. I rifled around in his drawers without luck.

"Will this help?" Ting-Yan came in with a broken chalice—the cup sliced neatly from the base to form a funnel. In the other hand, she had a slender piece of garden hose. "There was a pump, before the war. There used to be lots of anti-opium pill smokers in this village. We used to have to do this sometimes."

"Where did you find those?"

She pointed toward a basin that held kitchen implements.

I washed the broken chalice and the hose as well as I could with boiled water, and fashioned them into a makeshift pump.

I dissolved the salts in the priest's cruet.

Somehow, I got the hose into the baby's throat. He screamed bloody murder as I attempt to insert the device, but once it was in, he was so alarmed, he was silent. I held his nose. I poured the potassium permanganate solution into his poor little stomach. He sputtered and choked. I pumped his stomach with my hand. The solution came back up out of him, bright pink.

I did the same to Emily. She coughed. Vomited it out. I did it again.

Her face grew very red.

Then very blue.

"Violet," she coughed. An almost human skin tone returned.

"Emily. Praise God."

Again, she was sick on the floor. I poured more into her. She puked it up. She was pale, but beginning to look like herself.

"Tak-Wing was here," she said. She reached for Raymond, who continued to wail. Emily began to wail too. "He tried—he tried—he ..." She sobbed. There was a lot of snot, and choking.

Courchene came and put his arm around her. As Emily held and comforted Raymond, Courchene held and comforted Emily.

CHAPTER 51

Typhoon Shelter
THE FINAL SECRET
June 30, 1997

O*phelia and Great-Aunt Violet are the last people in the restaurant, except for a young couple in the far corner. The girl is shouting and the boy is crying. The crab-pink lights flicker furiously, as though picking up on their volatile emotions.*

The grumpy server approaches the table. "It's nearly midnight," she says. "I have to close soon. You want some sweet soup before you go?"

"Nearly midnight already?" says Great-Aunt Violet. "We missed the entire handover ceremony."

"I forgot all about it," says Ophelia. "What happened to Courchene and Grandma Emily?"

"You want that soup?" says the grumpy server. "It's green bean with seaweed. Very cooling."

"Ho ah, ho ah," says Great-Aunt Violet. "Yes, please. We will eat it and then get out of your hair."

The tapioca pudding was hours ago, and Ophelia finds that she does in fact have stomach space. "What happened to Old Mah? And was that really how Cheung died? What happened to Tak-Wing? Is Auntie Macy really such a great businesswoman? Where is Uncle Raymond now?"

Courchene stayed in the village through to the end of the war to be with Emily. We survived the American air raids together, and helped countless escapees and refugees flee to Free China. The person who could write Cree syllabics and who worked with Izzy Davis Wong turned out to be Courchene's cousin, Philip Courchene, who had been in the Winnipeg Grenadiers with him. They weren't a full Cree code-talking unit, but they routinely sent notes to their colleague on Hong Kong Island, in support of work done by the East River Column and the British Army Aid Group. But after the war, when Courchene learned his mother was dying of tuberculosis back in Saint-Boniface, he went home to see her one last time. He promised to come back. But once he was home, Hong Kong became a distant and almost unbelievable memory. He wrote Emily a long, sad letter saying he'd changed his mind. She cried a lot.

Shortly after that, Tak-Wing began to visit Chek Keng. At first, we tried to drive him off. But he kept coming—every weekend through 1948, even if we never let his boat dock at all. After a few years, we let him land. He seemed his old self again. The war-madness had left him, and it was clear that he missed Emily. He begged her to come back.

He kept saying to her, "I want to have a family, Em. I want to have that family with you, and no one else." He brought her gifts—cases of Awakening Lion brand aerated lemonade, a radio, a new cheung sam.

"I will never come back to you, ever," she said. "You tried to kill me. You tried to kill your own son."

"I wasn't well," he said. "I was beside myself."

"I don't care," she said. "I could never trust you again. How could you ever imagine that I might?"

"I don't expect it," he said. "But we aren't young anymore. Who else will want either of us?"

She still held out hope that Courchene would come back, though she didn't tell Tak-Wing that. She wrote songs to will him back, and sang them to Raymond as she dressed the little boy and combed his hair.

Years passed. She wrote to Courchene, and he wrote her a nice letter back. "I think of you often, but my people need me here."

I received a much longer letter from him, one that I never told Emily about because I didn't know what to say. Courchene's old romantic rival, Thomas McMahon, had died on the Western Front, targeted by the Germans to stop transmission of the Cree code. After a period of mourning, McMahon's widow, Estelle, had come looking for Courchene, who was her childhood sweetheart. He found that he still felt about her the way he always had. They married. Courchene had never told Emily the early part of this story, and he saw no point in telling her the later part either. It would only hurt her feelings, which he didn't want to do. Besides, there really was work, scads of it, including helping his father on the traplines, and his aunt and Estelle with their secret midwifery and herbalist work. He felt really bad about it. He still cared for Emily, but the world of the war was like a dream, and his real life was in Manitoba. He wanted me to understand, and to protect Emily, as I always had.

Tak-Wing kept coming. He told us that Old Cheung had been tortured and killed by the Kempeitai, along with Tak-Tam who had survived in their prison much longer than we had originally thought. He found this out from one of the young cricketers who had been released from the same terrible basement where Cheung and Tak-Tam were held, and heard their story. "All those military police your father killed, what an extraordinary feat!" the young cricketer said. "He was an inspiration to all of us who were imprisoned at the Supreme Court in those grim years. But the Kempeitai who lived to continue their grisly work in that prison had their vengeance on him. I'll spare you the details."

Tak-Wing told Emily that if she wouldn't take him back, he no longer wanted to live.

"Are you asking me to rescue you?" she asked.

"Of course not."

"What Cheung did to those murderers, you tried to do to me and Raymond."

"I know. I'm sorry. I wasn't myself. Will you forgive me?"

"I don't think I can."

"Will you take me back without forgiveness?"

"Are you asking me to carry your grief for you?"

"I would never do that."

"It sounds like you are. But I won't. And I can't forgive you either. Why don't you just go die?"

But he didn't die. He kept visiting. We gave him tea and sometimes even dinner, but Emily didn't want him to stay and so we always made him leave.

As for me and Ting-Yan, we realized we were each other's nearest and dearest. For a few years after the war we stayed in Chek Keng with Ting-Yan's mother, Siu-Wai, as well as Cheung's widow, Yim-Fong, with whom Siu-Wai was close.

Emily remained with us, even after Courchene left, and Amah joined us, to help with Macy and Raymond. So for a few years, we were quite the community of women! I worked there as the village doctor, and patients came to see me from all over the Sai Kung Peninsula. We farmed. We burned spirit money and incense for Captain Lee, Old Cheung, and Tak-Tam, too, at the village altar. We bought a new tang tsai from a neighbouring family who had lost most of its members in the initial invasion. We called it the *Bo Nay*—another type of tea, you know, not as delicious as oolong, but the best for cutting grease. We put a new Tin Hau statue in it, and taught Macy and Raymond how to fish.

Grief-stricken by her losses, Yim-Fong threw herself into farming and fishing at Chek Keng. She thought Cheung was a hero for killing all those military policemen, but she thought he was a monster too. When she learned that Tak-Wing had tried to poison Emily and Raymond, she was horrified. She didn't know what to do with this knowledge. She decided to do what a lot of us did with our memories of an unbearable past: she tried to forget. She farmed, she fished, she cooked for us, and she spoke very little. When the East River Column asked her to help the Communist side in China's civil war, she threw herself into the work of smuggling gasoline, guns, and penicillin. She was so happy to be useful.

Through the duration of the war, Isadore Davis Wong conveyed so many escapees from the concentration camps through the Sai Kung hills to Free China. He assisted thousands of refugees too, acting as a go-between for the East River Column and the British Army Aid Group. The British promised to repatriate any of their allies who wanted to go home after the war, so Wong sold his flat and all his furniture in anticipation of a return to Jamaica. The British kept him waiting, one week, two weeks, six months, nine. In the end, he never made it back and died an early death by tuberculosis in a small room in a small flat shared with six other families, leaving his wife, Jane, and their children still stranded in Hong Kong. Emily and I went over there with food when we could, though I'm ashamed to say that when the American embargoes started and we experienced shortages, we went over less often than we should have. But we had dinner with Jane and two of Izzy's grown children just a few weeks ago. Jane has to use a walker now, and her hearing is nearly gone. But one of the kids is a manager at Lane Crawford, and one of the others is a librettist for a musical theatre company in Mombasa, back here like you to witness the handover.

Selwyn-Clarke was picked up again by the Kempeitai later in the war. This time they held him not for three weeks, but for a whole year. His friends and family gave him up for dead. But in the last days of the war, the Kempeitai released him. He'd been tortured and one of his legs didn't work at all well anymore. When he came out, he had a long filthy beard and weighed half of what he had before going into their prison. Hilda Selwyn-Clarke and their daughter, Mary, were overjoyed at his return, and nursed him back to health. After the war, and a period of recovery, he was sent to the Seychelles to be governor.

Kathy Duffy made it to Chungking, and from there, after a journey of several weeks, back to Dublin, where she taught at Trinity College until she retired sixteen years ago. She still sends us a card every Christmas, and often books too.

After the war, between 1946 and 1948, a British military court conducted a war crimes trial here in Hong Kong at the Jardine East Point

Godown, which was converted into a courthouse. Noma was convicted for his many atrocities and hanged until dead at Stanley. Many Kempeitai, Japanese navy people, and interpreters were tried, but it was a trial for crimes against British and Commonwealth nationals. But those of us who were only incidentally national got only incidental justice.

Tanaka was devastated by the way the war ended. He had a sister in Nagasaki, who died with her husband and children in the A-bomb blast. He had been thinking of going back to Japan, but after learning about his sister's death, he couldn't stomach the thought. So he came back to Hong Kong Island and worked as a translator for Japanese sportsmen during the golfing craze in the 1950s. He never got rich, but he made a decent living. I think you know his daughter from one of your classes at UBC?

After the war, Mah suffered because of his involvement with the Chinese Cooperative Council. He wasn't exactly called a traitor, but it became harder for him to make the business deals he needed to keep Dream Horse afloat. He became—what's that word you young people use—"toxic." No one would touch him. That's the way it was with the less powerful among the justices of the peace who'd sat on that council. The big players got away with it because the British needed them when they came back into power. But Old Mah was not so much needed. Dream Horse, which had already lost a lot of money because of Japanese raids on the godowns at the start of the occupation, declined rapidly and he had to sell the Kimblewick.

He moved back into the Stable, and the bedroom of his dead first wife, my mother, Eunice Liu Hei-Yu. He asked me and Ting-Yan to come back to Hong Kong Island to run the business, with the understanding that as soon as Raymond was old enough, it would go to him.

We felt bad for Old Mah, and, in the end, we all went: me, Ting-Yan, Emily, Amah, Raymond, and Macy too. This was the early 1950s, around the time of the Korean War and the American embargoes that devastated the Hong Kong economy. Ting-Yan left Siu-Wai and Yim-Fong in charge of the Chek Keng house, boat, and land and came to the Stable to live with the rest of us. Siu-Wai still didn't like being on the water, and so Yim-Fong did all fishing work that Old Lee, then later, Ting-Yan, once used to do.

Dream Horse kept losing money, and Father told Second Mother Polly he had to sell the Nest. She flatly refused, and told him to sell the Stable. Though Father let Second Mother Polly have her way in most things, he refused to sell the Stable. They had a royal row about it, but in the end, for once, Old Mah put his foot down. Second Mother Polly and her brood moved in and took over my room, while Emily, Ting-Yan, Amah, Macy, Raymond, and I crowded into Emily's. Old Mah lived with Mother's ghost in her old bedroom.

Packed like rice grain fish into a tiny omelette, we were not exactly a happy family. We didn't fight outright, but we bickered and politicked against one another. Sometimes it was Second Mother Polly and her brood against me, Ting-Yan, and Emily. Sometimes conflagrations would break out among family members living in the same room. We grew irritated and responded by doing our best to be irritating. We stole individual socks from one another to ruin the pair. We put brown vinegar in the soy sauce bottle. We cut holes in one another's mosquito nets. When someone was upset about a lost scarf or a nasty interaction with a shopkeeper we goaded and taunted them 'til they fled the house in tears. The war of irritation escalated until we inhabited it at a frenzied pitch. It was no one's fault and it was everyone's fault. It was the result of falling fortunes, lack of opportunity, crowding, disappointment, and frustration. Those were not happy years.

Emily in particular suffered during those bickering years. Second Mother Polly was always kind to her, but her real feelings for Emily were expressed through her children, who stole her lipsticks and Florida water and worried the threads of her cheung sams so they would wear out quicker. When she sang to soothe herself, they screamed, or they aped her.

Father pressured her to take over Dream Horse, but she had no mind for business. My work as a doctor was more needed and made more money than Dream Horse, so I primarily did that. These conditions left Ting-Yan to run the company as best she could, though its products were no longer fashionable and her heart wasn't really in it. Because she was dutiful and competent she kept it afloat, which was good, because between both our family and Second Mother Polly's we needed the income to survive. As the effects of the embargoes deepened, however, the business declined badly. We were as poor as we had been during the Japanese occupation.

After the Japanese surrender, China had her civil war. Some of the guerrillas from Chek Keng who'd fought as Maoists during the Japanese occupation were happy about this. They believed China was finally free of foreign interference, and that the people were truly represented by their government. Some were not because they thought Mao was a dictator. A lot of East River people were purged during the anti-localist directive from the Central-South China Bureau of the CCP, including Ting-Yan's mother, Kwan Siu-Wai, and Tak-Wing's mother, Ng Yim-Fong, as well two more of Ting-Yan's cousins, and also her uncle. More East River guerrillas died during the Cultural Revolution. A lot of the bodies washed into the Hong Kong Harbour. When we saw them, it reminded us of the Japanese occupation all over again. Some of them lived, however, to participate in the leftist riots that took place in Hong Kong in 1967.

In 1952, when she was only ten, your precocious auntie Macy encouraged Ting-Yan to bring a small quantity of penicillin in from the United Kingdom to export to China. She read the papers every day and pored obsessively over the business section. It turned out her advice was good. With the Korean War raging, antibiotics were making a big difference in terms of whether injured soldiers lived or died. Ting-Yan made a small profit by investing a little bit of money in the companies Macy suggested. She would have made more if she'd invested more, but she didn't quite have the nerve. However, dotty Old Mah discouraged Macy's interest in Dream Horse. He wanted Raymond, as both a boy and his biological grandchild, to take over the business. At twelve, Raymond was extremely clever, easily capable—at least intellectually—of beginning to learn how to run Dream Horse. Mah called him into his old office, where the fan still turned and the papers still rattled. He placed columns of numbers in front of the boy and tried to show him how to balance an accounts ledger. Raymond said he said he wasn't interested. He said Tak-Wing wasn't his father. He said he was going to Canada to find Courchene, who was the closest he'd ever had to one. He took the parcel of inheritance money Old Mah had given him the week before and disappeared. We think he stowed away on one of the big freighters that still came into the Hong Kong Harbour, maybe from Ceylon or Egypt, since neither Americans nor Canadians were trading with us. We searched for him for months, spending our days on the docks, stopping every sailor we ran into to ask if they'd seen a Chinese boy with angry eyes and a birthmark in the crook of the elbow. We begged our way onto ships to search, and filed a missing person's report with the Royal Hong Kong Police Force, but we never found a trace. It was as though Ting-Yan's long-ago curse were finally being set in motion. Raymond's disappearance broke Old Mah's already ailing heart, and Mah left this world shortly after that.

With Old Mah no longer around to keep the peace, life at the Stable became unbearable. Uncle Peanut started snooping through Emily's things when she was out. She caught him at it once, when she came back early from visiting Auntie Jane, and gave him such a tongue lashing that he spent the rest of the day under his blanket crying. But the next day, she found her favorite cheung sam snipped to shreds. That night, in the darkest hours when everyone else was asleep, Emily was visited by Mother's hollow-eyed ghost, coughing and shivering in a tattered dressing grown. Mother tried to touch Emily's hair. Emily was not comforted, she was terrified.

That was when she agreed to go back to Tak-Wing, who was still living by himself in the Tai Hang house. This would have been around 1954. Though they were together again, the relationship was completely changed, as if it were a relationship between two different people. Their hearts were broken in so many places that they could do nothing but bicker and fight. They threw things at each other—dishes, toys, books, clocks—anything within reach when their mutual uncontrolled rage took hold of them. Their second child, a girl, died of cholera, and after that, they moved into separate rooms. Still, they tried for more children, wanting a son to remind them of Tak-Tam, and to help them forget Raymond. But this was not a gift the universe was willing to bestow. They had five more children, all girls, including your mother.

Macy worked with Ting-Yan to keep Dream Horse afloat, and in the early 1960s, Ting-Yan officially made her president of the company. By then the big money to be made in antibiotics had already been made by other people. But Macy was not daunted. She changed the name of the company from Dream Horse to Strong Horse. She made Strong Horse profitable by dumping the morphine-based products and focusing instead on some of the newer antibiotics and other innovative medicines like diazepam and thalidomide. I never said the new products were better than the old, Feelie! All they were was more modern. With the profits, she started an artificial-flower factory, then built a couple of casinos, then got into real estate. As you know, she became a rich lady, which is how Ting-Yan and I managed to afford that nice flat in the Mid-Levels after we sold the Stable for the land value. You're in no place to look Strong Horse in the teeth! It's how you have your False Creek condo in Vancouver.

Horace, along with his hero, W.E.B. Du Bois, recognized that he'd been wrong about Japan, and that Asians, especially the Chinese and Japanese, are as capable of vicious imperialism as any Western nation. In the sixties, he got deep into the civil rights movement and did support work for Black war vets on leave in Hong Kong from the war in Vietnam. He became less idealistic and more attuned to the messiness of life, and in that attunement, he grew more committed than ever to the work of building a better world. He married a woman from Tai Kang and built a headquarters for Screech Owl in Hong Kong. With backing from one of the Witt-Weatherall subsidiaries, he made a good living selling rum until he retired. His son runs it now, and brings us a bottle from time to time. Screech Owl rum is still our drink of choice. You want to try some? I know this restaurant stocks it. It's nice in a Cuba libre, especially with a good squeeze of lime.

Eight years ago, when all her girl children were long gone and had children of their own, Emily became quite ill. Tak-Wing took care of her for as long as he could and as well as he could considering his own deficiencies, but it was clear she was suffering from dementia, brought on early by all she had suffered in her younger years. When he couldn't take care of her anymore, he consulted us, and we all agreed she'd be better off in a home. A year after that, he, too, became ill and had to join her. By then, thanks to Macy, the family was doing quite well, and we found a comfortable place with private rooms and twenty-four-hour care out in Aberdeen.

Well, in the end, he went first. He died of a fentanyl overdose. We found him in his room, Emily stooping over the body, and not a nurse in sight. I'm not saying she killed him. Don't ever suggest that to anyone, especially not your Auntie Macy! But I'm not saying she didn't either. Her illness altered her sense of time. She thought she was living in the 1940s, and tried to escape the home on several occasions. She said Tak-Wing was beating her, though each time the doctors checked, her body was unharmed. We found her standing over him as he lay on the floor, having rolled out of bed in his dying moments. We didn't know what to do. We took her back to her room. We put Tak-Wing's body back in the bed. It wasn't right, what we did, but we were in a panic. The night nurse found him several hours later and the coroner ruled the death an accidental overdose. The night nurse was fired, and the home offered us compensation. We took it, to protect Emily. But we didn't hang on to it because it seemed disrespectful to the night nurse who had lost her job in spite of having done nothing wrong. I donated it to the Po Leung Kuk home for wayward women and girls. Don't tell Macy this story. She doesn't know. She'd be devastated. Anyway, I'm an old lady now, maybe my memory is flawed. Maybe we never found Emily stooping over the body at all. Maybe Tak-Wing's death really was an accident. What good would it do anyone if the truth came out? No good. No good at all. I shouldn't have told you. You'd have been better off not knowing.

Emily died a few weeks after Tak-Wing. It was then that we began to search for Raymond in earnest. We know he lived in Vancouver for a while, then Winnipeg. But we still don't have a current address for him. If you have any interest in helping us, we'll all be in the same flat tomorrow, though that flat will no longer be part of the British Empire but will belong to the new China that was born while Hong Kong was away.

Well, you'll have to watch the rerun of the handover ceremony on TV tomorrow. I hope Macy won't be too upset that we never showed up today. I hope she went down to the waterfront without us.

In the far distance Ophelia hears the old Kowloon–Canton Railway clock chime midnight. As it echoes, an unsung group of people who love the city gather in Chater Garden, where the old Hong Kong Cricket Club once stood. Though no one sees them, they silently take one another's hands as they bear witness to the great change.

Before a massive crowd at the Hong Kong Convention and Exhibition Centre down on the waterfront, ceremonial guns go off, and ever so faintly Ophelia can hear the band of the People's Liberation Army playing the "March of the Volunteers." She hears the loud boom of fireworks, and the clouds above the Typhoon Shelter Restaurant flash their reflected light right into the dining room.

The grumpy server approaches. "Sik bao mei, ah?" she says. "Did you get enough to eat?"

"Thank you, yes," says Great-Aunt Violet.

"So much," says Ophelia. "Way more than I should have eaten. I'm so full."

The grumpy server brings the bill, which Ophelia wants to pay. Great-Aunt Violet forbids it, and pushes her gold card into the server's hand. When the bill is settled, they put their coats on, take their blue and yellow umbrellas from the umbrella stand, and step out into the gently falling rain.

Acknowledgments

This book had its inception at the start of the COVID-19 pandemic, when my father was stranded in Calgary because of the virus. Our conversations about old Hong Kong got me wondering anew, as I have off and on since my earliest years, what the lives of my grandparents and great-grandparents were like prior to and during the Japanese occupation, as well as how my parents' lives and, by corollary, my own were shaped by it. Though that was a period of tremendous violence and suffering, it was hardly the first endured by the peoples of that city, which at the time of the invasion had already been held by colonial Britain for a hundred years and was plagued by both local unrest, and unrest over the border in China. I am grateful to Mom and Dad for the ideas they shared in the writing of this book. One particular inspiration was a photocopy my mother gave me of a cookbook that instructs Chinese cooks on how to make Western food. It belonged to my great-grandfather, who was head steward at the Hong Kong Cricket Club before—but not during—the Japanese occupation.

Though this novel is the product of my search for knowledge about family, it is not a story about my family as such. Nor is it a book that purports to accurately represent historical personages, though a number of them do appear. Rather, it is a fiction imaginatively brought into being by reading between the lines of such texts as Philip Snow's *The Fall of Hong Kong: Britain, China and the Japanese Occupation* (Yale University Press, 2003); Edwin Ride's *BAAG (British Army Aid Group): Hong Kong Resistance 1942–1945* (Oxford University Press, 1981); Sir Selwyn Selwyn-Clarke's memoir, *Footprints* (Sino-American Publishing Company, 1975), *Buck Clayton's Jazz World*, by Buck Clayton with Nancy Miller Elliott (Macmillan, 1986); *A History of the Hong Kong Cricket Club 1851–1989*, edited by Spencer Robinson (Centurion, 1989); Andrew F. Jones's *Yellow Music: Media Culture and Colonial Modernity in the Chinese Jazz Age* (Duke University Press, 2001); *W.E.B. Du Bois on Asia: Crossing the World*

Color Line, edited by Bill V. Mullen and Cathryn Watson (University Press of Mississippi, 2005); *Cree Code Talker*, a short film about Charles "Checker" Tomkins by Alexandra Lazarowich (NSI IndigiDocs, 2016); Liam Nolan's *Small Man of Nanataki: The True Story of a Japanese Who Risked His Life to Provide Comfort for His Enemies* (E.P. Dutton, 1966); W.H. Auden and Christopher Isherwood's *Journey to a War* (Random House, 1939); Rana Mitter's *Forgotten Ally: China's World War II, 1937–1945* (Mariner Books, 2014); and Chan Sui-jeung's invaluable *East River Column: Hong Kong Guerillas in the Second World War and After* (Hong Kong University Press, 2009). In addition, I read (or at least looked through) quite a number of accounts of the war by British, Canadian, and Australian soldiers, as well the work of Eileen Chang, Han Suyin, and of course, the wonderful Madeleine Thien. Inspiration for Old Mah's Dream Horse company came from the article "Narcotic Culture: A Social History of Drug Consumption in China" by Frank Dikötter, Lars Laamann, and Zhou Xun in the *British Journal of Criminology* (Spring 2002). For more on Hong Kong's role in the 1936 Berlin Olympics, see "China's 1936 Olympic Football Team: Eight of the Players Were From Hong Kong" by Vincent Heywood in the *Journal of the Royal Asiatic Society Hong Kong Branch* (2008). I relied extensively on news articles from the 1930s and 1940s in the *South China Morning Post*, and the archival photographs and facts of interest on David Bellis's website, gwulo.com, were immensely helpful. Also helpful was the website for Hong Kong's War Crimes Trials Collection. Readers wishing to dig deeper into this subject might begin with *Hong Kong's War Crimes Trials*, edited by Suzannah Linton (Oxford University Press, 2013).

Many thanks are due as well to those who read drafts of the novel, particularly Nadine Attewell, who generously shared her research on Percy Davis Chang, a mixed-race Black and Chinese radio worker in pre-war Hong Kong who was a major figure along the escape route for many refugees and internment camp escapees during the occupation. Having read about his life and work in Anthony Hewitt's *Bridge with Three Men: Across*

China to the Western Heaven in 1942 (Jonathan Cape, 1986) and seen his photo on gwulo.com, I was already excited about him. But Nadine showed me a fragment of a letter written by Chang to the British government, trying to get passage from Hong Kong to Jamaica, that she'd found in the Lindsay Tasman Ride Collection at the Australian War Memorial in Canberra. The British had offered passage home to all those who assisted the Allies during the war. In light of the fact that Chang died of tuberculosis in Hong Kong shortly after the war, leaving a large family to make their way without him, I found this letter unbearably moving. His story provides the inspiration for the character Isadore Davis Wong, though Wong is not Chang. Gratitude to Nadine as well for her thoughtful and encouraging feedback on the novel's first draft.

I relied once again on the brilliant and generous Warren Cariou, this time for his understanding of Métis history and culture, the particular experiences of Métis residential school survivors, and his knowledge of the city of Winnipeg and of vintage cameras. Without him, the character of William Courchene would not be who he is, and Violet's photography hobby would be a bit of a mess too. Warren also helped me think through the history of Cree code talking in the Canadian army and how it might have had echoes among the Winnipeg Grenadiers in Hong Kong, where it was not officially practised, at least not in any documented way. (Cree code talking was employed in the European theatres; in Asia, the Americans engaged Navajo speakers to encode their communications. See the film *Windtalkers* starring Adam Beach and directed by John Woo to learn more about the Navajo code talkers.)

Gratitude to Lillian Allen for helping me develop the letters between Chang and Horace, for thinking through with me the po-ethics of writing them, and for her wonderful ear for both poetry and dialogue. Through conversation with her, the novel grew in important and necessary ways.

As a team, Monika Kin Gagnon and Scott Toguri McFarlane gave me wonderful feedback on the flow of the narrative and on the ethics of Japanese and Japanese Canadian representations. I'm especially grateful to Monika for helping me round out the novel's women characters and to Scott for his thoughts on Raymond, the boy who disappears.

My friend and former graduate student Rebecca Geleyn gave me excellent feedback on character, structure, and flow. She's a wonderful reader, and I'm truly appreciative.

Much appreciation to Zaynui Nagji for his sharing his expertise on the game of cricket and making sure I didn't make a fool of myself. Gratitude also to his daughter, Anushka Azadi, for connecting us. Many thanks, too, to Peter Quartermain for sharing his love and knowledge of the game and for helping me to make the language of the cricket passages flow.

Many thanks to Kirsten Emiko McAllister and Nadine Chambers for brief but meaningful conversations about this book, and to Yilin Wang for her generous assistance in thinking through how to handle transliterations.

Rivers of appreciation to the ever-generous Brian Lam for publishing this book and those that came before it. I thank him so much for his ongoing belief in me and my work.

Catharine Chen was an incisive and thorough editor. I thank her for her sharp eye, brilliant attention to narrative logic, and thoughtful, generous critiques.

Appreciation to Rebecca Rosenblum for a careful and intelligent copy edit. Great thanks to Alison Strobel for her eagle eye in proofreading.

Thank you to the talented and generous Jazmin Welch for the beautiful cover and elegant interior design. I really appreciated her willingness to take my suggestions on board and develop them in her own original and creative ways.

Many thanks to Cynara Geissler and Jaiden Dembo their excellent work in publicity—that includes the work they've already done (they started early!) and all the work that I know will happen after this book is born. I appreciate the care, wisdom, and hard work that goes into all they do.

Appreciation as ever to Robert Ballantyne for all his work in distribution.

Thank you to my parents, Tyrone Lai and Yuen-Ting Lai, for their generous storytelling and their forbearance with the way I do things. They've seen so many changes in their lives—not least the changes in the relationship between what is possible to say and what is better left unsaid. Thanks also to Mom for her last-minute fact checking and bestowal of precious details, like the kinds of boats Violet sees when she looks down onto Victoria Harbour from the Peak.

Gratitude as always to my sister, Wendy Lai, and her partner, Karel Maršálek.

Edward, sorry about the giant mess, especially the book towers in the middle of the living room floor.

Though many people were generous with advice and support for this book, any errors, omissions, or missteps are my own.

Notes on Spelling, Transliteration, Naming, and Language

This novel is an attempt to capture the feel of a time and place in fiction. Particular difficulties arose around the issue of romanization, as different styles of transliteration have been in play at different times in Hong Kong's history. Rather than standardize to any one system, I have chosen to spell Chinese transliterations idiosyncratically, in favour of what feels right— that is, in favour of the spellings that evoke time, place, and character. These are often, though not always, Wade-Giles spellings. Though pinyin spellings are more accepted these days, Wade-Giles was the accepted mode for the milieu addressed in this novel. Hence, "Chungking" rather than "Chongqing," "Nanking" rather than "Nanjing."

In terms of character names, for Chinese names, I've followed the family-name-first order, e.g., Cheung Chiu-Wai, where Cheung is the family name and Chiu-Wai is the given name. Many names in Hong Kong, however, include both Chinese and Western given names. In this case, I've followed the convention of listing the Western given name first, then the family name, then the Chinese given name, e.g., Violet Mah Wai-Man. All-Western names use family-name-last order, e.g., Kathy Duffy. Chinese names with only Western given names use family-name-last order, e.g., Sutton Ngai. Some Chinese names also use the family-name-last order if they are historical figures who are best known that way, e.g., Shouson Chow.

Note that it is traditional for married women in Chinese families to keep their maiden names. Hence, Kwan Siu-Wai still uses the family name Kwan even though she is married to Lee Cho-Lam. Note also the tradition of uxorilocal marriage, which allows a man to marry into his wife's family and take the wife's family name, if both parties agree. This is the case for Grandfather Cheung, who marries into the family of his wife, Cheung Wan-See.

In Chinese systems of naming, children of the same generation share a name with all the others of the same gender and generation in the same family, and have a personal name of their own. Hence Tak-Wing and Tak-Tam.

When they are speaking, thinking, or writing letters, my characters take up terms that may strike readers as dated—for example, "Negro" rather than "Black," "coolie" rather than "labourer." In this context, I hope readers will not find these terms offensive, but will recognize the need in fiction to be accurate (within reason) to the speech conventions, ways of knowing, and habits of people inhabiting a particular historical time and place.

All of the characters in this novel are fictionalized, including the ones based on historical figures. While for the most part I've attempted to stay true to historical trajectories, some have been altered in the service of narrative logic and fictional truth.